OUR PUCKING WAY

RICH DEMONS OF HOCKEY BOOK 2

C.R. JANE
MAY DAWSON

Our Pucking Way by C. R. Jane & May Dawson

Copyright © 2024 by C. R. Jane

All rights reserved.

For permissions contact:

crjaneauthor@gmail.com

maydawsonauthor@gmail.com

This book is a work of fiction. Names, characters, businesses, places, events, locales, and incidents are either the products of the author's imagination or used in a fictitious manner. Any resemblance to actual persons, living or dead, or actual events is purely coincidental.

Cover Design: Emily Wittig

Photographer: Wander

Editing: Hannotek, Ink

JOIN OUR READERS' GROUP

Stay up to date with C.R. Jane by joining her Facebook readers' group, C.R.'s Fated Realm. Ask questions, get first looks at new books / series, and have fun with other book lovers!

Join C.R. Jane's Group

Join May Dawson's Wild Angels to chat directly with May and other readers about her books, enter giveaways, and generally just have fun!

Join May's Group

For the good girls who like their book boyfriends best when they have a million red flags….

PLEASE READ...

Dear readers, please be aware that this is a dark romance and as such can and will contain possible triggering content. Elements of this story are purely fantasy, and should not be taken as acceptable behavior in real life. This is a reverse harem romance, which means that there is more than one love interest and the heroine will end up with all of them. Our love interests are possessive, obsessive, and do a lot of crazy shit. Red Flag Renegades rejoice. These men will do anything to get their girl.

Themes include ice hockey, stalking, a non-consent flashback (NOT INCLUDING ANY OF HER MEN), a flashback including parental self-unaliving (not detailed), parental neglect flashbacks, manipulation, birth control tampering, dark obsessive themes, sexual scenes. There is no cheating involved.

Prepare to enter the world of the Devils...you've been warned.

OUR PUCKING WAY

Sometimes the past is best left forgotten...or at least that's what I'm learning.

The men I love lied to me...but I can't seem to let them go.

And Greyson's enemies are determined to destroy us all, once and forever.

To survive, Sebastian, Carter, and Jack will have to join Greyson and his Jackals...even though they thought they left their criminal past behind forever when they joined the NHL.

When Greyson demands they prove themselves to him, it turns out that despite their years of living as pampered superstars...they still know how to fight, torture and kill.

The only thing the four of them agree on is...me.

The mafia boss and the three NHL stars will do anything to protect me...even work together.

My memories are slowly returning of how the five of us once formed our own strange little family though...

Can we find our way back to the way we used to be so we can have the future I'm so desperate for?

Because I'm learning that the only thing I want more than my memories, is all of them...forever.

Asheville

Devils
TEAM ROSTER

CARTER HAYES, CAPTAIN	#1, GOALIE
JACK CAMERON, ASSISTANT CAPTAIN	#27, LEFT WING
SEBASTIAN WRIGHT, ASSISTANT CAPTAIN	#14, DEFENSEMAN
DAVID WEISS	#42, DEFENSEMAN
JONATHAN MACHOWSKI	#18, LEFT WING
MICHAEL LOGAN	#12, DEFENSEMAN
FOX ANDREWS	#2, GOALIE,
ADAM RODRIGUES	#31, RIGHT WING
SERGEI IVANOV	#22, DEFENSEMAN
DAVID SMITH	#14, CENTER
MICHAEL WILLIAMS	#19, DEFENSEMAN
ROBERT ANDERSON	#17, FORWARD
MATTHEW BROWN	#42, RIGHT WING
PATRICK LEWIS	#3, DEFENSEMAN
JAMES TAYLOR	#11, FORWARD
ANDREW MILLER	#8, FORWARD
RICH CLARK	#88, FORWARD,
BENJAMIN HALL	#6, DEFENSEMAN
AKIHIRO TANAKA	#26, FORWARD
VIKTOR HENRIKSSON	#24, FORWARD
IVAN PETROV	#16, FORWARD
DIEGO FERNANDEZ	#20, FORWARD
BILL KING	#4, FORWARD
DANIEL STUBBS	#60, WING
ALEX TURNER	#53, CENTER
PORTER MAST	#29, DEFENSEMAN
LOGAN EDWARDS	#9, DEFENSEMAN
CLARK DOBBINS	#63, WING
KYLE NETHERLAND	#23, DEFENSEMAN

COACHES

KEVIN HARRIS, HEAD COACH
MICHAEL "MIKE" SULLIVAN, ASSISTANT COACH
XAVIER MONTGOMERY, ASSISTANT COACH
TIM REED, GOALIE COACH

OUR
PUCKING
WAY PLAYLIST

TRAINING SEASON
Dua Lipa

COMPLETE MESS
5 Seconds of Summer

HANDS TO MYSELF
Selena Gomez

BURN IT DOWN
Parker McCollum

TOO GOOD TO BE TRUE
Kacey Musgraves

YOU ARE IN LOVE (TAYLOR'S VERSION)
Taylor Swift

HIGH
Stephen Sanchez

EVERYWHERE, EVERYTHING
Noah Kahan

I MISS YOU, I'M SORRY
Gracie Abrams

TAKE ME TO CHURCH
Hozier

OH MY GOD
Adele

TURNING TABLES
Adele

SAY YES TO HEAVEN
Lana Del Rey

TIMELESS (TAYLOR'S VERSION)
Taylor Swift

LISTEN TO THE FULL PLAYLIST HERE:
HTTPS://OPEN.SPOTIFY.COM/PLAYLIST/7YZQU3I9S5IPPIJOY29QDM?SI=613EEC38FC224BD7

"Yeah, I'm cocky and I am arrogant. But that doesn't mean I'm not a nice person." - Jeremy Roenick

CHAPTER

Kennedy

O ne moment, I was lost in dark, rainy streets. It felt like I needed to run from something following me, but my legs were exhausted and my head ached. I stumbled, lost.

And then I heard Carrie's voice in the distance.

It was just a dream. The streets faded to darkness.

Then I heard deeper voices. The world began to brighten. But I couldn't pick out any of the voices until I heard Carrie's cheerful prattle.

"Before Keith, I dated some absolute duds," she said. "One guy had the most lickable abs—like yours, I've heard a lot from Kennedy about your abs—but while he was nice to look at, it wasn't worth it. The guys with the abs never are, are they? He would try to turn every date into a workout session. He surprised me with a half-marathon registration for my birthday! Running is not a present!"

This felt so familiar. What was happening?

"He always told me how many push-ups I'd need to do, or miles I would need to run to burn off the calories of anything I ate. I even caught him looking in the mirror over my dresser once when we were doing girl-on-top, and then I realized he was staring at his biceps while he held me up because it gave him a good flex."

I had the most powerful sense of deja vu. I'd been in this moment before, right?

I'd been hit by a car, I'd had amnesia, and Carrie had been there, telling me about her bad boyfriends...just like this. A sense of horror pressed into my chest. I couldn't make myself wake up. It felt like I was stuck in the past.

"I can't believe some of the men I let myself get involved with!"

"Why are you telling us this?" The deep, masculine voice sent a shock straight up my spine.

"Because I'd rather date the guy who wore socks, not just with sandals, but also for sex. Those bozos still make y'all look bad!"

"Is she smiling?" It was a deep, concerned voice.

Maybe I was, because Carrie wasn't telling *me* about her bad boyfriends. She was using them to shame some men who very much deserved it.

"Wake up, sweetheart." A big hand wrapped around mine, holding my fingers gently. Softly, he added, "Please."

My eyelashes fluttered open until I could see a concerned, handsome face staring down at me.

Jack.

Carrie pushed him out of the way. "Hey, Kennedy. You just live to terrify me, don't you? I swear it's harder to keep you alive than Charlie. And he's taken to picking up spiders! He thinks he's Wednesday Addams...I swear he's going to eat one next. Raw."

The guys stared at her.

She talked a lot when she was worried. And every other time too, but I could tell this was Worried Carrie in action.

"What happened?" I asked.

"You were almost hit by a car, but from what I gather, this big bozo pushed you out of the way." She gestured vaguely, which didn't narrow down which big bozo it was. "Of course, he doesn't know his own strength and hit you too hard—"

"None of us said that," Carter interrupted.

"And you hit your head on the pavement! Like you need more head injuries." She shook her head. She grabbed my chin and tilted my face, holding my jaw steady. "Keep your head still. Use your eyes to track my pen."

She moved the pen back and forth. "Pupils look good," she murmured, mostly to herself.

She continued to check me over. She'd gone from my slightly goofy, upbeat best friend to the serious professional she was.

"Did they ask you to come?"

"Girl, I was on my way." She shook her head. "You texted me for help, remember? Nothing could've stopped me from coming to get you."

"Thank you," I told her gratefully.

"I would've been too late though if it weren't for this big lug who tackled you." She smacked Sebastian's shoulder.

Sebastian stuffed his hands in his pockets. Now that I knew these men were hiding so much from me, I wondered just how deep the lies went. Were they always manipulating me?

Still, my heart leapt despite itself as my gaze tracked over the three of them. We were in Carter's dark bedroom.

Jack hovered behind Carrie, broad shouldered and tousle-haired, desperate to be close to me it looked like. He kept bobbing from side to side behind her like a car trying to pass on the freeway. Meanwhile, Carter paced, his face intense under his dark hair.

Sebastian had a look on his face that I couldn't read and didn't trust.

And we were missing one of the four psychos.

"Where's Greyson?" I asked.

The guys exchanged a quick glance that told me they were preparing a lie, and it made me so furious I could barely breathe.

"He had to check in on his mom and sisters," Jack said guardedly.

I sat forward. Were they in danger too? But when I moved, my head screamed. It felt as if my brain was a brick sliding around in my skull. I winced, and Carrie leapt to push me back down in bed.

"Rest," she said. "You don't have signs of a concussion, but you were knocked out, so there's damage...you need all the rest."

"Did you lose your memories?" Sebastian asked as he crouched next to me, his eyes serious with concern.

He'd set the fire that terrified me.

Dark anger rushed over me. Through me. "You'd like that, wouldn't you?"

Sebastian frowned, looking hurt. "Of course not. I was worried because I know how hard it's been on you, losing your memories."

Even Carrie looked at me with vague horror on her face, as if he were a puppy I'd just attempted to kick into the stratosphere, although it was replaced the next second as she remembered she was always on my side.

"You don't get to give me a sad puppy face," I told him. "You burnt down my apartment, you psycho!"

The cloudy look on his face cleared. "Kennedy. I'll buy you your own place, better than that shitty apartment—"

"It was my own apartment!"

"You burnt down her apartment?" Carrie shrieked. She looked as if she were about to hit him.

Jack and Carter exchanged a look, as if they might just have to kill her in case she ratted him out. I didn't like that look one bit.

"No," I said grudgingly. "He left a candle burning in my apartment when he was over there. He apparently thought it was more important that my apartment smelled like a seaside bakery than to follow basic fire safety rules."

"It did kind of smell," Carrie said sympathetically. "There was wood rot everywhere in that old apartment building."

"It did not!"

"Have I mentioned how much I like her," Jack mouthed at Carter.

The last thing I needed was to lose my best friend to these charming psychos. I needed her firmly anchored on my side. "Carrie, I think I need some time to rest. Can we catch up later?"

"Of course," she told me. She cut her eyes at them. "And she does need *rest*. In case you were thinking of what depraved things you would do to her next."

"I would never," Jack said innocently.

It was remarkably unconvincing.

But I knew they wouldn't tell me the whole truth while she was there. I needed to know where Greyson was, and what had happened. Was it just a story that one of them had pushed me out of the way?

Carrie gave me a big hug and told me she could come back to check on me. She waved at the guys, slightly awkward, and they grumbled goodbyes at her. As soon as she had headed into the living room, Jack said, "One of us should make sure she gets home."

"I'll walk her to her car," Carter told me, looking concerned.

Fear squeezed my stomach.

Carrie was my person, my best friend. Was she in danger because she was close to me?

"Follow her home," I said quietly.

Carter looked as if he wanted to argue with me, but whatever he saw on my face stilled him. He gave me a quick jerk of a nod. "I'll make sure she's safe."

He hesitated for a second at the doorway, as if he wanted to stay with me, but then he was gone.

Once I heard the door to the condo shut in the distance, I asked again, "Where's Greyson?"

Jack was already sinking onto the edge of the bed, looking as if some of his tension unwound the second he was close to me. He stretched out alongside me, his big, hard body radiating warmth. As mad as I was right now, I was also bone-tired and aching, and I wanted to curl up against him. It took every ounce of self restraint I had not to wrap myself up in his powerful arms.

"He'll be back soon," Jack said. "He really is checking on Alli and Alexa."

"Why?" My voice was sharp. "Why did that car almost hit me? You told Carrie I was in the street, didn't you? Like I'm the most careless idiot when it comes to cars, to get hit *twice*—"

"You didn't get hit, though." Jack's voice was soothing, but it didn't soothe me. It made me want to smack him. "We were there."

"You weren't there last time," I said, and Jack tensed. "The car leapt the curb. It was coming straight for me, trying to kill me. Why?"

"I don't think they were trying to kill you."

"No? Why's that?"

"Because you've never been any threat to anyone," Jack said quietly. He gently ran his hand over my hair, smoothing it back, as if he couldn't resist touching me. "Look at you. You're sunshine and light. There's never been any reason anyone would hurt you...except to get to us."

He said it like he meant it.

And yet, something about it felt wrong...I tried to remember why.

My memories had come flooding back, or at least...some of them. I needed peace and quiet and for my head to stop pounding so I could think. Why would anyone try to hit me with a car...twice?

Sebastian moved to the floor to ceiling windows. Against the dark outside and the glitter of city lights beyond, his reflection was thrown back by the windows, revealing his dark expression. "We think they were trying to kidnap you."

"To get to Greyson or to get to you?" I asked sharply.

"I don't know," Sebastian admitted. "I always thought it was Greyson…that if we stayed on the straight-and-narrow and stayed away from you, there was no reason anyone would ever come looking for you."

"You're the reason we stayed out of trouble," Jack told me earnestly.

"Mm, wouldn't want to go to prison when Kennedy needs you." Sebastian's gaze flickered to Jack's in the reflection, and Jack stared back at him with wide eyes. It was an unspoken conversation I couldn't make sense of now.

"Why would any of you go to jail?" I asked sharply.

"Because we were mixed up with Greyson."

My head still ached. I needed to sleep. To make sense of what was happening. "Give me a few minutes, alright?"

"You can have all the time you need, sweetheart." Jack wove his fingers through mine. His big shoulder against mine was a comforting presence, even before he rested his head lightly against my forehead. "But don't ask us to leave you alone when we thought we'd lost you."

"I just need…" I yawned, my voice lost.

"I'll wake you up when Greyson and Carter come back," he promised, because Jack always knew just what I needed.

And then I was asleep.

———

I woke up curled against Jack's side. My head was pillowed on his broad shoulder, and my hand rested on his muscular thigh, my fingertips just grazing his enormous, hard—

I jolted away. But he kept sleeping. His face was handsome in profile, his eyelashes resting above those hard-angled cheekbones, his lips soft and kissable and faintly parted in sleep. I dared another look at the anaconda tenting his gray sweatpants; that part of him did not seem to be asleep.

Despite myself, a surge of desire ran through me, and my heart was pounding as I laid back down with a little space between us—though he took up so much of the bed that his broad, tattooed bicep was still against mine. I laid with my head on the cool pillow and stared up at the ceiling.

My head still thrummed with pain.

Pieces of my memory had come back to me. As I stared at Jack, his face was in my memory too. I remembered lying next to him, the wind whispering through my hair. He'd been staring up at the stars, but I hadn't been able to take my eyes off his handsome face. I'd been so nervous he would kiss me, and so nervous that he wouldn't.

Where had we been that night? I tried to remember the details, but all I could remember was how focused I'd been on him.

Then I remembered—we were lying on the trampoline behind his house. His big, fancy house had been in the distance, smoke still rising from the fire pit and dancing off into the night. I'd always felt like I didn't quite belong when I was at his beautiful house with his family that adored him and tolerated me.

Maybe that's why I couldn't quite help feeling that way in this glamorous condo, too.

I felt the moment he woke, as if his presence expanded. He turned onto his elbow, and his hand skimmed across my stomach through the blanket, as if he had to keep touching me. "Are you alright?"

"Yeah." My voice came out soft. Too soft, as I remembered everything they'd done to me, from hiding my identity, to burning down my house. "Despite all your bullshit."

I sat up. The world reeled around me dizzyingly. Jack scrambled to sit up too, and he had the most horrified look on his face. I thought it was because he was offended until I tried to stand up and swayed. Then he was sweeping me up into his arms.

"I don't need you to carry me."

"Please, Kennedy." His always sexy, low voice had a broken edge. "I almost lost you again. Don't push me away."

His forehead rested gently against mine for a second. I squeezed my eyes shut, trying to resist him, but then I sighed.

Jack was hard to resist.

"Are Greyson and Carter back?"

"Yeah," he said, looking incredibly unenthused. "Greyson wants to see you, but he didn't want to wake you up."

"And Carter..."

"Carter came and slept on the other side of you for a while." He looked at me as if he wanted to kiss me, but thought better of it.

Sebastian must have realized he had better stay away.

"Where is he now?"

"Once Greyson got here, he..." Jack trailed off.

Right. These four couldn't stop fighting. Carter was watching over Greyson, because he didn't trust him, but I was sure Greyson wouldn't leave me. Not after what happened last night.

"Carry me into the living room?" I asked. "Since you don't trust me to walk?"

"Is being ferried around like a princess by an NHL star really so terrible?" he said, a hint of Jack's usual light-hearted mischief peeking through.

"It is when the NHL star is a—"

He kissed me.

His lips on mine were soft, but his mouth was firm. He kissed me hard, and I gave in and kissed him back, my arm twining around his neck. I was barely breathing when he pulled away, a mischievous twinkle in his gaze.

"You're always so sweet," he told me. "I figured you didn't really want to finish that sentence any more than I wanted to hear you call me names."

"Stop trying to win her over when she has every reason to be pissed," Greyson called.

Jack rolled his eyes. He'd been carrying me down the hall as we spoke, and now we emerged into the sumptuous living room. Dawn streaked the sky, painting the skyline pink and gold. From here, the city was beautiful.

"She has every reason to be pissed at you too," Jack reminded Greyson as he stepped into the room.

"And I'd rather hear about it," Greyson's gaze met mine, a spark kindling in his dark eyes. "I'm not trying to shut my girl up."

"Hey," Jack frowned. "I'm not trying to get her to shut up."

"And everyone can see what you're doing," Carter told Greyson, turning away from the window. I didn't think Carter was ever that obsessed with scenery before.

Carter's gaze met mine and softened. "Kennedy—"

"Did Carrie get home alright?" I trusted Keith to look after her.

"Yeah. Of course."

"Because you'd tell me if she didn't?" My voice was acerbic.

I pushed away from Jack, and he set me down carefully on my feet, hovering behind me as I crossed the treacherous three feet of plush rug to sink into the sofa.

"We need to talk." Carter paced back and forth; he was still moving with a faint limp, almost unnoticeable.

But I saw Greyson noticing, his keen, icy blue eyes tracking Carter.

He was the reason Carter was limping, after all. He'd known about his old injury and made sure to take advantage of it.

"Yes." Sebastian sank into the couch across from me, though he didn't meet my gaze. "Where were you going last night, Kennedy?"

"Home."

He chewed his lower lip. "Home? But—"

"You burnt that down?" I asked crisply.

"That wasn't your home," Sebastian looked up, his gaze meeting mine for the first time, and his eyes were crystal clear with certainty. "This is your home. With us."

"I don't think so," I said. I held up my hand, before they could start to argue with me. "I was going to go with Carrie last night. Because you weren't going to help me. And then—this car jumped the curb and came straight for me. It felt just like… before…" I trailed off, feeling assailed by the memories, as if I were back on that rainy street running the second before the car slammed into me. "I remember that now."

"I'm sorry." Carter ran his hand through his hair. "You should never have felt like you needed to go off on your own."

I didn't want their apologies. "I want answers. What happened last night?"

And more importantly, what happened all those years ago?

But I needed to understand one piece at a time.

"I went after you. When we realized you were gone." Sebastian's face was pale as he replayed the memory, and it made my heart melt…just a little. There was no hiding how emotionally impacted he was by almost losing me. "We all split up. I was the one who went out the front, and I saw you. Frozen. Staring at the car that was racing toward you…."

I bit my lower lip. Why did my malfunctioning brain apparently have no survival instincts? It was as if when my brain was unlocking memories, everything else turned off.

"I tackled you out of the way," he said. "I'm sorry, Kennedy. I didn't mean to hurt you."

It was the second apology of the day and it wasn't even fully sunrise yet. But they weren't the apologies I wanted or needed. Sebastian obviously didn't need to apologize for saving my life.

However, he owed me for so many other reasons.

"Greyson, where did you go afterward?" I asked.

Greyson's jaw flexed. He didn't want to tell me.

I would've loved to storm from the room, but I might've passed out. And as much as I hated to admit it, I was safer with these men around me. I needed them…until I figured out what the hell was happening and how to fix it.

"We told her about how you were going to check on Alexa and Alli," Jack prompted him helpfully.

"Yes," Greyson said, taking a seat beside me. He spread his arm across the back of the couch, not touching me. "I did. But that's not the whole truth, is it?"

"Really campaigning hard for favorite status," Carter muttered. "And it's transparent as fuck."

"Oh, you've all got a long way to go to get to good standing, forget favorite status," I assured him.

"Kennedy, I think someone came after you because of me." Greyson's ice blue eyes met mine. "I checked on my sisters and my mom because I was afraid maybe they'd gone after them to get to me. But they're okay." He answered the question I'd been about to ask, as if he knew what I would ask. "Then I went to try to find the man who did this."

"You told me that you could protect me," I said softly.

His face twisted as if he were in pain. "I'm sorry."

"This was why we never claimed you," Jack burst out, as if it had been weighing on him this whole time. "It killed us all, Kennedy. Knowing you were out there, and we couldn't see you."

"We should've just killed our way through the splinter group that betrayed the Jackals," Greyson growled. "We could've done it together. If you three hadn't turned chicken shit."

Carter scoffed. "If it were that easy, Kennedy wouldn't be in danger after all this time. If you'd been able to clean up after yourself, to protect her, we wouldn't have had to hide her away—"

"It didn't fucking work, did it?"

"It worked for years!"

"And I was miserable for years!" I cried out. They were so frustrating. "I needed you! All four of you!" I glanced around at them, but they still looked stubborn as fuck.

And then they were arguing again.

"Stop!" I shouted. The second I yelled, my headache ripped

through my mind, worse than ever. I raised my hands to my temples as if I were trying to keep my head from exploding, because that was how it felt.

Instantly, all of them went silent. Jack rushed to me, sinking onto the opposite side of me from Greyson and wrapping his arms around my body as if he were going to protect me. Sebastian looked stricken. Carter's hands bunched into fists as if he were ready to throw punches, but there was no one to attack.

"You're hurting me." I said quietly. "Every time you fight."

"I'm sorry." Greyson had slipped to his knees, and he was staring up at me now, impeccable in his gray suit, his crisp white shirt just barely revealing the tattoos that climbed his powerful neck. "What do you need from us, baby?"

"I need you to work together," I told them, looking around at their faces. "I need us to fight *together*. And since none of you seem to be able to work together…I need you to follow my lead."

I was done being the victim they protected. The sweet girl they kept secrets from, so I never even knew about the nightmares that lurked behind me.

But this was my fight. I was the one in danger.

These four alpha males all thought they needed to be the ones who led, so they couldn't work together…not even to protect me.

It was time for me to be the boss.

CHAPTER

Kennedy

"Whatever you need," Greyson promised me. "You know you're our queen."

"I wish I knew that," I said, jumping to my feet.

But it was a mistake. Moving so quickly left me in terrible pain.

As soon as my face crumpled with pain, all four of them shut up. They leapt to try to get me to sit down, ready to sweep me off my feet again.

In their silence, I could finally hear my own power.

They'd been manipulating me all this time, keeping secrets from me. Greyson claimed they had good reasons to keep my past from me. He thought that if I didn't remember on my own, I'd never truly get my memories back. I would just have a shadow of memory, created from whatever they told me.

But I could manipulate them just as easily.

I didn't think Greyson meant it when he called me their queen. Not yet. But maybe one day…

"I'm going to make breakfast," Carter said abruptly, standing up. He had the most reason to hate Greyson.

"Kennedy, please sit down," Sebastian said. "You look like you're in pain."

"I probably should have gone to the hospital," I snapped at him. "But you all don't want to let me out of your sight, do you?"

"Kennedy, you're being ridiculous," Sebastian said firmly. "If you needed to go to the hospital, we would have brought the hospital to you. We want to protect you. You have to believe that."

It was true, that was something I couldn't really argue.

I was exasperated with them all though, and when Greyson opened his mouth, I knew he was going to feed me more lines. And so would the rest of them.

I stormed off in Carter's wake, proud of myself that I didn't collapse.

I wasn't done arguing with him. He couldn't get away from me just by marching off to the kitchen, even if he made my favorite chocolate chip pancakes.

Though it wouldn't hurt.

When I walked into the kitchen, Carter's broad shoulders were toward me, and he didn't turn around. He was rummaging through the cabinets, though he didn't seem to find whatever he was looking for. Sanity? Normal, non-psychopathic-alpha-male masculinity? Baking powder? Whatever it was, it did not materialize.

My mind buzzed with all the different things I could say to him. But what came out of my mouth was just, "Are you all right?"

Because he didn't look all right. There was so much tension in his shoulders and how he carried himself right now.

"Yes."

A long, pregnant silence followed. He reached the end of that cabinet, and moved on to the next one, never looking at me.

He was such a great conversationalist.

I was about to give up on him and go back to the living room.

Greyson would feed me a bunch of lies and manipulative nonsense, but at least he'd be cute about it.

But as soon as I made a move to leave, he blurted out, "I'm glad it was Sebastian."

My mind was still very much focused on how Sebastian had burnt down my apartment, causing the loss of all my worldly goods. So, I just stared at him for a few seconds, lost and confused–my normal state of being around these men.

He still didn't turn around. His broad shoulders and tight ass, while very cute, did not provide any answers.

"Why?" I demanded. "Because I'm pissed at you too."

Now he finally turned around, confusion written across his handsome face. "What are you talking about?"

"I'm mad at you too," I reminded him. "You let me sit in a hospital with no memories, no family, no sense of who I was...I thought no one loved me. I thought I had been a terrible person. Someone who wasn't worthy of love..."

My voice cracked. I hadn't realized how much I was still carrying the pain of that day until I could hear it in my voice. The pain of slowly trying to figure out, not just who I was and what I liked, but if I could be worthy of having people close to me when no one had ever claimed me.

He rushed to me and wrapped me in his arms. "Oh, Kennedy. You were always worthy. We never meant for you to feel that way." He looked stricken. "Everyone fell in love with you in that hospital...not just Carrie. People rallied around you. They thought you were great, because you are. There's no one like you."

It was a lot of words for Carter, and he said them with conviction.

"That doesn't mean I believed it," I said, my voice thick with tears. It was like getting almost hit by that car had taken down all my defenses, and I couldn't stop the words from spilling out. "Not when nobody ever came for me. Who has that happen to them? Who goes unclaimed?"

His face looked stricken. "I'm sorry, Kennedy. I had no idea. I never wanted you to feel that way..."

"I needed you," I whispered, and then he seemed to break and he pulled me into his arms.

"And we needed you the whole time too," he whispered, his voice low and husky, as if he were emotional too.

For a few long seconds, we clung to each other. I was still pissed, and yet there was comfort in his arms even when he was the reason I was angry.

"I'm glad it was Sebastian," he said, "because I can't move fast enough right now to have protected you."

A shudder ran through his body as he held me, and it startled me. I tipped my face up to see his. He looked wrecked with guilt. "I'm not good enough for you...but I'll become good enough. I'll be able to protect you."

Hearing him say that filled me with sadness, and then I had a flash of memory. Carter, as a teenage boy, serious and quiet like he was now, but sensitive. Holding my hand and walking with me one night, down the pitted streets of the trailer park. But the moonlight had scattered silver across the stream that ran behind the double-wides, and everything had looked beautiful that night with Carter by my side. It hadn't mattered where we were.

"I don't need you to shelter me, Carter. I need you to help me. Those are two different things."

He still didn't look like he believed me, so I took the hard angles of his jaw in my hands. His five o'clock shadow was rough against my palms. "You're already good enough, Carter."

He didn't look as if he believed me, so I added, "This is why you've needed me these last five years. Apparently, even being an NHL star couldn't be enough for you without me there to remind you how much I love you."

The second the words were out of my mouth, a blush of embarrassment rose to my cheeks. I felt as if now that my memories were coming back, so were deep, intense feelings. They were the feelings of Kennedy in the past who'd had more time with these boys.

"Sorry," I started, trying to explain, but it wasn't as if I could take back what I just said.

"Don't be sorry. I'm sorry." He wrapped his hands around my thighs and boosted me up onto the counter. I let out a breath at the sudden movement, but then his lips were on mine, and the two of us were just kissing.

He certainly kissed me like he didn't mind my confession of love.

When he pulled away, he tilted his forehead against mine. "I'll do anything for you. You know that."

"Even make up with Greyson?"

I could feel the tension through his body.

"After what he did? He's the reason I can't move..." He began. I pulled back, and when he saw my face, he stroked my cheekbone gently with one of his big, scarred thumbs. He seemed to contemplate for a second as he tried to ease the tension out of my face with his gentle touch. Then he said, "Yeah, even make up with Greyson."

Well, we would see about that. I had some thoughts about how to test Greyson and Carter's willingness to work together and forgive the past.

"I'm sorry we left you, Kennedy," he said, and his voice sounded rough and broken. "You're right. It's felt like we barely survived without you, all this time. Everything we accomplished didn't mean much when you weren't there to see it."

Then we were kissing again, and I didn't want to ever stop.

"I hate to break up the party," Greyson's voice was sarcastic, and I had the feeling he very much enjoyed breaking up the party. "But some of us have shit to do. I can't just laze around all day, waiting with you all to hear your names on ESPN while you eat pancakes."

"It does kind of sound like the perfect day though," Jack said coming in behind him, "You know, if there was any chance of having your name mentioned on ESPN."

"Sure," Greyson drawled. "If my girl hadn't just been almost killed."

"And if you hadn't given up on hockey," Jack said, an answering flare of heat in his eyes.

"If I was an NHL pretty boy who was only capable of violence on the ice," Greyson agreed.

I couldn't take it anymore. But before I could say anything, Carter turned to face them, looping his arm around my waist. "Can you all cut the bullshit out?"

Jack gave him an affronted look. It certainly wasn't like Carter to come to Greyson's defense—not anymore.

Carter turned to Greyson. "Look, we all want the same thing. To protect Kennedy. There's no reason we can't work together."

Greyson gave him a long look. Then he slow clapped, twice. "You think you're being magnanimous, don't you?"

"Yeah," Carter said, "I think I am."

"You have everything to lose protecting Kennedy the way we need to," Greyson said flatly. "I'm already a criminal. I will kill anyone I have to protect Kennedy."

He looked at me directly. "I'd burn your fucking house down to get you into mine, and I wouldn't apologize about it like Sebastian will. I'd kill these three stupid motherfuckers to have you to myself, if I thought you wouldn't be sad about it forever."

"I would," I said. "No killing. You're all mine."

"But you three, you could lose everything, you get convicted of murder and there goes your NHL careers. So, I don't fucking need you. You don't bring anything to my fight to protect Kennedy except for liability. You're a weakness."

"No." Carter shook his head. "You don't have anyone you can really trust in the Jackals. Not like you can trust us. You can't do this on your own."

"And you think I trust you?" Greyson sounded skeptical. "I'll have my men watching Kennedy constantly from now on. My only mistake was thinking she was safe when she was with you."

When he threw out those words, his tone dripped with revulsion, Carter bristled, and I laid my hand gently on his forearm, trying to anchor him to his better self.

Greyson was a dick. Now that my memories were coming back, I had the sense he had always been a dick. But we'd always all loved him anyway.

"We're not going to let you do this on your own," Carter said.

"I'm not looking at teaming up with the Jackals again," Jack broke in. "That almost destroyed our lives once. I don't see a reason to let it destroy my life now. We could talk to the cops—"

"Yeah, and when they start digging into what happened to Kennedy in the past, because that's sure as hell tied to what's happening now, they might just unearth everything we did before," Greyson growled at him. "Everything *you* did before. So, why don't you pretty boys just sit your asses down and let me do the work."

"That's not an option," Carter growled. "We work together."

"He's right," I cut in before Greyson could go on. "Greyson, I need you, but I need them too."

I held his gaze. Greyson's intense blue eyes softened when he stared into mine, and I thought I had him.

But then Sebastian walked into the kitchen and asked, "Do you really need him, though?"

Greyson shook his head. "I don't need them. I've been on my own all these years, since they walked out on me. And on you. We don't need them, Kennedy."

"I do," I whispered.

Greyson seemed to be battling internally. Then finally he said, "You're going to have to prove yourselves."

Sebastian scoffed. I wasn't sure where he stood—Carter side or on Jack's side of the idea of teaming up with Greyson. But Sebastian said, "We don't have anything to prove."

"You sure as fuck do," Greyson said. "You think you're

badasses when you're in the rink. But you can't protect Kennedy from the ice. And I don't think you have what it takes to protect my girl."

"*Our* girl," Carter gritted.

Sebastian crossed his arms over his chest. "What kind of tests are we talking about?"

Greyson smiled thinly. "We've added some new things to the Jackal initiation since you three walked out on us."

CHAPTER 3

Carter

E ven when our world was on fire, we had practice.

I could feel Greyson's radiating judgment, but he didn't say a word. He knew Kennedy, and he wanted to stay on her good side. The fact that he had wanted to find her all these years—and probably the fact that he hadn't recently committed arson in order to manipulate her—had him on her good side. He wasn't going to lose that.

Still, he insisted on riding with us to the ice rink.

And Sebastian, the traitor, even wanted him there. He said it'd be good for Greyson to keep an eye on Kennedy whenever we couldn't be there.

I was still struggling with the idea that we needed Greyson in any fucking capacity. But then, Sebastian told me quietly, "You don't get it. I saw her get hit by that car once, and we lost her for five years. Seeing that car barreling toward her..." He gave a short shake of his head, his shoulders stiff.

Well, that answered my question about whether he was Team Greyson or not. He'd sign on for anything he thought would keep her safe.

"We'll be right here," Jack promised Kennedy.

He was clearly looking for a hug, but she crossed her arms over her chest. "I know."

Still, as she walked away, she glanced over her shoulder at us. As if our presence was comforting even if she was still pissed at us.

I told myself it was alright, I knew how to win my girl back. But having Kennedy mad at me bothered me, more than I wanted to admit as someone who took hits on the ice, and abuse from the coaches.

It didn't help that Greyson had a twinkle in his eyes as if he was enjoying it all.

As Kennedy walked into the bar, the girls that she worked with greeted her exuberantly.

Greyson turned and his gaze found the two men who had just walked in, looking not at all sketchy.

And I said that with all the sarcasm I possessed.

"How do we know that we can trust them?" I demanded.

"You should worry about whether I can trust *you*," Greyson responded.

I didn't like the idea of men trailing Kennedy that weren't us.

"We need to talk about some things," Sebastian said tersely.

"There's no one else here yet. Let's head down to the locker room." Jack, always the peacemaker, when he wasn't being a homicidal maniac, agreed.

Walking into the locker room, Greyson's shoulder stiffened, and I wondered if Jack had realized the location would bother Greyson so much. This was our turf, after all. It was a reminder of what we were able to do that he couldn't. Greyson had money now, but he'd always live life in the shadows, doing things that would offend Kennedy's good-girl sensibilities.

Our team's flags hung from the ceiling, and each of us had a luxurious locker area, with our official team photo on a poster hanging above our red and black lockers.

"It's a bit nicer than when we were in high school, huh?" Jack asked, and I had to wonder if maybe he knew exactly what he was doing.

"If you have to be a grown man playing games, this certainly seems like the way to do it," Greyson said with mock agree-ability.

I remembered when playing hockey was the only thing Greyson had for himself. He was so busy trying to take care of Alli and Alexa, trying to get their mom straightened out. He'd always been working, always been stressed, then he'd run home from practice to make sure Alli and Alexa had dinner. But for a little while every day, he was free, and on the ice.

He hadn't been a dick with Alli and Alexa, and he hadn't always been a dick with us, either. It made me feel a little less disdain toward him when I remembered the younger version of Greyson, with his dark hair curling around his ears as it grew out during hockey season, and the quick smile he had for his little sisters. He'd been cold-eyed and sarcastic back then too, but it had all been an act. I wondered if some of it still was.

Not that I would trust my life to that. Greyson probably meant it when he said he'd kill all of us for the chance to have Kennedy to himself, if he could get away with it.

"Feels like old times," Jack said, eyeing Greyson as if he wanted to throw his arm around his shoulders, but Greyson turned his back, and Jack clearly thought better of it. "We should all get out on the ice together sometime. Just for fun."

"I don't skate anymore," Greyson said shortly. "Now, focus, assholes. We all agree on one thing, right? We'll let Kennedy think that she's in charge."

Jack said, "Kennedy has every reason to be involved. She's the one who was almost mowed down last night. I think we should be done cutting her out."

"Obviously we don't cut her out." The memory of her tears last night when she talked about being abandoned and alone still wrenched at my heart. "But she's going to want to go into every-thing with us. And we can't have that."

Sebastian still looked tense and troubled. "We can't put her in danger anymore. I don't even fucking like being here right now."

"Well, you heard Kennedy. She's not going to let us throw away our hockey careers. We'll figure out a way."

"I already have," Greyson said.

The three of us all turned to stare at him.

"Go on," I growled.

"No." Greyson said. "You're not Jackals anymore. I'm not telling you shit until you prove yourselves to me and you're back in."

"You're a fucking asshole," I began, trying to hold on to my promise to Kennedy to try to work with Greyson, but God it was difficult when Greyson was Greyson.

"Let's be honest," Greyson said. "Right now, you don't have any skin in the game. You haven't had any ties to the Jackals since we were kids. Jack's got that one body in his past—"

So, Greyson only knew about the one body. We should keep it that way.

"Are you going to keep saying shit about that around Kennedy?" Jack demanded. "We promised that we wouldn't tell her what happened with her stepfather."

"Ohh, we pinky promised," Greyson said with a mocking tone in his voice. "I don't trust you three not to use me to take out anyone who's a danger to Kennedy, then turn me into the cops so that you can have her to yourselves."

"We wouldn't do that," Jack said, sounding exasperated.

"And I'm going to make sure," Greyson said.

"What do you want?" I demanded.

"A return to the fight nights of our youth," Greyson said. "Only now, the stakes are a little higher and it's all a little more public. Jackals always fight when they're being initiated."

Jack looked troubled, knowing what it would do to our reputations if anyone ever found out we were mixed up with the Jackals. Before he could say anything, I said, "Yeah. Easy."

"Is that so..." Greyson drawled.

"And then that's it," Sebastian said. "You let us in on all the shit you know."

We didn't have the connections we used to. Even then, Greyson had been our connection to the Jackals, the one who brought us in.

Sebastian sounded like he would have let go of the glory of the last five years, if he could still have the connections that would have made it easy to find out who'd attacked Kennedy.

"And then I let you in as long as you're going to keep getting your hands dirty," Greyson said.

"And we make sure Kennedy is involved enough to feel like she's got control back," Sebastian said, clearly worried about Kennedy's wellbeing. "But not to let her be in danger. They're already coming after her to get to us..."

"Obviously, we're not going to let her into the fight with us," Jack said.

"And I want one of us with her at all times," I said. "I don't trust anyone else."

Greyson's irritation was evident, but he just smiled coolly. "Eradicating the threat is the best way to make sure Kennedy is safe. But yeah, obviously we're not going to let her anywhere near the danger. Especially when she could be pregnant with my baby."

It was obviously on his mind, given the fact Greyson blurted it out.

Which was not exactly the first time we'd heard that, although it had been five years since we heard about Greyson's fantasies for Kennedy.

I crossed my arms over my chest. "Technically, she could be pregnant with any of our babies."

I hadn't realized how good that would sound until I said it. Maybe there was something to be said for Greyson's breeder kink. At least when it came to Kennedy.

"What did you do?" Sebastian demanded.

"What are you talking about?" Greyson asked.

"It just sounds like you tampered with her birth control, so you have every reason to think she might be pregnant."

"Birth control fails all the time," Greyson said blithely.

"Yeah, but we know you," I reminded him. "You've been obsessed with getting her pregnant one day since we were sixteen."

"But I was smart enough to wait," Greyson pointed out.

"Yeah, you've been waiting eight years," I said dryly. "I have the feeling you decided that was enough time to wait. You've never been the patient type."

"I think I've been very patient," Greyson said, his voice cold and deadly. "I didn't come after you to tell me where Kennedy was. Even though she's mine."

"She's all of ours, asshole," I reminded him. I hated the thought of following "the Jackal." The softness I'd felt toward Greyson earlier while remembering when we were kids melted away.

It seemed like all the good parts of Greyson had been burnt away the last five years. I'd missed him, but I didn't miss the man he was now.

Greyson didn't seem offended by being called an asshole. He seemed amused. "You might want to be nice to me. Because you're gonna have to prove yourselves to me tomorrow night."

"Tomorrow night? We've got a game the next night," Jack said.

"I don't really give a fuck," Greyson said.

Of course he didn't. I was sure he would do everything he could to sabotage our fight. But I wished I could go out and fight *him*.

I was so pissed, that I couldn't take it anymore. I walked away, but as I headed through the arena, I saw Kennedy.

She was sitting at a table, helping one of the other girls wrap silverware. Kennedy was smiling, and that smile always melted away everything else for me. She was the center of my world.

Even when she hadn't been in it, for me everything still revolved around her.

I'd do anything for her. And Greyson might be an asshole, but he knew how to help us end this threat to her. I was pretty sure that with Greyson's help, we wouldn't all end up in prison. I didn't want to lose my hockey career, sure. But most of all, I didn't want anything to ever take me away from Kennedy again.

So, I guess I'd play Greyson's stupid games.

Whatever it took to protect my girl.

And, strangely enough, a whisper inside me corrected, *Our girl.*

CHAPTER

Kennedy

That night, and the next day were a blur that I spent lost in thought so that it felt like I was sleepwalking through my life. I kept finding new threads of memories and I didn't want to let any of them slip away.

After work, I had the feeling Sebastian, Carter, and Jack all had so much they wanted to say to me, but I didn't want to hear it. I kept moving, kept smiling, kept them at a distance.

Still, I slept with them at night. I'd felt like I was going to die, and I felt safe when they were with me.

The next night, I stepped into the shower in Sebastian's ensuite bathroom. I was still fuming about my apartment. Sebastian thought Greyson was a manipulative bastard, but he would never have told me he committed a little light arson, then played hero.

But anger wasn't the only emotion—I felt a wicked thrill at the thought of invading his space. I knew Sebastian; he liked his routines, his space. For some reason, I felt like I could feel so much more about him now that my memories were coming back, even without the little details. I had the feeling it would drive him nuts to have me in his bathroom…and that was before considering how much he would obsess over the thought of me naked in his space.

I lathered up with his body wash, knowing it would annoy the others to have me smell like Sebastian. There was fun to be had all around.

I heard the door creak open over the rainwater fall of the shower. I could almost sense his brooding presence, feel his gaze trying to pierce through the frosted glass that shielded me from view. My heart thrummed a little faster, and for the first time in two days, I felt a surge of defiant excitement—the kind of electric feeling I only felt around these men.

I wanted him to see, to know, to feel what he couldn't have—not until he made amends for what he'd done. Not that I could imagine now how he even would.

Pretending to be oblivious, I leaned back against the cool tiles, my fingers trailing down the curve of my stomach. I closed my eyes, blocking out everything except the heat and the sound of the water falling around me. Slowly, deliberately, I let my hand wander lower, imagining the look of hungry frustration that would be etched on Sebastian's face. The thought alone sent a spark of arousal through me as I ran my fingertips around my folds and then focused on my clit.

Through the hazy glass, I saw his silhouette stiffen, his posture changing to rapt attention. I bit back a smile, knowing full well the effect I was having on him.

My movements became more purposeful, more deliberate, as if each motion were another sentence in our silent conversation. I imagined it was Sebastian's hands on my body as I massaged my clit, that his hard-angled, muscular body was looming over mine in the shower, pinning me to the cool tile as he touched me.

My breath hitched and my skin flushed, hotter than even the hottest shower water. Sebastian shifted, the faint sound of his uneven breath barely audible above the water. It was an intoxicating feeling, wielding the power of his desire over a man who always seemed so sure of himself and confident.

"Kennedy," he murmured, though whether it was a plea or a reprimand, I couldn't tell. His voice vibrated through the steamy air, adding an edge to the already charged atmosphere, but I didn't respond.

Instead, I continued to touch myself, pushing myself closer and closer to the brink until my toes curled against the pebbled floor. My back arched, my shoulders pressing against the cold tile, and I let out a moan.

The heat of release washed over me in a wave, my body shuddering as I clung to the brink of pleasure before tumbling over. My breaths came out in ragged gasps, the sound mingling with the patter of water against the shower floor.

I dared a glance through the glass, catching sight of his hand moving in a familiar rhythm below his waist. His desire was an electric current that seemed to carry a charge across my skin even as the last tremors of my orgasm faded.

I turned off the water, letting the silence settle between us for a heartbeat before I pushed open the shower door. The steam billowed out around me as I stepped into the cooler air of the bathroom. My nipples pebbled at the cool air, but the sweep of his intense gaze felt hot on my body.

His eyes devoured me. He seemed momentarily lost for words, which almost made me smile when he was always so composed. The raw need etched into his expression satisfied me.

He swallowed hard, and then, as if compelled, he closed the distance between us.

"Let me." His voice was rough as he reached for a plush towel from the rack. His touch was gentle but charged as he wrapped the fabric around me. His hands lingered, tracing the outline of my curves through the towel, drying me off in slow, deliberate strokes.

"Sebastian," I teased, feigning annoyance though the playfulness in my tone betrayed my true feelings. "You're getting awfully handsy for someone who's still on my shit list."

"Can't help it," he admitted, his gaze locked onto mine. "I

didn't expect to walk into the most beautiful woman I've ever seen in my shower. You might give a guy some warning."

"As much as you gave me before you burnt my home to the ground?" I arched my eyebrows at him, leaning into his touch despite what I said.

His proximity was intoxicating, and I felt myself being drawn into the familiar push and pull that always existed between us.

"Fair enough," he murmured. "But if your idea of revenge is going to be making me want you…well. You already won a long time ago."

He took my hand and guided me to the enormous hard bulk of his erection, pressing against his jeans.

Then he pressed a lingering kiss to my forehead before stepping back. "Come on. Come see my presents."

I followed his broad shoulders out of his ensuite. I couldn't help but linger for a moment at the threshold of his bedroom.

The room was spacious and smelled faintly of cedar and cologne. It was a masculine haven with an expansive view of the city that turned the skyline into a glittering tapestry as night fell. Floor-to-ceiling windows revealed skyscrapers, their reflected light dancing on the glassy surface of the river far below. The river was as dirty as everything else in this city, but from far enough away, it looked magical.

I padded across the plush carpet. My gaze landed on the bed —or rather, what lay on it. A dozen high-end shopping bags were arranged neatly, each bearing the logo of a designer brand. They were like offerings, even though what I wanted most was a genuine apology.

Sebastian was terrible at apologizing though. Jack used to force him into it when we were kids, because Sebastian had needed a lot of babysitting to turn into a good boyfriend.

I sifted through the contents with a mixture of curiosity and reluctant appreciation. There was a silk blouse from Versace that slipped through my fingers like water, a pair of black Louboutin heels, and a selection of La Perla lingerie that made me think Sebastian expected to be forgiven soon.

Sebastian had remembered everything—the colors I favored, the cut of clothes that I preferred, even the shade of lipstick that I'd always borrowed from Carrie.

"Kennedy," Sebastian's voice was hesitant, almost tentative, a tone I had never heard from him before. It came from the doorway, where he leaned against the frame, looking every inch the remorseful sinner.

And looking good enough to sin with, in his dark jeans and black t-shirt that strained over his muscular chest and tattooed biceps.

"Sebastian, I need to get ready." I turned back to the clothes, even though when he looked so hot, forgiving him was more tempting than it should be.

"You're kicking me out of my own room?"

"Yep."

"Can we talk?" His request hung between us, charged with unspoken emotion.

"Later." The word was a dismissal, cutting short whatever plea was on the tip of his tongue.

The door closed softly behind me. When I turned back, he was gone. Unexpected disappointment swept through me.

I pulled over the enormous bag from Sephora and began to prepare for the night ahead. I curled my hair and deftly applied the smoky eyeshadow and lined my lips red. The girl I'd been before amnesia, had known how to apply makeup well, and it had been a miracle to me to find I was good with makeup when I didn't remember anything about my past.

Now, I remembered hanging out with my best friend in high school, doing each other's makeup and watching tutorials. It was a sweet memory. Then I remembered I'd always washed it off before I went home, because my stepfather would get angry and say I looked like a whore.

For every sweet memory, there seemed to be a dark one. But

maybe it went the other way too—for every dark memory, there was a sweet one.

Finally, I stepped into the outfit I had chosen—a dress that clung to my curves like a second skin, its hem scandalously short, paired with the Louboutin stilettos. Call it *mafia elegant*. I wanted to fit in tonight.

But most of all, I wanted all of their attention.

I strode into the living room, the sharp click of my stilettos announcing my arrival.

Carter, Jack, and Sebastian turned in unison, their gazes locking onto me like heat-seeking missiles.

Carter's jaw clenched noticeably, as if all his protective impulses had just gone into full red alert. Jack's eyes smoldered. Sebastian smiled faintly.

"Kennedy," Carter said, his voice strained.

"We're not going to make it into the ring before we end up fighting," Jack said with a chuckle. "You're not going to make this easy on us, are you? Having every man stare at you?"

"Consider it a strategic move," I teased. "I'll distract Greyson from how much he wants to punish you all."

Actually, I thought it went deeper than punishment. I was pretty sure Greyson's rage came from a sense of grief and loss—of our time together, but maybe deep down, he mourned what he had given up when he became the Jackal.

Their collective disapproval made my smile a little wider.

Jack's phone chimed, and he clearly struggled to tear his eyes away from me to look at the phone. "Greyson's here."

"No time to change anyway." As if I had any intention of doing so. I headed for the door, a sway in my hips that I could feel all of them watching.

When we stepped outside, there was Greyson, leaning against his car, looking sexy as hell.

He straightened from the car and approached with a predator's grace, his gaze locked onto me as though we were the only two people in existence.

His lips captured mine in a possessive kiss that left no room for doubt about his confidence in claiming them. He was kissing me before I could have the chance to reject him.

"Kennedy," he breathed against my lips, finally breaking the kiss, his hand lingering at the small of my back. Only then did he offer a cursory nod to the others.

"Blindfolds, gentlemen," he ordered, and two of his men from the car parked behind came forward with long black blindfolds draped over their palms. The bulge of their handguns were visible when their jackets shifted, but Greyson didn't need to threaten my men.

They looked irritated, but they picked up the blindfolds.

"Really?" Carter asked, his voice acerbic.

"It's standard for non-Jackals," Greyson assured them. "It's not personal. You just can't know where we meet yet."

He didn't even try to sound convincing.

I reached for one, and Greyson took my hand in his instead. "You don't need to be a Jackal, Kennedy. You're mine, and that's enough."

Carter's gaze met mine. Then he tied the black fabric over his eyes, his fingers steady despite the tension in his arms. Sebastian's expression tightened, but he did it anyway. Jack winked at me, and I didn't realize how tense I was until I felt my shoulders relax. Jack's easy, carefree ways always made me feel a little more carefree too.

"Let's go. We have a busy night ahead," Greyson said, a sly smile curving his lips.

His hand on my lower back guided me toward the car. The guys cursed and followed, groping their way off the sidewalk and into the car, and I pulled away from Greyson, so I could take their hands and help them in.

I raised my eyebrows at Greyson, silently trying to encourage him not to be a dick. He raised his eyebrows back, as if he were rejecting the idea.

"Passenger seat, Kennedy," Greyson ordered.

Since I'd said I would cheer him up and keep him well behaved, I slid into the smooth leather beside Greyson. The scent of his cologne was dark and intoxicating, and his gaze was heated as it fell on my short skirt, my bare thighs.

Greyson tore his gaze away with difficulty, and we pulled away from the curb. He drove with his usual speed and aggression, but it was always controlled. I felt safe sitting beside him as we sped through the dark city street.

Carter, Jack, and Sebastian were statues in the backseat, stiff with tension, the lines of their mouths and sharp jaws stoic under their blindfolds.

Greyson's fingers brushed against my bare thigh, a hint of a promise before they found the hem of my dress. It was a deliberate tease, and I caught my lower lip between my teeth, stifling a gasp. I could tell Carter heard it, though, because he leaned forward, looking irritated.

"Relax, Kennedy," Greyson murmured, his voice a velvet threat that sent shivers down my spine. His fingertip traced the edge of my panties before slipping beneath the fabric, lighting a sudden hum through my body. "Tonight will be fun."

Greyson's movements were skilled, and his faint smile was full of dark confidence. I leaned into him, my breath hitching in my throat as his finger delved deeper, circling with a rhythm that had my pulse racing to match.

From the corner of my eye, I could sense the rigid set of Carter's jaw, the way Jack's hands clenched into fists on his knees, and Sebastian's quiet, controlled breathing. Each noise from me, every shift in my seat, was a tease they were forced to endure.

With effort, I tried to shift away from him, and tried to close my knees. Greyson's hand spanned my thigh, his touch firm, pulling my legs back apart.

"Keep still," Greyson ordered. "Let them hear how much you enjoy this."

His command was a blade slicing through the last threads of

my restraint. My hips bucked against his hand involuntarily, seeking more, craving the release that he was working me toward with devilish intent. I bit down on my lip to silence the moans clawing their way up my throat.

Greyson's thumb worked my clit expertly, as if he had taken that quiet as a challenge, and my answering inhale sounded so loud in the silence.

"You could put the radio on," Jack said dryly.

"This is my favorite thing to listen to," Greyson answered.

Greyson continued his relentless pursuit, the pressure of his fingers unyielding, sending waves of heat coursing through my veins. His thumb kept toying with my clit, and I closed my eyes, a kaleidoscope of sensation blurring the city streets outside and even the figures behind me in the car.

"Good girl," Greyson praised, his voice laced with satisfaction as he felt my body tighten around his invading fingers. The sound of my own ragged breaths filled the car, and then, with a final, deliberate flick of his thumb, he shattered my control.

Waves of pleasure crashed over me as my hips bucked, and I wrenched down on my lip, but I could barely remember now why I had to keep quiet. It didn't matter anyway, my breathing was ragged. My nails dug into the leather seats, my whole being focused on blinding ecstasy.

As the tremors subsided, the car rolled to a stop. I raised my head, the world blurry, to find we had parked outside an enormous old mansion.

There were already dozens of cars here.

"Welcome to the home of the Jackals. You can remove the blindfolds now," Greyson said.

I raised my gaze to the rearview mirror and saw the tension on the faces of my three other men. I'd intended to play a game to loosen Greyson up and put him in a better mood. Instead, Greyson had made a claim of dominance at every turn.

When it came to the game I'd tried to play, I had the feeling Greyson had won.

CHAPTER

Kennedy

As we unfolded from the car, the hurt in Carter's green eyes cut through me like a blade. Sebastian, stone-faced and unreadable, stared out the window, set in a hard line.

I chewed my lower lip, but didn't bother to apologize. They owed me far more apologies than I did. I just hated the thought that I'd let Greyson rattle them before they went into the ring.

I crossed my arms, because the night had turned cool, and the dress I wore left so much skin vulnerable to the air.

Then Jack's arms enveloped me, pulling me into the sanctuary of his warmth. "You're perfect, Kennedy," he murmured against my hair, his breath hot on my ear. "And you look perfect tonight."

The timbre of his voice, low and reassuring, warmed the night…and chased away my guilt and anxiety. I leaned into him, soaking up his comfort.

"Thank you, Jack." I breathed out, pulling back reluctantly to meet his intense hazel eyes, which sparkled with an emotion I couldn't quite decipher in the dim light.

Greyson held out his arm, his raised eyebrow a silent call back to his side. I resisted the impulse to blurt out that I was humoring him to protect my other men. Greyson had an aura that was intimidating even to me at times, even knowing that he loved me.

Armed men roamed the perimeter, a reminder that the Jackals were always at war. The house in front of us was enormous, and Greyson led us up the steps; two of his men scrambled to open the doors wide for us. They glanced at me and then stared at the ground, their cheeks coloring as Greyson's eyes passed over them.

The fight club was alive with a thrumming energy, pulsing like a heartbeat through the sprawling old mansion. With my arm looped over Greyson's corded forearm, I was acutely aware of the deference directed his way; the subtle nods, the cautious distance maintained by others, the way they whispered his name with respect.

The foyer was vast, its high ceilings lost to shadows, with chandeliers casting a golden glow over the scene. Thick, velvet curtains draped the windows, while the scent of cigar smoke and expensive cologne mingled in the air.

Men in sharp suits had beautiful women on their arms, all scantily clad. I was glad I'd clocked the dress code right, and Greyson gently squeezed my arm as if he appreciated me.

As we made our way through the crowd, I noticed the way women stared at me hard—in a way men didn't dare—as if they were curious why Greyson had selected me...and not them. When we were crossing the massive foyer, I looked up at the catwalk and to the closed doors on the second floor and wondered what happened behind those doors.

I glanced at Greyson, whose face was as mysterious and closed as ever. Then he smiled faintly.

"What is it?" I whispered, leaning close to him.

"I love having you on my arm," he told me as we reached the sweeping staircase that led down to the basement.

I believed him. But I glanced back at Carter, Jack, and Sebastian, who didn't share Greyson's current pleasant mood, and I thought having his old friends trail him was quite the pleasure for him, too, at the moment.

The air grew cooler and carried the metallic tang of anticipation as we went below ground, and I felt unsettled.

When we reached the bottom, the transformation was stark. The opulence above gave way to a raw, brutal aesthetic below. The room stretched out, dominated by an enormous ring set in the center, its ropes reminding me of chains. Seats rose up around it, amphitheater-style, slowly filling with spectators. Electricity permeated the air.

"You can warm up in there until you're called," Greyson's voice cut through the noise. He gestured toward a door off to the side of the arena, his tone brokering no argument. "And the medic will meet you there after your fight."

The unease in my stomach twisted as if it were alive.

Carter nodded, his face expressionless. Sebastian, ever stoic, gave nothing away as he followed Carter. But Jack lingered, and our gazes met.

"Come," Greyson ordered, and Carter watched me until Greyson had pulled me away toward his own special seating area, with the best view of the house.

Not that I wanted to see my men fight.

Greyson sprawled back in his seat...or maybe I should say throne. It felt like a throne for a king or the god of his underground realm. His arm snaked around my waist, tugging me closer until I was forced onto his lap, and it felt like a display of possession as much as affection.

I tensed, feeling the urge to run to Carter, Jack, and Sebastian and check in on them. But I would only distract them now. Meanwhile, Greyson's touch was unexpectedly gentle, almost protective.

"Kennedy," his lips brushed against my ear, sending an involuntary rush down my spine. "Weren't you going to distract me?" His tone was teasing, but there was an edge to it, reminding me of the stakes.

"I'm worried about them," I confessed, my voice barely above a whisper.

His lips grazed the back of my neck, sending heat flooding through my body. His voice in my ear was warm, the tone Greyson only used with me. "Don't worry, Kennedy. I'll humble them, but I'm not going to hurt them. Not when they matter to you."

The same warmth in his tone glowed in my chest. I leaned back into his arms, letting him hold me close.

Sometimes, I felt like Greyson could either ruin me or make me his queen. There was no in-between for him. It felt like that was the case for all of us; we were all tied together, and we'd rise or fall together.

The announcer stepped out into the center of the ring and started to pump up the crowd. His voice boomed through the arena, even louder than his bright green mohawk or his electric orange blazer.

"Ladies and gentlemen," he bellowed like a circus ringleader, "tonight, we have three prodigal sons stepping up to claim their place among the Jackals again! Who will challenge them?"

One by one, fighters came out from the crowd, accompanied by cheers. A mountain of a man with a beard straight from the Viking era. Another had a scar running down his face, his gaze ruthless. The third—a tower of muscle and sinew whose head seemed too small for all that bulk—gave the crowd a sinister smile. All of it made me freak out.

Then I saw Carter, Jack, and Sebastian, shirtless now, in all their tanned, muscular glory. My breath caught in my chest. I hated for them to think I was siding with Greyson. I cared about all of them—needed all of them—and I wanted them to go into the ring knowing how much I loved them.

"Excuse me," I murmured to Greyson, sliding off his lap with urgency. "I'll be right back."

"Kennedy." His voice was stern. He reached for me, but I slipped away and melted through the crowd. People moved out of my way, parting like a sea until I reached where Carter stood. His posture was stiff with apprehension, his tattooed arms crossed over his chest.

I wrapped my arms around him in a tight embrace, my cheek pressed against his hard muscles. "Good luck."

Carter's hug was comforting. I clung to the warmth of his body for a moment longer, drawing strength from his resolve, before releasing him.

But Jack didn't hesitate. When I turned away from Carter, I turned into him, and he gripped me fiercely, pulling me into a tight hug.

Our lips crashed together in a desperate kiss that spoke volumes of the stakes tonight. It was rough, demanding, filled with an urgency that left me breathless.

"Thank you for doing this for me," I murmured between our lips.

"Kennedy, I'd do anything for you." His voice was low and filled with promise.

I turned, my gaze landing on Sebastian. The air between us was charged, heavy with unsaid words and tangled history.

I stepped towards him, closing the distance with a tentative heart. Our hug was awkward at first, until his arms encircled me tightly, almost fiercely. It felt as if he was trying to convey all the things that had been left unspoken between us.

"Good luck," I whispered into his ear.

"I don't need luck if I have you cheering for me," he told me, and I smiled, feeling relief flood through me. Sebastian still owed me groveling, but something about tonight made me nervous.

He touched my cheek tenderly. "I love that smile. Now, get back to Greyson before he boils over with jealousy and finds us a fucking lion or something to fight."

Sebastian grinned slightly, and I grinned back.

When I made my way toward Greyson, the crowd melted away, making sure not to touch me. It felt like a gauntlet though, the crowd pressing away to leave me a space, with Greyson at the end, still on his throne.

I couldn't read his face. But he held his arms out to me.

Settling onto his knee, I leaned in close, trailing my fingers through his hair in a deliberate act of seduction.

"All these mafia men," he said, his voice a rumble of dark amusement, "and I'm pretty sure you're the most dangerous thing in here tonight."

Before I could answer, the crowd roared. I turned to find Jack stepping into the ring. His muscles rippled beneath his tanned skin.

He faced the first challenger, a hulking brute with a shaved head and all his chair on his chest.

Jack moved to meet him.

Pride swelled within me as Jack landed a crushing blow, the thud echoing through the cavernous room. The brute stumbled, faltered, and then crumpled to the ground, unconscious. The crowd erupted. I felt myself grin, but when I started to jump to my feet, Greyson's arm around my waist held me rooted.

"Too early to celebrate," Greyson told me.

My heart seized as another man stepped up without hesitation.

I turned to Greyson, my eyes wide in horror. The casual brutality of it was too much. He was going to make them face opponent after opponent until they were beaten? "What's he doing? Another challenger?"

Greyson met my gaze, unflinching, the corner of his mouth quirked upward in a half-smirk that didn't reach his steely eyes. "If they can protect you, they can protect themselves."

His indifference to their safety was so cold it stung. Greyson measured the worth of those around him by their ability to stand in harm's way. For him, for me. It was twisted.

Before I could protest further, the man charged Jack. Jack moved with lightning speed. The two of them traded punishing blows. But Jack was quick and agile, even bloodied from facing multiple opponents.

I started to think Jack could win. I glanced at Greyson. "How many more?"

"Let's not ruin the fun surprises," he murmured.

"Nothing about this is fun!"

His arm around me was protective and hard. "They kept us apart for five years, Kennedy. Let's be honest. It's a little fun."

Jack landed a blow, and the other man rocked back. As Jack was pressing forward, throwing punches to take that man down, a third man lunged into the fray.

The third man edged toward Jack from behind. Jack was so focused on his first opponent, he didn't even see him. The roar of the crowd meant he couldn't hear the footfalls behind him.

"Jack!" I screamed.

He turned just in time to react to the punch. But not in time to dodge it completely. The punishing blow knocked him backward.

He was outnumbered as he fought off the relentless assault from both sides. Sebastian and Carter started forward, only to be blocked by some of Greyson's men.

I watched, horrified, as Jack took a hit that sent him staggering.

Fear was bitter on my tongue, a stark contrast to the heat that had coursed through my veins when he held me close. Jack was more than a fighter; he was a part of me, and seeing him stagger, bloody-faced, burnt through my soul.

"Please," I begged, turning to Greyson, my eyes pleading for mercy where I knew there would be none. "Stop the fight."

"They wouldn't appreciate that, Kennedy," Greyson said, sounding sorry, as if he weren't the one who had put this all into motion. "They want to be able to protect you."

The violence unfolding before me was raw. Jack's fists were relentless, connecting with a satisfying thud against the jaw of the man who attacked him from behind. For a fleeting moment, triumph surged through me.

But while that opponent fell to the ground, unconscious, the other one tackled Jack to the ground in a move that expelled the air from my lungs. They grappled on the grimy floor, a tangle of limbs.

The other man pinned Jack down and slammed his fists into his face over and over.

"Please!" My voice broke.

Greyson's arm tightened around me, his voice cutting through the chaos with a command that silenced the crowd. "That's enough."

I barely registered the words, my eyes fixed on Jack's still form. The room spun, the cheers of the crowd fading into a distant echo. This was all my fault.

Jack rolled onto his stomach and got to his feet. Slowly, but surely, he stood tall. Blood dripped from his face onto the floor.

But when his eyes found mine, he grinned through all the blood streaking his face, then gave me a wink.

Love swelled in my chest, along with relief.

I would have done anything for Jack.

Maybe I didn't have to feel guilty that he would do anything for me.

CHAPTER

Kennedy

My heart hammered against my ribcage, echoing the deafening roar of the crowd as Carter ... into the pit. Every muscle in my body tensed.

"Easy, Kennedy," Greyson murmured, his breath ... against my ear, his fingers daringly inching up my thigh.

He ignited a wildfire of sensation that clashed with the anxiety curling in my gut. I should have pushed him away, scolded him for making the guys prove themselves like this, but the truth was, his touch stroked a rush of reluctant arousal.

Carter stood defiantly in the center of the ring. Bare to the waist, I could see every chiseled ab and the hard angle of his hips above his faded denim jeans.

"Just send them all out!" he shouted.

Greyson frowned as the crowd responded with a frenzied cheer that vibrated through the house. It felt as if my three were winning the crowd over, and I smiled.

The three of them stepped into the ring. The first had a cruel glint in his eyes, his knuckles already wrapped and blood-stained…both his and Jack's blood. I chewed my lower lip as I searched the faces of the other two, but they were both fresh, not sweaty or bloodied like Carter would be soon. The second was a mountain of a man, as big and powerful as Carter. The third was leaner, but he moved with lethal grace.

Carter didn't flinch, didn't hesitate. He launched himself at them with sheer fury, turning to block blows and moving with relentless violence.

"Carter's an asshole, but he's got guts," Greyson muttered, grudging admiration in his voice.

His hand traced the contour of my hip, sending a fresh wave of heat through me. But I barely noticed when my whole heart was in the ring with Carter.

"Come on, Carter," I whispered under my breath. Watching him, for a moment, I forgot everything else—my amnesia, the past that was just beginning to return to me, the dangerous game we were all playing.

All that mattered was Carter, fighting not just for himself, but for all of us.

Carter's fists were a blur, and the sound of flesh hitting flesh echoed through the underground club like thunder. Every strike he landed was precise, every block a narrow escape from the relentless assault of his three attackers. I chewed my lower lip, feeling every punch in my chest as if it were my own heart taking the beating.

Greyson's hand slid up my thigh, distracting me for a moment with its possessive pressure, but my eyes remained locked on Carter. He was a whirlwind of violence.

He ducked, a fist whizzing past where his head had been a split second earlier, and retaliated with a vicious uppercut that sent one of his opponents staggering back. But even as the man reeled, the other two moved in, coordinated and cold.

Carter's presence was magnetic, and I felt even Greyson tense behind me as his three opponents closed in on him, moving in tandem. Carter fought without ever giving up.

But the numbers were against him. For every opponent he knocked away, another was there to take his place before Carter could follow up.

A cut opened above his eye, blood streaming down his face, painting him scarlet.

And then he was on the ground, the final blow knocking the breath from him as surely as it stole the air from my lungs. The crowd erupted, but all I could hear was the rush of blood in my ears.

"He almost had them," Greyson said, in a tone I couldn't quite read.

Carter didn't stay down long. With a grimace of pain, he pushed himself to his feet. He swayed slightly but held his swagger as he left the ring, defiance clear in every step as he headed straight toward us.

"You lose some—" Greyson began, his voice tinged with sarcasm.

But neither Carter nor I heard the rest of what he said. Carter pulled me into a kiss that tasted of iron and salt. I kissed him back fiercely, pouring my worry and admiration into the embrace, wanting him to feel everything I couldn't say out loud.

"Enough," Greyson finally grunted, releasing me from his lap to stand. With a reluctant nod, he motioned for Carter and Jack to flank us.

I thought the guys might refuse to stand at the sides of his throne, but they didn't hesitate. And it seemed to me that for someone who didn't know about the history between these guys and the tension, it would seem like we were a united front.

"Sebastian's up," Greyson said, his tone satisfied.

The taste of Carter's blood still lingered on my lips, a coppery reminder of the violence that had just unfolded, when the announcer's voice boomed through the underground arena once more.

"And now, our final contender of the evening—Sebastian! Is he worthy to join our ranks and become a Jackal?"

My gaze locked onto Sebastian as he stepped forward, his stride confident, undeterred by the prospect of what was to come. By now, he'd seen what had happened to Carter and Jack. He knew what he was facing.

The crowd's roar built into a crescendo of anticipation as his eyes found mine across the chaos. Mischief flashed across his face, an insolent grin stretching across his features.

My heart stuttered at the sight. I believed what Jack had said earlier, when he could tell I was wracked with guilt. Sebastian knew the pain waiting for him between those ropes, but he didn't care. To him, proving himself—to me—was worth paying in blood.

"I don't have all night," Sebastian called out, rolling his shoulders back and turning away from me to face his fate.

As if on cue, three new mafia brutes emerged from the crowd.

Greyson pulled me back onto his lap. I could feel Jack and Carter's presence, warm and comforting to either side, and I could tell from the way they stood that they were just as tense as I was.

Greyson's lingering touch was forgotten as my entire being focused on Sebastian.

As Sebastian took hit after hit, I felt each one as if it were my own body absorbing the impact.

"Would it matter if he gave up?" I asked Greyson, my voice bitter. "Is there any stopping the fight?"

"He wouldn't," Jack said, his tone gentle, grounding. "He'd never give up. That's how much you mean to us."

I expected Greyson to say something again about how they'd kept us apart for five years, how they half abandoned me. But he glanced at me and then just dropped his head to kiss my bare shoulder, his touch sending a wash of warmth through me.

Maybe instead of focusing on what Greyson and I had lost, I should remember what they had given up too.

As Sebastian parried and weaved, I could feel the tension radiating from Greyson, from Jack, from Carter—all of them bound by the same relentless determination that now fueled Sebastian's resolve.

He fought with a ferocity that left the crowd in awe even as he took one punishing blow after another. Yet, despite his valiance, it was clear the tide was turning, the numbers against him too great. And though my heart ached with every strike that sent him reeling, it swelled with pride.

I might not be ready to entirely forgive Sebastian. But I knew I would, eventually. Watching him fight, for me, I knew Sebastian and I would never be over.

The metallic taste of fear lingered on my tongue as Sebastian's fist connected with the jaw of his second opponent, sending him sprawling to the mat. His victory was short-lived—another man punched him from behind, a blow that echoed through the arena. The crowd let out a collective breath then fell silent.

It was a hit that would have felled anyone else, but Sebastian just staggered, shook his head, and turned back into the fight.

But he was moving slower now. He took a punch from one side, and as he struck back at his opponent, another danced in behind him.

His opponent threw another brutal punch to the back of his head, and Sebastian crumpled. He lay there, motionless, the fight draining out of him along with the blood from his split lip.

I scrambled off Greyson's lap and ran to him. Greyson leapt to his feet and strode beside me as I fell to my knees, reaching for Sebastian. He was unconscious.

"Enough!" Greyson's command cut through the noise, and the remaining fighters backed off, their chests heaving.

Standing over the two of us, Greyson looked out over the assembled Jackals. "These are our fellow Jackals now. Our brothers."

I glanced around at the violent men who made up this volatile brotherhood. Jack's jaw clenched, and he looked so worried about Sebastian that it made my heart melt. Carter's eyes were cold and unreadable, but he gave a small nod.

Greyson's gaze met mine, full of a fierce protectiveness that sent a shiver down my spine. They all had mixed feelings about being reunited. But they would all fight for me, and that struck me with awe.

Someday, I hoped they would fight for each other.

The medic came out to see Sebastian, carrying his bag over one shoulder. He knelt across from me, and Sebastian began to revive, letting out a groan. I grabbed his hand, and he seemed to force himself to come alive again. His gaze met mine, and he managed to smile through cracked lips.

Carter and Jack helped get him up.

"Clean up," Greyson said. "I'll have my men bring you upstairs when you're ready. Welcome home."

His voice was mocking. Carter's fists clenched, but he nodded. Carter and Jack half-carried Sebastian as he staggered back with them.

"Come with me," Greyson murmured, his hand finding mine. He pulled me away from the scene that had unfolded in the ring and the blood still smeared across the floor.

"I never want to see anything like that again," I said quietly.

"Then you don't want to come with us when we face the people who attacked you," Greyson warned me, his voice cold and steely. "That was nothing compared to the blood that will be shed."

When we emerged onto the first floor, the party upstairs was a stark contrast to the violence below. Servants were beginning to circulate with cocktails, champagne, and food.

And no matter how sick I had felt downstairs, I could always summon some excitement for crab rangoons. But Greyson pulled me through the crowd, single minded.

Greyson's attention never left me. His fingers brushed the small of my back, sending sparks dancing across my skin. People tried to snare him, but his focus remained laser-sharp on me.

The intensity of his gaze was disarming. It was as though the rest of the world faded to nothingness when he looked at me like that.

As we ascended the staircase, his grip tightened, possessive and demanding. And when we reached the top, he didn't pause to greet anyone else; instead, he led me straight to one of the bedrooms, closing the door behind us with a click that seemed to seal us off from the rest of existence.

In the muted silence of the room, away from the chaos of the party, Greyson's hands found my hips, pulling me flush against him. I could feel every line of his body, hard and unyielding, pressed against mine. My breath hitched as I looked up into his eyes, the blue of them dark with desire.

"Kennedy," he breathed, and his lips met mine in a hard, claiming kiss.

I kissed him back, because no matter how maddening he might be, he was mine and always would be.

But the door opened before things could go further. The music and talk from downstairs bled into the room.

Greyson's hands stilled on my hips as Carter, Jack, and Sebastian filed into the room. The air was thick with the scent of antiseptic and something more metallic, like blood, lingered on them despite their attempts at cleaning up.

"Alright, boys," Greyson's voice cut through the tension. I followed his gaze to the tattoo equipment on a small table by the window. "Time to make it official."

His gaze flicked over each of us, lingering on me for a moment too long before he poured shots of liquor into glasses.

"You're going to tattoo us?" Jack asked in disbelief.

Greyson handed him a shot glass. "Touching, isn't it? I always tattoo my Jackals."

We tossed back the fiery liquid, the burn in our throats momentarily distracting us from what was to come.

Jack exhaled sharply and said, "Let's get this over with," his voice laced with an undercurrent of dread.

He stripped off his shirt, revealing the canvas of his taut skin, marred only by scars and bruises.

I couldn't help but admire the way the dim light played across his muscled torso, shadow and light accentuating the lines of strength that defined him. But the uncertainty flickering in his gaze reminded me how uncomfortable he was with returning to the Jackals. He'd left this part of his past behind, and the darkness my boys had once been submerged in was beginning to come back to me in wisps of memory, of their split open knuckles as their hands caressed my skin, of learning to stitch them up again.

Of the dangers that had ultimately pulled us apart.

"Come here," I murmured, gesturing for him to sit down in front of Greyson. As he settled onto the stool, I moved towards him. I brushed my thumbs across his jawline before sitting down on his lap. His arms instinctively circled around my waist, drawing me closer as if I were his anchor.

His eyes, deep and searching, met mine. "Go ahead, Greyson." His voice was low and calm, and his gaze was all mine. He ignored Greyson and the buzz of the tattoo gun.

I pressed my mouth to his in a slow, deliberate kiss.

My fingers tangled in his hair, pulling him deeper into the kiss as I let my tongue glide against his. I felt Greyson's hot gaze as he leaned in with the tattoo gun.

Jack responded with fervent intensity, his hands roaming over my back, pulling me even tighter against him. The world narrowed down to the heat between us.

Jack's breath hitched as the needle touched skin, but his lips never left mine. His grip on me tightened, and I arched into him, stoking the fire that threatened to consume us both.

"Done." Greyson leaned back, crossing his arms. But when I met his gaze, Greyson just quirked an eyebrow at me. He rose and moved to the bar again, and I had the feeling he was even more amused than he was annoyed. Greyson enjoyed the little games between us.

Then once again, the clink of shot glasses echoed in the thick air. The burn of the whiskey chased away the lingering tension.

Sebastian was up next, and he cast a challenging glance at me as he settled onto the makeshift chair.

"Do I get a distraction too?" His voice was light, but the undercurrent of need wasn't lost on me.

"Always," I murmured, moving to sit in his lap, my hands finding the warmth of his bare shoulders. The room seemed to blur as I locked eyes with him, and the buzz of the tattoo gun started up again.

"You make anything bearable," he breathed into my hair. His muscles tensed beneath my touch as Greyson began his work.

"Oh, it's not that bad, is it?" Greyson asked. "Knowing you're one of my men now…and that everyone can see that."

I leaned into Sebastian, our connection a silent rebellion against the pain etched into his skin. I kissed along his jawline, tasting the salt of his skin, feeling the thrum of his pulse against my lips.

It wasn't long before it was Carter's turn, his expression a mix of bravado and barely concealed apprehension.

As the first line of ink marred his skin, he winced visibly, drawing a chuckle from Greyson.

"I forgot you were such a baby," Greyson teased, his voice laced with mockery.

Carter's lips parted, and I knew from the stubborn look on his face that whatever he intended to say next might plunge them into yet another argument. I gave Greyson a scolding look and put my hand over Carter's lips, feeling the hard angle of his jaw and the stubble covering it.

"Let me help you get through this." As I sank to my knees in front of him, I found myself enveloped by Greyson's intense gaze, heavy with expectation and something darker that sent a thrill down my spine.

Making Greyson watch me as I distracted Carter was Greyson's punishment. But memories were teasing at the back of my mind, making me think he had enjoyed it, once upon a time.

I met Carter's eyes. My fingers traced the lines of his forearm, feeling the coiled strength beneath his skin.

"Focus on me, Carter," I told him. "I'll distract you. You'll barely feel it."

I stroked my hand over the hard length that pushed against his jeans.

Greyson's stare never left me. "I'm going to tattoo you, too, one of these days, Kennedy," he murmured, though he seemed to be trying to brand me with just his burning gaze.

I gave him a saucy smile. Carter watched me, his pupils dilating as if he were taking a hit of drugs, as my fingers stroked over him again.

I pushed my hair back over my shoulder to make sure Greyson could see every movement of my lips, my jaw.

And then I wrapped my hand around Carter's cock and squeezed.

Carter's sharp intake of breath pulled me back to another time, another place where obsession and pleasure blurred together in the shadowed corners of our reckless youth. Greyson had watched like a dark prince overseeing his court. He had wanted things to be the way they were now back then, too.

"Kennedy," he'd said, his voice a low growl that resonated through the room, "show them how good you are." His voice turned teasing. "Be Jack's good girl."

And I had. With each touch, each moan that escaped my lips, I had performed for him, my body moving in rhythm with Jack's or Sebastian's or Carter's—sometimes all three. They had worshiped me with their hands, their mouths, their relentless desire, but it was always Greyson's gaze that seared into me.

The memory ignited a fire within me, a fierce heat that spread through my veins as I returned to the present, to the expectant eyes fixed on me. Carter winced again, his skin now adorned with the beginnings of the Jackal's emblem.

Greyson's hand was steady, but nothing could hide his laser focus on me.

"Keep your eyes on me," I whispered to Carter, my voice sultry and reassuring. My fingers danced over the waistband of his jeans, unbuttoning them slowly, deliberately. His breath hitched as I freed him, the air thick with anticipation.

Leaning forward, I wrapped my lips around him. The room fell away, leaving only the sound of the tattoo machine, the scent of ink, and the thrumming pulse of desire as I moved. Carter's hand tangled in my hair, guiding me with a gentle urgency.

I could feel the weight of Greyson's attention, the same intensity from years past, now laced with a possessive edge.

Carter groaned, his grip tightening, hips lifting to meet my mouth with a growing fervor. I savored him, taking him deeper, drawing out his pleasure until he was desperate for release.

"Kennedy," Carter gasped, his voice strained, "I'm—"

I pulled back just enough, my eyes locked on his as I brought him the rest of the way over the edge. He let out a groan of pleasure as he shattered.

As Carter's heavy breaths subsided, I rose from my knees. He pulled me into his lap and pressed a kiss to my lips. My lips tingled, and I felt powerful as Carter looked at me with flushed cheeks and a gaze full of affection.

Greyson's eyes were dark with need, his body tensed like a coiled spring. He laid aside the tattoo gun and then stood.

"I hope you've enjoyed your games tonight, Kennedy," he said.

"I have," I told him with a smile. His eyes smoldered at me, with a mix of desire and the need to dominate.

Then he surged forward, his large hands grasping my waist with an urgency that left no room for doubt. His mouth crashed against mine in a primal claiming that seared through my senses. I gasped into the kiss, my fingers curling into the fabric of his crisp shirt as he pressed his arousal firmly against me.

I melted into him, every inch of my body crying out for more.

His hand slipped beneath the hem of my dress, trailing fire up the length of my thigh. I arched into his touch, a soft moan escaping my throat.

He pulled away from me with great difficulty, the tension evident in the lines of his shoulders and arms.

"Keep an eye on our girl for me tonight," Greyson said, his voice husky with desire. "Everyone I need to talk to is here. I have work to do."

Work. The word carried implications of blood and violence after our conversations earlier.

I shook my head. "I want to be by your side. I want to be involved."

"I know. But you distract me." His lips tilted up. "You win, Kennedy. But that means you can't be here tonight."

CHAPTER

Kennedy

O n the way back to the penthouse, silence fell over the four of us. The night felt like an odd dream, full of violence and desire.

But I knew there would be plenty of violence in the cold, hard daylight too.

My men tensed walking across the parking garage to the elevator up to their penthouse. It seemed as if they couldn't relax now in their own building, after having me attacked just outside. It bothered me.

I knew how much they wanted me. I knew they felt I was worth it. But it still seemed as if they were losing so much to try to protect me and to guarantee our happy ending.

We walked into the hushed beauty of their living room. The view always took my breath away. I stared out at the serpentine river, and its reflection of the city lights as my men moved stiffly around behind me.

"Come sleep with me," Jack told me quietly.

"She can sleep in my room," Carter disagreed.

"*You* can sleep in my room," Jack told him. "I have dibs."

Jack's voice was warm, as if he was already letting go of the chaos of the night, despite how he held himself with his ribs guarded.

"You can't argue with dibs," I told Carter lightly, feeling warmed by the thought of sleeping between the two of them.

Carter let out a grunt. It wasn't exactly an enthused sound, but it certainly wasn't a no.

I glanced down the hall at Sebastian, who was closing the door to his room slowly. Knowing Sebastian, he needed time and space to process the night. But it still bothered me.

And then, Sebastian and I hadn't exactly made up yet, either.

Soon enough, I found myself falling into a deep, comfortable sleep. I felt safe between the two broad-shouldered men who slept on either side of me.

In the middle of the night, I woke to find Jack had pulled me against his body, wrapping himself around me as if I were the little spoon. Then I woke again to find Carter's leg thrown over mine, his arm around my waist as if he were trying to pull me away from Jack in his sleep.

The three of us so close together was so warm—too warm, but their competitiveness even in sleep made me smile drowsily before I succumbed to sleep again.

But during the night, as I overheated, I found myself lost in dark dreams. I was in my old apartment again, with flames crackling along the ceiling. I was frozen, open eyed, unable to move no matter how much I screamed internally.

And no one came.

There was no Sebastian in this dream.

Or maybe in this dream, there was only the Sebastian who set the fire, and not the version of him who rescued me.

I sat up, heart pounding, and felt the weight of their muscular arms and legs roll off me abruptly. Carter reached for me again, but I slipped out of bed. I was so tense that it felt like I couldn't catch my breath after that nightmare.

I stumbled out into the hall. The lights were on low in the living room, and I could feel someone's presence there even before Sebastian lifted his head up from the sofa. His gaze met mine.

My eyes must have been wild, because he was on his feet and to me in the hall in seconds. I would've darted back into the bedroom to avoid a deeper conversation with him, but it was too late.

"Kennedy, are you alright?" he asked quietly.

I shook my head. "Nightmare."

My voice was tight. I walked away from him.

He followed me through the living room and into the sprawling kitchen. "About the fire?" His voice was tense. Of course he'd seen right through me.

"Yes." There was no point in lying.

He might as well know what he had done.

I put on the kettle, my back still toward him. The silence stretched so long that I thought he was gone.

"I'm sorry."

I turned, my lips parting. Not because of the apology, but because he sounded destroyed.

"I just wanted to protect you, Kennedy. You are the best thing that ever happened to me, and losing you was the worst. But sometimes, those impulses lead me to do…the wrong thing. I'm…" He trailed off.

I helpfully provided, "A psychopathic alphahole?"

His brows knit, but then he shrugged. Without any rancor, he admitted, "I suppose so."

God help me, but maybe I loved a psychopathic alphahole.

At least it was never boring.

He wrapped his arm around my waist, and I let him pull me against his body. "I just couldn't stand having you sleep anywhere but under my roof."

"A girl needs her independence, Sebastian."

"No." He shook his head. "I don't know what *girls* need. But I know *you* need us, just like *we* need you."

His voice turned husky when he said, "And I'm sorry I let

you down when you needed me. I was a selfish, stupid bastard. It'll never happen again."

"Okay," I said softly.

"That's it?" he asked, his hand cupping my cheek gently. "That's all the groveling I have to do?"

"Oh, no," I said, widening my eyes at him. "But the rest you can do with presents and compliments and calling yourself more names. Oh, and orgasms. You can give me lots of orgasms."

He let out a husky laugh, and then he pulled me into his arms and he was kissing me.

CHAPTER

Kennedy

Greyson had insisted on accompanying me to the game, even though I'd told him, what felt like a million times, that he didn't need to. I highly doubted I was going to be attacked in the second row of an NHL game, but apparently they thought I was wrong. Everyone had agreed that Greyson should come.

"You're not allowed to cause trouble," I told him, side eyeing him as I tried to keep a strict face despite the fact that he looked like sex on a stick. While I loved Greyson in a suit...there was something about his snug jeans and tight white v-neck that had me actually swooning.

Judging by the looks every female in the nearby vicinity was giving him...they were all swooning too.

"I have no idea what you mean by trouble," Greyson drawled, "never heard of it."

He said that as he pressed a kiss against my neck...right as Carter skated by the glass to meet up with the team before the game started.

Carter gave him a snarly look, and Greyson chuckled.

"That's exactly what I'm talking about," I sighed as Greyson winked at me. His smile faded when he glanced at the jersey I was wearing—Jack's. I was trying to avoid distractions tonight so wearing Jack's jersey seemed to be the way to go. If he could even see what I was wearing out of the giant black eye he was sporting.

"Don't even think about it," I growled as Greyson reached for his beer. I could just see him "accidentally" spilling it—all over me—so I had to change into something else.

He made a big show of bringing the beer bottle to his full lips and taking a long draw from the bottle. "You're feisty tonight, baby."

I rubbed my eyes, dragging my hands down my face before I focused back on the ice where Jack was lined up for the puck to drop.

"I'm just thinking that tonight's going to be hard enough without you antagonizing them the whole time," I sighed as I watched Jack, normally a fierce forward, skating sluggishly across the ice after he'd lost the puck, his movements lacking their usual grace and speed. Every stride seemed to be a battle against his own body, his face contorted in pain with each shift of weight. That final guy he had fought last night had gotten in some good hits.

Sebastian wasn't faring any better. He was a shadow of himself. His usually stalwart defense was riddled with hesitations, his body moving with a stiffness that betrayed the bruises and cuts that I knew were hidden beneath his uniform. I winced as I saw him grimace with every collision against the boards. They'd all refused to go to the doctor last night, but I didn't need to be a doctor to know that the crack I'd heard last night in the middle of Sebastian's fight had most likely been his rib breaking. I'd helped him wrap his chest before he'd left for the game, but it had clearly not been enough.

"They do look terrible out there, don't they?" Greyson drawled, not sounding concerned about that in the slightest.

"Don't you think last night was at least a little bit of a cruel and unusual punishment?" I asked, wincing as Jack got checked into the boards and fell to the ice.

Greyson slid his arm around my shoulder, glaring down at the armrest between us like it had mortally offended him when he couldn't get closer to me.

"Well, I think that it was cruel and unusual punishment that they kept me from you for five years, so I'm not feeling too bad about that, baby." His hands tightened on my shoulder, and he pressed a firm kiss to the side of my head like he was trying to calm himself down.

I still didn't understand all the dynamics at play obviously...but maybe he'd made a little bit of a fair point.

My fingers were practically white from gripping the edge of my seat as I watched one of Tampa Bay's forwards skate towards Carter on a breakaway. Carter, who was usually a brick wall in front of the net, resembled more of a broken barrier tonight. His reflexes were slow, his movements awkward as he attempted to block the shot. The puck sailed past him, into the net, and the whole crowd groaned.

Carter slammed his stick against the goalpost, yelling "fuck" even as he winced from the movement.

As the game progressed, the frustration in the arena grew palpable. The fans, once roaring with excitement, now murmured discontentedly as they watched their team falter— their all star players struggling through every play.

"What the hell is going on out there?" Coach Harris screamed, his voice echoing even through the barrier between the bench and where Greyson and I were sitting. His face was red with fury as he glared at Jack as he heaved himself onto the bench. "You call this hockey? What the fuck is wrong with the three of you!"

Jack and Sebastian exchanged weary glances before they both turned towards Greyson and glared at him.

I held up the finger foam exuberantly, trying to distract them with the team spirit I'd come up with for the night.

A small grin slipped across Jack's lips before one of the assistant coaches started ripping into him again.

Jack's shoulders were slumped as he nodded at whatever the coach was saying, clearly not disagreeing with whatever insults he was hurling at him.

Coach Harris stalked along the bench, his eyes narrowed as he surveyed Jack and Sebastian before his gaze slipped over to where Carter had made a miserable looking save that lacked any of the finesse he was usually known for. "Get your heads in the game or I'll find someone who can!"

Greyson giggled next to me. *Giggled.* In absolute joy.

I gave him my best glare. "Can you be happy about this on the inside?" I snarled, elbowing him ineffectually in the ribs.

He smiled at me fondly like I'd just stroked his dick. "Now, why would I want to do that?"

Greyson insisted on nachos in between periods, and I tried to drown myself in cheese as I watched Jack, Sebastian, and Carter gather themselves for another grueling shift on the ice.

The game only got worse.

At one point Jack, who was normally the fastest guy on the ice, was struggling to keep up with the Tampa Bay forward who had the puck. He tripped over his own skates, sending himself sprawling across the ice in a spectacular fashion. I couldn't help but let out a snort of laughter, quickly covering my mouth with my hand as if he could hear me. I saw Coach Harris shake his head and throw something.

That was not good.

Sebastian, determined to shake off the stiffness in his movements, attempted to make a rush up the ice, only to lose control of the puck and crash headfirst into the boards. His helmet went flying, revealing a head of disheveled hair and a sheepish expression.

The scene honestly reminded me of when the basketball players had their "talent" stolen by the little aliens in *Space Jam*, a thought I would carry to my deathbed.

I'd lost my appetite for the nachos, but Greyson wasn't having any such problems. He was now snacking away on a tub of popcorn as big as his head as he watched the game like he was having the time of his life.

Carter made a desperate, wild dive to block a shot, only to miss it entirely and end up sprawled across the ice in a heap.

The whole crowd booed.

"This is entertainment right here," said Greyson, booing along with everyone else. I grabbed some popcorn and threw it at him.

He just smirked at me.

"So, does this make you guys even? Have they proven themselves to you yet?" I asked as Jack had the puck stolen from him by one of Tampa's worst players.

"Let me think about that," Greyson mused, mockingly tapping his chin as if he was in deep thought. I winced again as Sebastian got pounded into the boards. He was limping as he dragged himself off the ice. "That would be no."

People began to file up the steps as the clock ticked down its final minutes, the Devils down by three. I gave out dirty looks to all of them as I held my foam finger up, determined to cheer on my ailing guys until the bitter end.

Half the arena was gone when the buzzer sounded.

Assholes.

Carter slowly skated towards the bench, the other players dejected and unhappy.

"Alright, let's get out of here," Greyson said, practically hoisting me out of my seat.

"Nope. We're going to meet them outside the locker rooms," I chided, and he rolled his eyes like I'd just given him the most annoying news ever. "And no...you can't just drag me away."

That felt like an important point based on how he was now eyeing me, like he was coming up with some devious plan.

He sighed and let me lead him down the tunnel to the hallway where the guys would eventually be coming out.

And it felt like a victory.

CHAPTER

Kennedy

G reyson and I waited for the guys in the hallway outside the locker room. Greyson still had a goofily wide grin on his face from watching the guys fight their way through the game.

"You can stop smiling any time now," I murmured, watching the people around us who were milling around waiting for their players.

"I don't know what you're talking about. I feel just awful about it," Greyson drawled in the most insincere voice I'd ever heard.

I glared at him, but he did that hot winking thing of his, and I found it a little bit harder to be mad.

Jack sidled out of the locker room, his black eye large and in charge as he made a beeline towards me, scooping me into his arms and pressing a hard kiss against my lips.

"Good game," Greyson offered, and Jack rolled his eyes so dramatically I was a bit afraid they were going to get stuck like that.

"If I thought you meant that at all...I would probably have your head checked," Jack said sarcastically.

Greyson did his smug grin again, and Jack shook his head

tiredly. "I don't even have the energy to call you out for being an asshole."

I got up on my tippy toes and pressed a kiss against his injured brow, and his arms squeezed me closer to him.

"Let her go," griped Sebastian a second later as he grumpily pulled me from Jack's arms. "I need some kind of reward for enduring that."

"First rule of fight club...we don't complain about it," Greyson grinned.

Sebastian pulled me into his chest with one arm while he flipped Greyson off with the other.

"You could be a little nicer," I muttered to Greyson. "Since they are injured because of your demands."

Greyson shrugged, eyeing Sebastian's arms around me like he wanted to grab me away. "They should have fought better."

I grabbed Sebastian's shirt before he could lunge at Greyson.

This was going well.

Carter limped out, his face the picture of pain. "Can we get out of here? I just got the ass chewing of the century from Coach."

"You weren't that bad!" I said indignantly.

The four of them stared at me with matching raised eyebrows.

"You were watching the same game as me, right?" asked Greyson.

"I hate you," snapped Carter, tiredly pulling me from Sebastian's arms and walking me down the hallway towards the double doors that led out into the parking lot. I was aware of a mass of eyes staring at me as we walked, since they'd all seen me passed between four different men, but I found I didn't care in the slightest.

Carter helped me into his car and put on my seatbelt as I sat there amused. "I think I could have handled it under the circumstances," I said lightly.

He "mmmhed" and brushed a kiss against my lips before

closing the door and walking around the front of the car and getting in.

"I think they were wanting a ride," I commented as he pulled away, and I heard the faint sound of Jack yelling something from a few feet away.

"They can go with Greyson," Carter murmured, a smile building on his face. "That will give me time to call dibs."

"Dibs?"

"Dibs on your pussy," he commented dryly. "If I'm already balls deep inside you when they get to our place, it will be a little hard for them to claim you for the night...don't you think?"

"I literally just watched you limp your way across the ice for hours. I don't think that your dick should be going anywhere but under the covers...while you sleep...alone."

He huffed and began softly stroking my thigh, his fingers inching higher and higher with every pass.

My core gushed as if his fingers had somehow programmed me to respond to their touch alone. "I'm feeling a second wind," he teased as his movements stroked upwards, grazing the crease between my thigh and my pussy. "And I'm pretty sure that you riding my face and my dick won't be any strain on my knee," he said innocently.

That was a good point. His fingers danced along the seam of my leggings, rubbing teasingly on my clit until I was squirming in my seat.

"Hmmm. Maybe you're right. I should rest," he said as he stopped and began to pull his hand away.

I clamped my thighs together, catching his hand before he could move all the way away. "Don't you dare stop," I breathed and he laughed like I'd said something funny.

"Tell me you want me to fuck you, Kennedy," Carter said roughly, his hand still not moving.

"Please, fuck me," I responded, my voice coming out in an embarrassing whine.

"Good girl," he said mockingly as he yanked on my leggings

until I helped get them under my ass. Carter slid his hand between my legs so that his fingers were moving through my folds.

A ringing sound filled the air, and it took me a second to realize that it was his phone ringing through the car speakers.

"Please don't stop," I begged as he pushed me closer to the edge with every pass of his fingers over my clit.

"Wouldn't dream of it, sweetheart," he murmured as he thrust a finger inside of me, and my moan filled the car—right as he answered.

There was a soft curse on the other end of the line, and I should have tried to stop...but I was too close.

"Can I help you, gentlemen?" Carter asked as he continued to fuck me with his finger.

"Remember that time I told you in fifth grade that you were my best friend?" Sebastian's voice filled the car. I moaned again as Carter hit that spot inside me. I could feel a puddle collecting under my ass, and I was hoping that they ruined his leather seats. The asshole.

He stroked against my clit.

The glorious, perfect god of an asshole.

"I do remember that, Wright. What about it?"

"I take it back. I *so* take it back," Sebastican growled as I fell off the cliff into a mind melting orgasm, my cries echoing around me.

Carter chuckled evilly and slid his fingers from between my legs, making a big show of licking the juices. His lips made a loud smacking sound. "You know, Bas, I think I can live without that 'bestie' title if it means I get to keep tasting this perfect pussy," he drawled.

"I'm literally sitting right here," I tried to growl, but it came out all soft and warm because fuck...that orgasm had been amazing.

And by the dark hunger in Carter's gaze...that was just the beginning.

He turned off the engine and I stared around, a little amazed when I saw that we were already back at the guys' place. Had he really been finger fucking me for the entire drive?

"Let's go, baby," Carter grinned, like he could read the thoughts in my head.

"I've most likely ruined your seat," I told him seriously. "Your leather is never going to be the same."

He scoffed like that was the most ridiculous thing he'd ever heard me say. "Like I would ever want to clean the smell of your pussy out of my car."

I gaped at him as he slid out of the car and walked around to let me out. I realized my pants were still stuck under me, and I struggled to get them back over my ass before he made it to my door, pulling them up right as the door opened.

"Come here, sweetheart," he purred, and I melted as he took my hand and helped me out. There was a feral glint in his gaze as he stared at something behind me, and when I turned to see what he was looking at, I flushed in embarrassment.

I had kind of been joking about the puddle on his seats, but I was staring down at the evidence.

"Not a word," I squeaked as I pulled him away from the car. His laugh followed me as I hurried to the elevator where the doors opened and...

There was Greyson.

"What are you doing here, Jackal?" Carter growled sarcastically, all traces of amusement gone from his face. "I swear if Sebastian had that call on speaker in an Uber..."

Greyson scoffed. "I would ask what the hell you're talking about, but Kennedy smells like sex. So, that's self explanatory." We got into the elevator and the doors closed behind us. A second later we were ascending. "I gave Stooge One and Stooge Two the keys to my car and hitched a ride with my second-in-command. I may have had a head start since they had no idea where I parked."

I snorted, shaking my head. It was impossible for me to

pretend like that wasn't at least a little funny. Judging by the way Carter's face was twisted up, he was not having the same problem that I was.

"You can head back to your mansion, fancy pants. I'm sure your *second* is still crawling around here somewhere and can give you a ride home. Kennedy is mine tonight," snapped Carter, pulling me against his chest.

Greyson was lounging against the elevator wall across from us, completely ignoring Carter as he pinned me with his stare.

I squirmed against Carter and he huffed in pain, his hard dick burrowing into my back.

Greyson's tongue peeked out, and he slowly slid it along his bottom lip. I rubbed my legs together, need building inside me again.

"You know," I murmured, right as the elevator dinged and the doors slid open to reveal the guys' penthouse. "I think that you all have been doing a really good job of trying to get back in with Greyson...but not a good job of getting back...with *me*."

I stepped into the dark apartment, glancing at them over my shoulder. It was heady, to have their attention like that, to have their gazes burning into my skin desperately, like I was everything they could ever want.

"What did you have in mind, angel?" Greyson murmured as he finally stalked towards me, Carter close behind.

"I think you should show me tonight that it's possible for you both to be good boys and work together...for the greater good so to speak." I turned around so that I was facing them, the light of the elevator slowly slipping away as the door closed. Until finally, I was standing there in the shadows.

"I'm thinking you left a word out in that sentence, sweetheart," Carter murmured as he prowled past Greyson. "I think you meant 'your' greater good."

"Hmm. Maybe I did mean that." I grabbed the jersey I was wearing and slowly began to slide it up, a thrill moving up my spine as I pulled it over my head until I was just in my tank top. I tossed it at Greyson who let it hit him before it fell to the floor.

I took a step back, and both of them tracked my movement like I was prey. "So, what's it going to be? Do you think you can provide a little demonstration tonight that you can play nice together?"

Carter huffed, but the sound came out rough. These two seemed to have the most animosity between them, so I knew that this was a hard sale. Which was fair...Greyson had intentionally injured Carter's weak leg...and he'd knocked Carter out in the bathroom and kidnapped me while I was on a date with him.

"I'm game," said Greyson. "I think I've made it pretty clear that I'll do whatever it takes to make you happy. Even share your pretty cunt with this asshole."

My gaze flicked to Carter...who was clearly torn about the situation. He suddenly grabbed me and slammed his lips against mine, his tongue pushing between my lips. I moaned against him, grabbing at his shirt desperately. His hands slid to my hair, and he tugged on my roots as he directed my head just how he wanted.

He pulled away and turned my head so his lips were brushing against my ear. My gaze locked with Greyson's over his shoulder. His cheeks were flushed, and his hand was slowly rubbing along the massive bulge in the front of his pants. Why was that so hot?

"I can be a good boy, princess. Share this pretty pussy while we try and see how many orgasms you can have before you pass out," he growled.

I whimpered and they both laughed. "Come on, Greyson. Let's make our girl scream," Carter said, not bothering to look at him as he scooped me up into his arms and threw me over his shoulder before stalking towards his bedroom. He smacked my ass as we got to the threshold of his room and slowly slid me down his body before setting me down on the floor.

"I have some rules," he announced, and I raised an eyebrow as he started walking me towards his giant bed.

"I'm not very good at following rules, Carter, I think we both know that," Greyson commented as he strolled into the room, staring at everything disinterestedly.

"One...no knocking me out or doing anything that prevents me from participating. At no point in the night are you allowed to kidnap *my* girl and take her away."

Greyson scoffed at his rule like the thought was preposterous...even though we all knew it had happened before. "Fine," he said with a shrug, "No kidnapping or knocking people out. Got it."

"Two..." Carter stopped for a moment and pursed his lips. "Actually, I can't think of a 'two' at the moment. Hopefully rule number one covers all the important stuff."

I laughed and they both stared at me. "You think that's funny, sweetheart?"

"Maybe a little," I smirked. I grabbed my tank top and began to pull it up. "But I think that's enough talking. I'd like to get to the fun part of the evening."

"I can do fun," Carter murmured as I lifted the tank top over my head and revealed the skimpy lace bra that really had no function beyond looking sexy.

"Fuck," Greyson growled, lunging towards me and sinking to his knees as he began to knead and massage my breasts. He leaned forward and nipped at my nipples, which were poking through the thin lace.

"Yes," I breathed, my head falling back as he drew my nipple into his mouth and suckled it, lapping and biting until I was writhing against him.

My gaze met Carter's, and my lust only spiked when I saw how turned on he was, his gaze locked on what Greyson was doing to my breasts.

"You're so fucking hot," he said, peeling off his shirt and revealing his perfect abs which I was suddenly desperate to lick.

He threw the shirt to the floor and walked towards us, leaning over Greyson as he claimed my lips in a possessive kiss, his tongue licking into my mouth.

I sank into his kiss, yelping a second later when Greyson bit down hard on my nipple, obviously not liking losing some of my interest. When I glared down at him, he just grinned, his tongue soothing away the bite of pain.

"Let's get these off," Greyson growled, pulling away from my chest and yanking on my leggings until I sat up enough for him to slide them down my ass and legs. He stared at my pussy for a minute, and I squirmed. Reaching with one finger, he softly traced along my folds, his finger dipping inside.

Carter captured a desperate sob as his hands went to work on my breasts, squeezing and pulling at my nipples in a softer way than Greyson had been playing with me.

A vision hit me then.

Of me laying in bed, my head hanging off the bed, hockey posters on the wall above me. Greyson's head was between my legs as Carter hovered over me feeding me his dick with a groan.

I gasped, wetness flooding my pussy as the...memories...combined with what was actually happening sent me into a devastating orgasm.

"Yes," I gasped as I felt the weight of their stares.

"Fuck. We were barely touching you," Carter growled.

Greyson was studying my face, his fingers still trailing lazily through my pussy, occasionally sliding inside just an inch or two. "Tell me what you were just thinking about," he smirked.

Carter's hand gently gripped my throat. "Dirty thoughts, sweetheart? They better have been about us." His finger traced my pulse as his glittering gaze stared at me possessively.

"We've done this before," I whispered. "Haven't we?"

Carter and Greyson exchanged a quick glance. "What did you remember?" Carter asked carefully.

I blushed just thinking about it. Even with Greyson playing with me, and the fact that I was currently splayed naked in front of them, there was something erotic about whatever had just popped into my head.

"I was laying on a bed with navy-blue sheets. There were hockey posters all over the walls. Grey—Greyson was eating me out while you..." I flushed harder. "While you slid your dick into my mouth." I glanced between the two of them, gasping when Greyson suddenly slid two fingers all the way inside me. "Did that—" It was hard to find words with the way he was fucking into me, his fingers brushing against that perfect spot every time. "Did that happen? Did you used to...share?"

I fell back against the bed, my eyes widening further as Greyson pushed a third finger inside me. "Yes, yes, yes," I chanted, my head thrashing as Greyson sucked hard on my clit, at the same time as Carter started feasting on my breasts once again.

"I remember that day, princess," Carter grinned before he sucked hard on my nipple. "I came so hard that I almost passed out. You took every inch of me like such a good girl."

I gushed all over Greyson's mouth, and he chuckled as he lapped up the essence that was shiny across the bottom half of his face.

"You like hearing how we were obsessed with you even as teenagers, baby? How we fucked you every chance we could get? How I was obsessed with seeing how many of your fucking holes I could fill on a daily basis."

I moaned as a small orgasm flitted through me, and Carter laughed darkly.

"Should we act it out, sweetheart? Show you what it was like that time?" He licked between my breasts up to my pulse point. "Have to say, Kennedy. I never imagined that I could be more obsessed with your body than I was then. But here we are."

"Scoot back," Greyson ordered, slipping his fingers out of me and shoving them into Carter's face. "Want some?" he taunted.

Carter kept his gaze locked on mine as he slid his mouth over Greyson's fingers, sucking up my cum that was all over his skin.

Have I ever seen something hotter?

"Dirty girl," Carter murmured as he slid his mouth off Greyson's hand, deliberately letting his tongue trail along his skin for added effect. A low moan slipped from my lips. "You'd probably die if this was his dick instead, wouldn't you?"

I squeaked at the thought, and they both laughed at me.

Carter bit down on my shoulder. "Sorry to disappoint, baby cakes."

"I'm not waiting any longer," Greyson snarked, pushing my thighs apart, his hands gripping my skin. His tongue slid up my core in a long, slow lick that had me trembling and shaking.

Something warm and soft brushed against my cheek.

Oh...there was Carter's enormous dick.

"Open up, sweetheart," he teased, sliding his dick along my lips. I hadn't realized it, but somehow they'd gotten me from the position I'd been in, to the position I'd been in that memory, my head hanging slightly off the bed. Just like in my...flashback...I opened wide and he pushed his dick into my mouth as Greyson continued to feast on my core. Two fingers slid inside, finding that sensitive spot as his mouth latched onto my clit and sucked hard.

I groaned around Carter's dick which was still going into my mouth...like it was a freaking mile-long anaconda instead of a cock.

Carter groaned as he hit the back of my throat.

I was discovering that however many times we'd done something similar to this in the past...it was difficult work. Greyson was pushing me closer and closer to an orgasm with every pass of his tongue, and brush of his fingers, and it was hard to concentrate on Carter's dick.

"Just a little more, sweetheart. Let me in," he purred, stroking a soft hand down my cheek before he gently massaged my neck. Whatever he was doing helped me to relax the back of my throat and he was able to slide in so that my lips were wrapped around his base.

I coughed, tears gathering in my gaze as he pressed in for a second before finally withdrawing to the tip, and allowing me to breathe.

"Fucking perfect," he growled as Greyson's tongue and teeth worked on my clit until I was screaming around Carter's dick.

"I have to get in this tight cunt. I want to feel you choke my cock, baby," Greyson said in a rough, feral sounding voice as he got off his knees, notched his dick to my entrance, and surged in...right as Carter pushed into my mouth.

They were fucking each other, but their gazes were ravenous on my body, focused on where the other's dick was entering me.

"These fucking breasts," Carter moaned as he bent over me and licked at my tips, his dick once again pushed down my throat.

"Have to say, sweetheart. I think this even beats back then," he said, his voice slightly slurred as he thrust in and out of my mouth in earnest. Precum was sliding down my chin and it was all I could do to keep up, my tongue and my lips working to make it as good as I possibly could even while Greyson drove into me.

"Move over," Greyson snapped, pushing my legs up as he leaned into me and sucked on the breast that Carter had just released.

I screamed as I came again, and Carter snarled as his cum was suddenly flooding into me, surging into my throat and filling my mouth until it was spilling down my chin and splashing against my chest.

"Fuck," Greyson cursed, his fingers playing with my clit as he stared at me feverishly. "Come again, baby. Give me what I want."

Carter slowly pulled his dick out, his hands playing with the cum that had streamed from my mouth, spreading it all over my neck and chest as if it was lotion instead of bodily fluids.

"I want you just like this," Carter murmured. "Covered in me night and day. Think you can be a good girl and let me do that?"

I whimpered in response as my insides began to pulse and yet another orgasm hit me. How many had that been?

"Fucking finally," Greyson said through gritted teeth as he surged into me once more, hot bursts of cum suddenly coating my insides as he threw his head back and moaned in what could have been the most erotic sound I'd ever heard in my life.

We stayed like that for a minute, Carter's fingers still tracing my skin as Greyson pulled his attention forward and stared at me like he wanted to eat me alive.

"I love your cunt," he finally growled, acting like it was the hardest thing he'd ever had to do as he drew out of me.

Instead of cleaning up, he dropped to the bed next to me, his face nestling in my chest as Carter stared at us.

"Fucking heathen," Carter muttered as he stalked towards his bathroom, reappearing a second later with a wet washcloth. He carefully cleaned between my legs, and I was too tired to do anything but let him. Greyson made no move to help and his face was still pressed against my skin, his arm wrapped around my waist tightly like he was afraid I was going to run away. He didn't seem to mind that Carter's cum was still drying on my chest.

Carter sighed in mock exasperation, some of his anger seeming to have evaporated during what had just transpired.

Greyson's breaths became light snores, and I huffed out a laugh even though I was exhausted.

"My chest?" I asked, ducking my chin at where he'd covered me in his cum. It was a little itchy.

"I'm not washing that off," he said with a cheeky wink, tossing the washcloth through the doorway, so it hit the tiled bathroom floor.

There was no hope to get Greyson to move so Carter could yank the sheets out from under us, so he grabbed the comforter and pulled it over our bodies. Carter wrapped an arm around me, right above where Greyson was holding me.

"The asshole needs to share," he said, arranging me so I was on my side facing him.

Greyson growled in his sleep, and Carter smirked at the sound.

"I don't know...I think he did a pretty good job of sharing. Don't you think?" I teased. Carter rolled his eyes before leaning forward and brushing a kiss against my lips and nuzzling his nose against mine in a way that was very cute, especially for my rough-edged Carter.

"Tell me, sweetheart. Did the real thing live up to the memory." he asked, cocking an eyebrow at me. I grinned, blushing at the reminder even though I was currently naked...with cum dried all over my chest.

"Most definitely," I whispered.

He seemed to hesitate for a moment, and I stared at him tiredly. "What is it?"

"Did you have any other flashbacks?" he finally asked.

I shook my head, a pang of longing hitting me. Every flashback I did get was like a little tease, hinting at a life I was beginning to understand was a complicated mix of beauty and...a darkness I still didn't understand.

"Can I ask you something?" I whispered.

"Anything," he swore, his earlier grin faded.

"Did you all love me back?"

The question hovered in the air. I guess I had assumed it all this time. That because I had loved them, they had loved me. But that didn't necessarily have to be true. I don't know why it was this moment that my heart was choosing to be whiny and needy, but here we were.

"Yes," he answered, his emerald eyes staring at me soulfully. "I've never loved anyone, like I loved you—like I *love* you. I'm not capable of it. You took my heart all those years ago, and you've never given it back."

I relaxed into the bed, my heart singing in my chest. I hadn't realized how much I'd needed to hear that.

"I didn't plan on declaring my undying love for you after a threeway," Carter snarked, pressing into me, his dick hard and pressing against my stomach.

"Don't get any ideas," Greyson drawled, snuggling even closer. "Her pussy needs to rest after what I just did to it...even if you are as you say...'declaring your undying love.'"

Carter scoffed and somehow a second later...Greyson was snoring again, his breaths tickling my neck with every exhale out of his mouth.

"I love you too," I whispered. "And even though I don't remember...I'm pretty positive...I loved you then too."

As much as I struggled to keep my eyes open to get Carter's reaction—I couldn't. I fell into the deepest sleep I'd had in a long time, wrapped in the arms of two men that I loved...and that I was more confident each day...also loved me.

CHAPTER 10

Greyson

I hated always being in Carter, Sebastian, and Jack's penthouse. I wasn't just a guest in their world. I was as much a part of Kennedy's life as they were, and her home should be here with me. Which unfortunately meant letting them into my home—and my life—as well.

The car rolled up, its headlights slicing through the dusk. Behind the car, the gates closed again, and I glanced back at the roofline of my mansion, but I couldn't see the sniper I had up there ready in case a different car rolled through the gates. I would never let any danger get near Kennedy again.

Though Kennedy seemed determined to go find the danger. Just the thought of how she insisted she needed to be in with us for any fight made me think Jack had all the right ideas when it came to spanking her ass.

I stepped forward and opened the car door for her, and her legs slid out of the backseat, long and gorgeous in her short skirt, before she rose to her feet with a sunny smile. She looked like a vision crafted from every desire I tried to keep in check.

I pulled Kennedy into my arms, and my lips found hers with urgency. Even in her kiss, I felt her strength, her intelligence, and that undying spark that set her apart from anyone else I'd ever known.

Behind her, Carter, Jack, and Sebastian climbed out of the vehicle, each one favoring some hurt they'd earned in the fight club. They didn't whine about it, at least.

As we entered the mansion, Sunny stood by the entrance, his silhouette limned by the soft glow of the lights against the dusk. My right-hand man, and one of the few people I trusted—at all —since I gave up on my friendship with Carter, Jack and Sebastian. We'd risen up together, both found a home within the Jackals.

Sunny gave a curt nod, his gaze lingering protectively on Kennedy before returning to the perimeter surveillance.

"Everything's secure, Greyson," he assured me with that gravelly voice that sounded like it chewed up bullets for breakfast.

"Good," I replied, clapping him briefly on the shoulder. That touch spoke volumes—the shared history, the unspoken understanding that if the world went to hell, we'd be back-to-back facing down the flames.

"Let's get down to business," I announced, leading the way into the living room. I had the sense that the guys were gaping behind me at the mansion and at the many armed guards—probably more the guards, given how rich they were—but I didn't bother to look back.

I didn't care much about the house, beyond a fantasy of fucking Kennedy on every surface. That would make it a home.

In the living room, I poured the drinks with practiced ease, and ice clinked against the glasses in the silence of the room. Whiskey neat for Carter, a Classic Lager for Jack, and a Martini drier than Sebastian's usual sarcasm. I wondered if Kennedy was beginning to remember what she'd liked before her amnesia. She ran her polished red fingernails along the tops of the bottles.

"Chocolate Martini?" I asked her. She'd always had a sweet tooth, and she rewarded me with a smile.

"Never thought I'd see the day when Greyson would play bartender for us again." Jack eased himself into an armchair, nursing the ache of bruised ribs beneath his shirt.

"Only the best for my guests. Especially those who bleed for the cause."

Sebastian's impatient, tense posture as he leaned forward on the leather couch cut through the brief levity. "Can we get on with it?" His voice was terse, every word laced with the concern that haunted him.

"Speaking of bleeding," I asked, handing him his drink, "are you having nightmares about Kennedy almost getting clipped by that car? Twice?"

He bristled, his jaw clenching as if ready for a fight, but his eyes betrayed his fear lurking beneath the surface.

"I don't have nightmares," he snapped, not bothering to hide the protective fury in his tone. "Except ones where we waste time instead of making sure no one ever comes for our girl again."

I reached for the remote. The big screen came to life, casting an ominous glow over us as I pulled up the files I'd compiled.

"Meet my three least favorite people," I announced, gesturing towards the images on display. "They managed to supplant the three of you."

First, there was Marcus Velasco, a wiry man with cold, calculating eyes. He'd been my father's best friend until my father took over the Jackals. Next, was Ivan Borovsky, a muscle-bound brute whose loyalty to Marcus was matched only by his love for causing pain. Lastly, Eduardo Santos, who was almost as committed to his grudge against me as he was to coke.

"Velasco, Borovsky, and Santos. Velasco pretended to go clean a while back, but he wasn't quite as good as faking it as you three. I think he's the ringleader, but all three of them play a big role in trying to raise up an...alternative... to the Jackals."

"Why didn't you kill them already?" Carter leaned back in

his chair, tilting his drink back and forth. His casual posture belied his intensity.

"Rome wasn't built in a day," I said. "I've needed to consolidate power. Make allies."

"But now you're ready to go to war," Kennedy asked. "Or are you? Is it just that you feel you have no choice now?"

"A little of both," I admitted.

"Maybe the attack was a kidnapping attempt and they never meant to hit me at all, or at least, not hard enough to kill," she mused, "They must think that would give them power over you."

A smirk played at the corner of my mouth as I leaned back in my leather chair. I admired her and the way she was always piecing together puzzles. She wasn't just a pretty face.

And she was too right. Kennedy was the ultimate bargaining chip. For her, I'd go to war. I'd risk the kingdom I'd built.

"I'm not wildly excited about furthering your fiefdom," Sebastian said. "But we should end them."

Jack and Carter nodded in agreement, their faces etched with the same resolute determination. Kennedy's brows furrowed, a touch of concern lacing her question. "How can we be sure they attacked me?"

"Doesn't matter," Jack snorted. "They're not exactly good guys. If they might be the threat...we might as well eliminate them. We'd be doing the world a favor either way."

Kennedy shot me a glance, clearly offended by the implication. She still saw something in me worth defending. It was touching, really, but I knew what I was.

The corners of my lips quirked up in amusement. "I'm not a good man," I admitted, my gaze never leaving hers. "I only really care about one person...and luckily for you, that person is you, Kennedy."

The air between us crackled, charged with an electric current only we could feel. The others may love her too, but my obsession ran deeper than simple affection. I was the head of the Jackals, and Kennedy was my queen.

I would burn the world down to keep her safe.

I just hated that anyone else knew she was my weakness.

"Kennedy." She wouldn't like what I planned, but that wasn't going to deter me. "Once we take the first man, we can use him to get information about the others. Torture can be...persuasive."

Her eyes locked onto mine, conflict playing out on her face as she chewed her lip—a nervous habit that betrayed her discomfort.

I leaned back in my leather chair, feeling its familiar creak. "The three of them used to be close, but the others are sick of Santos's addiction and the trouble he causes. They won't come looking for him too soon if he disappears." The thought of exploiting the weakest link sparked a cold satisfaction within me. "And he'll crack."

The tension in the room was thick. I knew what Kennedy wanted: a united front, all for one and one for all, and a plan that made us all the good guys. But we weren't heroes, and the four of us weren't friends anymore. We were just allies who shared one common obsession—Kennedy.

"Here's the plan." I stood to command full attention. The four of us—me and my once brothers-in-arms—would go in under the cover of night. We'd hit Santos where he felt safest, probably as he emerged from the sex club where he was more invested in drugs than debauchery.

Two of us would cause a distraction, a fight or a commotion. Maybe I could get Sebastian and Carter to beat each other up; that would be amusing. Meanwhile, the other two would grab Santos. I just needed to make sure we were far enough from the club. I wasn't going to risk getting on the wrong side of Cain and company. Those allies were important to me.

"Then?" Carter's voice was gruff, expectant.

"Then we take him for a picnic in the woods," I continued,

feeling the predatory grin tugging at my lips. "We've got a cabin there, remote and soundproof. Perfect for...questioning."

Sebastian's jaw clenched, the muscles in his neck tensing. "And after?"

"Nobody finds him. Ever again. Given how questionable his life choices are, as long as no one sees us take him, I think we have a lot of time before the others get too curious."

I could see it play out in their minds, followed by the quiet resignation that comes with understanding the necessary evils of our world.

Kennedy was silent, but she was trying to be the tough woman I knew she could be. It was an act I didn't want her to perfect.

"Let us handle this, Kennedy." Jack rested his hand lightly on her thigh. "You don't need to see it."

She shook her head, determination setting her jaw in a firm line. "If all this violence is to protect me, then I should be there. I *need* to be there."

Carter grumbled something under his breath, likely cursing the day we entered into this life. But Kennedy's resolve was clear, and in that moment, she was every bit the fierce mafia queen.

"Alright," I conceded. "You're in. But you stay back. You watch, you learn. You do not engage."

"Understood," she said, but the fire behind her words told me she'd do whatever it took, just like I would for her.

My soul was already tarnished, and I'd let it burn in hell before I let anything hurt Kennedy again.

But I hated the thought of letting her be corrupted. If there was anything good left about me, anything pure, it was the way I loved Kennedy.

———

The leather of the steering wheel was cool under my grip as we waited outside the club—just outside the reach of Cain's cameras. I stole a glance at Kennedy. Her long brown hair cascaded over her shoulders, a serene expression on her face despite the dance of shadows on it from the streetlights outside. She was always my peace, even with violence simmering in the air.

Sebastian, Carter, and Jack were all quiet, their focus razor-sharp as we waited with predatorial patience for Eduardo Santos to slink out of his hole.

The second car, filled with some of my most loyal men, sat idling down the street. They were the hammer, there if we needed the extra muscle. But I wanted to let these three get their hands dirty.

But when Santos emerged, he was being dragged out. Several of Cain's ruffians sent him on his way with a shove.

"We'll follow him and grab him when he's out of range," I said, but there were more people exiting the club.

Behind him, was an enormous, blonde-haired man, covered with tattoos. His presence drew every eye to him.

He wasn't alone; Aurora, his blonde obsession, clung to his arm. Her gaze was watchful, and she clocked me in the car as soon as he did. She was sharp and dangerous, and I both wished for Kennedy to grow like that…and hated the thought.

"Change of plans," I muttered, more to myself than anyone else.

"Kennedy, come with me." My voice was soft, calm, hiding the storm that brewed beneath. Her puzzled look didn't last long before she nodded. Her trust sent warmth rising through my chest.

"What's going on?" Carter demanded.

"Your lucky day. Kennedy and I will be the distraction." I tossed Carter the keys, already regretting it.

"I'm touched you trust me," he said sarcastically.

"Fuck up my car, and I'll fuck up you."

As we stepped out into the night, the air felt cold. The city's pulse seemed to throb beneath my feet as I touched the bare skin at the small of her back exposed by Kennedy's little dress, leading her toward Cain.

As we approached, Cain's lips lifted in a greeting that never reached his eyes. That was his way.

"Kennedy, this is Cain and Aurora," I introduced them. The two women eyed each other, warmth igniting as if they both recognized something familiar in the other.

"Nice to meet you," Kennedy said,.

"Likewise," Aurora responded, her smile genuine. "How did you come to know this devil?"

"Jackal, you mean? I suppose it's the same thing," Kennedy said with a smile.

They began to chat, an effortless flow of conversation that made them seem like old friends rather than strangers standing in the looming shadow of the city's most notorious club.

"What are you up to?" Cain asked me bluntly.

"Nothing on your turf," I promised him. By now, Santos was out of sight, having stumbled along down the street to his own car. Driving under the influence was very naughty. But I knew he would pay as Sebastian, Carter, and Jack caught up to him. "But someone threatened my girl."

"I heard," he said. "I'd expected you to deal with it."

"I will."

I was half listening to the girls, who were deep in conversation—about nothing, really, but I had the feeling they both recognized the strength in each other it took to stand beside men like Cain and me.

My eyes flicked over to Cain. His gaze softened when he looked at her.

"They're both very sweet," I remarked, a rare smile tugging at my lips. "Unexpectedly so, in our world."

Cain's eyes never left Aurora, but he responded with a gruffness that belied the love written clear across his face.

"Don't be confused, Greyson. They're just as dangerous as we are."

"Wouldn't dream of underestimating them," I agreed.

When we finally parted ways, Kennedy and I walked down the street.

"I like her," Kennedy said warmly. "Maybe we can have a double date."

"I don't think Cain dates...at least not like a normal man."

Kennedy scoffed. "I'm sure he does whatever Aurora wants."

She gave me a meaningful look, as if that was exactly what she expected from me, and I chuckled. "Perhaps."

When we reached the car, I opened her door before I slid into the driver's seat.

Inside, Sebastian's knuckles were split, Carter had a fresh cut above his brow, and Jack was nursing his side with a grimace that didn't quite hide the satisfaction in his eyes. They looked like hell, but it was the victorious kind.

"Everybody in one piece?" I asked.

"And the groceries are in the trunk," Jack said lightly.

"Then let's roll out," I commanded, the engine roaring to life beneath my hands.

As I pulled away from the curb, the adrenaline that had been coursing through my veins was replaced by the cold focus of what was to come.

We sped off into the night, the darkness of the road swallowed by the headlights. My cabin was the perfect place to peel back the layers of a traitor's deceit. Or simply to peel back the layers of a traitor.

Santos was going to talk, one way or another.

In the silence of the drive, I found my attention drifting to Kennedy—the way her brown hair cascaded over her shoulders, the haunted look that sometimes flickered through her eyes. My grip tightened on the wheel. She was a constant light in the darkness of our lives, and I'd do anything to keep her just the way she was...safe, and a little more innocent than any of us.

A sudden thumping from the trunk cleaved through the quiet, followed by Santos' muffled shouts. His voice was laced with panic.

Kennedy's face was pale but composed. She knotted her hands in her lap, obviously determined not to show any weakness.

An hour later, we pulled up to the cabin. When I cut the engine, the sudden silence felt heavy, expectant.

When I popped the trunk, Carter and Sebastian pulled out a groaning Santos. His face was a canvas of bruises and swelling, and Kennedy winced.

"He wasn't that pretty to begin with," I assure her.

"Greyson..."

"Kennedy, go inside, start a fire. Warm up the place," I said, trying to divert her attention from the ugliness that was about to unfold.

"Stop." There was steel in her words now. "Don't treat me like I'm made of glass. I know who you are...who *we* are."

I met her gaze, searching for any sign of the girl I wanted to protect, but instead, I saw the resolve of a woman who had come too far to turn away now. Her words, *who we were,* lit a glow of warmth in my chest.

I nodded.

We hauled Santos inside, his pleas for mercy falling on deaf ears. Kennedy swallowed, and followed us like she would follow us anywhere.

We dragged him through the comfortable cabin and down into the basement. I had a room ready for him. And anyone like him.

As Carter and Jack secured Santos to the chair, the clanging of metal echoed off the sterile walls. Stainless steel surfaces shone everywhere, and plastic sheeting crinkled underfoot. Santos's face was alive with terror, and some small part of it seemed to be reflected on Kennedy's pretty features.

As Santos groaned behind us, I was glad to steer Kennedy back into the warmer room outside.

"Suit up," I instructed as I tossed white painters suits to all four of them.

I could feel her gaze on me as I stepped into the suit, the material whispering over my clothes. There was a question in her eyes, as if she wasn't sure how I could be both the man she knew who brought her tiger lilies and chai tea lattes, and the one who had an entire room set up for interrogation.

I turned away from her, but my peripheral vision caught the flash of her skin as she shed her outer layers, revealing the delicate curves of her body clad only in her underwear and bra. My heart clenched at the sight. She was an angel surrounded by demons.

"Looking good, Kennedy," Jack's tone was light. He never missed the chance to ease the tension. "Who knew crime-fighting could be so chic?"

A soft chuckle escaped her lips.

"Thanks, Jack," Kennedy replied, zipping up the front, but leaving it cut low enough to expose the curve of her breasts. The painter's suit bagged on her frame, and yet, somehow, she managed to make it look appealing. Her ability to find grace in the grit of our lives never ceased to amaze me.

Jack pissed me off so often, but I appreciated the way he eased things for Kennedy. As they finished suiting up, exchanging playful banter, I forced my attention back to Santos, pushing aside the swell of emotions that threatened to surface.

"Let's get this over with," I said, my words slicing through the air. We had a threat to deal with, and erasing that threat mattered more than Kennedy's comfort or how she looked at me.

When we walked back in, I locked eyes with Santos, his wiry frame trembling against the stainless steel chair. "Greyson, please—"

His voice trailed off as if he knew how hopeless it was to beg me for mercy.

Jack, once our high school's beloved class clown, kept Kennedy engaged in hushed conversation, his voice a soothing murmur that couldn't quite fully command her attention. Her gaze kept flickering toward us..

"Talk," I demanded. "You betrayed me, Eduardo. And I didn't come looking for payback until you traitors compounded that error by attacking me. Now I want to hear all about it."

Santos's gaze flickered toward Kennedy, then back to me, desperation clawing at his throat. "Greyson, man, I'm clean now, I swear it—"

"I don't care. Who attacked her?" I pressed, my hands itching to inflict pain, to rip the answers from his soul if necessary.

"Greyson, please," Santos whimpered, but I had no patience for weakness, not when Kennedy's safety hung in the balance.

Without another word, I grabbed the pair of pliers from the tray beside me, the metal cold and unforgiving in my grasp. Santos's eyes widened as he realized what was coming.

"Last chance," I growled.

"Man, I didn't—" He cut off with a scream as I clamped the pliers onto his fingernail, the sound echoing off the walls.

"Wrong answer," I said, emotionless, and pulled.

The nail came off with a sickening pop, blood welling up instantly. Santos thrashed against his restraints, his cries slicing through the sterile room. I dropped the bloody prize onto the plastic sheeting covering the floor.

"Who?" I demanded again.

"It was Borovsky!" he choked out, tears mixing with sweat on his pallid face.

"Go on," I prompted, absently fidgeting with the pliers.

"Kennedy...she's just a distraction," Santos gasped between sobs. "They want you off-balance."

"Who wants me off-balance?" My grip tightened, ready to escalate the lesson.

He said something unintelligible, his voice garbled by pain. "Borovsky's work..."

I nodded, a grim sense of satisfaction settling in my gut. As much as I loathed this part of our world, it was necessary. Necessary to protect what was ours, what was mine—especially Kennedy.

"I have more questions," I warned him, and because he had been part of hurting what was mine, I took another finger. He screamed.

Santos's eyes, wild with pain and desperation, found Kennedy across the room, and I felt her flinch from across the space.

"Kennedy," Santos's voice cracked, a beggar's plea. "Help me, please."

She jumped at the sound of her name. I hated that he fucking dared to use it, and I picked up a knife from the tray.

He only knew her name because they had targeted her. Because she mattered to me.

Her gaze flickered to mine as she caught her lower lip with her teeth. I wasn't sure she realized what his pleas meant. He should never have known her name.

"Greyson will hurt you too," Santos spat, his voice laced with bitterness. "You think you're special? They'll turn on you just like this."

The words struck a nerve. She snapped upright, her eyes widening. "You don't know anything about them!" she fired back. "There's almost no one in the world I trust like I trust them —and there's nothing I trust in the world like their love."

Her words hung in the air. Our love was twisted, knit from darkness, but it was ours. I could feel the heat of her emotion radiating across the room, the fierce protectiveness that matched my own.

Maybe she didn't remember all of our past. But she trusted us, believed in the love that had grown between us despite—or perhaps because of—the shadows that clung to our lives, then and now.

Santos's mouth worked soundlessly for a moment, his

gambit crumbling before the conviction in Kennedy's stance. She believed in us, in me, with a ferocity that belied her gentle appearance, and her faith fortified my resolve.

"Quiet now, Santos," I murmured, my voice deceptively soft. "You've lost the game."

With a tremor in her hands that she fought to control, she stepped forward, her eyes never leaving Santos's terrified gaze.

"Greyson," she whispered.

"Kennedy, you don't have to—" I started, but she cut me off with a shake of her head.

"I do," she stated simply, her voice void of any doubt. "You wanted to make sure we all had bloody hands, didn't you?"

Not her. I'd never intended for her to have bloody hands. But she reached and took the knife from me.

The air crackled with tension as she approached Santos. He began to beg, but it was clear that it didn't matter to her now.

"How do I do it, Greyson?" she asked. "What would you do?"

"I'd stab him and leave the knife in," I admitted. That was why there were a dozen small blades gleaming on the tray. "That way he doesn't lose blood too quickly."

"Alright." She zipped her suit the rest of the way up, until it was snug at the top of her throat.

"Please, you don't have to do this," Santos begged. "I'll tell you everything."

"You will," she agreed.

And then she stabbed him through the thigh.

He let out a scream, and Kennedy winced, pulling away. But she still reached for another knife.

"Enough," I said quietly, taking the knife from her trembling hands. "You've done more than anyone could ask. You're one of us, Kennedy. You don't have to prove that."

She never had to prove herself to us. She looked up at me with wide eyes. As much as I wanted to gather her in my arms and take her away from the dark side of our world, I just offered a tight nod of respect.

Kennedy stepped back, her chest rising and falling with shallow breaths, and I saw the glint of tears threatening to spill over. She was strong, impossibly so, but even the strongest have their limits.

"You're stronger than you know," I murmured, my compliment laced with an ache for the innocence she had just shed.

And while I was talking to her, Carter stepped up to continue the work.

Behind us, Santos had begun to repeat himself. "It's Borovsky...he orchestrated everything. The threats against Kennedy—it's all a ploy to break you, to distract you, to bring you into a trap!"

"Go on," I prompted, my voice cold as ice.

"Your weakness is her," Santos spat, venom in his gaze. "Borovsky knew that. He's targeting Kennedy to get to you, to take advantage of the fact you can't trust anyone—"

Kennedy wiped her trembling, bloody hands on her white trousers, but squared her shoulders, ready to listen to anything.

"Thank you, Santos," I said, although gratitude was the last thing I felt.

I leaned in close to him. The dim light from the single bulb overhead cast shadows across Santos's pain-wracked face. His eyes, bloodshot and filled with resignation, met mine one last time. "Where is Borovsky? And Velasco?"

Santos coughed, a trickle of blood seeping from the corner of his mouth. "Borovsky..." he rasped, "hiding out...old distillery...east side." Another labored breath. "Velasco's gone underground since..."

I nodded, etching the location into my memory, ready to unleash hell on those who dared threaten what was mine. But a crooked smile twisted Santos's lips.

"Doesn't matter now," he whispered, blood bubbling with

the words. "You're already distracted, Greyson—fixated on the girl, on us. We've won..."

He didn't understand what Kennedy did for me. She wasn't a weakness. She was my greatest strength.

"What would you know about winning, Santos?" I asked, my voice low and dangerous. "When you've definitely lost."

He let out one final shuddering breath, his body slumping. I stood back, watching the light fade from his eyes, feeling nothing but cold satisfaction. He had made his choices, and in this dark world we navigated, every choice had its bloody consequence.

"Greyson?" Jack's voice cut through my thoughts, a concerned edge to it as he watched me closely.

"Let's clean this up," I commanded, my focus already shifting to the hunt for Borovsky. "We have a distillery to case and a visit to plan."

As we moved to clean up, I felt Kennedy's gaze. I turned to her, and for a moment, the world narrowed down to just the two of us.

Her eyes were wide with a mix of fear and admiration.

"Let's go home," I said softly, offering her my hand.

She took it, her touch igniting a warmth that contrasted sharply with the chill of the steel room and who I was now.

CHAPTER

Kennedy

It was strange to return to the normal world—at least, comparatively normal—world of hockey, but the guys had a game the next day. They played fiercely, clearly out to prove themselves after the debacle the other day, and guided the Devils to victory. They always seemed like they didn't really want to be at the parties afterward, but the party that night was raucous.

"I'm going to use the restroom," I said to Sebastian who was wrapped around me, his hands brushing all over me, and driving me crazy.

He frowned like I'd just given him the worst news ever.

"I'll walk with you," he said.

Slipping into the stall, I sighed and sat down. The restroom door opened and I heard the clacking of heels.

"That girl's a joke if she thinks she can keep them all happy. An innocent little girl like that...she has no business with that type of man. She's setting herself up for failure."

It took me a second to realize that they were talking about *me*.

"Them all" should have clued me in, obviously. Not a lot of women out there trying to balance four men like I was.

Her friend snorted, and I saw her shaking her head through the crack in the stall.

"I mean take Jack for instance...you have to be a special kind of girl to keep up with what he likes in the bedroom."

"What do you mean?"

If you could hear a smug smile in someone's voice...that was what I was hearing right then.

"Well...Jack likes to be in control in and out of the rink," she practically purred.

"Oooh, tell me more. I love a little slap on the ass."

The girl cackled, and I felt a weird kind of rage while I was sitting there, listening to a woman who'd obviously been with Jack.

While I was out wandering around, not sure who I was...he was with her.

"A slap on the ass. That's nothing. That night...I'm never going to be the same. I've never had anyone else who made me feel like that." There was a long pause, and I watched as her friend stroked her arm comfortingly.

"She won't be able to keep him. If he's that kinky, there's no way that a girl like that would ever be enough."

The other girl laughed, the false tinkle of it seeming to echo around me.

"Come on. Let's go flirt with them while she's gone."

"Where did she go anyway?"

There was a pause, and I saw them peering at the bathroom stalls, suddenly realizing exactly where I'd gone.

The girls both laughed again and hurried out, the door sliding shut behind them with a thud.

I dragged myself off the toilet, the sparkliness of the evening completely dissipated.

What had they been talking about? What was Jack into that was so...crazy...that girl was never going to forget it?

I mean just regular sex with Jack was mind-blowing obviously...but she had definitely not been talking about that.

I slowly unlocked the stall and walked to the sink, washing my hands in a slight daze.

Sebastian was waiting for me in the hallway when I walked out and he raised an eyebrow. "Fall in, princess?" he drawled. I tried to smile at him but it fell flat. He pushed himself away from the wall. "What's wrong?" he barked.

"Nothing," I said, not wanting to ruin the big win the guys had just had. It was fun to pretend that there wasn't someone after me, and I was just enjoying the night with my hot hockey-god boyfriends.

Or at least it *had* been fun.

"Tell me what happened, so I can fix it," he said in a silky voice that had me melting against him and accepting his kiss eagerly. When he used that voice I was pretty sure that I would give him whatever he wanted.

"Come on," I said a bit breathlessly after we separated. I began to pull him down the hallway. The momentary glow disappeared when we got out into the main bar, and I saw Jack. The two girls from the bathroom—or at least I think it was them from what I could see through the bathroom stall crack—were gathered in front of the table where Carter and Jack were sitting, talking to them.

Or maybe talking *at* them was the better way to phrase it. Carter was staring at the game playing on the TV behind Jack's head...and Jack was staring at the table, fingering a knife in a way that would have made me a little nervous if I was those girls.

"Come on, princess," Sebastian said, kissing the side of my neck as he led me back to the table. Carter and Jack immediately glanced up the second we were back, their features changing from disinterested to...obsessed.

That was a weird way to describe it. But the feral glint in Jack's gaze seemed like it could only be described like that.

"I was about to come hunt you down...or hunt Sebastian

down if he'd left with you," Jack said...and I didn't think that he was joking.

"No need for that," I said in that same, terrible fake voice I'd been using since I'd come out into the hallway after hearing the women. Jack lifted an eyebrow, and I elbowed Sebastian...just in case he decided to say something. I did not want my business aired out in front of these women. Women who were both staring at me like I was shit they'd just wiped off their shoes.

Jack stared at me with a frown as I slid into the booth and pretended to study the table. I'd had a pleasant buzz before I'd left for the bathroom, but it had faded.

That needed to change.

I grabbed one of the shots that had been brought out while I'd been gone and threw it back.

"Jack, you had a really good game tonight," one of the girls said, and I eyed how her hand had just landed on his arm.

He shrugged her touch away and continued to stare at my face. "Do you need anything, pretty girl?" he pressed, leaning towards me across the table.

"Nope," I said, popping my "p" as I shook my head. "I've got exactly what I need right here." I grabbed another shot and threw it back, enjoying the burn and the light feeling that was once again spreading through my veins.

That was nice.

"Jack, I was thinking about that night..." the girl began, and I stiffened in my seat, my gaze shooting up where I saw she was smiling at me, a triumphant gleam in her eyes. Had Jack called her a pretty girl too? Because she was pretty. Really pretty. She actually looked like she belonged hanging around famous hockey players with her wavy blonde hair and pretty brown eyes.

She looked nothing like me.

I did *not* have enough alcohol for this.

I grabbed another shot glass, and Sebastian gently grabbed my wrist. "Maybe we should slow down, princess," he murmured, leaning in close until his lips were brushing against my ear. "I'd rather not fuck you while you're comatose."

I scoffed and threw the shot back because I wasn't interested in sleeping with any of them at the moment—except maybe Greyson. But he wasn't an option tonight thanks to the "business" he'd had to take care of.

I snuck a glance at Jack. He didn't seem to have heard her since he hadn't taken his gaze off me. I was aware I might have been acting a little unreasonably, but I couldn't help it. I'd seen girls hanging off them those first few weeks at the hockey rink.

But it felt different now. I knew what they felt like against my skin, how their dick fit perfectly inside me...I knew the taste of their cum.

And I hated the idea that some other girl did too.

"Jack," the girl whined insistently.

"Fuck this," I whispered, grabbing another shot.

"What are you still doing here?" Jack snapped, as if he'd literally just realized the two girls were still standing there.

They both gaped at him.

"I was just telling you—" she began, reaching out to touch him again.

He leaned away from her hand and a literal growl came out of his mouth. "If you touch me again, I will get you kicked out of this bar. News flash, you cunt, I don't remember anything about you, and I have no wish to repeat something that I probably had to be blacked-out drunk to take part of in the first place. Now get away."

I gaped at Jack as the girl's eyes welled up with tears. Sebastian and Carter didn't look shocked at all. They had wide grins on their faces, and Carter winked at me from across the table when he saw how shocked *I* was.

The two women ran away, Jack's former fling sobbing as they escaped to the bar entrance and out into the dark night.

"Alright, now that that's taken care of...what's wrong? What did they say?" Sebastian pressed.

"Do we have to do this? I'm fine. It's just always a pleasure to run into the women you guys were fucking while I was out there wandering around the city for the last five years because you'd left me." My words came out far more emotional than I'd intended.

I blamed the alcohol.

Sebastian was glaring at Jack whose face was the picture of devastation.

"Well, I can't speak for the others, princess. But my dick and other women were never in the same picture. He's only loyal to you...as am I," Sebastian purred, taking my hand and brushing his lips across my skin like he was my knight in shining armor and not the boy who'd burnt my apartment building down so I had to move in with him.

"Really?" I asked, a tiny flicker of happiness melting away some of the hurt I'd been feeling for the last little while.

He stared at me, brushing a piece of hair out of my face as he pressed a soft kiss against my lips. "How could I have had anyone else, when I'd already tasted perfection?"

Jack smacked his beer bottle on the table, shattering the little moment Sebastian and I had been having. "Thanks, asshole!" he snarled at Sebastian who flipped him off.

Carter wasn't saying anything, but he looked worried and pissed off too.

Jack slid his hand towards me frantically. "Will you come home with me? Can we talk?" he begged. He looked so miserable sitting there that I reluctantly nodded.

"I had plans for tonight," Sebastian said grumpily, slinging his arm around me possessively.

"Let them talk," Carter growled, his gaze promising that he and I would be having a talk in the near future as well.

Sebastian was muttering to himself, something about always getting the short end of the stick, as he slid out of the booth and let me out. I moved to step towards the exit, but he grabbed me before I could get far, pulling me into his body and taking my mouth in a brain melting kiss that set my entire body on fire.

"You're mine tomorrow night," he ordered, and I nodded, just as desperate for him as he seemed to be for me.

"See you later, sweetheart," Carter murmured, his hands sliding into my hair as he directed my lips away from Sebastian to his greedy ones. I sank into his kiss, sighing a little as I did.

I was aware of all the eyes on us as they passed me around, but at that moment, I couldn't find it in myself to care.

I wanted them all to see. I wanted them all to know that these men belonged to me.

Jack waited silently until they were done and then pressed his palm to the small of my back and led me towards the door.

"I love you, Kennedy!" Sebastian suddenly yelled, his voice rising above the crowd of his teammates and puck bunnies. I flushed and blew him a kiss, thinking how ridiculous it looked that he'd yelled that as I was leaving with his best friend.

This was a weird life.

I shivered as we walked out into the cool air. Jack tentatively put his arm around me, like he was afraid I was going to shrug him off. I cuddled against him, his body warming me up as the wind blasted against my face.

We got to his new truck, and he opened the door for me, helping me up into the cab before he pulled the seatbelt across my lap and buckled me in.

"I'm never going to get used to that," I remarked and he grinned, his first one of the past half hour.

"Eventually, we'll do it so much that you will."

Jack closed the door and walked around the front of the truck, hesitating for a second before he opened his door, like he was trying to prepare himself. I watched him take a deep breath and then he pulled on the door and hopped inside.

He slid his arm behind me as he glanced behind us and backed out of the spot. We were silent as he pulled out of the parking lot and headed down the road towards our place.

I realized that was one of the first times I'd called it that in my head.

Look at me...getting used to the high life.

Maybe I would get used to them buckling my seatbelt after all.

"I'm sorry," Jack said suddenly, breaking me out of my random thoughts.

"I mean it's stupid for me to be mad," I whispered, pushing my hair out of my eyes and staring at the passing streets sullenly. "I was supposed to be out of your life. It was to be expected that you would move on."

He braked so suddenly that I flew forward in the seat, the seat belt locking across my chest.

"Shit. I'm sorry," he growled. "Are you okay? I wasn't paying attention to the lights."

"Yeah, I'm fine," I told him, hating how awkward we were being with each other.

"But it's not like that. Not at all. I didn't move on. I—I was trying to forget the biggest mistake I'd ever made in my life. How I'd ruined the best thing that I'd ever had."

I bit down on my lip, watching his profile as the street lights reflected across his gorgeous face.

"After we left, I went a little crazy. I had to get black-out drunk to sleep, and then I'd walk around all day with a hangover, barely able to put two steps together. I got into fights. Carter and Sebastian had to drag me out of bars because I'd either get into brawls or I'd be passed out at the counter. Which obviously wasn't fair to them because they were hurting just as much as I was." He shook his head, his fingers digging into the steering wheel like he was about to rip it from the dash. "I was just trying to forget," he whispered. "That's all I was trying to do...forget your face. And the sound of your voice. And the fact that I saw you in my head every second. I would dream about how you felt, and your laugh...and everything..." A broken sob came out of his mouth, and I flinched, unable to do anything but stare at him as I listened to his pain.

For the first time I wondered if they'd gotten the worse end of the deal after all. Because if they loved me, like I was thinking they did...then they'd been stuck all those years remembering everything that had made us...*us*. While I hadn't remembered anything at all.

"I almost killed myself the first time I went to a girl's apartment. I took a bunch of pills she had and then took a few shots, and when I woke up there was puke all over the bed and the floor and I'd been asleep for over a day."

A tear slid down my cheek, and as if he could hear it, he looked at me for the first time. "Don't cry for me. I don't deserve it," he whispered.

"That girl at the bar—did you really not remember who she was?"

He shrugged. "I can't remember anyone but you."

I huffed at that, but he didn't smile. I guess that hadn't been a joke.

We pulled into the parking garage, and I debated bringing up the question I had about what the girl had said in the bathroom.

I let the silence linger as we got out of the truck and into the elevator, and as we started to ascend.

It was only when we'd stepped into the darkness of the penthouse that I let the words come.

"I got upset because those girls were talking about you when I was in the bathroom. They didn't know I was in there—or maybe they did and they just didn't care—but regardless...one of the girls..." My voice faded away, because I didn't like anything about this conversation.

"What did they say?" he asked.

"They were talking about how I wasn't going to be able to handle you guys. That your sex drives, so to speak, would be too much for me. And that I'd never be able to satisfy you—

"That's fucking ridiculous—" he began...his voice fading away as I shook my head and held up my hand for him to stop.

"She talked specifically about *you*. How you—you like certain things in bed and that I wouldn't be able to keep you happy."

Jack's face was torn, his forehead scrunched up. His lips pursed in displeasure.

"She said you like to be in control," I whispered.

There was a tic in Jack's cheek as he studied me, his eyes glittering in the dim light.

"What did she mean by that?"

"It's not a big deal," he said after what felt like an enormously long pause. "Having sex with you is a dream. The best thing I've ever experienced. I couldn't ask for more."

"But you do like *more*," I pressed.

He tore his gaze away and studied the floor.

"Jack—" I said softly. "Please, tell me."

"I couldn't stand for them to touch me. I would throw up when they did. So, I figured out the best way to get the distraction I needed...was to prevent them from doing that. I would tie them up, so they couldn't touch me at all..." His words faded away.

"And you ended up liking it," I finished for him.

CHAPTER 12

Jack

Since Kennedy had come back in our lives, I'd treasured every second. Life had meaning again. It felt like I could finally breathe after five years of feeling like I was drowning.

But this...this was torture. Having to admit to my soulmate that I'd tied up pretty girls, so I could try and fuck away the memory of her was like dipping my dick in hot acid.

Knowing that I had wet dreams about doing the same thing to her...that felt even worse.

I hadn't been lying that I didn't recognize that girl. I wouldn't be able to recognize any girl from that time. They were all nameless faces. With each one, I'd had to picture her face to even get off.

But it was what I had turned to when I realized that my other habits were going to kill me.

Maybe it had been the worst habit of them all though.

Because while the other habits might have killed my body, every interaction with those girls killed my soul.

"Jack?" she whispered.

I realized she was still waiting for an answer.

"It was something I was interested in…" I said vaguely, not

wanting to tell her that every time we made love I had thoughts of her on her knees, her face in the pillows, ass up. Her hands tied behind her back as I pressed a plug into her ass while I fucked her from behind.

With her history, that wasn't a place I could go with her.

Even if she didn't remember that.

"Why haven't you tried that with me?" she asked, her voice hurt, her ocean green eyes welling with tears as she stared at me like that fact was how I'd betrayed her—not the women that had come before.

Oh, I don't know...maybe because your stepfather raped you as a teenager, so you could be triggered at any second.

The thought of what had happened made me want to puke.

That was the one thing I'm glad she couldn't remember.

"I don't think that's something you would be interested in," I said carefully, trying to keep my voice blank.

"Why?" she pressed, scrunching up her nose and making my heart physically ache because of how adorable and perfect she was. "I want to try it."

"What? No!" I snapped, even as my dick hardened over the fact that my deepest, hidden fantasy was being presented to me on a silver platter.

"This isn't going to work," she said softly, wrapping her arms around her body like she was trying to comfort herself.

"What's not going to work?"

"This. Me. You. Us."

My mouth dried up as I stared at her in horror. What was she talking about?

"If you have this thing...that you really like...and I can't fulfill that for you. Then how could we ever work?"

"You're not allowed to leave me," I growled. "Now that I have you back...nothing is going to take you away from me again." I took a step towards her, my hands itching to grab her and never let her go. "And also, what kind of asshole do you think I am? Sex with you is the most mind blowing experience of my life. But if you cut that out of our relationship, I would still follow you around like a lost puppy, content to just be near you."

Kennedy's lip quivered and I cursed, finally lunging at her and pulling her into my arms. I buried my face in her hair and breathed in the comforting scent. My favorite smell in the world...besides her pussy.

"Please, just let me try it. Whatever you're worried about— it's in the past. I can't even remember it. I want to know if this is something that I like. I need—I can't stand that you've done this with them, but you won't do it with me." The words came out muffled since her face was pressed against my chest. But the words were clear enough for me to flinch.

Fuck. I hated myself. If I wasn't such a selfish bastard, I would have wanted to die for making her feel that way. But I couldn't bear to be somewhere that she wasn't.

So, I was just going to have to work through this somehow.

I mean she was right...she didn't remember anything about back then. And since we weren't supposed to be talking to her about memories so that she could bring them back herself...there wasn't really a way to warn her. I'd start slow, hold her wrists a little bit, see how she reacted to not being able to move.

Yeah. That's what I would do.

And I'd watch her closely and stop as soon as I noticed anything.

This could work.

Fuck...my dick was the hardest it had ever been. Like it was going to burst out of my jeans if it didn't get inside her imme- diately.

"Okay. But you need to tell me to stop if…" my words trailed off because an image of my hands wrapped around her fuckwad stepfather's neck, his skin slowly turning purple as I squeezed...it was assaulting my brain.

"If what?" she whispered, pulling back to stare up at me.

Fuck. She was so beautiful. The kind of beautiful that tore

you up inside. Rebuilt you so you had no choice but to worship it for the rest of your life.

"If you're uncomfortable at all," I finished, trying to say it lightly even though there was an alarm going off in my brain that this was a terrible idea.

"Alright. Come on," she said suddenly, pushing away from my chest and grabbing my hand as she yanked me down the hallway towards my bedroom.

We got inside the room, and I was starting to feel sick.

And turned on.

Which was honestly a really weird combination.

Kennedy dropped my hand and took a few steps away from me while holding my gaze the entire time. Slowly, she lowered herself to her knees.

Fuck.

Maybe I *was* going to die.

———

Kennedy

Jack liked this.

Correction...I was pretty sure he *loved* this.

His eyes, usually a light hazel color, seemed darker somehow, as if a storm was brewing behind them. I couldn't tear my gaze away from his, captivated by the raw emotion I saw flickering there.

Jack's whole demeanor had shifted. His pupils, normally a mere speck against the vast expanse of his irises, dilated ever so slightly, expanding like black holes drawing me in. He was hungry. He wanted this more than he had let on.

A faint blush crept up his cheeks, barely noticeable against his sun-kissed skin, but enough to betray the emotions simmering beneath the surface. His lips dropped open and it looked like he was having trouble remembering to breathe.

I felt my heart race in response, the tension between us crackling like electricity in the air. Every fiber of my being screamed with want.

I needed him.

"What—what are you doing?" he asked roughly.

I cocked an eyebrow, trying to be playful even though my panties were soaked, and my thighs were trembling as I knelt there.

"What does it look like, sir…" I purred, my voice coming out breathy.

He dragged a hand down his face, taking a deep breath…and then he was suddenly someone different. Someone…more.

"I want you to crawl over to the bed," he growled, and apparently I was a big fan of *Captain* Jack…because I swear I almost came.

"Okay," I breathed.

"What was that?" he asked, his voice changing into something silky…something dark.

Something that twisted my insides and made me want to lay down and call him *daddy*.

"I said, yes," I corrected.

"Yes, what?" He crossed his bulging arms in front of him and I squirmed.

"Yes, sir."

"Good girl."

Fuck. A small orgasm slid through me, and I closed my eyes in embarrassment…hoping he hadn't just seen that.

"You just came, didn't you? Fuck, just when I think you can't get any hotter."

I bit down on my lip, and he shook his head as if he was trying to clear it.

"Now, crawl."

I wasn't sure how sexy I looked in my jersey and jeans…but the guys seemed to like it. I turned and started crawling to his enormous bed, well aware of his gaze imprinted on my ass.

"Stand up," he said gruffly, and I tried to smoothly get to my feet without reminding him that most of the time I was lack-ing...grace.

Once up, I glanced back at him over my shoulder. "Did I say you could look at me?" he said softly.

I'd always thought that a scream or a yell was the best way to get attention...but I was learning fast that it was when the guys spoke like this that they were at their most dangerous. I yanked my head forward and stood there, my legs shaking as I waited for what came next.

"Take off your jeans."

Finally.

I unbuttoned my jeans and began pulling them off, well aware that I wasn't going to be able to look sexy while I did that.

I managed to get them off and then he was walking towards me...or should I say prowling.

That was a better word for what he was doing.

His palm went in between my shoulder blades and he gently pushed me forward.

"Lean over," he ordered.

I bent over obediently, and he kept pushing me forward until my cheek was pressed against the bed.

"Up on your tiptoes."

This felt weird...but my insides were zinging, everything inside me tightening in anticipation of what he was going to do. *Touch me. Please. Make me come.*

"Soon," he said with a dark laugh, and I realized that I'd said that out loud.

Oops.

Jack pulled at my underwear, slipping them under my butt and down my legs as I pushed it up in the air.

A second later his hand cracked against my ass and I yelped, a wave of heat pulsing through my core.

His hands squeezed and kneaded my bottom, soothing away the sting.

I moaned, moisture trickling down my thighs.

"This is the most perfect ass I've ever seen," he growled, right before his teeth sunk into my skin. My eyes rolled back in my head. Had I ever been this turned on in my life?

I felt him shift behind me and then his tongue was dipping through my folds, sliding *everywhere* as he gripped my ass hard.

He held me to his mouth as his tongue caressed and licked at my puckered flesh. I gasped and squirmed against the bed.

Jack immediately stopped and a cry tore from my lips.

"Don't move," he chided. "Every time you move...I'm going to stop."

"Please," I begged.

"Please, what?" Jack asked cruelly.

"Please, sirrrr."

His tongue slipped in my core, dipping inside me as his fingers played with my clit, pinching and massaging until I was coming again, screaming as I came all over his face.

"Up," he snarled, as if he was angry with me.

I stood up and he grabbed my jersey, ripping it off me until I was standing there in nothing but my bra. A second later Jack ripped the back open.

"Hey, I liked this one!"

"I'll fucking buy you a million more," he promised as he pushed me forward again so that I was falling on the bed. Jack grabbed my arms and pulled them behind me, gripping them in one hand as he forced my legs apart. "Don't move," he ordered, leaning over me as he angled his cock and pushed inside me roughly.

I cried out, my core tight and swollen from the orgasms I'd just had. He felt enormous, and I had to actively think about breathing because I felt so fucking full.

"Fuck. You're tight," he huffed, stilling for a second as he let me adjust to his size. "You're going to be my good girl. Let me fill all your holes. Are you going to be my little cum slut?"

I whimpered as his tongue licked up my back before he withdrew and slammed back in. His grip on my wrists was tight.

With him pressed against me like this, I couldn't move. He seemed to thrust deeper every time he pushed in.

"You like this, don't you? You little slut," he whispered, trying to stay quiet so my mother wouldn't hear where she was passed out in the next room.

"Please. No," I cried, thrashing around desperately as I tried to get away from him. But he was so much bigger than me.

I couldn't do this. Not again.

"You want this. I see how you look at me. You can't wait for my big fat cock to be in your tight cunt."

"No!" I tried to scream, but he slammed his grimy, sweaty palm over my mouth before the words could go anywhere.

Not that it would have mattered.

My mother wouldn't do anything.

I was all alone.

"No! Stop!" I screamed again.

"Kennedy!" Jack's voice cut through the...flashback? My eyes shot open to realize I was on my back now, Jack hovering over me with frantic eyes, his hand softly caressing my hair.

I was in his bedroom. On his bed.

I was safe.

He wasn't here.

I wiped at my face, realizing my skin was soaked with tears.

"You had a flashback...didn't you?" Jack asked in a tortured voice. "I knew this would happen. Fuck. Fuck!" he yelled. He wiped at his eyes angrily, before staring down at me.

"Someone was...someone was hurting me," I whispered.""They were about to—I think they were about to..." A hitched sob escaped from my mouth as Jack sank to his knees in front of me.

"I'm so sorry," he said in a strange, flat voice. "I'm so sorry."

There was a savage snarl, and a second later Frank was ripped off me, his body thrown to the floor with a loud crash that reverberated around the room. I scrambled to my feet, pulling at the scraps of my dress as I turned around and saw Jack straddling him.

Jack's fists few at Frank's face, his hands a blur of motion fueled by pure adrenaline and rage. His normally composed demeanor was replaced by a primal ferocity, his muscles coiled like a spring ready to unleash its fury.

The air crackled with violence, the sound of flesh meeting flesh echoing through the small room like a symphony of pain. There was a wildness in Jack's eyes, a fire burning bright.

Frank's fists were raised as he feebly tried to defend himself against Jack's onslaught. But it was like trying to stop a hurricane with a cardboard box, futile and ultimately doomed to fail.

I watched in awe as Jack moved with a grace that belied the brutality of his actions, each strike landing with precision and purpose. There was no hesitation in his movements, no mercy in his gaze, only a relentless determination.

Jack's hands wrapped around his throat. Frank struggled, his limbs wildly thrashing around as he tried to get out of his grip.

But Jack was a man in peak physical condition. Frank, with his years of booze and drugs...he didn't stand a chance.

The air was heavy with the sound of choking, his gasps for air mixing with the sickening sound of flesh against flesh as Jack's grip tightened with each passing moment. A garbled sound was coming from his lips as he tried to beg for Jack to stop.

I should have been horrified. I should have told him to stop. But instead I watched in calm satisfaction as life slowly began to fade from Frank's gaze, replaced by a vacant emptiness that I would remember for the rest of my life, the memory of it like a scar that would never heal.

That I would never want to heal.

And then, just as suddenly as it had begun, it was over. Jack released his grip on Frank's throat stood up, Frank's body slumping to the ground in a motionless heap. The room was silent save for the sound of our ragged breathing, the aftermath of violence hanging thick in the air like fog.

Jack's gaze met mine, the anger and ferociousness fading as we stared at each other.

"Kennedy," he breathed as he threw himself at me, gathering me *into his strong arms as I began to sob, my entire body shaking against him as it really hit me what had just happened.*

I looked beyond him, a numbness settling into my veins as I stared at the dead body laying on the floor.

Jack had just killed him for me.

"Kennedy, baby. Are you—I mean fuck, of course you're not okay. Fuck. Did he...?" He made a retching sound, like he was going to throw up.

I had thrown up in the past after he'd—it was hard to even think the words.

But something had settled in my chest as soon as the last breath had left that asshole's body. The man who had been torturing me since almost the moment my mother had brought him home...he was gone.

"Kennedy, say something," he breathed, his voice breaking as he tilted my head back so he could stare at my face.

"You killed him," I whispered.

A savage look crossed his features. "I should have given him a much more painful death." He cursed. "You're terrified of me, aren't you? Fuck. I should have taken him outside, I—"

I slammed my lips against his, trying to put every ounce of my thankfulness and love into that kiss.

His tongue slid into my mouth and I moaned as my hands tangled in his hair. I wanted him. I wanted to show him just how much I loved him.

"Fuck. Kennedy," he said in between our frantic kisses. "I really love where this is going, pretty girl...and I definitely want to pick this up later..." I sucked lightly on his tongue, trying to catch every taste of him that I could. "Kennedy," he growled. "I think I need to get rid of this body." His lips danced down my neck and I pulled on his shirt, trying to get it off him...because I'd clearly lost my mind. "Baby. Seriously. I haven't exactly...murdered someone before...but..." Another kiss. "I need to get this party started."

"Yes, exactly. That's what I'm trying to do. Get this started," I breathed, barely recognizing myself. There was some strange, crazy energy surging through my veins.

Something buzzed between us and I cried out when Jack jerked
himself away, his breath coming out in ragged gasps. He pulled the
phone from his pocket. "It's Greyson. He'll know what to do..."

"Greyson knows what to do with a dead body?" I asked, confused. I
mean I'd heard the stories about Greyson, but we'd never talked about
it. Who heard of a high school hockey player that was in the freaking
mafia?

"Hey...we might have a problem."

I came back to the present with a gasp, my head spinning,
and my stomach feeling queasy as I went over everything I had
just...remembered.

Everything I wish I hadn't...remembered.

Frank—Frank had been my stepfather. I could remember
small flashes of the past. A small, hot room with no air condi-
tioner. Faded flowered wallpaper peeling off the walls.

And a flimsy lock.

That never worked the entire time I'd lived there.

My stepfather had been trying to rape me. He *had* raped me
in the past.

Thank fuck I couldn't recall those specific moments now.

Jack had...killed him.

"You killed Frank," I whispered.

"What did you just say?" Jack asked in shock.

"You killed my stepfather. He—he'd been hurting me. And
you killed him."

Jack searched my face, his skin pale and his jaw tense. "You
remember?"

"Like it just happened yesterday," I whispered, my hand
reaching up to gently stroke his face.

I'd been searching for some link to the past.

Something that gave me a hint of the bond we'd shared
before...one that I couldn't remember.

Murder apparently was enough to solidify that. At least with
Jack.

Not sure you could ask for more of a bond than that.

"I would have done anything for you back then," he whispered, brushing a tender kiss across my lips. "And I'd do anything for you now."

"Make love to me, Jack. I need you," I whispered, a sense of calm settling over me.

His face blanched and he tried to move away. I grabbed his face and forced him to look at me. "Please."

I took his hand and stepped back towards the bed, leading him with me.

"Kennedy. Sweetheart. I—"

"Just trust me, Jack. Remembering now...I think I'll be okay. I just have this feeling."

"I feel like the biggest asshole that I'm hard right now," he growled, his tone frustrated.

I laid back on the bed, pulling him with me as I did so until he was hovering above me. I put my arms above my head, my hands clasped together. "We can work our way into more. But for now...we'll do this. Take me, Jack. I'm yours."

Maybe murder turned me on.

I'd have to analyze that at a later date.

Jack studied me for a second, before that earlier commanding presence settled over him. His hands moved to my thighs and he slowly moved them upwards until they were settled right under my core. Jack's thumbs idly slid along my skin, each brush coming achingly close to where I wanted him.

"I can't resist you," he finally murmured. "I would give you whatever you wanted. Be whoever you wanted me to be. Die trying to keep you." His hands glided around my thighs until he was gripping my ass, squeezing as he leaned forward and captured my lips in a deep, desperate kiss.

My hands came down to grab his hair and he broke away. "Hands above your head," he growled, one hand coming out from under me to grab both of my wrists in a tight grip. He had me pinned under him, but it didn't feel quite as intimidating as it had before I'd had that flashback. Like knowing he would kill for me had quieted something inside me, assured me that he would never hurt me. That I would always be safe with him.

'You're my sweet, perfect girl, aren't you, baby? You're going to choke my cock, take my cum. Give me whatever I want."

"Yes," I cried, and we both groaned almost in unison as he slid into me, his face burying in my neck as he held my arms above my head. We stayed like that for a minute and then he lifted his head, a fierce, desperate hunger in his gaze...right before he bit down on my pulse point, his hips beginning to hammer in and out of me. My pussy throbbed and squeezed at his dick and I whimpered. He was so big, it was almost painful. But the bite of hurt only amplified the pleasure.

"Fuck, yes. Squeeze my dick. Just like that," he begged. My core tightened hearing how desperate he was.

My insides began to flutter as an orgasm built deep inside me. He still had me pinned down, my hips barely able to move as I took every inch of him, over and over until I was flying— pleasure shooting through me—the edges of my vision darkening from the exquisite intensity of the moment.

"One day I'm going to shove a plug in this perfect ass. Stretch that hole out while I fuck you until you pass out. Choke you with my dick while I fuck your face. My gorgeous, little fuck toy."

I groaned as his words sent me flying over the edge. Again.

"That's my sweet pussy. How are you even real? Fuck. I love you." His cock slipped through my wetness, battering in and out in long, hard strokes.

I arched against him as he continued to mutter filthy, perfect words, until finally, his thrusts turned erratic. "Fuck. Yes," he breathed as his cock pulsed inside me. A second later, I could feel his liquid bursts of heat filling my core, the sensation of it sending one last orgasm rushing through me.

He'd collapsed on top of me as he came and we laid like that for a second, until it became a little hard to breathe—he was so much bigger than I was.

"Are you okay?" he finally asked in a gruff, pinched voice as he lifted my head with a somber expression on his beautiful face.

"Okay?"

"I was rougher than I'd intended. Did you have any flashbacks? Did you even like any of that?"

My eyes widened. "You did feel me having multiple orgasms around your dick, right?" I huffed with a small laugh, whimpering softly when his dick twitched inside me like it was up for another round.

"Kennedy, I love you," he whispered.

And I felt the words all the way to my soul.

He carefully rolled us so that we were on our sides, facing one another. He was somehow still inside me.

"Tell me about that day," I whispered, my hand cradling his cheek as we stared deep into each other's eyes. "I've already remembered the important part," I pressed when he seemed to hesitate.

"You'd acted weird at school and hadn't wanted to hang out afterwards, which was something we did every day—we couldn't get enough of you, so we would try and get you to hang out with us as much as we could. But you hadn't wanted to that day." His eyes grew hazy, like he was back in that moment. "I'd made it two minutes away from your place before I'd decided I couldn't bear to not see you until the morning. I was going to beg you to hang out if that's what it took."

I snorted, and a small smile slipped across his lips. "You've had us wrapped around your finger for a long time, pretty girl." His dick began to thicken inside me, but he continued talking like he hadn't noticed.

His smile dimmed.

"I thought you were alone...he was usually drunk at a bar somewhere, or pretending to work at the tire shop. So, I hadn't bothered knocking. I just walked in. I heard you crying and rushed down the hall and—" His words faded away and he squeezed his eyes closed.

It was a strange thing. I could remember it. But it felt like it was something that had happened to someone else. Maybe later when I was alone, what had happened would sink in and feel real. But right now, connected to him like this...it felt like a dream.

A terrible, bad dream for sure.

But just a dream.

"I lost my mind, I guess. But I don't regret it."

"I remember you, Greyson, and Sebastian leaving with the body while Carter stayed with me. But where did you take the body?"

"Greyson had connections. A pig farm got rid of all the evidence. Your mother didn't call the police until he hadn't come home for a week. And a guy like that...well the police hadn't cared if he'd disappeared. Everyone agreed the world would be better off if he was gone."

I nodded, remembering bits and pieces of that. A police officer at the door. My fear we would be discovered. Crying coming out of my mother's room.

And me finally being able to sleep at night.

"I'm sure I said it back then...but thank you," I murmured.

"I know you don't remember it," he whispered. "I know we've made so many mistakes, that we've done so many things wrong. But my world begins and ends with you. I love you so much it hurts. I would do anything to prove that to you."

"I love you," I answered as he smoothly rolled us over and pushed further into me once again.

We made love again, and I cried.

It finally felt like things were starting to make sense.

CHAPTER 13

Sebastian

The next night was going to be my night with Kennedy. I knew I'd have to fight the others for my time with my girl, but I was ready.

But first, we had a fucking family dinner. Even with Greyson. We really would all do anything for her…and I could tell it made her happy, so I was perfectly content.

It helped that Carter could cook.

In our dining room, the exposed brick walls felt sturdy and cozy. The savory scent of barbecue and charcoaled steak hung in the air. When Kennedy rose from her seat and settled herself into Carter's lap to kiss his cheek with appreciation for the good meal, I couldn't even summon any jealousy.

"Man, that was good," I said, pushing my plate away. There was a collective sense of contentment at the dining table, glasses of whiskey reflecting the soft glow of the pendant lights overhead.

Greyson raised his glass in a silent toast to Carter.

Kennedy, her laughter the most intoxicating sound in the world to me, beamed at all of us, her eyes sparkling with an irrepressible mischief.

"Thanks guys, but who actually did the dishes last time?

That's where you show your gratitude." Carter said with a grin. Of course he looked happy, when Kennedy was looking at him like that, and she was perched on his leg. He wrapped his arm around her waist, nuzzling his lips against her throat, unable to resist touching her.

It was a rare moment of peace and comfort for all of us.

But of course, Greyson still had to be Greyson.

"Not you, Sebastian?" he asked, faux innocently. "I bet Kennedy would rather have someone who cleans up after themselves, right?"

Kennedy rolled her eyes so dramatically I almost laughed. "That wouldn't be you, would it, Greyson?" she asked before I could respond to him.

"I don't live here," Greyson said. "Speaking of which. We'll have to talk about that at some point."

Greyson was obviously not going to be content to have Kennedy here all the time.

She pushed back from the table and stood up, shaking her head as if we were children squabbling over the last piece of candy.

"Put away the ruler, boys. I'm not impressed with any of you," she teased, tossing the comment over her shoulder as she sauntered off toward the living room, hips swaying in a rhythm that my pulse jumped to meet.

"Hey, I'm coming with you," Jack called after her, his voice laced with a playful arrogance that always seemed to amuse her. "I know how to impress you!"

"Prove it," her voice floated back to us, full of teasing.

Jack gave us a grin and ran after her.

"I think we all know how to impress Kennedy." I frowned.

Carter shrugged and followed them, leaving the dishes on the table.

I sighed and got up. "Help me out here, Greyson. You're the one who talked us into dish duty."

Greyson scoffed, but he started to stack the plates, no matter what he'd said.

In the kitchen, I leaned against the cool granite of the kitchen island, my gaze fixed on the array of half-empty wine glasses and stack of dirty dishes. Carter had apparently managed to use every pan we owned in the pursuit of dinner.

The penthouse held the echo of laughter from the living room, where the rest of our unlikely family had migrated. In this moment, it was just Greyson and me, the tension between us hanging in the air.

"The housekeeper comes in tomorrow," I said, shrugging.

Greyson shook his head. "And what precautions are you taking after having someone else in Kennedy's home?"

I didn't argue with him about whose house it was. The minute Kennedy walked into our home, it was hers.

"Velasco and Borovsky won't stop until they get what they want," Greyson stated flatly, his voice low and dangerous. "And they *want* Kennedy."

"Borovsky is still holed up in the distillery?"

Greyson nodded.

"Is he hiding from you or someone else?"

"Word on the street is he and Velasco are on the outs. I'm really curious what put a crack in that friendship."

"Maybe we should go ask him," I suggested.

Greyson's lips smirked in a faint smile of approval.

For all our differences, this protectiveness over Kennedy was a shared connection that neither of us could deny.

The shrill ring of a phone shattered the quiet understanding between us. Greyson drew his cell from his pocket with a swift motion, his expression morphing into one of steely anticipation. "Yes?"

He paced the confines of the kitchen with a predator's stride as he listened. Every terse word he uttered tightened the coil of unease in my gut.

"When?" A pause. "No, don't engage. Keep your eyes on him." He glanced at me, his blue eyes flashing.

"Understood." His hand squeezed the phone, knuckles whitening. With a decisive click, he ended the call and faced me, a predator ready to strike. "Velasco's been spotted heading toward the distillery on the east side. Want to go...observe?"

My heart hammered against my ribs with sudden adrenaline. Greyson had the look of a man who intended to get his hands bloody tonight. But Kennedy would want to go with us if this were anything but a simple observation mission.

The urgency to protect Kennedy pulsed through me like an electric current. "Seems convenient. Could this be a trap?"

"It's possible," he conceded, his eyes hard as flint. "But it's a risk I'm willing to take."

He paused, glancing toward the doorway. "Not Kennedy, though. She stays put."

"Agreed."

"Coming with me?" Greyson leaned against the island, his arms crossed over his chest, which pulled at his jacket and revealed the shape of the gun hidden beneath.

Rolling my shoulders back, I shot him a wry grin. "Oh, Greyson, we're still BFF's deep down. I wouldn't miss it."

When we stepped into the living room, the soft glow of the lamps cast a warm aura around Kennedy, who nestled comfortably between Jack and Carter on the plush leather couch. She was laughing at something Carter said. Jack's hand moved in slow, soothing circles over her sock-clad feet, which were pulled into his lap. I felt an ache in my chest over how badly I wanted to join the three of them.

"Hey, guys," I called out, feigning nonchalance. Just going 'out'. No chance of violence. "Greyson and I have to step out for a bit. Just going to check on things at the distillery."

Kennedy's laughter faltered, her gaze snapping to mine with an intuitive sharpness that saw too much. "What's going on?"

"Everything's fine, Kennedy," I reassured her. "We just want to get our own eyes on the place and make sure Velasco is there."

She didn't look entirely convinced, but she nodded, allowing us to maintain the façade of a harmless outing. "You'll be careful?"

"Always am," I promised. I leaned over the couch to press a hot, fierce kiss to her lips.

Nothing could stop me from coming back to my girl.

As we stepped into the parking garage, the chill of the night wrapped around us like a shroud. Greyson pointed to his car, a low-slung sleek black sports car. The silence seemed to stretch between us.

As we snaked through the desolate streets leading out of the city toward the distillery, my hands fidgeted on my knees, craving the feel of Kennedy's soft hair between my fingers. The silence between Greyson and me was charged, each of us lost in our own grim thoughts.

I was trusting Greyson to help protect Kennedy and to protect us from losing everything while we did so. But could I really trust Greyson?

Could he really resist the opportunity to ruin us if he saw the chance to have Kennedy to himself?

We pulled up to the outskirts of the distillery, which loomed against the night sky. A perimeter had already been established. Greyson's men communicated with subtle gestures as they prowled the invisible barrier, many of them armed with machine guns.

Sunny, Greyson's right hand, approached as we stepped out of the car. There was deference etched into the lines of his face as he addressed Greyson. But beneath that, I caught the flicker of concern in his eyes, a concern that echoed in his hushed tone, meant only for Greyson's ears.

"Trap," Sunny muttered, casting a wary glance at the abandoned structure before us. "Velasco seemed to be alone, but it's too convenient."

"Could be," Greyson conceded with a shrug. "But we're not turning back now."

The respect these hardened men showed Greyson impressed me. So did the weight of their trust in his decision, even when it might lead them straight into hell.

"Let's move," Greyson said, a note of finality in his voice that ended any argument.

Sunny nodded, pressing his lips into a thin line but falling in behind Greyson as we made our way towards the skeletal remains of the abandoned distillery.

"Want to stay warm in the car, or are you coming with?" Greyson's voice was laced with a mocking challenge.

But he was already handing me a gun from his collection. The weight of it settled into my palm, which had a familiar heft, bringing me right back to my youth. I'd had to make a decision which way to go with my life—crime or hockey.

I'd been so sure I had chosen right until Kennedy was in danger.

"Let's just get this over with," I grunted, checking the safety before tucking the gun into my waistband.

Greyson's men fanned out ahead of us like the wings of a deadly hawk. The distillery loomed ahead, windows blank and empty, telling us nothing about what waited inside.

The men breached the building with military precision. I was impressed. The Jackals had come a long way since I'd known them under Greyson's father and the boss before that. I was glad there was more to Greyson's changes for them than just vicious fights and pretty tattoos.

Inside, the air within was stagnant, thick with the scent of old spirits and rotting wood. As we swept through the shadows, the voices of Greyson's men echoed from every corner, calling that each area they searched was clear.

But something felt off. Even though the distillery was empty, the sense of a presence still seemed to linger here. I looked toward the large, hulking silhouette of the grain silo outside.

"Think they made it all the way out, on foot?" He didn't need to say more; his question hung between us, heavy with implication.

"It looks like they knew we were coming. But they didn't get a lot of advance notice, or they would've taken the cars we passed by on our way in." My pulse thrummed in my ears, the way it did during the start of a game, even though the stakes were higher. I nodded towards the silo, "That way."

His eyes followed mine. He nodded silently, and we were moving again, exiting the false stillness of the distillery into the cool night air.

"Could be nothing," Greyson said as we approached, though the set of his shoulders told me he was ready for anything.

His men were already streaming out into the woods, starting the search for our two targets even as others set up new guard stations in case they emerged from fighting.

"Could be everything. Could be our chance to keep Kennedy safe."

As we neared the silo, I could feel the charged air of potential violence wrap around us, waiting to be unleashed.

We reached the silo, our weapons drawn. The gun was heavy in my hand. For Kennedy, there wasn't a line I wouldn't cross.

And with Greyson by my side, I felt an unexpected kinship. We were two sides of the same coin—we had always been so different, never more so than now, but we shared the same unwavering determination to protect our girl.

"Ready?" His eyes met mine, and for a moment, there was no mockery, no rivalry.

"Always," I replied.

The rusted latch of the silo door gave way under my grip. The metallic screech cut through the oppressive silence of the night, and I winced; it'd warn anyone inside we were coming if this was where they'd sheltered.

The air was thick with the scent of damp earth and decay.

Corn fell at my feet when I pulled the door open, joining other hard kernels that crunched underfoot.

My stomach knotted, every sense warning me that we weren't alone.

Before I could fully process what was happening, instinct took over. I lunged at Greyson, my body slamming into his with the force of a body check on the ice. We hit the ground hard, corn dust billowing around us.

Just as the gunshots cracked over our heads. Once, twice. The noise was unbelievably loud in the cavernous silo.

Greyson's breath was quick and hot against my skin. I'd have felt embarrassed, but I had no time. I rolled off him, swiping the gun from the floor where it had skittered away.

There was almost no cover in here. I lunged for an abandoned palette, with Greyson on my heels. Someone had thrown a bunch of trash into the silo when it was abandoned, and that created a labyrinth of hiding places.

Lucky us.

It also meant, though, that we didn't know where our enemies were.

For a few seconds, our breaths were loud in the silence. I found a piece of broken concrete and rose to lob it, knowing that someone was sighting in on me and would track the movement with their rifle. I needed to figure out where they were shooting from. A shot went off, loud—following the path of the concrete. It was a split second mistake, but it was enough for me to know where the shooter was hiding.

I ducked as two more shots rang out overhead. They came from a different angle than the other two, as I replayed them, and I signaled to Greyson.

He nodded.

The two of us were up and running, parting ways. Greyson fired off shots, trying to cover us both. I was pretty sure we were taking shots from behind a pile of abandoned copper tanks, so I came up on the side, already firing. If I was wrong, I was exposed. I knew a bullet would punch through me before I had time to recover. The noise of Greyson's covering fire echoed through the silo.

A surprised face, a gun raised toward me.

I fired. Again and again.

Velasco's body leapt back, each shot punching him backward. He looked at me in astonishment as he fell onto his back, blood blooming across his chest.

The last of Greyson's shots faded. I looked up to find him still standing, and I checked Velasco's pulse before moving to join him.

Dust hovered in the air, motes dancing in the sparse light. The coppery scent of blood was thick, mingling with the musty aroma of corn.

Greyson's boots crunched softly on the scattered kernels that littered the floor. Ahead, Borvosky's body lay sprawled, the life seeping out of him and staining the yellow beads of corn.

"Looks like I've got a hell of a guardian angel watching over me, Sebastian," Greyson quipped, a wry smile tugging at the corner of his mouth as he nudged one of the bodies with his foot.

I glared at him, my heart still hammering from the adrenaline. "Don't mention it. Seriously."

I wasn't sure when or how my protective impulses had extended to Greyson, of all fucking people.

Greyson's expression sobered as he surveyed the mess before us. "We needed answers from these two. This is inconvenient."

"Tell me about it." I crouched down, scanning the pockets of Velasco's jacket. "We need to know if anyone else is gunning for Kennedy, or if taking out these three is enough."

"Exactly." He ran a hand through his hair, frustration etched on his face. "Now we're flying blind again."

The drive back to the penthouse was quiet, the hum of the engine soft. This time, though, the silence didn't carry the simmering tension that had been between us earlier.

As the city lights began to twinkle in the distance, I thought of Kennedy, safe and warm in our place, probably laughing at something Jack said or cozying into Carter's side. That image, the thought of her safe, made all this worth it.

For her, I would walk through the shadows, so my girl could stay in the light.

And I knew, without a doubt, so would Greyson.

When we walked into the penthouse, Kennedy could tell something had happened. She jolted off the couch and ran to us, and I wasn't sure if it was the scent of gunpowder that clung to us or the looks on our faces.

"What did you do?" she demanded.

"We ended up having to go in," Greyson said, lying to her without a second's hesitation. We could've waited. "It became urgent."

"Greyson—" she looked ready to tear him apart, and then her gaze flew to me, and suddenly she was ready to tear me apart too.

But Greyson gripped her shoulders, caressing them gently. There was a mischievous look in his gaze. "I know, baby. I'm sorry you weren't there. But if it makes you feel any better, we were never in any real danger."

"How so?" Carter asked dryly from the couch. Of course he'd want to get us in trouble, even though he'd had the pleasure of spending all night with Kennedy.

"Well, I feel very safe when I'm with Sebastian," Greyson began.

"Shut up," I told him.

But Greyson's eyes twinkled. "He saved my life. Tackled me out of the way of danger...like he was my brother."

"Shut up," I said again, but then Kennedy was turning to me, her eyes lighting with warmth.

She folded into my embrace, tilting her head to kiss me, and I drew her against my body, savoring her kiss.

As if I were her hero.

And maybe I didn't regret saving Greyson's mangy life.

CHAPTER 1

Kennedy

The car hummed along the familiar stretch of highway, the rhythmic thud of tires against asphalt lulling me into a trance-like state. I stared out the window, my gaze fixed on the passing landscape, but my mind a million miles away.

Memories pricked at my mind like small drops of rain right before a storm began, each one a sharp pang of nostalgia mixed with pain.

We were on our way to the home I'd lived at with my parents —before my father had died, and before Frank had been a plague in my life.

I didn't know how I felt about that.

Greyson had learned everything he could about me in the years I was gone, searching everywhere he could just in case I was there. This house in North Carolina was apparently where I'd lived before the trailer park.

Now that my memories appeared to be unlocking, it seemed the obvious thing for me to try and visit as many places from my past as I could in an attempt to unlock even more.

I leaned my head against the cool glass, feeling a sense of unease as we drew closer.

Based on what I knew about my trailer park days...I wasn't sure that I wanted to uncover more memories.

But maybe it had been better before.

Maybe without Frank, my mother had been a mom.

Maybe I'd had a dad who'd loved me.

They had all continued to be tight lipped about anything to do with my past, not explaining situations until I at least remembered some of it on my own.

We turned off the highway, and I struggled to pull anything up. Had I gone to that Taco Bell on the corner? Had it even been there back when I'd lived here?

That elementary school, with its flag beating in the wind...had I played on that playground, had I walked through those front doors, did I have any friends?

Nothing was coming to me.

"Anything?" Sebastian asked, his thumb rubbing my skin soothingly as he held onto my hand.

I shook my head, sighing and hoping that this two-hour drive hadn't been for nothing.

Greyson snored loudly from the back and shifted in his seat, as if he was trying to remind me that we could have been on a private plane and not stuffed into a car.

"Got a permanent marker?" Sebastian whispered, a mischievous look on his face as he glanced away from the road.

"He will kill you," Carter said from next to Greyson in the back seat, shooting Sebastian a look, and not bothering to keep his voice quiet at all. He was still pissed that he'd lost rock-paper-scissors, and I was sitting in the front seat instead of in the back with him.

Sebastian rolled his eyes at him through the rear view mirror.

I blew Carter a kiss and he smirked at me. "He won't kill you, sweetheart. So, go ahead and do your worst."

"I can hear you, fools," Greyson drawled in an annoyed, tired voice. He'd been "taking care" of something last night and hadn't gotten back to the penthouse until we were getting ready to leave this morning. "And Kennedy likes my face too much to do anything to it. So, good luck trying to get her to do anything."

"I like your face too much? Are you sure about that?" I teased, glancing over my shoulder where he was staring at me, amused.

"You must like to be spanked, baby. Jack's corrupted you."

I flushed, and turned back around, decidedly not looking at Jack who was lounging in the third-row of the SUV. I was not going to think about how he'd fucked me in the shower yesterday, convincing me to try out the new butt plug he'd bought for the occasion.

Nope. Wasn't going to think about that at all.

All of them laughed at me as I squirmed in my seat.

We came to a stop sign, and my throat went dry at the Oak Street sign.

This was it. This was where I used to live.

The whole car went quiet, and I stared at the passing houses, each one a stranger in the landscape of my mind.

And there it was.

A faded yellow two story nestled among a row of similar homes. Its weathered facade seemed to whisper secrets of the past, inviting me to unravel the mysteries hidden within its walls.

Or at least that's what I imagined it was doing.

There was a *For Sale* sign in the front yard, a swinging banner underneath it that advertised "Amazing Floor Plan!"

"I've arranged for a realtor to meet with us. The home is vacant. She knows to unlock the door and leave," Greyson commented, and I glanced back at him, surprised.

"That's convenient."

His eyes glittered and then I was wondering just how "convenient" it really was.

I was distracted from asking him though when a woman in a tight gray pencil skirt and sky-high heels appeared on the sidewalk in front of the SUV.

A sense of anticipation swelled within me as Sebastian shut off the car, my heart fluttering with the possibility that this house could hold the key to unlocking more of my past.

I was having trouble getting out of the car though.

"Either way, it's going to be okay, princess," Sebastian murmured. I took a shaky breath and nodded my head, right as Greyson opened the door and practically yanked me out.

"I will throw the biggest fit this world has ever seen if you don't sit by me on the car ride home," he growled, smashing his lips against mine in a kiss that left me breathless. "And we're never going on a road trip again. We will be flying everywhere."

I giggled and his gaze softened, and I realized that he'd been trying to make me laugh. Mission accomplished.

"I've already unlocked the door. Obviously, take as much time as you need," the realtor commented, keeping her gaze averted from Greyson.

"Thank you," he said flippantly as he grabbed my hand and led me towards the front door, its wood badly in need of a paint job. Greyson stared at the rusted handle in disgust, sighing as he grabbed it and pushed the door open. The interior of the house was shrouded in darkness, the faint glow of sunlight flickering through the dusty windows casting long shadows across the floor.

"I could see you in here. I bet you were the cutest little kid ever. I would have had the biggest crush ever and showed up at your door every day asking you to play," Sebastian joked, slinging an arm around my shoulder as we walked down the front hallway.

"Mmh," I murmured absentmindedly, staring around the main living room.

"Daddy!" I screamed happily as the front door opened. I'd been sitting on the living room floor, playing with a doll. I jumped up and raced down the hallway, coming to a stop when I saw he was still facing the door, his shoulders slumped.

"Daddy?" I repeated, uncertainly.

"There's my girl!" he said, spinning around. But it wasn't with his usual excitement. He looked tired and sad.

I didn't want my daddy to look sad.

"Don't tell me," my mother snapped from behind me. "Please, don't tell me." Her voice was worried and mean.

"We'll talk about it later," he said to her firmly, nodding at me.

They needed to have a grown-up conversation. That's what that meant.

Daddy scooped me up before I could go anywhere and carried me into the kitchen. "Spaghetti, my favorite," he said lightly.

"Will you play with me after dinner?" I asked. "Pleaseeee."

He smiled at me, and again, it seemed all wrong. His eyes still seemed so sad.

I put my hands on both his cheeks and squished his lips together like the pufferfish I'd seen on a show the other day.

That did make him laugh. And I was proud of myself because that time his eyes smiled too.

"Of course, sweetie-pie," he said, smacking a kiss against my cheek as he set me down in my chair. "Let's eat!"

Later that night I heard screaming. I crept down the stairs and peeked through the railing, into the kitchen where they were yelling at each other.

"You're a good for nothing joke, Paul. You're a fucking joke. That's three jobs in two months. You're pathetic!"

"Fuck you!" Daddy snarled, and I jumped because he never sounded mean like that. "You think this is easy? You think I can concentrate knowing you're popping pills here at home, spending money we don't have, neglecting our baby girl."

Mom scoffed and rolled her eyes. "She's perfectly fine."

"Well, at least you're not denying it. You're a fucking addict."

"Better than being a loser."

Daddy backhanded her and she fell to the floor. I'd let out a little scream when he did that, and I froze, sure he'd heard me. But he didn't turn around.

I came back to the present, my fingers trailing over worn

furniture and peeling wallpaper, shivering because it felt like I was surrounded by more than bad memories. It felt like I was surrounded by ghosts.

"Remember something?" Jack asked hopefully, his nose wrinkled as he stared around the room. Sebastian's arm was still around me, and I nestled closer to him, wondering if every moment of my past was carved in misery.

"A little," I murmured, my gaze on the floor, seeing myself as a little girl playing there on the faded and worn carpet.

I sighed and walked into the kitchen, my eyes immediately ꞏꞏꞏꞏꞏꞏꞏ ꞏꞏꞏ ꞏꞏꞏꞏ ꞏꞏꞏꞏꞏ ꞏꞏꞏ ꞏꞏꞏꞏꞏꞏ had fallen to the ground after he'd hit her.

I could remember her more now. She'd been a cold, selfish woman. She would pop pills, and go lay down, staying in her room all day while I fended for myself. I remembered dragging the wooden chair to the counter, trying to make myself a sandwich, the too sharp knife I'd been using to spread the mayo cutting into my hand.

"Ow," I cried, blood dribbling from my cut onto the counter, splashing on my bread. Big tears fell off my face, dripping down and mixing with the blood until the sandwich I was making was nothing but a soggy mess.

I was really hungry, and that just made me cry harder.

My hand really hurt too. I got off the chair and moved it to the other counter where there were some paper towels. Mom would get mad if I got blood everywhere. And there was a lot of blood dripping from my hand right now.

I tore off the paper towels, wrapping it around my hand and crying some more when I saw how it was already soaked.

I almost fell off the chair, trying to get down. I needed to tell Mom that I cut myself. She was going to be so mad.

I walked to her closed door, the faint sound of the TV flickering through the wood. "Mom," I called softly.

She didn't answer.

I knocked with my other hand. "Mom!"

Still nothing.

Staring at the door, I debated what I was going to do. She didn't like me to walk in without permission. But I really needed help. This was an emergency, right?

I slowly opened the door and peeked through the crack. The window was open and the breeze was blowing the curtains. I couldn't hear anything but the TV.

"Mom?" I called again, wishing she would just answer.

I tentatively walked down the hall, taking a deep breath when I saw that she was still asleep in the bed. Her covers were pushed down so she was uncovered. Which was probably good because it felt like it was a hundred degrees in here, even with the window open.

"Mom," I whispered, coming up beside her. There was an orange medicine bottle lying on its side on the table next to the bed. It was the kind of bottle I wasn't supposed to ever, ever touch, Daddy had told me.

"Mom!" I said louder when she still didn't move. Why wasn't she answering? She would usually have gotten mad at me already. I glanced at the TV. One of her soap stories was on—or whatever they were called. People always seemed really unhappy on those shows. Daddy called them trash. But Mom loved them.

My hand throbbed and some blood dripped on the floor, and I was starting to feel dizzy. That feeling like when you got off a ride at an amusement park and your head felt crazy and your stomach felt like you were going to throw up.

"Mom," I said, shaking her arm this time. Her head lolled to the side, and I realized for the first time that she looked weird. Her face was the color of my white sidewalk chalk, and there was some sweat beaded on her lip. I started to cry harder, and I began to shake her arm more, trying to get her to wake up.

"Kennedy?" my dad's voice called.

"Daddy!" I cried as I heard him enter the room and then a second later he was there. He almost tripped when he saw me and Mom.

"Kennedy, what happened, sweetheart?" he said, rushing to my side and carefully grabbing my hand. The paper towel was completely red, and I whimpered as he removed it and stared at the cut.

"I was trying to make a sandwich. It was an accident. I'm sorry," I whimpered. He seemed so mad. But it really was just an accident. I'd been hungry.

I was still hungry.

"Fucking hell," he snarled, his gaze going to Mom, who was laying there, so still it was scary...even with all the noise.

"Don't move, sweetie," Daddy said in a gentler voice as he went into their bathroom, coming back a second later with one of their towels. He wrapped it around my hand. "Keep that tight," he ordered before he leaned over Mom, slapping her face a few times. "Wake up! You stupid bitch, wake up!"

I sobbed because I didn't like when he was mean like that, and he cursed before glancing back at me with a sad look on his face.

"I'm sorry, baby. But she should have been taking better care of you. She isn't supposed to leave you by yourself!"

"Kennedy?" Sebastian's voice filtered through my consciousness and I was once again standing in the present. The linoleum counters under my fingertips were cracked where they'd once been in pristine condition.

"I think I've been sad...forever," I said quietly, turning and burying my face in Sebastian's chest because everything felt so heavy.

I'd been nervous on the drive here...that I would find memories I didn't want. But a part of me had been hopeful that there would be some good things in my past too.

I guess I'd been right to be nervous.

I could feel the watchful gazes of the others on my skin, but I kept myself against Sebastian's chest, not wanting to see their looks of pity.

Taking a deep breath, I finally pulled away, my eyes immediately seeking Greyson's.

"I suppose you know all sorts of things about what happened in this house," I said quietly.

He studied me for a second, probably trying to decide how much he wanted to reveal. Hell, he just needed to tell me everything. I was quite sure I would be good with not having any more of my past in this house coming back to me.

"Your dad was in and out of jobs. There were police reports that detailed constant calls to your house. Sometimes CPS would be called, reports from your school coming in that you seemed hungry, and you were sneaking food in the cafeteria."

A tear slid down my cheek. I stared at the long white scar on my palm. I guess I knew where that had come from.

"My mother was addicted to prescription drugs. She would go into her room and leave me alone all day. One day, I hurt myself pretty bad, and she'd overdosed that same day," I said in a blank voice as my gaze trailed along the scratched cabinets, all done in that yellow-oak color that was so popular back in the day.

This house hadn't been considered on trend even when I was growing up here.

It would have to be gutted by whoever ended up buying it if they didn't want a relic from the 90s.

"My dad stitched up my hand himself and then made me hide in my room while the paramedics came to get my mom so that they wouldn't know something had happened to me." I glanced at Greyson again with a sad smile. "I guess that tracks with those CPS visits if that was happening all the time." Greyson's face was angry looking, like he was offended on behalf of my little kid self.

"You say the word and we're gone, sweetheart," Carter growled. His lips were also curled in animosity as he stared around the kitchen.

"I guess we might as well keep going," I said with a sigh. I strode out of the kitchen and across the living room, to where I now remembered my parents' bedroom located. It was a funny thing, but walking into the room without knocking, it felt like something I wasn't supposed to do.

I took a few steps in and stopped, rubbing at my chest, and

then my head, because the flood of memories was almost too much.

"*Fucking look at this,*" Mom screamed as I listened through the door. *I'd snuck out of my bed again when I'd heard them yelling. This had been happening more and more often lately. I think I'd been woken up every night for the past two weeks.* "*We're going to be out on the streets!*"

There was a crashing sound. "*Would your life even change? You spend every day passed the fuck out anyway. You can just do it in the street.*"

My mother made a screaming sound, and I plastered myself against the wall behind me, fear clattering around in my chest.

"*Stop!*" *she yelled in a weird, garbled sounding voice.*

I ran away, back up the stairs and into my room where I threw the covers over my head. "*Please, stop. Please, stop. Please, stop,*" *I whispered, hoping that if I said it enough, that they would.*

A loud bang sounded from downstairs and I flinched. Shivering more when my mom screamed again. Over and over until I didn't think that I would ever get the sound of it out of my head.

"This was where my dad killed himself," I whispered softly.

"He kept losing jobs and the bills were stacking up, and my mom was drugging herself to death. I remember..." My words faded as a memory came of a rainy day, where I'd dressed all in black and cried at my father's grave. Because he'd been the only one who loved me. "I remember my mother once told me when she was high how he'd pointed it at her before pointing it at himself and squeezing the trigger." I glanced up at Sebastian who was watching me with wide, sympathetic eyes. "I don't think he meant to do it. I think he was just feeling overwhelmed. I think he would have stayed."

It was a big thing to say considering I only had bits and pieces of memories, but it felt like the truth. From the memories that I'd had, I don't think my dad had wanted to leave me like that.

I walked out of the bedroom and took a deep breath before heading up the stairs to where my bedroom had been.

Walking in, the room seemed much smaller than it had been in my memories.

"Pack your stuff up and put it in a box, Kennedy," Mother snapped as she appeared in the doorway, looking way more dressed up than she usually did. Her brown hair was brushed and shiny, and she had some pink lipstick on that made her look really pretty. She wasn't wearing a bathrobe either. Mom had on clothes that looked brand new.

"Where are we going?" I asked, looking up from the doll I was playing with. Or staring at—that was a better way for me to describe what I was doing.

"We're moving in with your new father," she said brightly, a smile on her face as if that was an everyday thing to announce.

My mouth dropped open in shock. "What?"

Her smile faded. "Are you talking back to me?"

"No, Mom," I said quickly, not wanting to make her angry when she seemed like she was in a good mood for once. "Who exactly are you talking about?" I'd noticed that she'd been disappearing at night lately. And a few times I'd woken up for school, and she still hadn't been home.

But that wasn't much different than her staying in her room all the time, so I hadn't thought much of it honestly.

"I met a wonderful man. He's going to take care of us. Frank can't wait to meet you!"

Frank. I didn't like that name.

"He's going to be here in twenty minutes, and I want this room packed up!" she snapped when I didn't say anything in response.

"Do we have to leave our house?" I asked, trying to keep the tears out of my voice, because I knew that would just make her mad. But Daddy had only been gone for a few months.

I couldn't imagine leaving this house. Leaving his stuff.

The cemetery was right around the corner. I'd been sneaking over there after school even though Shelby Ray had told me at school that it was haunted.

I just wanted to be near him.

Mom sniffed, her pink lips pursed disapprovingly. "We're leaving this place and I don't want to hear any complaining! You'll see. Everything is going to be better now." With that she turned and left the room, not caring that she'd left her little girl falling apart.

Twenty minutes later, I heard the murmur of voices and the front door opening and then closing.

"Kennedy," Mom called, and I hurriedly wiped at my face as I put my doll in the box.

"Coming," I called as I headed out of the room and down the stairs. My steps faltered when Mom appeared from the hallway, a man next to her that was holding her around the waist. He was tall and imposing, with a thick beard that hid his mouth. His eyes were dark and scary, like bottomless pits—nothing like the warm gaze that Daddy had. I watched him as he talked to my mom, his words dripping with honeyed sweetness that made me feel nervous.

And then he turned to look at me...and he looked...hungry. Like he wanted to eat me for dinner. I'd never seen a man look like that, and a knot of fear tightened in my chest.

"Well, come on down here," Mom said in a nice voice I normally didn't hear from her.

I hesitantly walked down the stairs towards them while they watched me.

"This is Kennedy," Mom announced to the man, and he smiled at me with yellow looking teeth, his hand reaching out to ruffle my hair. I tried my best to smile, knowing that's what Mom would want me to do.

"I'm Frank, Kennedy. And I have a feeling that you and I are going to be the best of friends."

I came back to the room, hunched over as I tried not to throw up. It was time to get out of here. I'd seen enough.

"Let's go," I told the guys weakly. They were all gathered around me with various expressions of concern.

They nodded, and Carter grabbed my hand as I headed out of the room. No one said anything until we were out of the house.

We gathered on the lawn, and I stared at the house, wondering how it could look so ominous now, like a dark cloud had settled over it while we'd been inside.

"You know, Sebastian," Greyson mused from my other side. "Now might be a good time to let that nasty little pyro habit of yours out." I glanced at him and snorted, because obviously he was kidding.

Except his face was completely serious.

Night had fallen, and the street was quiet. But I still stared around, sure that someone was nearby listening to every word we were saying.

Although, Greyson was a mafia boss. So, I bet burning down an old house in the middle of the suburbs wasn't really a big deal to him.

"Do you want me to?" Sebastian's voice cut through the tense silence, his words hanging in the air like a dare waiting to be accepted.

I hesitated for a moment, the gravity of his question sinking in. But then, fueled by a mixture of anger—that this was my past —and desperation for the reminder of it all to be gone, I nodded, my voice barely above a whisper. "Burn it. Burn it to the ground."

Sebastian wasted no time, walking back inside the house, his movements swift and purposeful as he set about preparing the fire, looking so at ease with everything, I was questioning just how much time he spent doing this sort of thing.

He broke off some cabinets and began to arrange them in a makeshift pyre, his hands steady like he couldn't feel any of the anticipation that was clearly coursing through every one else's veins. My hands were literally trembling. Carter was pacing around the room. Jack was staring between me and the pile of wood like he wanted to drag me out of here before it was lit. And Greyson was on the phone with the real estate agent from earlier—warning her that her listing was about to disappear. But she would be compensated.

Like I'd said before...this was a weird life.

Sebastian's eyes held a fierce determination, and I couldn't tear my gaze away from him. It felt like he was really ridding me of the demons that haunted this place.

"Grab some of that newspaper," he ordered Jack and Carter, and they got to work, gathering the random old newspaper that we'd seen stuffed in cabinets and scattered in some of the closet shelves.

As I watched, he arranged the newspaper around the cabinets.

Kindling, that was the word for that.

"How fast is this going to burn?" Jack asked. "I don't think the rest of the neighborhood will like their houses going up in flames."

Sebastian scoffed at him, like Jack's question had offended him. "I'm setting up a slow burn, so the fire department will get here in time to stop it from spreading to other houses, but the house will be too destroyed to be able to save it. Come on, Jack. Who do you think I am?"

"Oh, I'm sorry. Forgive me for forgetting you're an absolute psychopath," Jack drawled.

I snorted out a laugh and he shot me a wink. Like that had been his intention all along.

"The fire department is fifteen minutes away," Carter commented, squinting at his phone.

Sebastian huffed and shook his head.

Carter shook his head in disgust.

Well then, I was never going to question Sebastian again when it came to burning things up.

"Ready?" he asked me a minute later, glancing up at me expectantly.

I took a deep breath, my gaze darting around the interior of the house, everything looking far more sinister in the dark of night.

"Ready," I said firmly.

With a flick of his lighter, the flames erupted into life, dancing and licking at the air with a voracious hunger. The sound of crackling wood filled the silence, a soundtrack of destruction that echoed the turmoil raging within my own heart.

I watched the flames move for a second, before a hand slid into mine.

"Come on, princess," Sebastian said. "We need to watch the show from farther away." I nodded, ripping my gaze away from the fire as I followed him to the front door.

Once outside, I stood there for what felt like an eternity, watching through the doorway as the flames began to consume everything in their path, devouring the memories I no longer wanted to discover. It was a cathartic release, a cleansing fire that purged the darkness and left nothing but ash in its wake.

"Let's go, pretty girl," Jack said to me. "I'm sure someone has called the fire department by now."

I nodded, although none of them seemed too worried about the thought of someone finding us here.

We piled into the car, and I stared as smoke poured from the doorway. I felt a sense of relief wash over me as we drove away, like a cool breeze on a sweltering day.

I was so lost in my thoughts and the memories I'd discovered that it took me a minute to realize that Jack, who'd taken over driving, wasn't headed back the way we'd come.

"Where are we going?" I asked.

"Somewhere else that might bring back some memories," Greyson answered for him, his voice subdued.

"I'm not sure I can take any more," I told him, and that was the truth. I was having enough trouble trying to process the memories that that house had drudged up.

The car rolled to a halt outside a pair of heavy, wrought iron gates, the engine's low hum cutting through the silence of the night...and I realized where we were.

The cemetery.

Jack's hand clasped mine. "We don't have to do this, but…"

I smiled at him. "It's okay," I whispered.

Carter opened my door and I slipped out, taking his hand as we stepped out onto the gravel path.

We walked together, the night enveloping us in its cool embrace as we made our way through the rows of headstones. Each step felt heavier than the last, unfamiliar grief pressing down on my chest like a leaden burden.

Moonlight cast eerie shadows among the tombstones, turning the serene landscape into a haunting tableau. I didn't need anyone to show me the way, my footsteps echoed softly against the damp earth as we neared the spot where I now remembered my father lay.

Kneeling beside the grave, I felt a lump form in my throat as I traced the letters of his name etched into the weathered stone. "Hi, Daddy," I whispered, the words barely audible in the stillness of the night. "I'm sorry, I haven't been here."

My words ended with a little sob as I saw him in my mind, throwing me up in the air as I giggled and screamed "Again! Again!"

A strong pair of arms wrapped around me and I leaned into Jack's embrace. A rush of warmth washed over me, like sunlight peeking out from behind a cloud, wrapping me in a cocoon of comfort. Almost like Dad was here right then, reaching out to me from beyond the veil of death.

Tears welled in my eyes as I closed them, allowing myself to bask in the few good memories I did have. I could hear his voice in my head, the soft and reassuring way he'd always spoken to me.

I opened my eyes, and the reality of his absence was there.

I squeezed Jack's arms and then rose to my feet, a sense of emptiness gnawing at me. It was hell to be reminded that you couldn't miss what you couldn't remember...and now I was starting to remember so much.

We walked back to the car, and I decided my takeaway from this weird, awful day...would be the memory of his love, lingering inside my head now.

CHAPTER 15

Greyson

The crowd roared as the puck dropped, the energy in the arena already crazy as the game got underway. I sat beside Kennedy, my gaze fixed on the ice below, pretending that the longing stirring within me wasn't there.

"What if we went to Paris, again? Tonight," I asked, debating how much it would mess with this arrangement I had with the others if I absconded with her during their game.

Might be worth their anger if I didn't have to sit through this game.

Kennedy stared at me like I was crazy. "We're not going to Paris," she told me firmly. It was cute that she thought she was the boss of me.

The only thing she was the boss of was my dick.

I eyed her Diet Coke and then her stomach...wondering if she should be cutting off caffeine soon. Her period was due next week...and with how much time I'd spent inside her—and how much time the others had spent inside her...this could be the month.

Daddy Greyson here I come.

There was a whole list of things that needed to be taken care of in preparation for the baby, number one being needing to figure out who the fuck was after her. But besides that, there were nutritional concerns...and making sure we had a doctor who wouldn't accept pay outs from my enemies in exchange for hurting Kennedy.

Those sorts of things.

"You're staring at me all crazy like," she murmured as we watched Carter block a shot, his reflexes lightning fast. He was getting lit-up tonight, but he was a beast between the pipes, stopping every puck.

"I don't know what you're talking about," I answered in a bland tone, wrapping an arm around her, and feeling the familiar stirrings of my cock—a problem I always had anytime I touched her. "This is how I always look at you. Like you're the love of my existence, of course."

"Sweet words. But you're acting weird tonight," she said, taking my hand and holding it between both of hers. I stared at the discrepancy between our hands. My skin was dark tan against her paleness, and my hand was so much bigger than hers.

She was so fragile. Panic sliced through me as I thought about how easily someone could destroy her. I tore my gaze away from our clasped hands, glancing around like someone was going to pounce at us any second. Everyone looked like normal fans, stuffing themselves with popcorn and soft pretzels, or gulping down beer as they cheered or yelled at the players.

But you never knew.

The crowd roared, and I glanced back at the ice where Jack was a blur of motion as he streaked down the ice, his stick handling skills a sight to behold. With a flick of his wrist, he sent the puck soaring past Nashville's goalie, the sound of the goal horn echoing through the arena as everyone went nuts around us.

Kennedy sprang from her seat and started dancing around, distracting me from my lookout by the sight of her bouncing ass and boobs.

I held in a groan because fuck...my girl was the most gorgeous girl I'd ever seen.

"Stand up," she called at me, because I was literally the only person still in their seat after that goal. I begrudgingly stood up, because okay...she owned more than my dick, but I only clapped a little. Jack skated by where we were sitting and blew her a kiss and I pretended I wasn't jealous at all when Kennedy pretended to catch it and blew one back.

I tried not to care. I really did. But watching them play...it was a little torturous. I'd once thought that I'd be out there with them. That had been our dream. I'd once known what Jack was going to do before he even did it. I'd once been the one that the fans screamed for.

I'd never been the spectator sort of guy. I preferred to be in the action.

No one dreamed of being a mob boss.

Little kids dreamed of being professional athletes, of being on TV, of crowds screaming their name.

I wasn't bitter at all...that the guys' dreams had once been mine.

I was usually able to distract myself when I came to games with Kennedy, but I was having trouble tonight.

Hence, why I was thinking of Paris.

Because Kennedy and I—alone—that was the only thing that could distract me when my thoughts got like this.

As much as playing for the NHL had been my dream.

I'd always wanted Kennedy more.

"Holy hellfry. Did you see that hit?" she asked me, cocking an eyebrow when she realized I was staring at her again instead of the game.

"Holy hellfry?" I chuckled, forcing myself to watch as Sebastian delivered another bone-crushing hit behind Carter's net, clearing the puck and sending it to Jack.

"Do you think they have pickles at the concessions?" she asked...and I was once again watching her.

Absolutely thrilled...

Because pickles were a pregnancy craving, right? I couldn't remember her ever wanting pickles as a snack before.

"You want pickles?" I asked casually, once again studying every inch of her. Did her boobs look bigger? I'd just been sucking on them before the game as I fucked her in the car. But had they been more sensitive?

I'd been so caught up on what her cunt was doing to my dick that I hadn't been paying as much attention as I should have been.

Get your shit together, you idiot.

"They just sound really good. Don't you think?" she asked, tearing her gaze away from the game to look at me as she sucked down her Diet Coke.

"Let me get you a refill...and a pickle," I told her silkily as I reached out to grab her cup before she could take any more sips.

She was going to be a literal devil without caffeine...but maybe if we gave her enough orgasms we could withstand the storm.

Orgasms trumped caffeine...right?

"My cup's still full!" she said, trying to pull it away.

"Naw. I know how you feel about proper ice to soda ratio and the current ratio is bad," I told her.

Everyone jumped out of their seats, and I saw that Jack was once again on a breakaway. Kennedy forgot all about her soda as she got up too and started screaming wildly as Jack swung back and...his shot was blocked.

I took the opportunity to grab her drink, deciding the pickles had to be a sign.

The caffeine cutoff had to begin.

I was going to have to watch the guys, they got all googly-eyed and gave her whatever she wanted any time she looked at them.

I was...slightly better.

Okay, not really. But I could stick to a caffeine ban if necessary. I was, after all, responsible for pulling the goalie so to speak.

Carter would be amused at that joke.

"Come on," I told her. "Let's go get you that pickle." The buzzer sounded, signaling the end of the period, so she didn't have to miss out on any of the game to fulfill her craving. She slipped her hand into mine and as we walked out into the crowded hallway where all the concessions were, I dumped her soda in the trash without her noticing.

It was my lucky day that one of the reporters had caught Jack as he was going into the locker room and she was schmoozing up to him on the TV screen. Kennedy was distracted watching the girl try and flirt with Jack, and she didn't even notice when I got her a pickle and a Gatorade instead of a Diet Coke.

She could resume all the caffeine she wanted if the pregnancy test came back negative.

She would forgive me...in time.

We were walking back to our seats when she happened to glance back at my hands. "Oh, we need to go back...you forgot my drink."

I panicked, something I never did, and pushed her gently against the wall, my free hand coming up to cradle her head as I crowded her in with my body, my lips crashing against hers.

I'd just thought of one thing I could use for distraction...sex.

I let go of her head and slipped my hand under her jersey— the one I hated because it had someone else's name on it—and my cock somehow hardened even more just feeling her soft skin under my fingertips.

She moaned against my lips, my tongue tangling against hers.

"Get a room," someone coughed loudly from somewhere behind me, and I fought the urge to turn around and shoot him.

But it was a bit difficult to do what I wanted with a pickle and a sports drink in one of my hands, so we needed to find some place to remedy that. Pronto.

And then I had the best idea ever.

"Come on," I growled at her, yanking her down the hall to one of the doors that led to the tunnels where the locker rooms and other staff rooms were. I heard the faint sound of the buzzer signaling the start of the new period, but glancing back at Kennedy, she didn't seem to be too worried about getting back to the game. I had her lust drunk.

"Where are we going?" she asked as I led her down a flight of stairs. I kissed her against the wall again until she was all dazed and confused, because I knew she wasn't going to totally go along with my new, brilliant plan unless I had her really primed.

"Come on, baby," I murmured, leading her into the tunnel and down the hall where the team locker room was. They'd just gone out on the ice, so we had just enough time for me to make her cum a few times...all over Carter's locker...before they came back.

"Oh," she whispered, like we were going to get caught any minute as I swiped the card I'd stolen from Sebastian and led her into the locker room.

She glanced around. I knew she'd been in here before, but it was a little different mid game. Things were strewn everywhere and it...smelled. Worse than usual.

Brought back a million memories honestly. Of other times when I'd brought Kennedy into our high school locker room as teenagers and done things *very* similar to what we were about to do.

Just like I thought, the place was deserted, everyone out watching what was looking like a very close game based on the goal they'd just scored on Carter that had played out on the TV above us.

The three of them were probably all distracted, wondering where I'd taken Kennedy, and it gave me a little satisfaction that they were suffering a little since I was still feeling salty tonight about my brain's decision to take a walk down memory lane and think about the fact that I didn't play hockey anymore.

I mean seriously, I had more money than God, more power than the president, and I had the girl of my dreams...I wasn't suffering.

But maybe tonight I had to remind myself a little more of why I had given all that up, and who I had given it up for.

I dropped the pickle and the Gatorade on a chair and scooped her up in my arms, her legs wrapping around me as I carried her over to where Carter's locker was. It wasn't really a locker, it was more like an enormous open space. So, it was perfect for what I had planned.

"I'm going to fuck you right here, baby," I murmured as I pulled her pants down until they were around her ankles.

Her eyes widened. "What?! We can't do that." She squirmed against me though, making no real move to get away.

I smiled at her as I slid two fingers through her soaking wet folds, smearing her wetness around her clit and massaging it as she let out a soft moan, her gaze darting around like any second now, someone was going to walk in on us.

I mean they *could* walk in on us. It would actually be awesome if one of the guys was brought in with an injury—not a bad one obviously since I needed them to help me protect Kennedy, but maybe a muscle contusion or something. I could just imagine the look on Carter's face if he turned the corner and found me balls deep in our girl, her delicious scent soaking his locker.

She gasped as I slid my fingers into her tight pussy, a squelching sound delighting my ears from how turned on she was.

"I'm obsessed with this tight cunt. Have I told you that lately?" I whispered in her ear as I softly bit down on her earlobe, her body shaking with need against mine as she gasped.

"We really shouldn't do this," she said, but I could tell she'd already given in. My Kennedy loved what I could do to her.

I cupped her breast through her jersey, wanting to rip the whole thing off. It was one thing though for someone to see her face if they walked in...it was quite another for them to see her perfect body.

I would have to kill them and something told me that Jack, Carter, and Sebastian probably wouldn't be too happy about me ending one of their teammates.

I smiled in victory when her hand moved between our bodies, sliding under the band of my jeans and finding my aching cock.

"Please, fuck me," she whimpered, and I pressed a hard kiss against her lips because I loved when my girl begged.

"Anything for you, baby," I growled as I unbuttoned my jeans with one hand as I continued to fuck my fingers in and out of her. I breathed a sigh of relief when my cock was released from its confinement. I actually preferred suit pants for that reason, room for my dick to breathe in the event that Kennedy gave me a hard on for the millionth time in a day.

I pulled my fingers out and slid them into my mouth, trying not to pass out from how fucking perfect she tasted. Her pussy was all the nutrition that I needed. I would probably live forever if that was what I was eating every day.

"Fuck, you taste like my favorite fucking thing," I growled, shoving my jeans down further so I could get inside her easier.

I grabbed her hips and lifted her up, taking in the desperate look in her eyes right before I slammed into her.

Kennedy's mouth opened in a gasp, and I captured the sound in my mouth as I kissed her, holding her impaled on my dick so she could get used to the stretch.

If nothing else told me that she was made for me, the way my dick fit inside her pussy would have solidified it.

The perfect fucking fit.

She arched against me, her eyes squeezing shut as she breathed into me. I wished it was possible to keep her like this all the time, connected permanently.

"Are you ready for me?" I murmured, and those light green

eyes of hers finally opened as we stared at each other for a moment.

No one in my organization would ever believe I could act like this, living for every breath that a woman gave me.

It was the fucking best.

"Such a gentleman," she huffed. "But yes, please move. Please make me cum. Please."

I bit down on her bottom lip pressing her against the wall so I could balance her better as I slid a hand up her jersey again, needing to feel those perfect tits.

Her body was my heaven.

Who needed the pearly gates when you had Kennedy.

Not that they'd ever let me past those things anyway.

She cried out as I tugged and pinched at her nipple, still keeping her sheathed on my dick as she quivered and squirmed against me, exquisitely torturing my cock.

"Make me cum," she whimpered. "Why are you torturing me?"

I groaned as I pulled my hand away from her tits so I could get a better grip on her as I fucked her.

With one hand on the back of her neck, and the other on her hip, I slowly slid out, angling my hips before I slammed back into her. The tension seeped out of her and she closed her eyes as I moved, each thrust hitting deep inside her pussy. I pictured driving into her womb, my seed filling her.

Everyone knew that manifestation got you halfway there.

"That's it, baby. You feel so fucking good. I love you so much."

"Say it again," she whispered, her arms looping around my neck as I settled into a pounding, steady rhythm. I was aware that the clock was ticking down. I had to give her at least two more orgasms before that buzzer sounded.

"You feel so fucking good?" I groaned.

Her nails dug into my neck and I just about came from that. "Tell me you love me," she corrected me.

I pressed my forehead against hers, staring deep into her eyes as I pushed in and out of her. "I love you," I breathed. "I love you. I love you. I love you."

She came, her core choking my cock until I had to start thinking about dead puppies or I was going to embarrass myself real fast.

I licked up her pulse, savoring how wild and out of control it was. It was nice to sometimes see evidence that I had some kind of effect on her. I needed to know she felt at least a little of this exquisite torture. That maybe, she needed me at least a portion of how much I needed her.

"That's it. Such a good girl, coming all over Daddy's cock."

She'd had her eyes closed as she came, but they flew open then, staring at me with a mix of mirth and horror.

"Please don't ever say that again," she moaned as I tugged back her hair and my teeth sank into her skin.

I laughed, because she was going to be calling me "Daddy" here, very, very soon if everything happened like I wanted it to.

"Give me one more, baby. That game's going to end soon, and there will be a crowd of players coming into this room. And if they see you cum—because I'm not stopping until you do—then bad things are going to happen."

She cried out as I flexed my hips, pushing as deep inside her as I could get. I let go of her neck and reached between us, massaging her clit as I fucked into her. A moment later, her core pulsed around my dick, her teeth sinking into my shirt as she writhed against me.

"That's so good, baby. So good," I moaned, my words coming out strangled and broken as I began to cum.

Fire flowed through me and it was all I could do to not drop her and collapse to the ground because it felt so fucking good.

I was definitely waxing poetic as I came down from that high.

Somewhere above us was the faint sound of the buzzer, signaling the end of the game.

Fuck.

I withdrew with a groan, tucking myself back in my pants, rethinking my idea to do it here. I liked to cuddle afterwards and there was definitely no time for cuddling at the moment.

I swiped my fingers through her core, loving the feel of our combined climax. She shivered, burying her face against my chest, her breaths still coming out in small gasps.

I wiped my fingers across Carter's bench and on some of his practice clothes with a wide grin.

Kennedy didn't even notice I was doing it.

Perfection.

"Let's go, baby," I said urgently, pulling up her pants and hoisting her towards the door as I heard the sound of footsteps coming in from the tunnel.

I opened the door to a surprised looking trainer who'd just been reaching for the door.

"What?" he said, taking a step back and looking between the two of us, probably instantly guessing what we'd just done. "Are you two fucking serious?"

Kennedy's face was red with embarrassment, and she looked like she was about to bolt. Plus, I'd forgotten her drink and pickle in the locker room, so she was probably about to get incredibly hangry.

I'd need to fix that soon.

"Hey, great game," I told him, smacking three hundred dollar bills into his chest.

He stared at the money in shock, but like any good sheep, he was now bought and paid for. Sexscapades in the locker room be damned.

We strode down the hallway and there was a big grin across my face...not just from the incredible sex I'd just had.

I couldn't wait for Carter's reaction.

CHAPTER 16

Carter

Fuck. That game had been tough. We'd squeaked out the win, but I was fucking exhausted.

I needed Kennedy, a burger, and a beer.

In that order, please.

"You were a wall out there, Hayes," Jack said, smacking me on the ass as he pushed past me, obviously eager to get to our girl. She disappeared after the second period and we were all twitchy about it.

I may have been at peace with Greyson. I may have even agreed to share Kennedy with him...

But that didn't mean I trusted him implicitly.

I didn't think I could ever do that after everything that had happened between us all.

"We're going to need to be better than that for Toronto next week," Sebastian said tiredly as he made his way to his locker, plopping down on the seat and leaning his head back against the wall. Outside of me, he'd had the most time out on the ice to try and help me out. He was obviously feeling it.

I grunted as I finally made it to my locker and threw my gloves down. I was about to plop down when I noticed something shiny smeared across my seat.

What the hell?

I was exhausted. That was the only excuse I had for reaching down to see what it was instead of asking someone from the janitorial staff to clean it off. Fuck, it could have just been some of the menthol gel I'd rubbed on my wrist before last period to try and distract myself from the pain I was having thanks to that hit I'd gotten from one of their forwards as he tried to push the puck in.

I slid my fingers through, grimacing at the texture as I brought it up to my nose to sniff.

"Fuck," I growled when I smelled Kennedy's scent...and something else. "Fucking hell."

"What?" Sebastian asked, jumping up from his seat like we were under attack.

Fuck, is that what our life had come to now?

"Greyson had Kennedy in here. And I'm pretty sure he fucked her against my locker."

I thrust my fingers into Sebastian's face and he inhaled, his eyes growing hazy for a second as he took in Kennedy's scent.

"Ugh. That's not just Kennedy!" he snarled, wiping at his nose like I'd wiped some of it on him.

"I'm well aware," I drawled, grabbing a towel and wiping my seat, even though I knew it wouldn't be enough to cancel her scent.

I knew that because my room was soaked in the smell of her for weeks after she'd come on my leg that first day.

I glared around the room like any second now one of my teammates was going to lunge forward and get a whiff of Kennedy's scent.

Fucking Greyson.

"What's going on?" asked Jack, wiping a towel through his hair. Somehow he'd managed to shower in the five seconds we'd been back in the locker room...like a freaking ninja.

I held up my hand and he stared at it like it was a snake that was going to bite him.

Since it did have some of Greyson's cum on it...I guess it was like a snake.

I thrust my hand forward, so he had no choice but to smell it. If the rest of us had to, he had to as well.

"Fucking hell." Jack shook his head, sighing as he dragged his hand down his face. "I'm never going to be able to concentrate knowing she's been here. That she's cum in here," he whisper-yelled. He also eyed our teammates suspiciously, like they were all going to attack and start sniffing around my locker.

I studied my locker, realizing the asshole had spread it to other places as well. My practice jersey, my bag...I mean hell, how long had they been in here?

"Guess we know he didn't kidnap her during that last period," I remarked as Sebastian inspected his locker for anything.

Greyson hadn't done anything to his space. And Jack didn't find anything on his either. Which meant that Greyson had chosen to torture just me.

Which didn't surprise me honestly.

It was probably because my dick was half an inch bigger. He'd probably gotten a look at it in that threesome we'd had the other day and gotten all jealous.

"I'm going to have to take all my stuff back to our place to wash it because I don't want any of the staff smelling her," I complained, beginning to unsnap my pads. "I'm not going to be able to concentrate at all if I keep it on there. I'll be skating around with a hard-on. And we all know I won't be able to hide it."

Jack snorted, shaking his head and going back to get his bag. Fuck, he was going to get so much more time with Kennedy, getting these pads off was a fucking chore.

Jack disappeared out into the hallway as Sebastian dragged himself to the shower. I finally got my pads off and I followed, after covering the bench with a towel...just in case.

I knew from experience that Kennedy's scent was addictive.

Sebastian and I both finished around the same time and

found Jack, leaned over Kennedy, one arm propped against the wall above her head as he sweet-talked her. I glared at Greyson, who was scrolling through his phone on her other side, one hand holding her hand like he couldn't bear for Kennedy not to be paying attention to him at least a little bit.

I sidled up and pushed my way between him and Kennedy, so he had no choice but to let her go.

He growled and finally glanced up from his phone.

"Payback is a bitch," I whispered in Greyson's ear.

His nose flared and then his face went suspiciously blank. "Oh, something happen?"

I rolled my eyes. "You're a jackass. What if that had been my lucky jersey? What if I'd never been able to wash it? Where would I be then?"

"You'd be smelling like me forever then, I suppose," Greyson smirked.

"I hope you choke on a dick," I hissed, and the bastard just laughed at me.

"I'm sorry. I'm not very good at saying no to you guys," Kennedy said softly, a faint blush to her cheeks. She was biting down on her bottom lip and glancing up at me with a guilty looking expression on her face.

"Stop being an asshole," Jack hissed at me, before pressing a comforting kiss on Kennedy's lips.

"You're a perfect little sweetheart," I said soothingly.

"We're just mad that we didn't get to join in," Sebastian added, pushing in between Jack and I and stuffing his face in Kennedy's neck and squeezing her against him. People were looking at us—as usual—but we were beyond giving a fuck.

We'd gotten used to that sort of thing in high school when we were all mooning over her and following her around like lost sheep.

"I call dibs. I need sleep," Sebastian moaned...still attached to her.

"Yeah, yeah. That's not happening, buddy," Jack said, patting him on the back and pulling her away. "But let's get home."

I watched as Kennedy fawned all over Sebastian as we walked to the car, worried because he was acting so tired.

It was only when he winked at me that I got annoyed.

Getting her attention like that was a heady thing and I was thinking about showing her the cut on my wrist from that slash I'd taken...just so I could get more of her attention.

"I've got to go deal with something, baby," Greyson told Kennedy when we got to Jack's truck.

———

Jack

"You do?" she asked Greyson, her face falling, and her voice worried as Greyson pulled her away from Sebastian.

He met my gaze over her head as he hugged her tight, a silent warning in his gaze.

Fuck. I should probably offer to help the asshole, shouldn't I?

"I'll go with you," I told him and his gaze widened imperceptibly. Carter and Sebastian looked equally shocked.

"Okay," Greyson said simply as Kennedy turned to look at me.

"Maybe I should go too," she said. It was cute that she thought she was such a badass.

Greyson's mouth dipped into a frown as his gaze fell from her face...to her stomach.

Now, I was looking at her stomach too.

When was the last time she'd had a period?

"Why do you guys keep staring at me like that? You look like Greyson did the entire game," Kennedy complained to me. I did my best to make my expression innocent.

I wasn't sure how our girl was going to feel about pregnancy, but I did know that I was excited about it.

And terrified.

Since we still hadn't figured out who was after us.

Which was why I was going to go with Greyson tonight.

Because I suspected his "business" had something to do with tracking down the mole we'd decided was in his operation—in our operation I guess I should say.

I did have the tattoo now after all.

The death of Greyson's three main suspects hadn't stopped things from happening. Greyson had a weapons shipment disappear last week, and a threatening note had been on Carter's car a few days ago.

"We'll be back soon," Greyson said soothingly, pressing a succinct kiss across her lips before he stepped away. I could tell it was hard for him to do that.

It was hard for all of us to be away from her for a second.

"Take care of her," he growled at Carter and Sebastian. Carter rolled his eyes like he was going to punch him in the face. Sebastian straightened up, all signs of his tiredness fading away.

I smoothed Kennedy's hair from her face and took a second to take in her gorgeous features.

How had I lived without her for even a second?

The younger me must have been a better man, because there was no way that I could ever give her up again.

No matter what.

"See you soon, pretty girl," I murmured, knowing that I wouldn't feel sane until I was back in her presence again.

"Come on, Romeo," Greyson drawled, like he hadn't been fawning over her a second ago. The idiot was just jealous of anyone spending time with Kennedy that wasn't him.

I made sure to give her one more long kiss, just to piss him off.

But of course then I got carried away, because who wouldn't when they were tasting perfection. A second later, Greyson yanked me off.

We both waved one more time and strode towards one of Greyson's ridiculous sports cars.

"You really need to get a truck," I told him as I slid into the sleek interior.

"You wouldn't say that if you could afford this car," he snarked. And I rolled my eyes.

Bazillionaires.

Fucking unbelievable.

I glanced back to see that the others were already pulling out and I sighed. Feeling twitchy that she was gone.

"This shouldn't take long," Greyson mused, flipping on some indie playlist that had me rolling my eyes. Because, of course, he would think he was too cool for regular music. I went to change the song to...honestly anything else.

"I will throw you out of my car," he said, side-eyeing me.

I rolled my eyes even more.

But I didn't try to change the song again.

Because I knew he really would.

Greyson and I had been co-captains all throughout high school. Both used to being the top dogs.

If I was honest with myself, it had been strange when he hadn't been there anymore to help shoulder the load.

Sometimes it still felt strange.

"So, are you going to tell me where we're going?" I asked, when he hadn't offered anything ten minutes later. We were in the warehouse district, a place I didn't make a habit of frequenting when I had the choice. The streets were lined with towering structures of rusted steel and crumbling brick. Shadows danced along the graffiti-covered walls, casting eerie shapes in the dim light of the flickering street lamps.

"Sunny found a lead...supposedly. He traced some of the messages we've been receiving to this number. I doubt he's the one behind anything since he was dumb enough to send messages outside of a burner phone, but I'm hoping he has some information. With the baby coming..."

My eyes went bug-eyed at what he'd just said, and he

grinned, because the bastard knew he'd just dropped a veritable bomb on me.

"She's pregnant?" I whispered, the words coming out rough and choked. The thought of Kennedy pregnant with my baby...with *our* baby...fuck.

"Hold your hard-on, *Cameron*, it's not for sure yet. I just think she is...she was craving pickles."

I scoffed, and adjusted myself because, okay...I may have gotten slightly hard at the idea of her pregnant. But obviously that was for nothing.

"Pickles?" I asked sarcastically. "You're thinking she's pregnant based on pickles."

"Has Kennedy ever asked for pickles before, at any point in the countless number of games she's attended since we were teenagers?" he asked pointedly as he pulled in behind a particularly decrepit looking warehouse.

I thought about it. I could not remember a single pickle in her past. She even picked the pickles off her chicken sandwiches—which was honestly a travesty because everyone knew that chicken sandwiches needed pickles.

"Huh," I muttered. "You might be onto something."

His answering smile was entirely too smug. "I think that I am." We hopped out of the car and I followed Greyson to the gray, metal back door that looked like someone had taken a baseball bat to it. "Her period is in a few days though. So, we'll know for sure."

"You *would* know that."

His grin this time was positively giddy. "Kennedy's the horniest on her period. You think I'm going to miss out and have meetings that interfere with that?"

Fuck.

The man might be a genius.

I resolved to pay closer attention to that as well. Get a few more "dibs" in on those nights.

A bulking giant of a man opened the door and nodded

respectfully at Greyson. He stepped towards me and Greyson held up a hand.

"He's fine, Tapper," Greyson murmured, and "Tapper" nodded again and stepped back into the shadowed interior of the building.

I was honestly a bit shocked he hadn't had me frisked just for fun.

The pickle had gotten to him.

We walked inside, our footsteps echoing off the empty walls like whispers in the darkness. Dust motes danced in the faint shafts of light filtering through broken windows, casting eerie shadows on the cold concrete floor. Ahead, a set of stairs beckoned, their descent into the depths below shrouded in darkness.

Greyson headed to the stairs, because of course, where else would we be going...

I followed Greyson down, my footsteps echoing against the concrete walls as we descended into the darkness below.

The air was cold and damp, heavy with the stench of fear and desperation.

"Is this where you kill me?" I whispered mockingly.

He stopped and glanced back at me over his shoulder, raising an eyebrow sarcastically—if that was really a thing.

Greyson's second, Sunny, was leaning against one of the walls as we entered the room, staring at the piece of shit in front of us. He gave us a head nod as we walked in.

In the center of the room, a man was tied to a chair, his face bruised and bloodied from the beating he'd already endured. His eyes widened in terror as we approached, a strangled sound coming out of his mouth as he tried to hold in a whimper as his gaze tracked Greyson's approach.

I was a little offended that he was so scared of Greyson. I was scary too. If I had my hockey stick I'd bet he'd be scared of me right now.

Greyson stepped forward, a predatory gleam in his eyes as he surveyed the man before us. He slowly walked around the chair, his finger trailing along the leather. I had to admire the man's talent—he certainly knew how to evoke fear.

"Who is he, Torrin?" Greyson finally asked in a soft, chilling voice.

The guy's eyes widened and some snot dripped down his face.

Disgusting.

He glanced around desperately, as if one of us was going to help him.

I smiled when he looked at me and finally got the squeak of terror I'd been looking for.

Torrin remained silent and Greyson sighed in annoyance, his expression hardening as he reached for a length of rope coiled on the floor beside him.

With a swift motion, he wrapped it around Torrin's neck, pulling it taut with a cruel smile.

He gasped for breath, his eyes bulging as he struggled against the rope. I could see the panic in his eyes, the realization dawning on him that Greyson wasn't playing around.

I mean Greyson's rope work needed work, but I guess we couldn't all be perfect.

"Do you have a name for me?" Greyson purred. Torrin remained stubborn, his lips sealed shut as he fought against the suffocating pressure of the rope around his neck.

Greyson's smile widened, and I kept my gaze firmly above his waist just in case this was something he got off on...he looked giddy enough that I wouldn't put it past him honestly. He leaned in close to the man's ear. "You have one last chance," he whispered, his voice dripping with malice. "Tell me what I want to know...or you're going to die. Miserably."

I watched as Torrin's resolve wavered, fear flicking across his face as he weighed his options. With a defeated sigh, and one more tug on the rope... "Okay! I'll tell you what I know. But please! I'm your loyal servant. I would never betray you."

Sunny shifted off the wall, his gaze narrowed on our captive.

"He never gave me his name. I promise. He would text me where you were—where Kennedy was!"

Whack! Greyson's fist pounded against his face, a loud crunch sound filling the room as his nose broke and blood splatter went everywhere.

Nose injuries were always so messy.

Torrin started howling, and I rubbed my temple where a headache was building.

"Don't say her name again," Greyson hissed, his gaze crazy-eyed and wild as he pulled on the rope.

"I'm sorry!" Torrin shrieked, his voice sounding...pathetic.

Greyson took a deep breath. "Continue."

"I thought it was a work thing. He would give me locations—"

"How do you know it was a *he*?" I asked.

Torrin gaped at me, confused.

"Well? He asked you something," Greyson snapped coldly.

"I—I don't know," he answered.

"Continue, " I told Greyson, gesturing benevolently.

Greyson rolled his eyes but turned his attention back to his prey. "How many times did this happen?"

"Did I get a text?" Torrin rasped, confused.

Greyson shook his head impatiently. "How many times have you followed us?"

"At least a couple times a week."

My eyes widened at that, and I felt sick.

One of us had been with Kennedy every second, but still...to think that at any point someone was watching us, watching her.

How the fuck were we going to keep her safe?

"I thought I was watching out for her. It was on my official phone. I swear!" he cried, blood and saliva dribbling everywhere.

Greyson was either employing really dumb people, or this guy was a terrible liar.

Either way, he'd been watching us, watching *her*.

And that was unacceptable.

Greyson listened to the man's crap, useless secrets that he thought would save his life. He probably should have been ⁣⁣⁣ since everything he was giving us was fucking pointless.

Greyson's expression would have been unreadable to most people, a mask of indifference at first glance...but I knew him well enough to know how angry he was.

With a cold determination in his eyes, Greyson stared down at Torrin, wrapping the rope several times around his hand as he began to pull.

"What?! No! You said if I talked you wouldn't—" Torrin's words cut off as Greyson tightened the rope.

"I don't believe I said any such thing," Greyson said calmly. "Regardless of what your reason was for spying on me—I don't employ idiots. And I certainly don't employ moles. And you, Torrin...are one or both of those."

Torrin's cries came out as choked coughs, and I got more satisfaction than I wanted to admit at the fear in his gaze, the panic rising within him as he struggled against the suffocating pressure.

Greyson's grip was relentless, his fingers like steel as he squeezed tighter, his expression devoid of any remorse. The man's struggles grew weaker and weaker with each passing moment, his breaths coming in ragged gasps as he neared the end.

It reminded me of how Kennedy's disgusting stepfather had sounded at the end.

With a final, desperate gasp, Torrin fell silent, his eyes staring blankly into the void as his life slipped away. Greyson finally released his grip, staring at the dead body disinterestedly for a moment before he turned away.

"Fucking useless," Greyson growled, picking up a metal tin and throwing it against the wall with a roar, the sound of it echoing around us.

Sunny shifted against the wall, obviously uneasy at his boss's loss of control.

Greyson had always prided himself on that, whether it was out on the ice, or when we were doing jobs as teenagers.

It was probably good for Sunny to understand Greyson wasn't messing around when it came to this. I'd never liked the guy—he was too far up Greyson's ass.

Greyson didn't bother saying anything as he stalked towards me, signaling with his chin it was time to go.

As we left the basement and started up the stairs, the memory of Torrin's final cries echoing in my mind, I felt no satisfaction.

Every new piece of information we got was a dead end.

And as we returned to the main floor to get back to Kennedy, I was well aware that that darkness I'd once tried to run far away from, it was back in full force.

I would do anything to keep her safe.

Anything.

———

We walked into Sebastian's room once we got back to the penthouse, the weight of our silence heavy between us. Greyson and I hadn't exchanged a single word on the drive home, each of us lost in our own thoughts and regrets that we hadn't found out anything to help put this danger to rest.

We stood at the foot of her bed, watching her sleep, surrounded on either side by Carter and Sebastian. They were wrapped around her, just like I would have been if I'd been in their place. She looked like an angel, her delicate features illuminated by the silvery beams filtering through the window. Her chest rose and fell rhythmically with each breath, and just watching it gave me some peace, like a comforting blanket settling over my shoulders.

But I also felt the familiar pang of guilt gnawing at my conscience, the one that had haunted me all those years ago...when I decided to let her go.

I pushed it away.

"There's no turning back," Greyson murmured, as if he could read my thoughts.

I nodded but I didn't say anything in response.

Her hair spilled across her pillow in a cascade of dark waves. I ached just looking at her, my cock stirring as I took in her perfection. Sebastian sighed and cuddled into her further. She stirred slightly at his movement, a faint smile tugging at the corners of her lips.

I moved forward, gently dislodging Sebastian from Kennedy's side. His eyes flew open and he snarled at me. He must have seen how close I was to the edge though, because he reluctantly slid to the edge of the bed, allowing me to make room for myself beside her.

Greyson had a little more difficulty getting Carter to move, and there was a quiet grunt as Greyson eventually kneed him in the stomach to push between him and Kennedy.

I glared at both of them for being so loud, but somehow she didn't wake up.

Our hands instinctively found her stomach, cradling her and possibly our baby in a protective touch.

"Things go that bad?" Carter whispered, his gaze alert as he stared at us, and then our hands, his eyebrow going up at the move.

I grimaced and he nodded, disappointment flooding his features.

She stirred again, a soft sigh escaping her lips as she nuzzled into me. Greyson followed her, until he was pressed up to her back, as close as he could get.

Surrounded by her warmth, it was easier to relax, to pretend like everything was going to be okay.

But I still didn't sleep.

Greyson and I stayed awake the whole night, watching over her together.

Keeping her safe.

CHAPTER 1

Kennedy

With the three would-be leaders of the Jackal splinter group off the board, my guys hadn't let up like I'd thought they would...

Today though, I was watching TV in the living room with Jack, Carter, and Sebastian. My head was on Sebastian's lap and Carter was massaging my feet.

This was the good life. What I wished we could have all the time.

Greyson was due home any minute, or so his text to me had said, and my gaze was flicking to the elevator doors every couple of minutes, hoping he would hurry up.

"Not enjoying *The Office*?" Sebastian murmured as he stroked my hair.

"Mmmh," I said lazily, too relaxed to form words properly.

Carter ran his finger down the center of my foot and I shivered, kicking lightly at his rock-hard stomach. He grinned at me wickedly, and I bit my lip, trying to keep my lust tampered down.

With four hot men around me all the time, my vagina didn't get a lot of breaks.

I wasn't complaining.

But...I was also really comfortable at the moment...so sex could wait.

"Feel like some...fun?" Carter asked casually...way too casually as he touched some erogenous spot on my foot that I was not aware that I had.

My breath stuttered, but I tried to play it cool. I lifted an eyebrow. "Why do I get the feeling that you mean something else when you say fun?"

"I have no idea what you're talking about," he said as his finger trailed from my foot up my leg. I squeezed my thighs together...because this had taken a turn.

"You could just tell me that your fun involves my vagina," I said lightly.

"When doesn't it?" Sebastian said suddenly, his voice in my ear as he wrapped his arms around me.

"I mean I'm really interested in what Dwight Schrute's doing right now," I insisted, as my foot passed lightly over Carter's erection.

He was wearing a pair of gray sweatpants that were basically a gift to my eyes, and there was no hiding how he'd suddenly gone full mast.

Jack leaned over the back of the couch, sipping at a beer.

When had he taken off his shirt?

I wasn't complaining. Watching the contours of his pecs and abs was a treat for the eyes.

"See something you like, pretty girl?" Jack asked, swiping his beer bottle across my chest where my nipples had suddenly become headlights peeking out from my shirt. I shivered again as the cold seeped through my thin bra.

I held in my groan, wondering how I got this lucky that this was my life. I mean there may have been some kind of crazy person after me...but I could forget about that on days like today.

Sebastian began massaging my shoulders at the same time that Carter's massage moved from my feet to my legs.

Jack was watching with a hot, smug look on his face, his gaze burning into me. He took a sip of his beer again and reached down with his other hand to play with the skin peeking out between my leggings and my shirt.

"Let's take this fun into the bedroom, princess," Sebastian purred.

I nodded...because I wasn't an idiot.

Jack grabbed me off the couch like I weighed nothing and threw me over his shoulder as he stalked towards the bedroom.

Strangely...the other two didn't follow.

Jack slid me down his body, making sure that I felt every muscle.

And the fact that his dick was ready to play.

My mouth watered just staring at it. The head was peeking out from his waistband, precum glistening on the hot, red tip.

"You look hungry, pretty girl," he purred.

"I am," I breathed, slowly beginning to sink to the floor.

The door opened right before my knees hit the ground...

And Sebastian and Carter dragged in a struggling, snarling Greyson, their faces alight with mischief and determination.

What the...

They threw him into the chair and Jack walked towards them, rope in his hand that he'd pulled out of nowhere.

"Guys?" I asked, straightening up.

"The three of you are dead men. Are you out of your fucking minds? What are you doing?"

"You really should have seen this coming," Carter drawled as he smacked Greyson's arm against the chair and Jack deftly secured the knots with practiced ease.

"This is how you properly tie a knot," Jack said and Greyson stopped struggling for a moment to stare at him with a lifted eyebrow.

"That's what this is about? You're signing your death warrant because you want to show me proper rope technique? This seems a bit...theatrical...even for you," Greyson said sarcastically.

I was just watching them in shock, not understanding what was going on at all.

"I thought we were all one big happy family now?" I asked, waving at the four of them. Greyson got loose from Sebastian and popped him in the stomach.

Sebastian grunted but wrestled his arm back into place as Jack quickly tied it to the chair.

"Oh we are one big happy family, princess. The happiest," said Sebastian, grimacing as he rubbed his stomach and squatting down, narrowly missing being kicked in the face.

Jack tied Greyson's leg down.

"Fucking hell. Let me out of here right the fuck now," Greyson seethed.

"It's just sometimes, families have to learn some lessons," Carter grinned as Jack finished tying Greyson's other leg.

"Why are you teaching him a lesson exactly?" I asked slowly, feeling like I was missing out on something.

"Think, Greyson. Think really hard," said Carter in a sweet sing-song voice.

Greyson suddenly stopped struggling, and his grin lit up the room.

He threw back his head and started laughing...loudly.

"This is for your locker having a little something extra in it," he said, sounding delighted.

"It is in fact for that," Carter snarled.

My face went red. My hands flew to my cheeks as I recalled the very hot moment we'd had in the locker room.

"Tell me, princess....should we punish you, too, for participating in torturing us?" asked Sebastian, coming up behind me and wrapping his arms around my waist, pulling me towards his chest.

"It was all his idea," I gasped as his lips trailed down my neck. He nipped at my shoulder, and I shivered.

"Did you notice right away?" Greyson asked, still sounding...euphoric. Like this was one of the best moments of his life.

Considering he was tied up at the moment, I wasn't sure what that said about him.

Or his life.

"Oh, let's see…" Carter began, pretending to think as he tapped his finger on his chin. "One second," he finally snapped. "One fucking second was all it took for me to realize you'd spread her cum all over my fucking locker! You fucking bastard!"

I gasped. Because I had not been aware of that.

Carter glanced over at me, along with Greyson…who winked unrepentantly when he caught my gaze. "Oh, you didn't know that he spread your fucking essence all over my locker, ensuring that I'm going to get a fucking hard on every time I go in my locker room. I sprayed everything with bleach…and I still smell you."

"I'm not sure if I should be offended right now. I—I feel like you're calling me smelly," I said indignantly.

All four of them stared at me like I was crazy.

Sebastian bit down on my neck again. "It's because you're the most delicious thing that any of us have ever smelled…have ever tasted. We're addicted to you. It's our favorite fucking thing."

Oh. Well that made me feel a little bit better.

"Don't forget that it also smelled like me," Greyson grinned, leaning back in his chair like he didn't have a care in the world and he wasn't in fact tied up.

Carter huffed. "I've been trying to forget about that."

"When you get that woody. You're partially getting it for me," Greyson continued.

Jack walked over to his dresser and a second later, had a pair of socks in his hand.

"It's time for you to shut up now."

"Don't you—"

Jack stuffed the socks into Greyson's mouth…and of course

188 C.R. JANE & MAY DAWSON

because Greyson's hands were tied...he couldn't do anything. Especially after Jack put duct tape on top of that.

"Looks like you're stuck with us for a while," Sebastian said happily.

"I'm really not sure that I should be going along with this," I said, but it came out completely half-hearted because Carter had just stripped his shirt off, and now there were two chests I was melting over.

A̶n̶d̶ ̶t̶h̶e̶n̶ ̶t̶h̶r̶e̶e̶

Sebastian moved out from behind me and slowly slid his shirt off. "I've gotta get some of your attention too," he purred.

I wiped my lips because I was pretty sure that some drool was slipping out of my mouth.

Greyson made a noise and rattled the chair...but apparently Jack was good at ropes. And the chair was exceptionally strong. Because Greyson wasn't going anywhere.

This was kind of fun.

"Let's get you a little more comfortable, sweetheart," Carter murmured, slipping off my shirt so that I was standing there in my bra.

The way all four of them were staring at me...you would have thought that I was wearing the most exotic lingerie available.

Greyson made another muffled growling sound and he almost tipped over trying to get out.

"I will leave you there if you fall over," Jack told him earnestly.

I snorted and he winked at me.

"Look at our girl, Greyson. You need to remember this moment next time you want to have some fun at our expense. The consequences will be twice whatever you've done," said Carter, coming up behind me and shoving down my leggings.

"Step," he murmured, removing them until I was then just in my bra and my tiny scrap of a thong.

I should probably wear pants more often...but leggings were much easier to get off in these types of circumstances.

Circumstances I found myself in a lot nowadays.

Carter dragged his hand down my chest, in between my breasts. He lightly brushed against my stomach before sliding towards my core. He pressed on my clit briefly before he moved to my cloth-covered slit, growling when he felt how soaked my panties were.

"She's soaked, Greyson. And you don't get to taste any of it. You can just get what the rest of us got that night...her smell."

Carter's finger moved under my thong, brushing through my sopping wet folds before he pulled it out and rubbed his finger right under Greyson's nose.

"Have fun," Carter said in a sing-song voice.

The chair rocked again and Carter, Sebastian, and Jack all laughed.

I was honestly a little scared for them. The threat in Greyson's eyes looked...scary.

Oh well, they could worry about that after they gave me some orgasms.

Jack gently grabbed my chin and his wet tongue licked into my mouth, thrusting against my tongue. He rolled his hips against me, and I moaned as I kissed him back hungrily.

"I think our baby girl is ready to be fucked now, aren't you?" he murmured against my lips, sucking on my tongue lightly and deepening our kiss.

A hand wrapped around my throat as rough fingers played with my breast, kneading and massaging and pinching at my nipple until I was writhing against Jack's mouth.

He laughed and captured my moan, his fingers lazily playing in my folds, brushing against my clit enough that sparks of pleasure were shooting through me.

I was feeling so much.

His abs clenched against my stomach, wet drops smearing on my skin as his heavy cock bobbed between us.

"Bring her over here," Sebastian said roughly, and I whimpered as Jack broke our kiss and stopped playing in between my legs.

"Shhh baby. We're going to take such good care of you," Carter soothed, giving one last tug at my nipple before he released my breast and turned me towards the bed.

I was faintly aware of Greyson making a racket with the chair again, but I couldn't take my eyes off Sebastian, sprawled out naked on the bed, looking like the most delicious daydream I could imagine.

Everything about these men looked unreal. Flawless, heavy slabs of muscle that literally made my mouth water.

"Get up on that bed and ride our boy, pretty girl," Jack rumbled, his hand coming down with a sharp smack on my ass cheek.

I jumped, a flare of pleasure streaking through me. I slid off my thong and put one knee up on the bed and crawled towards Sebastian who was staring at me like he was going to die if I didn't touch him soon.

Sebastian lunged forward when I was taking too long and suddenly I found myself perched above his dick, his tip pressing against my lips and sliding along my slit.

I mewled and went to grab his cock and put it where I wanted, but my arms were yanked away and pulled behind me, forcing my breasts to jut out obscenely.

"You're not in charge tonight, sweetheart," Carter said with a dark chuckle as he licked up the side of my neck.

"Am I ever in charge?" I pouted, my breath coming out in loud gasps as Jack leaned over and licked one of my nipples, sucking it into his hot mouth. My back bowed further as my pussy tightened with ecstasy. I shifted my hips, desperately trying to find some friction to help with the ache inside of me.

The bastards all laughed in response again like I'd said something funny.

Before I could say anything else, Sebastian fisted his dick and pressed it to my opening, pushing inside me in one smooth move.

"You're perfect," he hissed, his face curled up in erotic agony as we came together.

My eyes closed as I tried to adjust to the exquisite fullness of his dick inside me.

All of my men were too big to fit comfortably.

But the bite of pain never outweighed the pleasure.

"That's it, pretty girl. You're taking him so well," Jack murmured, his lips brushing against my ear.

Sebastian's hips surged even deeper and I gasped.

"You're going to take even more," Carter said from behind me. A second later hands were leaning me forward and I heard the pop of a lid. Cold liquid slipped down my crack and fingers were spreading it around my hole.

"I don't think—" I cried and Sebastian captured the sound in his mouth.

Another hand slid soothingly down my spine. "Yes. You're going to take all of us. You were made for us. Our perfect, gorgeous girl."

Our tongues slowly curled together, relaxing me as Carter pushed one finger into my ass...and then another, stretching me as he scissored his fingers in and out. He spread the cold gel all over.

"That's it. We're going to make you feel so good," Carter said.

Sebastian gently massaged my clit as we kissed, and I was having some kind of out of body experience as soft waves of pleasure took over my senses. Like my existence was only to feel now, and I didn't have any other cares or concerns in the world.

I felt Carter's dick push against my asshole, and I moaned into Sebastian's mouth when his broad head popped through the tight ring of muscle.

Sebastian laid back down, his head thrown back as his hands dug into my hips.

Carter pushed further in and a flood of unintelligible words were streaming out of my mouth because I thought I'd felt full before...

Tears slid down my cheeks at the overwhelming sensations. I felt like I was being split in half...but at the same time more whole than ever before.

How did that make sense?

"That's it, pretty girl. You're taking us so good." Jack purred as he slid his mouth leisurely over mine. Carter and Sebastian still hadn't moved, but Sebastian was still working on my clit, relaxing me with every pass.

"Look over at Greyson," Carter growled, and I turned my head towards our *captive* audience, completely forgetting about the situation thanks to the two dicks inside me.

Greyson's eyes were pure fire, his dick a huge bulge in his suit pants as he stared at me. A bead of sweat slid down his cheek. He wasn't struggling anymore, but his body was laced with tension. He was clearly suffering.

Something came over me and I blew him a kiss. He strained forward, muffled gasps falling from his mouth before he forced himself to relax back in his seat.

"Look how much he wants you, Kennedy. He's desperate for you. Look at the power you have over that mob boss. Someday, you'll have all of us. He just needs to learn this little lesson first about how we treat our *family*," Jack murmured, allowing me to look at Greyson for one more second before he tilted my chin towards him and began to kiss me.

A memory came, of a darkened room, their hands all over me. We'd done this before, all of us. Except I didn't think Greyson had been tied up in that instance.

Sebastian surged up into me and I moaned, and then Carter was following, his dick pulling out and pushing back into my ass.

"Yes, yes, yes," I chanted against Jack's lips, our breaths mingling together around my gasps and moans.

"Fuck, I can feel you sliding against my dick," Sebastian said through gritted teeth—presumedly to Carter because it was a given that he could feel me, there wasn't an inch to spare in my pussy at the moment.

"Think you can take me, too?" Jack asked as Sebastian and Carter moved in and out of me. I gaped at Jack and they all laughed again, as if the idea of me literally splitting in half was funny to them.

"We'll work up to that," Carter growled as he thrust into my ass as Sebastian pulled out. "Think of the four of us inside you at the same time. We've done it before," he murmured, and my eyes rolled into the back of my head as an orgasm hit me hard, my entire body overcome as my climax pulsed through me.

"Fucking hell," Sebastian moaned. "You're so fucking tight."

"Such a sweet girl," Jack praised me. All of a sudden his dick was tapping against my cheek.

Even though I hadn't gotten used to the two dicks currently spearing me.

But it was better than the other way I could have "taken" him.

"Open up, pretty girl," he begged, and as soon as my mouth opened...his dick surged in between my lips.

More tears fell down my cheeks as I tried to breathe around his cock.

Jack pulled out until just his head was between my lips, before he pushed forward even farther, his tip sliding into my throat.

I made a choking sound and Jack groaned.

Sebastian's movements were becoming frantic, his cock fucking up into me, suddenly out of sync with Carter's still steady movements.

"Please, come again," Sebastian begged, his fingers digging in so hard against my hips I would be wearing his marks for days.

He didn't have to ask twice. One more pass against my clit and I was coming. Hard.

"Fuck, yes," Sebastian snarled, and I felt his warm heat flooding my insides.

Carter abruptly yanked me off Sebastian's dick and Sebastian snarled as he laid back against the bed. Jack's cock slipped from my mouth as I was pulled against Carter's chest. One hand encircled my neck, the other hand grabbing my hip as he pounded into my ass.

His hand squeezed my throat until I began to feel light headed, the oxygen deprivation heightening every thrust of his cock against my nerve endings.

"Kiss me," Carter growled, releasing my neck enough so I could give him my mouth. His kiss was rough and demanding. I whimpered against him as fingers suddenly slipped into my core, sliding in and out and spreading around Sebastian and my combined cum.

Jack's fingers and Carter's dick thrust in time with each other, a rhythm that had my eyes rolling back in my head.

"Are you going to fuck her?" Carter asked as he slammed into me harder.

"No. I want her to myself," Jack answered in a rough voice as his fingers brushed on that spot inside me.

"Carter," I moaned as my muscles trembled and my core clenched as I came for him.

"That's it. That's my perfect girl," Carter groaned as his control slipped. "You feel so fucking good."

He released my lips, and my head fell back against his chest, my eyes locking with Jack's fiery ones as he watched me closely while he fucked me with his fingers.

Carter tilted my hips back a little more, his hand again locking around my throat as he pushed in and out.

His movements faltered. "Yes. Fuck. Fuck. Fuck. Take me," Carter said, surging forward until he was all the way in and it was almost impossible to breathe. His hot cum filled me to the brim, and I screamed as I somehow came again. The room took on a glowy, hazy look as Carter squeezed my throat.

Jack only gave Carter a second more to stay inside me before he ripped me off his dick. "Finally!" he growled, pulling me forward so that I was on my hands and knees and facing...Greyson.

Greyson's face was the epitome of sexual frustration, his entire body straining towards me as his gaze met mine.

"Lesson learned, oh great Jackal?" Jack said mockingly as he slowly pushed into me, making sure that I felt every inch of his giant, ridged dick. Greyson made some kind of angry—I assume sexually frustrated—sound. I whimpered as my hips tilted up, and Jack made it all the way in. I was sore, Sebastian and Carter had made a mess of me, but somehow Jack still felt so good.

"Yes," he groaned as he slid out and played with me, the head of his cock rubbing through my folds. Jack surged in again, and I was so exhausted. My arms gave out, making the angle even more intense as Jack made sure my hips stayed lifted up. He bent over and kissed my spine. "Such a good girl," he purred and I shivered as my eyes met Greyson's again. I licked my lips, envisioning him feeding me his dick from this position.

Another orgasm was coming as Jack's cock hammered into me, seeming to push against my womb with every thrust.

It was as agonizing as it was pleasurable.

He pulled me up higher so that my knees were barely brushing against the sheets as I shook around his cock.

"I can't. No more," I pleaded.

"Just a little more, pretty girl," Jack soothed as Sebastian appeared to the side of me. He reached under me and gently massaged my clit.

"Squeeze me, just like that," Jack panted as his thrusts went erratic. His climax was loud, his groan echoing around the room.

Jack allowed me to fall forward, and a second later Sebastian's hot seed was spraying my back as he came again.

The last thing I saw was the large wet spot in Greyson's pants that told me he'd come too.

And then I blacked out.

———

I woke up in a mess of limbs, lounging against a warm body.

I was sweaty and sore.

And my vagina was definitely out of commission for a minute.

I laid there for a second, soaking in the feeling of...being loved...of belonging...of feeling like I'd found my purpose in life.

And maybe it was being loved by them.

There was a small sound, and I glanced over to where it had come from, my eyes widening when I saw that Greyson was still sitting in the chair, his eyes glittering in the darkness as he stared at us indignantly.

"Crap," I whispered, struggling to move some of the arms holding me tight so I could get to him and try and get him out.

Jack groaned and pulled me closer, burying his face in my neck as he breathed softly against my skin.

His body felt like it was a thousand degrees.

"Jack," I whispered.

He groaned against my skin and I rolled my eyes, because hello, I was the one who'd been railed a thousand ways to Sunday, and yet I'd managed to wake up.

"Jack," I hissed again, gently shaking him. He brushed his lips against my neck, and his hand moved in between my legs.

"Nope," I whispered, locking my thighs together because he wasn't allowed to get anywhere near there.

Carter was breathing softly underneath me, so he wasn't going to be any help.

I turned towards Sebastian, who was also plastered to my other side. "Sebastian," I hissed. "Wake up!"

Sebastian's eyes slowly opened, fluttering a few times before they started to close again.

"Sebastian!"

This time his gaze flew open all the way and he looked at me frantically, his gaze weirdly going to my stomach. "Shit! Is everything okay? Do you need to go to the hospital?"

I blinked. "Why would I need to go to the hospital?"

Jack groaned and shifted against me, but he still didn't wake up.

"We need to let Greyson out. I think your point has been proven, and I can't do those knots myself."

Sebastian snuggled closer. "He's okay."

"Sebastian!" I whisper-yelled. "You need to let him out right now."

Sebastian sighed, like I'd just assigned him the worst task possible.

He tweaked my nipple, and I hissed at him.

Because those were sore too.

He smacked a kiss against my lips and slid out of the bed, grabbing a pair of sweatpants and pulling them over his bare, delectable ass before he walked over to where Greyson was absolutely fuming.

Sebastian reached into his pocket, coming up with a pocketknife that I didn't know he owned. "Don't move, Greyson," he said lightly. "I would hate for my knife to slip."

I rolled my eyes, because these guys were impossible.

Sebastian squatted down and steadied the rope around Greyson's left leg. He started sawing, but before he'd cut all the way through he paused and glanced up at Greyson's face. "Do not kick me," he snarled.

Greyson sniffed, nodding once, and then he resumed slicing through the rope. A few seconds later Greyson's leg was free.

Sebastian did his other leg and then straightened up, eyeing him again. He glanced over where I was still lounging against Carter and Jack, completely exhausted from the sex fest. "Sure we can't leave the socks in his mouth? I think it's a major improvement."

Greyson made a choking sound, and Sebastian laughed as he stripped off the duct tape and pulled off the sock.

"You fucking—" he began before Sebastian held up the sock.

"Don't make me put this back in."

Greyson's face went that angry, purple-red color again and he took a deep breath. "I lost feeling in my hands three hours ago. Get this rope off me."

I giggled and Greyson's glare sliced through me, gentling slightly as his gaze got caught on my breasts.

"Don't get any ideas," I warned. "I'm closed for business."

He scoffed like I'd said something offensive.

Sebastian carefully undid one of his wrists, and Greyson gasped as he flexed his fingers, shaking out his hand. "I could have lost a limb!" he snarled.

"Okay, whiny baby," Sebastian commented calmly as he finished sawing through the last knot.

A second later Greyson's fist connected with Sebastian's jaw, sending him sprawling backwards.

I sat up with a gasp as Greyson stalked towards me, his chest heaving as he stared at me.

"Hi?" I whispered, lamely waving.

Somehow, Jack and Carter were *still* asleep.

I was definitely going to give them a hard time for this tomorrow.

"You're not taking her anywhere," Sebastian snarled as he stood up and rubbed at his jaw. "Also, that was a really shitty way to thank someone for helping you!"

"I wouldn't have needed help if you hadn't tied me up to begin with," Greyson growled at him.

Very good point.

I snorted again, slapping a hand over my mouth when his gaze fell to me once again.

"You think that's funny, baby?" Greyson purred dangerously.

"Think it's funny that I came in my pants for the first time in my fucking life while I watched them fuck all the holes that *I* wanted to fuck? Think it's funny that I had the most painful erection of my life, and I couldn't even touch myself? Not to mention how uncomfortable it was to have a sock stuffed in my mouth for hours?"

I bit down on my lip. "Maybe a little bit," I told him. He lunged towards the bed to grab me, and all of a sudden Carter and Jack's arms went even tighter around me.

"You can sleep with us," Jack said in a drowsy voice. "You're not allowed to take her away. She needs...aftercare."

"That's exactly what I want to do...aftercare. After I fuck her," Greyson said sarcastically. His gaze widening incredulously as Sebastian slid into his original spot by my side.

"Come on in, Greyson," Sebastian said tiredly, rubbing his chin once more before snuggling into the other side of my neck.

I was going to memorize this moment forever, the day that Greyson the Jackal completely lost his mind.

He growled and huffed again, sounding more like a petulant child who'd lost his favorite toy than the mighty *Jackal*, but eventually he kneed up on the bed and crawled towards me.

I stared in shock as Greyson crawled between my legs, laying his head carefully on my chest—using my breasts as a pillow.

I knew that this was going to be uncomfortable in about three point five seconds as he settled against me.

But I didn't try to move him.

I soaked in all four of their closeness.

And to my immense surprise...I fell asleep.

CHAPTER

Kennedy

"C ome on, I have a surprise," I told him as we pulled into the hockey arena's parking lot.

"I can't imagine what kind of surprise I could possibly want in there," Greyson commented, putting the car in park anyways, because he was really bad at saying no to me. "Unless you're going to let me fuck you on Carter's locker again —or maybe we should do it on Jack's locker instead—"

"We're not fucking in the team locker room," I said quickly before he could get too much farther down that particular path...and he ended up convincing me to go in there again.

Greyson frowned, and I leaned forward and pressed a soft kiss against his lips. "Trust me," I murmured. He stared into my eyes for a long moment before finally nodding.

"Always," he replied back.

He took my hand after he'd opened my door for me, pulling me with him even though he didn't know what we were doing. Greyson raised an eyebrow once we'd made it inside.

"So, what's the surprise?" he asked.

"It's date night!" I said excitedly. "And you, sir, are taking me skating."

Greyson grimaced. "I will literally take you anywhere you want. Ask me for anything."

"You're being dramatic. This will be fun."

Greyson sighed and was definitely dragging his feet as we made our way into the rink.

I breathed in the smell of the arena. The ice stretched before us, a vast expanse of glistening white beneath the dim glow of the overhead lights. Greyson hesitated as he stared at it, uncertainty clouding his gorgeous features like a shadow.

I'd arranged...using my boyfriends' perks to have the rink to ourselves for the evening. I hadn't missed Greyson's longing looks when we went to games. He'd missed being out there. I was hoping he'd be able to let his mob boss persona rest for the night.

I was also selfishly hoping that maybe I'd get some more memories back of Greyson and I in high school. I loved these men so much. I wanted every memory of me and them that I could get.

We grabbed skates from the desk, Greyson staring at them like they'd personally offended him of course. "I could have brought my own skates, baby," he said, staring at them disgustedly. "Do you even know what kind of bacteria is in those things?"

"Pssh. You'll survive. I even left my skates home because I didn't want you to see them and ruin the surprise."

Greyson grumbled the entire time he laced up the skates while I just laughed at him.

"Ready?" I asked, holding out my hand.

He gazed at the ice and then back to my hand. "Anything for you, baby."

"This is for you, too," I said quietly.

We walked over to the entrance of the ice, and Greyson hesitated at the edge, uncertainty clouding his features.

For the first time I wondered if this had been the right move. He looked so...sad.

"Come on, baby cakes," I urged, offering him what I hoped looked like a reassuring smile. "It will be just like old times."

He glanced over at me. "That's what I'm afraid of," he answered, a hint of vulnerability across his features. There was a spark of longing in his gaze though too.

The usual rush of excitement coursed through me as we stepped onto the ice, anticipation thrumming in the pit of my stomach.

This was when I'd first felt a sense of familiarity. First felt that maybe my past wasn't locked behind a wall permanently.

The ice was smooth beneath my feet, the crisp air invigorating as it filled my lungs with each breath.

I took a few tentative strikes, the sound of blades scraping against the surface echoing in the stillness of the rink.

Beside me, Greyson moved with a grace born of years of experience, his movements slow and deliberate as he reacquainted himself with the sensation of gliding across the ice. I could see the tension melting away from his shoulders with each stroke, a sense of peace settling over him like a comforting embrace.

I smiled as I watched him, as I watched the hardened mafia leader slip away, and in its place the boy that I'd once known.

With a burst of speed, I launched into a series of spins, my body turning gracefully across the ice like I was a dancer in flight. The cold air whipped past my cheeks, the sensation exhilarating as I lost myself in the simple joy of movement.

A strong pair of arms caught me and held me in place. "Woah there. You're going to give me a heart attack!" Greyson exclaimed, his hands checking me like I had been injured moving around.

"I'm fine," I laughed, not understanding why he was freaking out.

And then he was laughing, too, the sound echoing around the empty rink like a beacon of light.

Greyson almost never laughed, and I marveled at the sound for a moment, because it could have been my new favorite thing.

He grabbed my hand and we skated around, Greyson taking the opportunity to feel me up every chance he got.

"Best date ever?" I asked hopefully, now that he seemed so happy.

"Depends if I end up in your tight pussy after this," he commented as I scoffed, my insides fluttering though just thinking about it.

"Well, who do we have here?" Carter's voice floated towards us from the side of the rink, Jack and Sebastian appearing with him.

"You invited those assholes?" Greyson asked, glancing over at me, but not sounding overly upset about them popping up for our date.

Jack held up a bag of gear. "Think you can keep up with us for a game?"

Greyson hesitated again.

"Come on, Grey-Grey. It'll be fun. Half the battle was getting you on the ice again," said Sebastian. "Grey-Grey." I hadn't heard that one before.

"Fine," he said, as if he was doing them a favor.

They suited up, and I settled onto the bench, trying not to think about how hot they were because a public orgy would definitely not be approved of.

Greyson stared at the stick Jack had handed him, the others already passing back and forth. Sebastian shot him a puck and Greyson easily handled it, skating towards the net and taking a confident shot that went into the net.

He whooped and pumped his stick in the air and my grin was so big I probably resembled a clown.

They began to play two against two, and I couldn't take my eyes off of them.

I closed my eyes, and a memory washed over me.

Suddenly, I could hear the roar of the crowd, feel the energy pulsating through the air as Greyson and the others took to the ice for our high school team. Girls around us were dressed in their best school pride and when I stared down at myself, I was wearing Greyson's jersey.

I gripped the edge of my seat, my heart pounding in my chest as Greyson streaked down the ice, the puck dancing on the blade of his stick. His movements were fluid and precise. With a sudden burst of speed, Greyson darted past the opposing defense, his eyes locked on the goal in front of him.

Suddenly, he glanced up to where I was sitting...and he winked at me.

Greyson closed in on the net and unleashed a powerful shot, the puck sailing through the air. The crowd held its breath, their eyes glued to the puck as it soared towards the goal.

With a resounding thud, it found its mark, slamming into the back of the net with a force that sent the goal post shaking. The arena erupted in cheers as the buzzer rang and the game ended, the sound echoing off the walls as Greyson raised his arms in triumph.

Sebastian, Jack, and Carter tackled him to the ice.

I came back to the present when Sebastian crashed Greyson into the boards as they fought for the puck.

"You still hit like a pussy," snarled Greyson, elbowing Sebastian in the gut as he tore the puck away from him and passed it to Carter who fired on the goal.

"And you obviously need to work out more," Sebastian retorted mockingly as Greyson gasped for breath.

Greyson kept his body perfect—his muscles were a work of art—but there was obviously a difference in working out in a gym and skating on the ice for hours.

And these guys were at each other's throats again.

Luckily, I'd discovered there were a few things that unified them all—worrying about me and fucking me.

I grabbed a stick myself and skated out.

"Oh, hell no," Greyson said, his eyes lighting up with worry. I'd planned on the *fucking* distraction, but apparently I was not allowed to offer even the lightest check to one of these guys.

I tried skating into Jack, as if I were an opponent checking him into the boards. He just caught me up in one arm, not moving in the least even on skates.

"You could let a girl pretend," I teased him.

"Maybe another time," Greyson answered with a frown. "I don't trust these idiots not to...hurt you "

I frowned right back at him. I appreciated their protectiveness...sometimes...but this was a little too much. I wasn't going to die from falling on the ice or getting pushed into the boards.

But then Jack lowered his head and kissed me, since he still had me anchored against his hard, powerful body. The two of us traded long, intense kisses. I smiled against his lips, because kissing him while we rocked on the ice like this brought up the ghosts of old memories.

Sweet ones.

Then, Carter was behind me—the puck clutched in his hand because he was too damn competitive to let anyone have the chance to get a puck in his goal, even when it was all for fun, and the game had basically come to an end—and he was kissing my neck. The puck pressed against my stomach, just above my hip, as he ran his lips along my throat.

I could hear the swish-swish of skates across the ice as Greyson and Sebastian joined us.

And suddenly, none of us could remember what had ever seemed worth fighting over.

CHAPTER 1

Kennedy

I sank into the plush leather seat of Sebastian's Aston
Martin Vanquish, listening to the low purr of the engine
when he touched the accelerator.

"Are you going to let me drive sometime?" I asked,
expecting that he would be protective of the car and feel the
need to be in control.

"Any time you want," he said instead. "You can drive us
home."

"Really?" I asked, unexpectedly delighted.

He glanced over at me. "Baby, you need a car of your own,
don't you?"

"You all don't let me out of your sight to drive myself
anywhere," I reminded him. "Despite you and Greyson going
rogue and destroying all my enemies."

"I hope so," he said, not apologizing for the destruction he
and Greyson had caused when they were supposed to just be out
doing some reconnaissance. They said they'd seen a chance to
eliminate a threat to me, so they took it. I couldn't really argue
with that.

But they still weren't exactly letting me go jogging on my
own, either.

Not that I wanted to jog. But I wanted to be able to jog, in theory, without being kidnapped.

The interior was as sleek as Sebastian himself, all black and chrome, with a hint of rebellion in the red stitching.

"So, where are we going again, Olive Garden?" he asked, even though he knew damn well we were headed to my favorite Italian restaurant. "Spending a day pretending to be normal people? Double dates and garlic knots?"

He had one confident hand on the wheel, the other resting casually on my knee. His touch sent a current through me, a delicious warmth that pooled in my belly.

"Normal can be nice," I retorted, unable to suppress the smile tugging at my lips. "And *everyone* loves garlic knots."

Sebastian shot me a quick glance, his eyes sparkling. I knew him well enough by now to know the tilt of his mouth, the creases that formed when he tried not to smile, even when he was being a grouch. He was thrilled to be the one I'd chosen for my double date with Carrie.

"Kennedy, your life is anything but ordinary," he said, shaking his head. "Just like you."

"Exactly why I need moments like this." I laid my fingers over his hand on my thigh, feeling the calloused warmth. "If you want to be my boyfriend, you have to do boyfriend stuff."

"Boyfriend stuff, huh?" He chuckled. It was the laugh of a man who could get almost any woman he wanted, and yet, he did anything to make *me* happy, and warmth swelled in my chest. "I'm pretty sure I do plenty of 'boyfriend stuff.'"

"Not everything is about sex," I reminded him.

The car pulled up to the restaurant, an upscale Italian place with a canopy of twinkling lights. Sebastian's foot barely touched the brake before the valet sprinted over, eager to open my door. I caught the way his eyes widened as he recognized the man behind the wheel—Sebastian Wright of the Demons, a legend on the ice.

"Mr. Wright, it's an honor!" the valet exclaimed.

"Call me Sebastian," he replied with an easygoing smile, offering me his hand out of the car.

I secretly relished watching Sebastian with his fans, even though I knew it frustrated him to have his attention pulled away from me. He always made people feel at ease, like they were part of his world. Sebastian often seems like he was knit of stoicism and sarcasm, but he was kind too.

"Could I, um, get an autograph?" The valet's cheeks flushed with excitement and embarrassment.

"Sure thing, kid." Sebastian fished a pen from his jacket pocket and scrawled his signature. "There you go."

"Thank you so much, sir!"

"Enjoy your evening," Sebastian said, tossing the keys lightly to the young man who caught them with a reverence usually reserved for holy relics.

As we turned towards the entrance, I looped my arm through Sebastian's. Normal was good. Here I was, walking into a restaurant for a meal with friends, close to a man who could make my heart race with nothing more than a glance. That was the best kind of ordinary.

Across the dimly lit street, I spotted Sunny, his eyes fixed on us, before he melted back into the shadows. It was such a quick glimpse of him that I wasn't entirely sure I'd seen him correctly.

A shiver crept along my spine. I knew Greyson would still have people watching over me. And I recognized Sunny, so why couldn't I shake off the eerie sensation?

"Kennedy!" Carrie's voice shattered my unease.

I turned to see her bounding toward me, her long hair bouncing with each enthusiastic step. Her arms enveloped me in a hug so tight it almost squeezed out my anxiety.

"Sorry we're late, but I cannot be blamed. Wait till you hear about the twins' latest escapade."

She launched into a story about how her mischievous toddlers had created a modern art masterpiece out of what used to be a boring couch, thanks to the gift of mashed carrots and a serious miscommunication about who was watching the kids. I found myself laughing, and my momentary freakout seemed rather silly. I knew Greyson had men watching me. He probably always would.

Keith stood by with an indulgent smile, clearly accustomed to being the audience to his wife's animated storytelling. His gaze shifted between Carrie and me before landing on Sebastian, who extended his hand in greeting.

"Keith, right?" Sebastian's voice was smooth, confident, and friendly.

"Sebastian Wright." Keith shook Sebastian's hand heartily. "Heard a lot about you. From ESPN and now from Carrie."

"Hopefully, all good things," Sebastian said, giving me a raised eyebrow.

"Absolutely." Keith assured him, and there was the faintest starstruck tone in his voice before he coughed.

Carrie's gaze met mine and widened, and I suppressed a giggle. Apparently, Sebastian could impress anyone.

But Sebastian quickly struck up a conversation with Keith, and the starstruck moment passed in seconds as the two of them started to delve into a discussion about cars. Warmth blossomed in my chest as Carrie went on to tell me about how she'd been researching au pairs on the drive over, because clearly the twins needed all new levels of supervision. The night already felt comforting, grounding, like exactly what I needed.

The warm, yeasty scent of freshly baked bread wafted through the air as we entered the Italian restaurant.

Carrie's eyes met mine, and we barely sat down before we descended on the bread basket. It held an array of crisp ciabatta, fragrant focaccia, and the garlic knots I'd been praising on the way over. Sebastian probably didn't want any of those, so I took his.

"Looks like you ladies have found your happy place," Sebastian teased.

"If you want any, you'd better stake your claim now," Carrie said.

Keith lifted his beer in a mock toast. "It's all you, ladies. We'll get our grains in the beer."

I stole a glance at Sebastian, who seemed more at ease than when we first started the evening. Keith's relaxed demeanor must have been infectious because they were starting to banter comfortably.

Our conversation was interrupted by a little boy around six or seven, who tugged on his mother's hand, eyes wide with awe as they drew closer to our table.

"Sebastian Wright, right?" the boy piped up, voice trembling with excitement. "You play for the Demons!"

I watched as Sebastian's features softened, his smile genuine. "That's me, buddy. What's your name?"

"Tyler," the boy answered, a mixture of shyness and thrill in his tone.

"Nice to meet you, Tyler." Sebastian extended his hand for a high-five which the boy eagerly met. "So, do you play hockey too?"

Tyler nodded vigorously. "Yes! I want to be a goalie."

"Goalie, huh? That's the heart of the team." Sebastian's eyes glinted with respect. "Takes courage to stand in front of those pucks."

"Sometimes it's scary," Tyler admitted, looking down at his shoes.

"Hey, even the best get scared sometimes." Sebastian leaned in closer, conspiratorially. "Between you and me, I still get nervous before every game."

"Really?" Tyler's eyes widened further.

"Cross my heart." Sebastian winked. "Just keep practicing, stay brave, and I'll be watching out for you in the big leagues someday."

"Promise?" The hope in Tyler's voice tugged at my heart-strings.

"Promise." Sebastian bumped fists with Tyler, sealing their pact.

As the family thanked us and returned to their table, a hint of red tinged Sebastian's cheeks.

Keith had been quietly observing the interaction. There was an air of awe mixed with a hint of intimidation in the way he looked at Sebastian.

Sebastian noticed it too. With an easy smile that seemed to put the whole table at ease, he leaned forward, shifting the spotlight from himself. "So, Keith, Kennedy told me you were in the Marines. Infantry?"

Keith nodded. "Yeah, that's right. Did a couple of tours overseas."

"Man, that's incredible," Sebastian said, leaning back in his chair, visibly impressed. The admiration in his voice was palpable. "That must've taken some serious courage. Tell me more about it."

I watched as Keith's posture relaxed, his initial starstruck tension melting away under Sebastian's friendly interrogation. Sebastian's effortless ability to make Keith feel valued lit a glow of warmth in my chest.

The waiter arrived, presenting us with an enticing dessert menu. Three decadent options caught my eye—tiramisu, panna cotta, and a chocolate torte so rich it looked sinful.

"Can't decide?" Sebastian murmured, noticing my indecision.

"They all look amazing," I confessed.

"Then we'll have all three," he declared with a playful wink, signaling the waiter. "One for her, one for me, and one for the road."

"Are you sure?" I laughed, both amused and touched by the gesture.

"Absolutely." His eyes twinkled with mischief. "Life's too short for just one dessert."

When the desserts arrived, Sebastian slid the plate with the tiramisu towards me. It was the one I'd eyed the longest. He picked up his fork, breaking into the chocolate torte, and after taking a bite, offered the next one to me. He fed me with a warm smile, full of charm and indulgence.

"Good, isn't it?" he asked, his voice a low rumble that sent a shiver through me.

"Delicious," I whispered back.

Carrie and I excused ourselves from the table, our heels clicking on the polished marble floors that led to the opulent bathroom. Carrie reapplied her red lipstick, then leaned against the long countertop, her eyes warm.

"Kennedy, you have no idea how lucky you are," she said as we checked our reflections in the ornate mirror.

I smoothed a stray lock of hair behind my ear, meeting her gaze in the reflection. "You really like Sebastian?"

"I really do. Trust me, I would tell you if I didn't. Emphatically."

Our laughter mingled, light and unburdened, because I knew she'd never lie to me.

"He looks at you like Keith looks at me," she said, reminding me of all the years I'd longed for the same kind of comfortable, happy relationship she had with Keith. I even secretly dreamt sometimes of having babies like her twins—though maybe without the baby food redecorating attempts. "And if you have four guys who all treat you like that, you just might be the luckiest woman in the world."

Our goodbyes were warm-filled, with promises to do this again soon sealed with hugs. I glanced at Sebastian, wondering if he really meant it.

Sebastian led me outside, and the cool night air brushed against my skin as we approached his sleek car.

Sebastian navigated through the city with an ease that came from years of driving these streets. A comfortable silence settled between us, and I cradled dessert number three on my lap in its white Styrofoam container.

"Sometimes," he began suddenly, reaching for his phone in the console, "I browse Zillow for fun."

A playful smirk danced on his lips as he handed me the device, screen alive with the image of a sprawling mansion surrounded by lush greenery.

"Really? What kind of things are you looking at?"

I scrolled through a few listings, each more extravagant than the last. Apparently, Sebastian was shopping for a mansion.

"Tell me about your dream house," he prompted.

"It's got to have character," I swiped yet again through the series of photos showing one particular house. "Like this one. It's got huge windows...and a library already, so it's ready for my books. Which I need to replace..."

"I'll buy you all the books," Sebastian promised, his cheeks coloring slightly.

"It's so cute."

"A garden?" Sebastian asked, glancing over briefly as the traffic light turned green.

"Yes!" I was delighted by the thought. "I was obsessed with 'The Secret Garden' when I was a kid. I'd love to have a garden that felt like its own little world."

"Sounds perfect," he said, his voice warm.

Sebastian was careful and watchful in the parking garage, then in the elevator up to the penthouse. He didn't unwind until we were inside with the doors locked. Then, he turned toward me and pinned me against the closed door.

"Kennedy," he murmured against my lips, his hands roaming over my back, pulling me closer. "Tonight was fun, but I've been longing to get you alone all night, too."

I leaned into him, deepening the kiss. We were lost in each other, the world around us fading until there was nothing but the heat between us. My fingers tangled in his hair as our kisses grew more fervent.

With a soft thud, the box slipped from my grasp, panna cotta splatting across the floor.

"Oh no," I said.

"Leave it, I'll take care of it later," Sebastian said, sweeping me up into his arms and carrying me toward his room. He gave me a mischievous smile. "Or Clean Freak Carter will find it, and I won't have to."

He carried me into his bedroom, where the panoramic window offered a voyeuristic view of the city. The scent of him was everywhere, dark and spicy.

I remembered the way things had been between us, complicated and awkward, last time.

"Shower with me," I whispered.

With a smoldering look, he carried me into the bathroom and set me down. He began to undress me. His fingers deftly worked the zipper of my dress, brushing against my spine. Fabric whispered to the floor, pooling at my feet.

He peeled away my panties, revealing inch by heated inch of my skin to the cool air of the room. There was reverence in his movements, as if he were unwrapping a precious gift.

My breath hitched when his hands cupped the swell of my breasts. His thumbs brushed over the sensitive peaks that ached for more. His eyes locked onto mine, dark with want, as he traced the contours of my body.

"You are so perfect," he whispered.

With the city lights casting a soft glow over Sebastian's chiseled form, our lips met in an urgent kiss. His mouth moved against mine fervently.

My fingers fumbled at the buttons of his shirt, revealing the sculpted length of his torso. His Jackal tattoo was still red, but it was sexy too. All four of my men carried the same tattoo. It made it feel as if they were finding their way back to being a family. My family. The only family I ever really needed.

I traced the hard planes of his chest, marveling at his muscles as they flexed under my touch. My hands lingered on his abs, dancing over the ridges. I pushed his shirt down his broad shoulders.

Sebastian gently pushed me into his steam-clouded shower. The glass doors closed behind us, cocooning us in a world of heat.

The heat from the water enveloped us, mingling with the heat of our bodies as he turned to face me. I couldn't help but admire the way the water cascaded down his perfectly defined abs and broad shoulders, glistening like diamonds on his deeply tanned skin.

He reached for the soap and lathered a washcloth. His hands were strong but gentle as they began to tenderly explore every curve of my body. He washed across my collarbone, down the valley between my breasts, and over the curve of my waist. Each stroke was a caress, each glide of his palms a silent declaration of care.

The way he washed me felt almost reverent, as if he were memorizing every inch of me with his hands. His eyes locked onto mine with an intensity that promised the evening had just begun.

Sebastian washed my inner thighs, and I moaned, my hips swaying forward against his, wanting more of him. He dropped the cloth and his naked fingers met the slick warmth between my thighs. He began to tease me, his fingers confident against my clit until I was biting my lower lip, my knees weak.

"Sebastian, I want you inside me," I whispered.

Sebastian grabbed my hips and spun me around with a groan of desire, as if he'd been waiting for those words. His hands were firm on my hips as I braced myself against the cool wall, my breath catching in anticipation. His cock pressed against my inner thighs, and I pushed back against him, wanting more.

He aligned himself with me, his tip teasing at my entrance. My heart hammered in my chest, each beat echoing his name.

And then, inch by deliberate inch, he slid inside, stretching and filling me in a rhythm that was both insistent and careful. I gasped, my fingers splaying out to find purchase against the wet wall.

Our bodies began to move together, and he found the perfect rhythm, slow and intense, his cock pressing deep inside me.

"Sebastian," I moaned.

He reached around to where my need throbbed the most, his fingers expertly coaxing the flame higher, hotter, until I was on the edge.

His breath was hot against my damp skin. "You feel so incredible."

The praise sent a jolt of pleasure straight to my core. His hand, his voice, his body—all of him enveloped me.

"Sebastian, I'm…" The rest of my words were lost in a strangled cry as the first waves of an orgasm crashed over me, my body tensing and then shuddering. I found myself chanting his name as he continued, unrelenting, chasing his own climax.

He tensed, his movements becoming more erratic, more desperate, until with a final deep thrust, he stilled, his body pressed flush against mine. He roared my name.

We stayed locked together, panting, for a long minute as the water poured over us. His arms wrapped around me, holding me close.

Sebastian's warmth enveloped me as he wrapped me up in a plush towel, the fabric soft against my damp skin. He lifted me with ease and carried me through the fog that lingered in the air from our shower. The city lights flickered outside the windows of his room, casting a dim glow that danced across his handsome, sharply angled face.

He laid me gently on the bed, the sheets cool against my back. His eyes held a promise of more as he leaned over me, his hands tracing the contours of my body with tenderness. I smiled up at him and he returned that smile with a full hearted grin.

Then, someone knocked on the door.

"Should I get that?" Sebastian's voice was low, husky, his breath brushing against the tender skin of my inner thigh.

"Is that okay?" I whispered.

"Princess, anything you want—I want," he promised.

Was it Jack, Carter, or Greyson? Or...some combination? All the possibilities made my heart swell with excitement.

"Open it," I whispered.

Sebastian rose, his movements fluid. He opened the door, revealing Jack standing there, his presence commanding as ever. There was no surprise in his eyes, only an intensity that seemed to amplify the heat between us. Jack's gaze met mine, and it was hungry.

"Are you coming in?" Sebastian asked, stepping back.

The simplicity and warmth of his easy invitation made me smile. Jack nodded, and he closed the door softly behind him.

Their gazes met mine as they approached, two pairs of eyes that burned with a hunger that matched my own.

My hands wandered over my body, my fingertips caressing the sensitive peaks of my breasts, trailing lower, teasing around the edges of my arousal. I let my legs fall open so they could see. I could practically feel their gaze on my body like heat, and they stopped, watching me eagerly.

"Kennedy," Jack murmured, his cock tenting the front of his jeans. It was an extra-large tent. Not the usual family of four-size, this was large enough for a reunion. "You are so fucking perfect."

As they moved closer, I could feel the shift in the atmosphere, charged with the promise of what was to come.

CHAPTER 2

Kennedy

Dusk was falling outside the arena, which felt like our second home.

"Fine, get our girl some food," Jack eyed G——— as if he were jealous of eating subs with me when he ——— out to warm up before stepping onto the ice for th——nds of adoring fans. "But get her back so she doesn't miss a—ything."

Greyson sighed, but didn't argue. "It's so boring," he said, convincing absolutely no one.

Sebastian held out his arms to me. "Kiss me for luck, princess."

"As if you aren't going to be staring at her and blowing kisses on the ice when you're supposed to be blocking for me," Carter grumbled.

"That happened one time!" Sebastian protested good humoredly.

When he turned to me, he pulled me into his strong arms, and I let myself sink into his powerful chest. His lips coaxed mine open with gentle insistence, and I kissed him back until Jack muttered, "Save some for the rest of us. We had to be on the ice three minutes ago."

We broke apart with a soft sound.

"Knock 'em dead, tiger," I murmured, my voice husky.

Sebastian's answering grin was cocky, lit by his confidence on and off the ice. "As long as you cheer me on, princess."

Jack's piercing gaze locked onto mine with a glint of pre-game adrenaline and something more raw, more primal. As our lips met, the world around us faded to a dull hum. My fingers threaded through his ash blonde hair, pulling him closer.

"Score one for me," I whispered against his lips, feeling his smile.

Carter grabbed my hips and spun me around to face him, claiming my lips impatiently. His touch was intense, his hand sliding to the nape of my neck to draw me impossibly closer.

"Play hard," I said breathlessly when we finally parted, my fingertips lingering on his jaw.

"Now or later?" he asked me, his lips parting in a faint smile.

From the corner of my eye, I caught Greyson's gaze on us. Amusement flickered across his features, a bemused quirk to his lips. He finally seemed to fit in with us, and to know this was where he belonged. I felt a surge of gratitude for his presence.

We watched the boys walk down the hall to the locker room. Jack looked back over his shoulder and gave me a wink.

"Let's grab something to eat," I suggested, reaching for his hand. He laced his fingers with mine.

"Lead the way," Greyson replied, his voice smooth as aged whiskey.

"Thai or Italian?" I asked, my heels clicking against the slick linoleum flooring as we navigated through the stream of fans headed into the arena.

"If you want Italian, I can have you in Tuscany by morning."

"You're impossible," I said, though I couldn't hide my smile. "I want a quick dinner and then to go cheer on the rest of my boyfriends."

"The rest of your boyfriends?" he sounded dissatisfied.

"What?" I asked, mildly exasperated. "You know they aren't going anywhere."

"Oh, I'm keenly aware," he said dryly. "They're even growing on me. They're not as useless as they seemed at first glance."

I felt a thrill of heat, thinking about some of the things Jack had whispered he planned to do to me tonight. "They're not useless at all."

"It's this *boyfriend* thing," he said. "It's such a ridiculous word."

"I told you all, if you want to be my boyfriend, you have to do boyfriend stuff."

"I don't want to do boyfriend stuff. I want to do husband stuff."

I stared at him, my lips parted, but Greyson just seemed amused by my response.

"Speaking of family," he said casually, "aren't you late for your period?"

I gawked at him. "How would you know that?"

"I pay attention to details," he said. "You can't exactly lead a criminal empire if you don't pay attention."

"To *menstruation*?"

"To you," he corrected. "My queen. Future mother of my children."

My head spun.

"Would you take a test for me real quick?" he asked. "I'll get it off to the doc, and we'll know ASAP."

"Greyson…" But suddenly, I realized I was a day late. Barely late. I held out my hand. "You psycho."

He let out a chuckle, producing a cup from inside his jacket. As soon as I emerged from the bathroom, feeling embarrassed, he handed it over to an even-more embarrassed Jackal to be whisked away to the lab.

I decided not to worry about it right now—to dwell on the good or the scary, which were both wrapped up in the possibility I was pregnant. I'd know soon enough.

We stepped out into the brisk evening air. Side by side, we

walked through the throng of fans and vendors hawking jerseys that carried my men's names. The sight of their jerseys always made me smile in pride. The energy of the night wrapped around us, lighting a warm glow in my chest.

He gestured ahead. "There you are. Best Thai food in town. Let's get something spicy enough to make you blush...that seems to get a little harder every day, and I do love it when you blush for me."

I laughed. "Spicy food. Is that a challenge, Mr. Tall-Dark-and Dangerous?"

"Do you have to make everything a competition?"

"I know who I'm dealing with."

But before we could reach the restaurant door, someone melted out of the shadows. Greyson reached for his gun instinctively, and it was in his hand in a flash before he recognized Sunny and relaxed.

My enemies were supposed to be dead. But I wasn't sure Greyson would ever relax, and the light banter and fun of the evening had suddenly melted away into darkness.

"Greyson, a word?" Sunny's tone held urgency, and beneath the streetlamp, his face was a mask of concern.

My pulse quickened. Trouble never did seem far from our lives.

"Can it wait?" Greyson's voice was a low growl. He holstered his gun in one fluid move and smoothed his jacket with a practiced motion, casting a glance around to make sure no one had seen.

Now, I could see more of Greyson's men waiting behind Sunny in a car down the street, ready for action. For violence.

"It's about Kennedy," Sunny said, and suddenly all the air seemed sucked off the street. "We thought Borovsky's man, Clint, was dead, but he was sighted a few streets away. I assume he's here to try to take you all out when you leave the arena after the game."

"Kennedy, go back to the arena," Greyson commanded

without taking his eyes off Sunny. "Now."

"Greyson—" I began, but he cut me off with a sharp look.

"Please, Kennedy. Trust me on this. Go watch the game, stay in public," he said, and the intensity in his gaze brooked no argument. "Sunny, you take her. Axe can catch me up."

"Fine." I didn't like it, not one bit, but if danger was knocking at my door again, I wouldn't be the one to slow down our response. I understood why Greyson wanted to deal with it himself, and make sure there was no question this time that all my enemies were dead. And I understood why he wanted me near Sebastian, Carter, and Jack.

With Greyson's command still ringing in my ears, I doubled back towards the arena, my heels clicking a rapid staccato on the pavement. Why the hell hadn't I worn flats? I knew what my life was like.

The chill evening air did little to cool my flush of unease. Trust didn't come easy for me, especially not since my memory was all cobwebs, wisps of memory that didn't quite come into clear sight.

Sunny moved quickly beside me, his eyes tracking over every possible threat.

The arena loomed ahead of us, bright lights shining out. We were so close. And the streets were crowded with hundreds of fans. It was no wonder Greyson had trusted the short trip back.

A van suddenly cut in front of us, going down a side street, so close that it almost ran over my toes. My heart seized. Before I could react, a heavy hand clamped over my mouth, cutting off my startled cry. A strong arm circled my waist, dragging me into the van.

Panic surged through me, igniting every nerve as I thrashed and kicked, trying to break free. But I still found myself pressed against the hard floor of the van, the world a blur through the open door as it sped off.

The cold bite of metal pressed against my wrist as a zip tie cinched it to its twin, rendering my hands useless.

"Sorry, love," a gruff voice whispered in my ear, one I didn't recognize, sending a shiver down my spine. "Nothing personal."

My mind screamed at being bound, bringing up a sudden wave of helpless fear, like an echo of what I'd felt as a child. But I wasn't a child. The next second, I lashed out hard with my feet, and heard a grunt as I connected. I rolled desperately toward the blur of light outside, even though the car was accelerating. I was better off fighting here than being taken to a second location.

The car door slammed shut with a thud that echoed through my bones, the darkness of the van swallowing me whole.

Escape was gone.

I was still for a moment, disoriented. My breathing was ragged. I looked up, searching for Sunny, and he stared back down at me—one of three faces leaning over mine, but every bit as much a stranger.

"Keep quiet," he grunted.

As the car lurched forward, I was thrown around the wide expanse of the open back of the van. Rough hands grabbed me, flipping me onto my stomach. Another zip tie—this one biting into my ankles. The tightness around my limbs dragged me back through time, to a darker place where I was just a little girl.

"Please," I managed, the words echoing now in the hollow space of the moving car.

But of course, no one came.

Tears pricked the corners of my eyes, both then and now, as I fought the bindings that held me, fought the memories clawing their way to the surface.

"Shut up," one of the strangers spat, and the world outside the tinted windows blurred into streaks of light and shadow as we sped away. My past and present collided in a dizzying spiral. Frank's cruel laughter might as well have been theirs.

Except...

The memory of Jack pulling Frank off me came to my mind, and I whispered the names of my men, fervent as a prayer.

I knew they would always come for me.

CHAPTER

Kennedy

The van jolted to a halt, throwing me forward. I rolled across the harsh carpet of the trunk.

They had blindfolded me, and the knot someone had made tugged at my hair painfully. I couldn't see anything, but that seemed to make all my other senses sharper. The universe of sound around me had become overwhelming—tires crunching gravel, then the van's engine idling down, and above all, the erratic symphony of my own breathing.

Iron hands clamped my upper arms and hauled me up. The grip was bruising as they dragged me down from the van into cold air.

My right high heel was almost as big a traitor as Sunny. It had twisted halfway off during my fight, clinging to my foot by one defiant strap. It buckled underneath me when I tried to stand, and my heel hit cold concrete, my ankle twisting painfully. Then my knees buckled. My legs and feet were numb. The drive had gone on forever. I collapsed with an undignified yelp.

"Careful!" The sharp command cut through my panic. It was Sunny, Greyson's second-in-command.

"Are you all insane? Don't hurt her!" His words echoed off

unseen walls as he knelt beside me and undid the zip tie. Hands, surprisingly gentle, reached for my feet and deftly removed the offending shoes. The coolness of the ground seeped into the soles of my feet.

"Come on, Kennedy," he told me kindly, gripping my arm, and I felt the other captor move away. He tugged me forward, but his grip was far softer.

I took slow, tentative steps forward, feeling as if I might slam into something.

The other man loosened his grip so he was no longer bruising me and let out a dark scoff of a laugh. "I guess she's not going to run barefoot. But those heels were probably better than the zip ties."

"Kennedy won't run," Sunny repeated, and the certainty in his tone hurt my feelings. I wasn't exactly a wimp. I'd been through more than most people could ever dream of—and I even remembered some of it. He went on, "Kennedy is going to wait for Greyson to negotiate for her...because she knows he will."

Greyson. The thought of his icy blue eyes and easy charm toward me—and his terrifying violence toward others when I was in danger—sent a ripple of feeling through me.

And Jack, Carter, and Sebastian had reentered the world of the Jackals, which they had never wanted, to protect me. The four of them had forged themselves into a team of dangerous men to make sure I was safe.

I knew they would come for me.

And I knew hell would rain down on anyone in their way.

But for now, I was lonely and afraid and so cold. I didn't even know where I was, or what they were dragging me so steadily toward.

The echo of our footsteps bounced off high ceilings and distant walls. I could hear the faint drip of water somewhere to my left.

"Up the stairs now," Sunny said.

My shin barked gently against the metal edge of a step as he pulled me to a stop. "There you go. Right ahead of you. One step, then another. That's it."

He sounded so fucking careful of me for a kidnapper. Clearly, no one planned to murder me today.

But I knew sometimes plans went awry.

We reached the top of the stairs, and they steered me down a hall.

"Sunny, what do you want?" My voice trembled less than I expected. My other senses sharpened in response to the dark. The air was heavy with the acrid scent of rust and oil, and it felt so thick with the damp that it seemed to lay on my skin.

"Keep quiet for now," Sunny's voice in my ear made me shiver, as if it were a violation. Only my men were allowed to be so close to me. "I'll keep you safe, Kennedy. Just...stay calm."

We kept moving. My other captor released me, and my skin seemed to burn where he'd touched me. I wished I wasn't bound so I could wipe away his touch.

A door jamb or wall brushed my arm, and then we stopped. Sunny's hands grasped both my upper arms, turning me. The knot that had caught up some of my hair pulled painfully, and then the blindfold fell away.

Blinking against the harsh glare of fluorescent lights, I squinted at the windowless office. It was stark—a desk, two chairs, and filing cabinets that were an olive-drab color that Crayola might label 'depression green.' Through the frosted glass partition, I caught a glimpse of a shadow moving past, carrying a long barrel that made my heart stop.

My eyes flew past him to the door. It was closed. We were alone.

"Are you working with Greyson?" My heart clung to a sliver of hope that I let him hear in my voice. Even if my optimism was misplaced, he might let his defenses down if he thought I was feeling safe with him. "Are you going to help me?"

"Of course," Sunny promised confidently, but something in his gaze flickered, a tightening around his eyes that betrayed his words. It was a microexpression, gone as quickly as it appeared, but it was enough.

"Good." I forced a smile, playing the part he needed me to play. "I trust you."

His nod was almost imperceptible, and I wondered if he saw through my façade as easily as I saw through his. But there was no time to question it further. Not now. Not when survival hinged on my wits.

My men would come through those doors, sooner or later. I intended to be there to kiss them hello.

And ideally, I'd like to be ready to end these stupid assholes who had taken me. I wanted to protect my men as much as they wanted to protect me.

"Stay here, Kennedy," Sunny said, his voice oddly gentle against the backdrop of my pounding heart. As if I had any choice. "Just hang tight."

"Sure," I murmured.

I watched him, noting the slight hesitation before he moved toward me. His fingers brushed against my wrists, and the zip ties fell away, leaving painful ghosts of the pressure where they had dug into my skin.

"Trying to stay on Greyson's good side, just in case?" The attempt at humor sounded embarrassingly fake.

"Kennedy," Sunny paused, and his eyes met mine, dead and empty. He might be pretending, but I didn't think he was capable of compassion for me. "If Greyson finds me, I know I'm dead."

"Why?" I asked. "Why are you doing this?"

He was standing close to me, too close. My gaze locked onto his face, and suddenly, it was as if the world tilted on its axis. I *remembered* his face, distorted by the flash of headlights and a surge of adrenaline, that had haunted my nightmares.

The memory punched through me like a fist. I almost stumbled backward, gasping for air, struggling to anchor myself in the present. I could feel the phantom ache of impact where none had occurred, the terror of tires screeching on asphalt.

"I'm sorry, Kennedy." His voice was filled with regret that sounded genuine.

But I had the feeling he was playing yet another game, just like I was.

Then he turned and walked out, leaving me alone with the cold truth settling into my bones.

Had Sunny been trying to kidnap me that night when Sebastian pushed me out of the way?

Or had he been trying to kill me?

I blinked, trying to remember the details of when I'd seen his face before.

Had that been the night Sebastian saved me at all?

Or was that an older memory, long lost?

Because I was sure that the man who had almost run me down last week had been wearing a mask.

Wasn't I?

I'd never exactly had the most reliable memory.

Clutching at the tendrils of memory, I tried to weave them into something coherent. But the harder I reached, the more elusive the details became, like trying to catch handfuls of mist.

I took a deep breath, focusing on the here and now. The pins and needles from being tied up were fading, but they left me clumsy. Gritting my teeth, I massaged my wrists, coaxing feeling back into my fingers. I worked down to my feet, wincing as each touch sparked trails of painful tingling sensation. It was agony and relief intertwined, an unwelcome reminder of how long I'd been held captive. How far had they driven me from the arena? It would be useful information, except that I was pretty sure every minute bound on that floor might've felt like ten.

Once I felt like I'd recovered, I pushed myself up from the chair. By now, Greyson must have gone looking for me, and he would know I was gone. The guys would be on the ice. Would he tell them? I pictured them charging off the ice in the middle of the game and bit my lip, knowing that would cost them professionally.

I'd made their lives so much harder since I came back into it. Maybe they were better off when they could pretend I was nothing to them.

I had to keep myself busy. I had to figure out what Sunny wanted, why I was here, and how I could help my men when they came.

And I kept imagining Greyson, Jack, Sebastian, and Carter, and what they were doing now...because every thought of them brought me so much comfort.

I almost didn't feel alone, knowing they were out there somewhere.

———

Greyson

Tires screeched as I ran down the alleyway and emerged just in time to see my men on the street with guns leveled. The car they faced skidded to a halt, inches from my unflinching men with their rifles on their shoulders.

Was this the car that had almost run down my girl?

I lunged forward, shoving past my own crew with a snarl. They parted, knowing better than to get in my way. One of them yanked the driver's side door open for me, and another waited with his rifle raised, ready to pull off a shot if the driver made the wrong move.

I didn't wait for pleasantries. My fingers wrapped around the collar of a jacket, and I hauled the driver out onto the pavement. He landed with a thud, his eyes wide with fear as he recognized me.

"Take it easy!" he begged. "I'm working for you?"

"Is that so?" I narrowed my eyes at him, taking in the scruffy beard and the panicked look of someone who knew exactly whose bad side he'd just found himself on. "Who are you?"

I knew everyone who worked for me. Having a good head for names and faces was a skill I'd developed purposefully, given my occupation.

"Ricky," he stammered, not even trying to get up from the concrete when I had put him there. "I work for you, Mr. Greyson, sir."

"Work for me? I think I would've noticed. You're not one of my Jackals."

"Boss," one of my men said quietly, urgently. "We're going to start attracting attention."

It wasn't every day a roadblock was set up like our city had turned into a warzone.

"Tell me something," I asked Ricky quietly. If this low-level thug thought he worked for me, then we had bigger problems than just a case of mistaken identity. "Who hired you?"

"I asked for a job years ago, a chance to prove myself," he said. "Then, I started getting texts a while back."

"You started working for a criminal organization based on text messages." My voice was deadly cold. "I suppose a Nigerian prince hired you."

"Sir?" Ricky looked confused.

"Take him and get off the street," I told my men. "Did the team meet up with Sunny alright at the arena?"

Luca gave me a tight shake of the head. "They didn't find them."

Cold fear rippled through my gut like a stone into ice water.

I strode away, already dialing Sunny. The persistent beep-beep-beep of a dead line hit me like a hammer.

"Keep him talking," I snapped at the Jackals who had taken custody of Ricky, their nods curt as they dragged him into a car.

I pocketed my phone and headed for the arena, my mind racing.

The roar of the crowd greeted me like a slap to the face as I burst through the hockey arena's doors.

My eyes darted over the sea of heads, searching for a sign of her.

The Demons were on the ice, clashing with the Bobcats. The noise of the crowd and the chaos of faces around me were a blur.

"Kennedy!" I shouldered my way through the throng, each step spiked with urgency. Faces blurred past—fans painted in team colors, children clutching foam fingers, vendors hawking beer and pretzels—but none were hers.

"Excuse me." I muttered. Once. "Move!"

That got more attention, my tone brooking no argument as I forged a path toward the seats where she should have been, where she should be watching our boys play.

Sweat coated my palms, and I wiped them on my jeans. It was impossible to see clearly, the press of bodies too dense, too alive with excitement when I felt a deep sense of terror.

"Kennedy!" I tried again, hoping beyond reason she'd hear me, that she'd stand up and wave, that this mounting panic was for nothing.

I pushed through the last of the crowd, hope swelling desperately that my girl would look up at me with bright eyes.

Our seats were empty.

A cold dread settled in my gut, heavier than the weight of the gun under my arm.

I scanned the rows again. Nothing. The ache in my chest tightened, and I palmed the back of a seat to steady myself.

My men were spreading through the arena, moving quickly and efficiently. Their dark suits and urgency didn't fit amid all the red and black jerseys of the fans.

I paced out into the quieter expanse of the lobby, hoping I'd see Kennedy getting a pickle or hell, I'd be happy to find her drinking Diet Coke right now.

I called my tech guy.

"Still working on it, boss. His signal's gone dark." The tech's voice, usually so calm, held an edge of concern that did nothing to ease my own.

One of my men had already clued him in on the situation.

All of the Jackals would be out searching for Kennedy. Who the hell would dare to take her?

Sunny. Either Sunny had died fighting to protect her, or he had betrayed me. Either way, Sunny's silence must mean he was a dead man.

"Keep on it," I snarled, spinning on my heel to face the ice. Jack, Carter, and Sebastian were playing their hearts out, oblivious to the chaos off-rink, although they might've missed Kennedy's smiles and blown kisses.

Carter was guarding the goal, a beast in his crease. Even from this distance, I could see the intensity in his stance, the readiness in the dip of his knees.

I strode to the edge of the rink, my presence alone parting the officials like a blade. They knew better than to ask questions. I waved down Carter, who finally looked my way. Behind his face mask, I couldn't tell if he understood me.

Fiercely pursued by Sebastian, two Bobcats were driving a puck up the rink. One of them shot on Carter, somewhat desperately because Sebastian was on top of him. Carter blocked the shot. The puck sailed off.

Then, with the grace of a practiced deceptor, he lurched, clutching his leg, and crumpled to the ice. The ref's whistle cut through the noise. Medics rushed forward.

So, he had seen and understood me.

I caught Jack's eye first, gave him a subtle tilt of my head. Understanding flashed across his features. Sebastian was next, following Jack's gaze to where I stood, grim and resolute.

They exchanged a look, a silent conversation passing between them before they peeled away from the play.

"Kennedy's missing," I barked, my voice barely carrying over the din of the crowd and the shrill protests from the coaches. Jack's stride faltered for half a beat, his eyes searching mine for a mistake, a misunderstanding—anything but the truth I'd just laid bare. Sebastian's jaw clenched, the easygoing defenseman

234 C.R. JANE & MAY DAWSON

replaced in an instant by the hardened man who'd survived too much to be easily rattled.

"We're going to find her." I said grimly.

Carter's exit was swift, and given all the media about his obvious injury—he could thank me later—no one was surprised by having the backup goalie step in. As soon as he limped off the ice, play began again—but not for Jack and Sebastian.

The puck slid by unnoticed as they broke formation, their skates carving hard into the ice, propelling them toward me.

Without a word, they vaulted over the boards. Behind them, a coach was yelling. Confusion rippled through the stands and across the ice, but none of that mattered. Only one thing did— finding Kennedy.

We moved quickly away from the curious gazes. Carter met us outside, his dark shirt clinging to his powerful body; he'd pulled off his pads and dressed as quickly as possible.

"Kennedy was in danger, I sent Sunny to bring her back to the arena, and she never fucking arrived. Sunny's gone dark."

"Any leads?" Jack's voice was steady, controlled, despite the fury in his gaze.

It was my fucking fault she was gone, but none of them said anything. All of us had a laser focus on getting our girl back.

"Working on it. We swept the arena, then branched out. The asshole who distracted us is being interrogated now."

"Got it," Sebastian's voice was clipped.

"Let's move," I ordered, leading the way.

The cold air of the arena bit at my skin, but I barely felt it. My phone vibrated against my thigh. I yanked it out, expecting it was Sunny with news about Kennedy, or at least news about Sunny.

Instead, I saw an unfamiliar number topped by the words "Lab Results."

I hadn't been willing to wait for the results after Kennedy took that test.

"She's pregnant," I mumbled to Jack and Sebastian, the weight of those words so heavy my shoulders tensed.

"Kennedy?" Sebastian's voice was tight.

"Yeah," I said, shoving the phone back into my pocket. It should've been a moment of joy.

But the joy was strangled before it could take its first breath, suffocated by the terror of not knowing where she was, if she was safe, and if our child was safe.

"We'll find her," Jack said. "*Them*. We'll find them, and they'll be okay."

"Right."

There was no time for fear or blaming each other right now.

Only one thing mattered.

Protecting our family.

CHAPTER 2

Kennedy

I paced the room, over and over again until I thought I was going crazy. The room was perfectly bare with the exception of the furniture and whatever was inside the locked filing cabinets, not even a pen lid for me to try and use as a weapon.

I tried to pick up the office cabinet, but whatever was in there weighed a thousand tons, so I couldn't even get it to move an inch.

My next efforts were to try and get the office cabinet doors open, but those might as well have been glued shut with concrete because they weren't budging at all.

I sat on the ground and tried to use my legs as leverage to push on the cabinet base while I pulled, but that didn't do anything but strain my abs.

Which made me nervous.

What if I *was* pregnant?

I didn't have any knowledge about pregnancy besides Carrie's twins, but Keith had been so protective of Carrie the entire time. He wouldn't let her pick up anything, even if it only weighed five pounds. Carrie had griped about it every time we met up.

But what if that was what was necessary to keep the baby safe?

I immediately stopped straining, my shoulders drooping as I stared down at the floor. I hated feeling so helpless.

It felt like that had been my role my entire life, whether it was with my mother, or my stepdad, or with my memory loss...or keeping myself safe.

My hands cradled my flat stomach, wondering if there was a baby in there.

I didn't want to be helpless in keeping my child safe.

I didn't want to be helpless at all anymore.

I got up from the floor and sat down in one of the office chairs.

If someone didn't come in soon, I was going to lose my flipping mind.

And I missed the guys so much.

I'm sure they were going crazy right now. Doing everything to find me.

But again, I wondered to myself...what if they were better off if they never did?

A memory hit, and I sucked in a breath as it filtered through me.

I navigated my way through the crowded halls, clutching my backpack tightly. The English classroom was on the second floor, and I made my way up a narrow flight of stairs. My heart raced with anticipation and nerves as I approached the door.

Just as I reached for the handle, a red-haired girl stormed past me without a word, her shoulder knocking me hard into the unforgiving metal lockers lining the hallway. Pain shot through my side as I stumbled and gritted my teeth to stifle a cry. I watched her continue down the hall, not bothering to glance back at me.

Confusion and embarrassment swirled in my chest as I heard more whispers.

I bent down to retrieve my fallen backpack, my vision blurred with unshed tears. My ribs were throbbing.

Just as my fingers brushed the worn straps of my backpack, someone else's hand reached down and grabbed it. Startled, I looked up, my cheeks flushed with embarrassment and tears threatening to spill over. To my astonishment, it was him—Jack.

This day was just getting better and better.

Our eyes met, his golden hazel gaze locked onto mine, and for a moment, everything else faded away. His expression was one of concern, and he held onto my backpack, not handing it back when I reached out my hand for it.

"Are you okay?" he asked, his voice soft and filled with genuine concern.

I bit my lip, struggling to hold back the tears that had gathered. Swallowing hard, I nodded, unable to find my voice.

Jack was an absolute heartthrob, a living masterpiece really. His ash-blond hair was a tousled work of art, effortlessly framing his face with an irresistible allure. Each strand seemed to fall into place as if guided by the hands of a higher power, giving him an effortlessly rugged yet sophisticated appearance.

But it was his eyes that were leaving me tongue-tied. They were a captivating shade of molten gold, like liquid fire burning with intensity.

He was the embodiment of desire, a temptation that no one could resist, and the hottest thing I'd ever seen in a high school hallway.

"Come on, pretty girl," he said, nodding his head to the classroom door.

Of course he would be in my first class. Seven hundred people in the school, and I ran into him in yet another embarrassing position.

I could feel Jack's gaze burning into the back of my neck as I made my way into the classroom. I immediately headed towards the far end of the classroom, but he grabbed my hip in a gentle grip.

"This way," he murmured, and I was a little afraid he had magical powers because I found myself letting him lead me to a desk in the back like he'd put me in a trance.

Or at the very least a lust trance. His fingers were branding my skin, sending heat shooting through my insides.

I rarely felt attracted to someone, my life was too hard to think about something as petty as that.

But he had me thinking all sorts of things at the moment.

I watched in complete confusion as he unzipped my backpack and pulled out my supplies, setting them neatly on my desk before setting the backpack on the ground. Then he slipped into the desk next to me, shooting me a sexy grin as he did so that zapped my brain.

"What are you doing?" *I finally asked.*

"I've designated myself your new best friend."

I gaped at him.

"What?"

"I'm assuming you don't have any other best friends at this school," *he said, his hand reaching out and pushing some hair out of my face like we really had known each other for forever.*

"No, I haven't quite made it that far," *I answered, a smile hitting my lips.*

"That's good, because you should know I take my best friend duties very seriously."

"Is that so?"

"Yes," *he said, nodding.*

"And what does this best friendship come with?" *I asked, realizing that I was actually...flirting.*

Who even was I right now?

"Let's see if I can make a little list for you...for starters, lunchtime buddies."

I nodded. "A good thing since I'd be sitting in the library otherwise."

"A very good thing," *he said as his fingers danced across my skin. Again.*

This guy was very familiar considering he didn't know me.

Was he like this with all the new girls?

The needy girl inside me soaked up the attention like I was a flower and he was the sun.

"There's also a guaranteed study buddy. As well as hockey tickets for all my games."

My eyes went wide at that.

He studied my face, his pupils looking a little blown out and dazed.

"Wow," he whispered, and I touched my cheek, wondering if I'd somehow gotten ink on myself.

"What?"

"You're just blowing my mind, pretty girl."

I came back to my windowless prison, a tear sliding down my cheek. I stared down at my stomach once again. If I was pregnant, were they ever going to know our baby?

Was I going to last that long?

I'd spent so much time trying to come up with the past, but right now what was most terrifying...was the fact that I could envision the future so clearly.

I could see long weekends in that dream house I'd told Sebastian about, my head in his lap as he stroked my baby bump.

I could see us in the hospital room, all of them gathered around me, the cries of our baby as he or she entered the world. Their faces when they saw her for the first time.

I could see them all gathered around me while I nursed her. Walking in, seeing one of them humming a lullaby as they rocked her in the middle of the night. Long walks in the spring sunshine as we pushed the baby carriage.

I could see the baby's first steps towards the guys, their big grins and shouts of encouragement. Greyson completely melting for our baby, wiping their tears and holding them close.

I could see us all gathered on the ice as they taught our child to skate.

I could see it all.

And the loss of that future I realized...was far scarier than anything I'd lost in the past.

I just needed to have hope.

That's what had gotten me this far in the first place, right?

The door opened, and I scrambled out of my chair, realizing that at the very least, I could push the office chair at someone if the situation called for it.

Sunny appeared in the doorway, that same blankness in his gaze that was more terrifying than any other emotion would have been. He came in and closed the door behind him.

He studied me for a second and I worked on holding his gaze, not wanting to show how scared I was.

"What are you going to do to me?" I finally whispered, when it appeared that he was just going to stare at me all night—or all day—I wasn't sure how much time had passed at this point.

The air was heavy with tension, the silence broken by the sound of my embarrassingly ragged breaths.

"I suppose that depends on Greyson, doesn't it? We'll find out exactly how much he cares about you when he finally figures out where you are," Sunny answered with a shrug. I guess the TV shows with the villains were right about something—the villain did always seem to be remarkably blasé about what they were doing.

Sunny was certainly playing that part well.

"Aren't you scared at all of what he'll do when he gets here?"

"I've been planning this for a long, long time. I would like to hope that I've finally got it right." He rubbed his chin, his eyes still piercing into me.

"Why?" I asked. "He trusted you."

The blankness finally disappeared at that question, replaced by a dark bitterness.

"I wasn't supposed to be anyone's second. Did you know that? I paid my dues for years under Matteo, and then Greyson's father. And promises were made." He shook his head angrily. "We may be criminals, but there's always been a code of honor, when you made a promise, you kept it. And those men promised me!" He banged his hand against the wall behind him, his voice rising.

Sunny took a deep breath, smoothing back his hair as he calmed himself down. "I was going to be the next Jackal. All of my work. All of the years I spent being the guy they could count on, who sacrificed everything...it was all going to be repaid.

Greyson's father wasn't in good health. And he made enemies left and right. He would have been gone soon enough. I was so close."

Sunny bared his teeth. "Greyson swooped in and stole it all from me. Stole the crown off his father's head, and out of my grasp. He betrayed his father's trust, seized control of everything, and made sure that I would be nothing forever."

"So, you decided to, what...betray him? So much for 'honor among thieves,'" I said sarcastically.

Sunny scoffed, shaking his head at me like I was an errant child, who just didn't understand.

"You have no idea how much power Greyson has. He's hidden so much from you. There isn't anything that happens on this side of the country that he doesn't have his hand in. Politicians and kings bow before him. He has unlimited resources. Unlimited wealth. Unlimited...power. That was all supposed to be mine. Any man would kill to have that."

"You've been his most loyal guy for all these years."

"And I've been trying to ruin him for just as long," Sunny growled.

I raised an eyebrow.

"It's taken time to build up the necessary tools...and men to take down a man like Greyson," Sunny admitted slowly. "Especially when he lost you...he became...a force to be reckoned with. Not distracted like he is now. He was building my kingdom, collecting all the power that would one day be mine. So, I worked behind the scenes while he did all the hard work," Sunny shrugged. "It was a smart move to let him have his fun."

"So, you just let bigger men do all the hard work and then you try and take credit for it, is that it?" I commented, thoroughly unimpressed. Which worked in my favor because *unimpressed* seemed to piss him off the most.

"You were the one to run me down that day? Right?" I asked, desperately hoping he would continue to be a chatty Kathy because I needed to know what had happened.

He pretended to look sorry, but it came across mocking—which perhaps had been his intent. "It's amazing what the brain does to protect us, isn't it?"

"What do you mean?"

"You overheard me talking to Greyson's father about getting rid of Greyson. You left immediately to tell him, and I had to run you down right before you made it to them, to stop you."

I stared at him, shocked. Because I may have been able to recover a lot of memories, but there was nothing involving him. No memories with his face, or his voice.

"You still don't remember, even now?" he asked, cocking his head, his smile predatory.

I shrugged. "Apparently you're just not memorable," I told him.

His smile dropped at that.

The ego of this guy. He really thought he was some kind of god. Or that he deserved to be a god at least.

"Alright, now that you've bared your soul...is this where you kill me?"

He rolled his eyes and sighed. "That would kind of defeat the purpose, right? I suppose it would be fun to send your head to him in a box or something like that. But that wouldn't get him here. Where I have men and enough firepower to finally bring him down."

"What's it like in that head of yours, do you just constantly think about how you wish you had Greyson's dick?" I murmured in an awestruck voice.

His face reddened and he snarled at me. "You know, I've always felt sorry for you. A little slut, desperate for someone to love her, with so many daddy issues a therapist wouldn't know where to start...but I'm not feeling so sorry for you at the moment."

He leaned forward, a small smile on his face.

"And believe me. With what I have planned, you're really going to want me to feel sorry for you."

With those kind tidings, he tipped his chin at me and left the room, the lock clicking behind him.

I sprung from my chair and threw it on the ground. It did absolutely nothing, and it didn't make me feel any better.

I went to the door and banged on it.

And then banged on it some more.

Eventually, I started screaming and banging at the same time, hiccuped sobs falling from my mouth.

I knew this wasn't doing anything for my situation. But it was making me feel slightly better.

I finally exhausted myself, and picked up the chair, falling into it with a huff.

I guess now, I would just have to wait.

———

At some point the lock on the door clicked open, and I sat up, staring at it hopefully. "I have a gun, so don't even think of trying something," a rough and gravelly voice warned sternly before the door creaked open, and an older woman shuffled in, her frizzy red hair haloed around her head like a fiery crown. Her eyes, sharp and piercing, scanned the room, taking in every detail with keen intensity, like I'd somehow figured out how to rig a booby trap in here.

She was carrying a tray of food in her freckled hands, the aroma of the meal wafting through the air, enticing and repelling at the same time.

How long had it been since I ate? My stomach grumbled and her lips pressed in a thin line, like the sound had offended her.

"Eat this," she snapped, setting the tray down on the office cabinet. I stared at the soup and bread, my stomach continuing to churn with a mixture of hunger and apprehension.

"I'm good," I said stiffly.

"I'm sorry. Did I say that in question form? I meant 'Eat the damn food,'" she growled.

I hesitated. Sunny had basically said they had no plans to kill me...yet, right? And I needed to keep up my strength, especially if there was a baby in there.

"This is a stupid question, but I'll just ask it anyway...since everything about this situation is, in fact, stupid. But is it safe?"

The woman laughed at me, the sound coming out more of a bark. "Eat the food, or I'll stuff it down your throat. Any more *stupid* questions?"

I frowned at her, and a second later her hand was whipping against my cheekbone with a loud smack. Pain exploded along the side of my face, a sharp, stinging sensation that left my head ringing.

I clutched my throbbing cheek as tears welled in my eye. My other hand went to my stomach, just in case she wasn't done.

The woman stood there, her expression unchanged, as if she hadn't just struck me.

"Eat," she ordered.

Let's see, get beaten by this crazy witch, or potentially get poisoned.

Decisions, decisions.

I immediately picked up the spoon and dipped it into the soup. Hesitating for one more second, I scooped some of it up.

It was salty and lukewarm...but not terrible.

She stood there watching me until I'd drained the whole bowl.

And then she made me eat the roll.

Which was not as good as the soup.

As I faded into unconsciousness, thanks to the drugs that had definitely been in the soup...at least I wasn't being beaten to death.

CHAPTER 23

Jack

The air in the war room was thick with tension. Maps and photographs littered the large table where Sebastian, Carter, Greyson, and I stood.

"Greyson!" The door burst open, slamming against the wall with an urgency that made us all turn.

"Felix," Greyson greeted him, clearly naming him for our sake.

Felix's glasses were askew above freckled cheeks as he rushed toward us with a tablet in hand. "I got something!"

My heart hammered at the possibility of news about Kennedy. Every second she was missing felt like a year off my life.

"Sunny's location. His phone just came online out of nowhere," Felix announced, tapping on the screen to zoom in on a map.

A red dot blinked back at us from an industrial part of town, an area riddled with abandoned factories and warehouses. The factories and our city had crumpled at the same time.

Sebastian's brow furrowed as he leaned in, his instincts kicking in. "You think he took Kennedy?"

"Could be. Or maybe they took him too." Greyson said.

"Either way," I said, staring at the blinking dot, "this feels wrong. It's too convenient."

My gut twisted at the thought of Kennedy being alone and afraid, and I fought the impulse to rush to act. We had one shot.

"It's a trap," Greyson muttered, arms crossed over his chest. "No doubt about it."

Felix nodded, adjusting his glasses nervously. "For him to have gone dark like that and then suddenly pop up...someone's baiting us."

We exchanged glances, each of us processing the possibilities. Given the trail of bodies we'd left trying to protect Kennedy, there should have been fewer pieces left on the chess board.

But I didn't trust any of Greyson's Jackals.

Any of them but us, I guessed, though I didn't like thinking of myself as a Jackal...or Greyson's.

We knew the risks, but we also knew what was at stake. Kennedy—our Kennedy—needed us. The thought ignited a burning need to act, to protect her at all costs. It was a struggle to keep myself under control.

But we had to be smart.

"Alright, so it's a trap," I said. "Let's figure out how to turn their trap into our advantage."

Greyson nodded curtly, his eyes sharp and calculating as he turned towards the door. "I'll send Hawk and his team out for recon. They're discreet, they won't raise any alarms."

With a few swift strides, Greyson was out of the room, barking orders.

"I'll get you the building's layout, just give me a minute." Felix gave us a sympathetic look and rushed after him.

The air crackled with barely suppressed energy, like the moments just before a storm. Carter stood stock still, the goalie ready and waiting, while Sebastian paced impatiently.

"They'll be expecting recon," I pointed out, running a hand through my hair in frustration. "They're waiting for us to make a move."

Greyson re-entered, his expression unreadable. "I'm aware," he admitted, his jaw tight.

He leaned back against the heavy oak table that dominated the space and crossed his arms. "And frankly, I don't know who I can trust within the Jackals anymore."

I wouldn't have expected him to acknowledge that to us. Greyson always had to be in control. It must have killed him that he couldn't trust his Jackals, but he didn't show it.

"What are we going to do, then?" Sebastian asked, his tone cautious.

"I've called in some other help," Greyson replied, his gaze meeting mine for a moment.

Someone outside my usual circle."

Carter nodded, but I had a bad feeling when Greyson started calling in favors.

I couldn't shake a vision of Kennedy with her eyes wide, and her face tense with terror.

I moved to the smartboard on the wall, bringing up the schematic showing the layout of the factory. "Where do you think she is?"

"We can't trust the layout. That's from when the building was built," Greyson said. "But I would hold her deep inside the factory. Make my enemies fight their way through it."

"Maybe one of the offices," I said, tapping the schematic of the second floor layout, which was narrower than the first floor.

"Maybe. We'll find out." Greyson's voice was grim.

The thought of her trapped in that factory, her heart hammering with fear, tightened something in my chest until I could barely breathe. Each second we spent planning was another second she was alone, possibly terrified, and full of... No, I couldn't let myself think about the fact she was pregnant.

The heavy door to the war room swung open with a decisive thud that echoed off the walls.

We needed to be focused. Still, I couldn't help saying, "Let's make sure this outside help understands what's at stake."

"I promise we do." The hulking figure in the doorway said. Inked skin stretched over corded muscles, and his eyes were an intense shade of green.

Behind him, a tall dark haired man sauntered in, his frame tall and leanly muscled beneath a fitted black shirt. He carried a leather bag that seemed heavy with equipment.

"Gentlemen, meet Cain and Remington," Greyson said, and there was a faint flicker of humor—the first I'd seen since he left the rink with Kennedy—when he said, "Try not to piss Cain off. Not when you've just started to grow on me."

"Greyson," Cain nodded, his voice deep and resonant.

"Thanks for coming," Greyson said, wasting no extra breath as he swept his arm toward the digital map projected on the wall. "Here's the situation."

I shifted while Greyson briefed them, my heart pounding in sync with the flickering of the red dot that represented our best lead on Kennedy's location. Remington unpacked his equipment as he listened, and his eyes scanned the data with a predator's focus.

"Damn." Remington finally broke the silence, his low whistle cutting through the tension. "You guys must be going crazy. If it were Aurora missing…"

He trailed off, leaving the implication hanging thick in the air.

His words hit me like a gut punch. I didn't think anyone could understand, but they had a girl too. Her face, her laugh, the way her long brown hair felt slipping through my fingers— all of it haunted me. Especially the…

"She's pregnant," I blurted out.

Sebastian's hand was a steady weight on my shoulder, grounding me.

"I understand." Remington pivoted to the computers he'd begun to unpack. "I can cut the power. Plunge them into darkness. It'll give you an edge."

My mind conjured images of Kennedy, alone in that pitch

blackness, her heart racing in fear. But the advantage was unde-niable. "Let's do it."

Beside us, Cain's imposing figure loomed closer. "We're going to need more than just the element of surprise. We can go in with night vision, but we're still looking at a high cost. We know they're expecting us."

"Understood," Greyson acknowledged, his eyes locked on Cain's.

"Friendship's got its limits," Cain said bluntly, crossing his arms over his vast chest. "Halting my entire operation to get every man massed out there…"

Greyson didn't hesitate. "We know. Whatever it takes."

Cain gave a short nod. I had the feeling he'd do the same for Aurora.

The pain I felt was muted by the blur of preparation. Greyson took us to the armory, where the scent of gun oil lingered in the air. Grimly, we loaded magazines and prepared ourselves for war.

Hawk and his team reported back. Greyson told his men that we would be planning an attack for the morning and to get some rest.

And then, unseen, we slipped out. Cain picked us up and brought us to the edge of the factory, where his people were gathering.

The abandoned factory loomed ahead. Cain's men were already there, figures draped in darkness, their movements effi-cient and silent. I could make out the soft-green glow of night vision goggles.

Remington held a heat gun. "I'm seeing at least twenty bodies in there."

I ran my hand over the weight of the gun under my arm, before pressing the butt of the rifle I carried into my shoulder. I hadn't carried a gun since we left the Jackals.

"Everyone's in position," Cain murmured, his voice barely above a whisper, yet it cut through the quiet like a knife.

My chest tightened at his words, anticipation and dread knotting at the base of my throat. We were here. This was where I would find her, or lose everything trying. The world seemed odd through the green night vision blur.

I stepped forward at Greyson's command, and he grabbed my arm, giving me a shake of the head. "For Kennedy's sake," he muttered, "hold back."

I hesitated, then nodded. He was right. As much as I wanted to get in there, Kennedy would be destroyed if she lost us.

The lights at the factory cut out, every one of them dying.

Cain's men melted out of the shadows, running up on the building in a practiced crouch, like special forces.

With every fiber on edge, I followed them. My hands were steady, gripping the rifle that had become an extension of myself.

The night vision goggles cast everything in a surreal green hue, narrowing my focus even more than my adrenaline already had.

Cain's men moved with practiced precision, years of training and hard-earned trust funneling our actions into silent choreography.

We advanced, room by room, clearing each space with swift and bloody efficiency.

A muffled sound caught my attention, and without hesitation, I pivoted towards it. Through the goggles, I saw distorted shapes. Then a flash of movement, and I squeezed the trigger. The sound of gunfire was shockingly loud in the confined space, followed by the softer thud of a body hitting the ground.

Then a bomb detonated. Bodies blasted back toward us.

Cain cursed, and it was the last sound I heard before my ears popped and the world became muted.

Greyson glanced at me again. If I'd been in the lead, I would've been caught in that blast.

With everything in a stark contrast of black and green, there was no color to the blood that now painted the floor, just darker shades of monochrome.

What were the odds that Kennedy was here? That each trigger pull meant we were that much closer to saving her?

Another figure loomed ahead, weapon raised, and time seemed to slow as I took aim. I squeezed the trigger, and the figure crumpled without a sound. I'd settled into a deep, dangerous calm I'd long forgotten.

"Moving up," Greyson signaled, and we pressed on, deeper into the factory.

And unexpectedly, being a Jackal felt like…coming home.

Just like loving Kennedy.

CHAPTER 2

Kennedy

The door was flown open so hard it slammed against the wall. "Shit, shit, shit."

I raised my head drowsily, startled out of my deep sleep, and blinked, feeling a dull headache pulse behind my eyes like what happens when you wake up too early.

The room was pitch black, but someone was pacing through the room. Then a narrow flashlight beam switched on—and into my face.

I squeezed my eyes shut against the painful feeling.

"There you are," Sunny muttered, and now I recognized his voice. He fumed, "You can thank your asshole *boyfriend* for what's going to happen next. He was supposed to send the Jackals in…what the hell is this?"

"You wanted the Jackals," I repeated, a bit slowly. I felt terrible.

"I needed it to be the Jackals, so Thane and Peter could turn on Greyson," he muttered, sounding as if he were talking to himself as much as me. "And then we'd take out the rest who are loyal to him, like Hawk, and we'd rebuild…"

The ground shook, the bed beneath me sliding across the

ground, and the sound of a *boom* was loud even through the muffled wall. Bed–they must have moved me while I was out.

It took my sleep-fogged brain a second to understand what was happening. Not an earthquake. Bombs going off.

"Greyson!" Fear spiked through my heart. So, that had been their plan to take out the Jackals who were loyal to Greyson. Explosives were set, traps in place to take them down."

"Not just Greyson," he snarled. "All four of your pretty boys are out there, you slut."

Fear clutched my heart.

"They cut the power to the building, surprised us by going completely around the Jackal chain of command, and now they've got a fucking ordnance team out there working through the booby traps," he snarled. He sounded as if he were coming unhinged.

Of course, he'd been unhinged in the first place to betray Greyson.

I felt a swell of pride in my men. They were psychopaths at times…criminals deep down…

And they were impressive.

They were coming for me.

"But that's slowing them down," he said, "so there's plenty of time for you and me to prepare a little surprise for them. And my team's coming in behind them, so they're going to find themselves enveloped in a trap."

"Oh?" I asked. "It looks like it's just you, Sunny."

"No," he disagreed. He shone the flashlight in my face again, blinding me, and I ducked away from the light. "It's you and me."

Still, he let out a groan of frustration as he pressed his hands to his temples, the gun still gripped in his hand. No matter what he said, he didn't seem like his new plan was going too well for him, now that the plan he'd spent five years putting into place had crumbled into dust.

Then, he flashed the light around again, an eerie smile coming over his face in the reddish glow of the flashlight.

He grabbed my arm and tried to yank me up from the bed. I let out a cry of pain as his fingers wrenched deep into my skin, because my legs wouldn't straighten underneath me. It was like my limbs were made of noodles after all the drugs they'd given me.

"You're not going to be any use to them, are you?" he chuckled, before dragging me over his shoulder. He staggered with me through the darkness.

Carter

I watched with coiled impatience as the ordnance team disarmed the booby trap. It was a crude, but deadly setup, wires strung haphazardly. Every tick of time that passed felt like an eternity, knowing Kennedy was somewhere in this hellhole.

"Careful," I heard someone mutter, their voice barely more than a whisper. The team moved with surgical precision, snipping wires and disarming mechanisms. It was hard to see what was happening through the eerie glow of the night vision goggles.

All I could do was stand there, clenched fists at my sides, feeling useless.

"Trap's clear," one of them finally said, and relief surged through me, replaced by a fresh wave of urgency. We needed to move, now.

As we advanced, my boots were silent on the concrete floor, all my senses on high alert.

Gunfire erupted from the shadows, bullets ricocheting off metal and concrete with deafening clangs.

Then a smoke bomb hissed. Gray smoke filled the air, blinding us, and I suppressed a cough as I took cover. More shots were pinging around us, but they were as blind as we were.

"Push up!" I yelled, my voice husky from the smoke.

Two of Cain's men signaled as they moved past, taking a position ahead and to the right to lay down covering fire. They disappeared into the smoke, but as long as I moved left, we should be able to leapfrog forward and lay down covering fire without walking into our own bullets.

"Going with you," Greyson muttered, his own voice foreign and harsh in the smoke. "Covering fire!"

The two of us rushed forward. I banged into something in the smoke, something big enough to hide behind, and grabbed Greyson's arm to yank him down too.

A muzzle flash, orange in all the gray, betrayed the shooter's position. I tapped Greyson's shoulder in silent communication. "I've got him."

Greyson called to Cain's men to hold so we wouldn't rush into the path of their bullets.

"Cover me," I told him.

As Greyson fired off bursts from his automatic rifle, I made my move, darting forward. I went wide and left, staying out of the path of potential friendly fire and trying to get wide of the shooter.

I found the shooter crouched behind an overturned desk. I was almost on top of him before I could see him through the smoke. As his head swiveled toward me, my finger tightened on the trigger, putting two shots in his body. He jerked back, his gun flying from his hand.

And then I raised my gun and fired one final bullet through his head.

I didn't feel anything. Not now, not when all this was for Kennedy.

"Clear," I called, scanning for more threats, already turning and moving forward.

And as I did, the smoke cleared…

And I saw Kennedy.

She was slumped over in a chair. Her brown hair hung all around her face, tangled, and she was so still...

She might be unconscious. She might be dead.

Panic surged through me, sweeping away all sense of strategy. Time slowed, my breath caught. She couldn't be...

"Kennedy!" I sprinted towards her, every other thought obliterated by the need to reach her, to see her eyes open and meet mine.

"Get down!" Greyson's sharp voice jolted me from my tunnel vision.

His hand clamped down on my shoulder, yanking me sideways with a force that sent us sprawling. The world tilted wildly, a blur of shadows and light.

A split second later, the crack of gunfire ripped through the air where I'd been standing.

"Ah!" Greyson's grunt was right next to me, muffled by the chaos, but unmistakably pained.

Scrambling to my knees, I blinked to clear the disorientation, only to freeze.

Sunny stood behind Kennedy using her as a shield, the barrel of his gun pressing coldly against her temple.

"One wrong move and she's dead."

From my position on the floor, I could see Kennedy more clearly now. Her wrists were free, no bindings to hold her—except for whatever cocktail of drugs they'd pumped into her system. The slight droop of her eyelids, the limpness of her posture...

She was drugged. What if those drugs destroyed her fledgling memories?

An unexpected thought jolted through me. What if someone had purposefully caused her amnesia with drugs?

"Greyson, you okay?" I whispered harshly, eyes locked on Kennedy, searching for any sign of consciousness.

"Been better," he muttered through clenched teeth, his hand

pressed to his shoulder where a dark stain was spreading across his t-shirt from underneath his bulletproof vest. But even bleeding, his gaze was fixed on Sunny.

Greyson was calculating, waiting for an opening.

"Good," I answered, because both of us had to keep moving. Greyson got to his feet, letting out a hiss of pain; blood splattered onto the floor from his shoulder.

"Let's talk this out, Sunny. Man to man," Greyson called out, his voice steady despite his blood loss. He took a measured step forward, hands raised in a gesture of peace.

No one who knew Greyson would buy that gesture.

I kept low, my heart hammering against my ribs as I edged to the side, desperate for a clear line of sight. Right now, Kennedy was in the crossfire.

Sunny's head turned sharply at the sound of my movement, and his finger tensed on the trigger. Bullets seared past me, but I lunged desperately and managed to dive behind an old piece of machinery. The bullets slammed into the metal instead before coming to an abrupt halt.

How many rounds had Sunny just fired? I tried to count them, hoping he'd run out of rounds soon.

Greyson had lunged forward in a burst of speed while Sunny was distracted. He grappled with Sunny, who let out a startled curse, their struggle a blur. It was impossible to take out Sunny without risking Greyson too..

"Kennedy!" I yelled, but the words were useless. She couldn't hear me, couldn't respond. All she could do was be the silent center of this deadly tug of war.

"Damn it, Greyson!" Sunny spat as he dragged Kennedy back, her body a ragdoll in his ruthless grip.

His arm locked around her neck, gun pressed to her temple with a cold finality that froze my insides. "The only way she's getting out of here is with me!"

The air felt thick with the scent of gunpowder. Rain had

begun to pound on the roof of the factory, deafening every other sound.

I held back, muscles coiled tight, knowing that one wrong move could end everything we'd fought so hard to reclaim.

Blood continued to seep through the fabric of Greyson's shirt, dark even through the monochrome filter of my night vision goggles. He seemed not to notice, his focus locked on Sunny as if the injury were nothing more than a nuisance.

We backed off slowly, step by measured step, creating the space that Sunny demanded with Kennedy held tight against him. She stumbled alongside him as she slowly regained consciousness, then her wide eyes were taking in the chaos in front of her. When her gaze locked on mine, time stopped. Fear radiated from her in waves.

"Sunny," I started, voice steady despite the chaos raging within me, "it's over. Your people are scattered, dead, or dying. There's nowhere to go."

Kennedy's muffled attempt at speech was stifled by Sunny's hand clamped over her mouth, her eyes pleading above his fingers. The raw terror in them dug into me like a blade.

Sunny's words cut through the darkness. "Greyson, drop the gun. You're coming with us."

Greyson's grip on his weapon tightened for a moment before he let it clatter to the ground. His eyes never left Sunny.

Greyson was dangerous even without the gun.

But so was Sunny, and he had Kennedy.

I could only watch as Sunny, with his gun still trained on my girl, began to back away into the swirling mist of smoke. Greyson moved cautiously beside him, blood soaking through his shirt.

Then, the haze enveloped them. Kennedy turned her head slightly, fighting Sunny's grip. Her gaze met mine, signaling desperately with her eyes, trying to tell me something.

The outlines of their bodies became ghosts in the smoke and fog, and then they were gone.

Kennedy

S unny yanked me along mercilessly. My lungs burned, my eyes watered, and I wasn't sure how he even knew where we were going in the dim light. At least some light came through the clouded factory windows, but the factory was full of smoke too. The acrid taste singed my throat and mouth.

In the smoke, it was hard to see until we were almost on top of someone. Shadowy figures loomed like wraiths out of the smoke. I searched for a familiar face, but the eerie glow of night vision goggles just stared back at me, blank and inhuman.

Greyson moved alongside us, lost in the smoke from time to time or to the watery vision that made it hard for me to see.

"Ambush!" I tried to call out, to warn him. But Sunny's hand was pressing over my mouth, and it was barely an audible croak.

"None of that, or I'll kill him now," Sunny hissed into my ear, his breath hot against my skin.

Fear tightened my chest even more than the smoke. He was using me to get Greyson outside, but once he did...I was sure he would kill Greyson. He was just trying to make the most of the brief peace he'd managed to force on Greyson.

Suddenly, Jack's voice cut through the haze. "Lights!"

Beside us, Greyson tore off his night vision goggles immediately.

The lights blazed back to life. The sudden illumination stabbed my eyes, but then as I blinked and cleared them, I could see more; the light filtered through some of the smoke.

And Jack was standing a few yards away, his rifle set in his shoulder, his face grim and watchful. He was frozen too, waiting for an opening when Sunny couldn't kill me instantly.

His familiar face brought a surge of relief. There was Greyson, and now Jack; my men were alive. Hopefully Sebastian 𝗐𝗮𝗌 𝖿𝗂𝗇𝖾, 𝗍𝗈𝗈

I just had to keep them all that way.

He met my gaze across the expanse of the factory floor, his eyes softening for a split second before he winked at me. It was a promise that everything was going to be alright, and it was ridiculous, and it lit me up with hope anyway.

Gritting my teeth against the pain radiating from where Sunny's fingers dug into my arm, I kept stumbling forward. His gun was cold and unyielding at my temple. My legs kept buckling as I moved forward, but he always held me up with that bruising grip until I managed to get some control of my limbs.

Greyson's form was lost in the fog, then emerged again, steadily keeping pace with us. "It's going to be okay. We'll get out of this."

His gaze flicked to Sunny, hardening with resolve. "You can't win this, Sunny. The Jackals are mine."

"Are they?" Sunny spat back, anger seething just below the surface. "You took what should've been mine!"

"If it was ever your right to be the Jackal, you'd be the one leading them," Greyson countered. "I fought for my place. If it's a challenge you want, I'm right here."

"Or I could just kill you now," Sunny said, his tone chillingly casual.

"No, you can't. Because we're your ticket out of here."

Greyson shook his head. "This was your plan? All these fucking years, and this was the best you came up with?"

My heart raced as we moved past more shadowy figures. Sebastian. He was ahead of us on our right as Greyson kept pace at our left. My heart lit up.

Sebastian's posture was rigid as if carved from stone, rifle nestled in the crook of his shoulder.

Sunny twisted, using me as a shield between himself and Sebastian. But I knew Sebastian wouldn't take the shot, not when it was too likely to hit me.

"Easy, Seb," Greyson muttered under his breath. "Let's move this party outside."

He sounded so confident. Did he think he'd be able to get a clear strike at Sunny once we were outside?

He didn't know that Sunny had an ambush prepared out there.

The moment Sunny dragged me outside was a disorienting shift from the smoky dimness of the factory to the glaring brightness of morning. I'd imagined emerging back into the sunshine to be a moment of power and relief. I'd thought I'd be free and safe.

But this dawn light didn't mean anything. Not with Sunny's hot breath on the back of my throat and the gun bruising my temple as he shoved it hard against my skin.

My body was still sluggish. But I wasn't stumbling anymore. The drugs were wearing off.

"Keep them away," Sunny called, his voice loud in my ear. Ahead of him, I saw the men he was fixed on, who had taken cover behind some cars, their guns fixed on him. "Get me a car!"

But while those men had all his attention—and no way of knowing Sunny's forces would try to envelop them—I saw Greyson's gaze shift upward.

Through the corner of my eye, up above on the rooftop, I saw a silhouette against the too-bright rising sun. A figure, lying on the edge of the roof. The tell tale glint of a rifle.

Panic surged through me. Greyson thought the sniper was his, but what if the sniper was part of Sunny's ambush?

I had to make sure Greyson knew an ambush was coming.

With a surge of desperate energy, I twisted against Sunny's hold. I was clumsy as I fought against the numbness in my limbs, my actions more of a distraction than an effective struggle. But it was enough. Sunny's hand slipped from my mouth to grab my chin, holding me against the muzzle.

"Ambush!" The words tore from from my throat my with limbs.

But Greyson heard me. I saw his face through my narrowed vision.

The world spun as the butt of Sunny's gun connected with my temple. Searing pain exploded across my skull. My vision blurred even more.

My knees buckled, but I was stronger now and stayed upright.

I snarled at him, "If you kill me, there's nothing to stop Greyson from killing you...I'm not going with you!"

Sunny didn't respond, but I could feel his chaotic desperation oozing through the air.

"Tell me about this ambush, Sunny," Greyson mocked. "Did you think you had that much control over my Jackals? That you could orchestrate a coup, and I wouldn't be able to figure out who was loyal to me?"

A single shot pierced the charged air between us.

Instinctively, I dropped, my fingers clawing at Sunny's gun, desperate to wrench it away. Sunny finally let me go, shoving me hard. I slammed into the ground on my knees.

Greyson tackled Sunny. The two of them rolled over and over on the ground, fighting for control of the gun that Sunny still gripped between them.

Dizziness swirled through my head as I stumbled up and forward, the world tilting precariously with each step as if I were in a funhouse. The drugs left a metallic taste on my tongue and turned my limbs to lead.

"Kennedy!" Jack's voice was rough with concern. His form was a blur as he, along with Sebastian and Carter, burst from the shadows of the factory, guns drawn and ready for a fight.

"I'm okay," I tried to say, but it came out slurred, lost beneath the ringing in my ears. I fell to my knees, the impact jarring, sending shots of pain up my spine. The ground was cool against my palms, steadying me for a fleeting moment.

Long enough to see the figures moving out of the forest and toward the factory.

A dozen men moved forward with quick, stealthy steps, all heavily armed.

"Watch out—" I managed to gasp out.

Gunfire cracked out, sizzling through the air around us.

Carter and Sebastian reacted with the precision of seasoned soldiers, returning fire with deadly accuracy. Their movements were fluid. They needed to fill me in on the misspent youth that I apparently still didn't remember.

Jack reached down to help me, his hands steady despite the cacophony of violence around us. He tried to pull me away from the line of fire, his big body shielding mine as he pulled me forward toward cover.

But that meant he was exposed to the men racing toward us and also to the sniper who was above us, if he were Sunny's ally.

The air was thick with the stench of gunpowder and the sharp tang of fear. I tried to shake off the cloud in my mind.

My knees trembled, struggling to support my weight as I watched the struggle unfold before me. Greyson's face was contorted with pain. He and Sunny were still scrambling for control, locked so close together neither side could take a shot without risking killing their own man.

"Stay," Jack whispered to me. "You're okay. I'll be right back."

He launched himself away, firing on the men who were attacking us, shouting to Sebastian and Carter and the other men in the chaos.

Greyson was fighting desperately, but the blood streaming down his arm was a weakness, even before Sunny began to slam his fist into the bloody wound.

Greyson let out a roar of pain and with one a sudden, violent twist, the gun they were fighting over broke free.

The metallic clang as it hit the ground reverberated through the chaos, and it skidded to a halt by my feet. My breath hitched as I stared at the weapon.

Sunny slammed his fist into Greyson's face, and a cut opened over his eye, blinding him partially. Greyson grabbed at him, trying to tackle him to the ground, as Sunny moved toward me.

My hand shook as I extended it towards the gun, every movement an immense effort. The cool metal felt strange as I wrapped my fingers around it, lifting it with trembling arms. Over the sights, I could see Sunny, who sneered at me.

Sunny's mocking laugh cut through the noise around us. "Can't even hold the gun steady, can you, sweetheart?" he sneered, a cruel smirk twisting his lips as he momentarily turned his attention away from Greyson.

Greyson dove after him again, but for one long second, I had a clear shot.

Time seemed to slow, my heart thundering in my ears as I steadied my aim as best I could.

Could I trust myself?

Slowly, I squeezed the trigger.

The gunshot was deafening. Sunny's body jerked violently, flung backward onto the grass.

In the silence that followed, only the ragged sound of my own breathing filled my ears, my hands still shaking.

Then Greyson reached me. "That's my girl," he said softly. "Give me the gun."

I handed it over. He took it from me oh so gently and carefully and then, without hesitation, performed a double tap on Sunny's body—two quick shots ensuring no chance of survival. I flinched, the sound of gunfire ringing in my ears.

I hoped I'd never hear that sound again.

But then I caught sight of the figure lining up a shot from the roof. "Sniper!" I screamed, reaching for Greyson, trying to shield him.

Greyson twisted, his lips parting in surprise. He grabbed me, shielding me with his own body. "Crazy girl." But he sounded affectionate, not afraid.

Bullets began to punch into the grass around us—not aimed at Greyson or Jack, but finding their marks in the bodies of renegade Jackals emerging from the forest.

It was over in moments that seemed to stretch on forever. Before I could fully grasp the sniper's allegiance, Jack's arms were around me, lifting me effortlessly off the ground. His chest was a solid wall against my cheek, his heartbeat a steady drum through the fabric of his shirt.

"Got you," he murmured, his breath warm against my hair as we moved away from the scene of death and betrayal.

I clung to him, the earthy scent of his jacket mingling with the acrid bite of gunpowder.

"Greyson?" I managed, my voice weak. "Sebastian? Carter?"

"Will be fine," Jack assured me, though I couldn't see his face. "Focus on breathing, Kennedy. Just breathe."

The drugs still lingered in my system, making the world tilt and blur, but when I was in Jack's arms, I couldn't be lost, no matter how deep the fog.

CHAPTER 2

Kennedy

I was laying in the bed, all of us waiting for the doctor to get here. They hadn't let me walk since they'd brought me back from that building. And they were insisting the other doctor come to the guy's penthouse because they didn't want anything to do with a hospital.

Greyson's phone buzzed and he glanced down at it. "She's here," he muttered, stalking through the bedroom door with his gun drawn. Because that was a great way to start a doctor-patient relationship.

By gunpoint.

"Have her look at your arm first!" I called after him.

"Not a chance of that, baby. I'm fine," he responded back.

The elevator dinged, and I listened to the murmur of voices, a soft one, and then the harsh tone of Greyson's that he'd had since they'd gotten me back.

"You guys should probably have changed," I mused, staring at the blood and dust that still covered them.

Sebastian glanced down at his clothes like he was just seeing himself for the first time.

"Naw, princess. I feel like this look is great for the vibe we're going with for this appointment," he drawled with a shrug.

I wrinkled my nose at him, but he was right, their appearance did go with Greyson's whole, let's point a gun at everyone attitude.

A few minutes later a dark haired woman in a pristine white coat came into the bedroom, accompanied by a terrified looking younger woman dressed in scrubs. The doctor looked nonplussed at the scene in the room—bloody clothes and all— but her assistant, or what I assumed was her assistant, looked like she was about to crap her pants.

She'd probably been the first person at the door when Greyson had opened it with a gun in hand.

The doctor had an air of quiet confidence, her steady gaze and gentle demeanor putting me slightly at ease as she walked in like people pointed guns at her all the time.

Knowing Greyson, I guess I couldn't rule that out.

Their appearance sent off a ripple of tension through the air though, as Jack, Carter, and Sebastian huddled close to me, all of them touching me in one way or another—Jack physically shielding me with his body.

I wondered how long it would take for us not to look over our shoulder and feel like someone was after us.

Hopefully, it wouldn't be like that when the baby came.

I softly rubbed at my stomach.

If there was still a baby in there.

Or if there had even been one in there in the first place.

It felt like this doctor held my whole future in her hands.

"Kennedy, I presume?"

I pushed Jack out of the way and struggled to sit up.

"No! Lay back!" All four of them were immediately jumping all over me, and I frowned as I settled back into the pillows.

The doctor glanced at the four guys, before lifting her eyebrow in amusement.

"Please move away from the patient," she said with a sigh as she approached the bed, where I was laying.

The guys were reluctant to move away from me. She finally

put her hands on her hips. "Move away from my patient. NOW!"

I heard a snarl come from Carter's mouth, but they reluctantly moved to my other side.

Greyson was still standing by the doorway...his gun drawn.

So, this was fun.

"Kennedy, my name is Dr. Freeman. I understand...you were recently *detained*."

Detained. That was a much prettier way to say kidnapping.

"Yes, I was."

She pulled a chair up to the side of the bed. "Can you walk me through what happened?" she asked. Her voice was very soothing, I would definitely give her an "A" for bedside manner.

"I was taken into a van and my hands and legs were tied. I moved around quite a bit in the van, sustained some bumps and bruises for sure on the drive. When we reached the building we were taken to, I was hit in the face. And then..." My words faded away as I tried to keep my composure. "They put something in the food they gave me. Something that made me pass out. I'm not sure what it was. I couldn't taste it in the food."

Dr. Freeman gestured to her assistant who hurried over with the huge bag that she'd come in with.

"I'm going to get some blood samples and have it sent to my lab for immediate review, okay?"

I nodded, grimacing as I held out my arm, and she got to work cleaning my skin.

"Just a small pinch," she soothed as she slid the needle in and started collecting my blood. She filled one vial, and then another.

"I'm going to have you give me a urine sample as well," Dr. Freeman said, pulling out a small plastic cup.

I moved to get out of the bed, and Carter lunged towards me. "Let me carry you!"

"I'm good," I told him, pushing out of bed on the opposite side as him.

The guys were falling all over themselves to accompany me

to the restroom, but I drew the line at letting them come in with me.

I almost laughed at their looks of dismay as I closed the door in their faces.

Almost being the operative word. I was still too tired from whatever drugs I'd been given to fully get one out.

I peed into the cup and then washed my hands, wincing when I saw my reflection in the mirror, noting how bad I looked. My hair looked like a bird had taken up permanent residence on my head, and my eyes were bloodshot with deep circles under them.

Not beautiful.

But alive.

I just needed to remember that.

I walked out, jumping when Jack popped in front of the door like a real life Jack-in-the-box.

My heart squeezed with how relieved he was at seeing me, like he'd been worried I'd disappear while I was in the bathroom.

He grabbed my hand and led me back towards the bed.

"Hand that to Alex," Dr. Freeman said, gesturing to the pee cup in my hand. "She'll take the vials to our lab and we should have results back within the hour."

The scared girl—Alex—took the vials and bundled them in a plastic container before striding out of the room.

"I'll accompany you," Greyson said in a scary voice. Any remaining color drained out of the poor girl's skin.

"Greyson, stop torturing my assistant. Let the poor girl work," Dr. Freeman said, sounding amused and exasperated at the same time.

Greyson flashed her his teeth instead of answering, and still followed the girl out of the room. A second later, I heard the door open and close.

"He thinks he's so scary," she said, rolling her eyes. "He forgets that I've known him since he was in diapers."

Carter grinned. "Well, Dr. Freeman. I would love to hear some stories one day when you have time."

Dr. Freeman grinned. "There are some good ones."

I climbed back into bed, feeling pitifully tired. Sebastian tried to pull the covers up to my chin like a mother hen.

"Depending on what it was, you could feel tired for at least another week," Dr. Freeman said, obviously seeing my exhaustion.

"What do you think it was?" I asked quietly.

"You haven't had a headache or anything like that?" she questioned.

I shook my head. "Just extreme exhaustion and a dry mouth."

Dr. Freeman nodded. "I'm sure it was just a little sleeping powder then. Nothing to be too worried about."

"Even if—" I glanced at Jack, Sebastian, and Carter who were hanging on my every word. "Even if I could be pregnant?" I finished in a whisper.

Jack's body was practically vibrating as he gripped my hand tightly, holding it in both of his hands as he lifted it to his lips and pressed a gentle kiss on my racing pulse.

"You think you're pregnant?" Dr. Freeman asked with a frown, rooting around her bag and pulling out some medical devices.

"She *is* pregnant," Jack said firmly.

I glanced up at him, shocked.

"That test you took with Greyson came back positive, pretty girl. We're going to be parents," Jack told me, the emotion in his eyes enough to take my breath away.

There was a moment where I felt euphoric, but it was immediately followed by a wave of fear so strong I could barely breathe.

Was my baby alright?

"Let's get you looked at," Dr. Freeman said soothingly, obviously sensing my building hysteria.

She took my temperature and examined my eyes and my throat before measuring my pulse.

"Pulse is high, but that's a good sign that whatever they gave you wasn't super harmful," she commented.

She continued her examination, explaining each step before she proceeded. She palpated my abdomen, feeling for any abnormalities, while the guys watched closely, their expressions a mix of concern and protectiveness.

I heard the distant ding of the elevator and then a minute later, Greyson and Alex appeared. She didn't look any less scared, and he didn't look any less stressed out.

Greyson at least had a fresh bandage on his arm though.

I wondered what the lab had thought of him looking like he'd just come back from war.

"They'll send you the results soon, Dr. Freeman," Alex commented in a trembling voice as Greyson stalked towards me, his gaze running up and down my body like he was making sure nothing had happened while he was gone.

"Can you grab the ultrasound machine, Alex?" the doctor asked in a level tone that seemed to relax her assistant...at least a little. "It should have been delivered just now."

"Yes, Doctor," Alex said, hurrying out of the room.

Greyson stared after her suspiciously before glancing down at me, his entire face softening.

"What did I miss?" he asked, his fingers trailing down my cheek. I leaned into his touch, still holding onto Jack's hand tightly.

"Well we're about to see our baby," I told him, trying to sound positive and hopeful.

There was a burst of fear in Greyson's gaze before he quickly shuttered his emotions, pasting on a smile I knew wasn't real. "I can't wait," he murmured.

Alex wheeled in the machine, because apparently doctors in Greyson's world brought ultrasound machines to their patient's houses, and she and the doctor worked to set it up and get it plugged in.

I stared at each of the guys while Dr. Freeman pushed up my shirt and spread gel all over my stomach. I wanted to memorize this moment, this before...just in case what she told us shattered my hopes and dreams.

She placed the probe on my abdomen, and the room was completely silent as we all watched the screen, anticipation...and fear building with each passing moment.

And then, there it was—a tiny flicker of movement on the monitor, so small, and yet so significant.

Life changing, in fact.

The sound of the heartbeat filled the room, strong and steady, a reassuring rhythm that echoed in my ears.

"There it is," Dr. Freeman said softly, her voice filled with warmth as she pointed to the screen. "Your baby's heartbeat. Everything looks perfectly fine and healthy."

I closed my eyes and a sob slipped from my mouth as relief washed over me, my heart swelling with gratitude and wonder.

I wiped some of the tears falling down my cheeks, trying to look at the guys and gauge their reactions.

They all looked emotional and awestruck, but it was Greyson's reaction that did me in.

"You're giving me a baby," he whispered, and then his shoulders were shaking, and his face scrunched up. Tears were falling from his eyes.

Greyson buried his face in my neck, his tears wetting my skin.

I never could have imagined my tough mafia boss reacting like this to becoming a dad.

I stared up at Jack, Carter, and Sebastian in shock, and their answering grins made my heart squeeze in my chest.

I thought I knew what happiness felt like.

But what I was feeling now surpassed anything I could have ever imagined.

It didn't matter that I couldn't remember most of my past. Because my future was all I needed.

CHAPTER 2

Kennedy

D r. Freeman got the blood test results and confirmed
that the drug they'd given me wouldn't have any
lasting effects for me or the baby. The guys made her
show us the baby one more time and then she and her assistant
left.

As soon as the elevator doors closed, the guys turned their
attention back to me.

I blushed, because having all four of their attention like
that...I didn't think it was anything I was going to get used to
any time soon.

"On a scale of one to ten...how tired are you?" Sebastian
mused, rubbing his bottom lip as he stared at me...hungrily.

I squeezed my legs together, realizing that I was surprisingly
experiencing a burst of energy, most of the sleepiness and pure
exhaustion I'd been feeling earlier was nowhere to be found.

"Heathens, we're all taking showers first," Carter growled,
grabbing the back of Sebastian's shirt before he could get any
closer to me. "No one else's blood is getting close to our princess
and our baby."

I snorted and he winked at me, but my smile quickly
dropped when I realized that he wasn't kidding.

They were going to make me wait.

I pouted and they all laughed at me as they went to their respective rooms, all of them except Sebastian—this was his room after all.

As soon as the others had left, he turned to me with a smirk. "Look how lucky I am," he purred, taking a step towards me.

"Don't even think about it," Carter snarled, popping his head into the room suddenly and throwing what looked like a shoe at the back of his head.

Sebastian growled and glared at him, rubbing the back of his scalp.

"Don't make me tie you up," Carter insisted, still staring at Sebastian with distrust.

"Fine," he sighed, rolling his eyes. But noticeably when Carter left, he didn't make any more moves toward me.

He knew from experience that the guys didn't joke around when it came to tying people up.

"I'm claiming your pussy," he growled as he slowly stripped his blood-covered shirt off in that hot guy way they all had, slowly revealing a set of chiseled abs and chest that made me want to get on my knees and beg to be able to touch him.

His smirk told me he knew exactly what he was doing to me.

Sebastian undid his jeans and slid them down his legs, and it was official—my panties were soaked.

His dick was peeking out the top of his tight gray briefs, the head already glistening with precum.

"I think I need a shower too," I murmured as I stripped off my shirt and then my pants, and he blinked, a wicked smile sliding across his beautiful face.

"I think so too. They won't be able to get mad at me for that."

"I agree," I said, nodding my head seriously as I slid out of bed in nothing but my bra and underwear.

He pursed his lips and looked panicked for a second before he bolted over to me and scooped me up in his arms.

"So, you guys think that I'm well enough for an orgy, but I'm not allowed to walk? Not sure that makes sense," I teased as he carried me towards his bathroom.

"It makes sense in my head," Sebastian answered with a laugh. "Evidently my dick thinks your perfect pussy is much more resilient than the rest of you."

I reached down and slid my hand into his briefs, grabbing his dick.

"I'm glad your dick feels so confident."

He gulped and stopped walking, a dazed look falling across his face as I continued to run my hand up and down his length.

"Are we going to...shower?" I asked, when he still hadn't moved.

"Oh yeah," he asked in a rough voice. "The shower. That's where I was going."

I laughed and laid my head down in the crook of his neck, breathing him in. I could smell dust, gunpowder, and salt from his sweat. But through it all, I could still smell *him*.

My favorite.

Still holding me, he reached into the cavernous shower and turned on some of the shower heads.

And yes, I said some—because like all the other showers in this penthouse, Sebastian's shower had a million features.

I'd been showering in this place for a while now, and it still took me some time to figure out how to turn on the features I wanted.

Perhaps, because I didn't shower by myself very much.

He pressed a soft kiss against my shoulder as we waited for the water to warm up. I realized I was still gripping his dick and I slowly released it, pressing against his chest for him to let me down.

Those briefs needed to come off after all.

He slid me down his body and watched me with glittering, feverish eyes as I grabbed onto his waistband and slowly moved it down his legs, my tongue moving down his cock as I did so.

"Holy fuck," he growled. "It's hard to be good, when you show me you're such a bad girl."

I grinned. "Then stop trying so hard."

He pushed his briefs the rest of the way to the floor and dragged me into the shower, forgetting all about how gentle he wanted to be as he did so.

"Yes," I breathed as he pushed me against the tiled wall, the steam from the warm water floating around us.

"Fuck. You're so hot. How did I get this lucky to have such a perfect girl," he purred as he dragged his gaze from my face down my body. "Let's get this bra off you." Sebastian ripped off my now soaked bra and underwear so that I was bare under his gaze.

He palmed my breast, watching as the water dripped from my nipple. Leaning over, he sucked the water off, licking and suckling my skin until I was squirming against him.

"You'd better hurry and fuck me," I told him breathlessly, "before the others come and want to share."

"Fuck," he groaned. His eyes widening as I slid down the wall to my knees, his pierced cock bobbing deliciously in front of me.

"You shouldn't be on your knees," Sebastian attempted to protest, but his words quickly cut off when my tongue flicked out and licked at his swollen head. "Fuck. They're going to kill me. But this is worth dying for," he rasped.

Sebastian's hand went to his shaft and he fed me his arousal, pushing it into my mouth as I greedily licked at his slit and along his shaft, the metal piercings rubbing along my tongue.

Water was dripping down my face, but there was nothing that could distract me from what I wanted.

His cum. His essence.

Him.

Sebastian groaned again, surging deeper in my mouth. "Fuck, you're mouth is perfect, princess."

I pulled back so I was suckling his slit again, and his hand smacked against the wall above my head as he leaned over me.

"Please," he begged, and I got wet from how needy he sounded.

I took more of him in my mouth, sucking harder, pulling him in deeper until he was hitting the back of my throat.

"So good. So fucking good," he panted as I gagged, tears falling down my face as I tried to open my throat.

His hand gripped my hair, and I could feel the tension in his grip as he tried to hold himself back from doing what he wanted to do—fuck my face.

Sebastian's breath was labored and harsh...and I was pretty sure that I was going to come just by doing this.

I tested different angles, taking in every moan and growl he made, my pussy absolutely flooding for him.

His dick was dripping copiously, and I drank every drop down and then...

Sebastian ripped me off his dick and hoisted me up, holding me up against the shower wall as his lips kissed me fiercely.

His hands dug into my ass as he lined up his cock and slammed in.

I gasped, my head tilting back as I came instantly around his dick, his piercings seeming to drag along every nerve ending in my core. I was flying, floating, so overcome with pleasure I'd forgotten how to breathe.

Sebastian bit down on my neck, centering me and bringing me back to the present where he was buried deep inside of me.

"I love you," he whispered. "You can't ever leave me again. I can't live without you," he said brokenly, lifting his head from my neck and staring deep into my eyes. "When you disappeared..." his eyes welled with moisture—unrelated to the shower.

His kiss this time was soft and romantic, breaking my heart with its perfection.

"I love you too," I whispered.

The shower door was thrown open, and an irate looking Carter stood there, his wet hair slicked back from his face, nothing but a towel slung around his waist.

"Are you out of your fucking mind?"

He seemed to notice then that Sebastian was still inside me...either that or he was just realizing that I was naked, because his gaze took on a sort of feral, crazy edge.

"Get her out of there right now, or let me join," Carter growled, dropping his towel and revealing his enormous, erect cock.

I was currently impaled by a delicious dick.

But I was suddenly ravenous for that dick too.

"Carter," I gasped, as Sebastian held Carter's gaze and started pumping slowly in and out of me.

Carter growled and stalked forward, gently pushing me forward and slipping behind me, so I was sandwiched between the two of them.

"You feel up to the two of us, sweetheart?" he said silkily, and I shivered as his fingers rubbed against my puckered flesh.

Sebastian wasn't stopping, pumping in and out of me with a determined look on his face.

One thing I could say for having four very alpha men as my boyfriends...baby daddies...they were very competitive when it came to handing out orgasms.

"Always," I gasped, which was true. My body always wanted them.

And so did my heart.

Carter slowly pushed into my ass and my head fell back onto his shoulder, the water pelting me in the face. My legs were still wrapped around Sebastian's waist as he pumped into me.

Carter fucked into me as Sebastian pulled out, an alternating rhythm that kept me close to the edge, but not quite able to come.

But it felt amazing.

I wrapped an arm around Carter's neck. "Kiss me," I pleaded

as Sebastian played with my clit between us. Carter's lips crashed against mine and I moaned into the kiss.

"I love you," he whispered in between each brush of our lips. "I love you so fucking much."

Once again, the shower door crashed open and there stood an irate Jack and Greyson.

"Out. Right the fuck now," Jack demanded, reaching in and turning off the water before any of us could move. "This is not a three-way situation tonight. Give her to me."

Sebastian growled, biting down on my shoulder as he continued to work my clit. Carter wasn't giving any indication that he wanted to stop either...but I was desperate for all of them.

"Bed," I gasped right before their movements synched up enough for me to finally come, Carter capturing every cry that fell from my mouth.

"Love the way you choke my fucking cock," Sebastian said through clenched teeth as he pushed Carter's head away from my lips and replaced them with his own. His tongue licked into my mouth, and I moaned because I loved the way he tasted.

I loved everything about him.

Carter dragged his tongue down my neck, like he was trying to remind me he was still there. But how could I forget when every slide of his dick was sending fire licking through my veins.

I let out a squeak when Sebastian was suddenly yanked away, and I was grabbed off Carter's dick, a strong pair of arms catching me before I fell to the shower floor.

Jack threw me over his shoulder, even though I was soaking wet, and marched towards the bed.

"Be careful with her!" Carter snarled after us.

"Says the guy who was just fucking her ass," Jack snapped back.

"I need to dry off," I said, feeling grumpy because I'd been really enjoying myself and he'd ruined my fun.

"No need to, pretty girl. I like you wet," Jack said as he somehow laid us both on the bed, rolling us so that I was sitting on top of him while he laid on his back. We stared at each other for a moment and I took him in. For a while there I was afraid that I was never going to see them again.

Out of the corner of my eye I saw the others approaching, but they let me have this moment with Jack. He gripped my hips and lifted me slightly, positioning me over his dick and then slowly bringing me down so every delicious inch pushed into my core.

I fell forward, my hands gripping his shoulders as I tried to take all of him. It didn't matter that I'd just been speared between two cocks in the shower, they were all just too big.

And it felt so good.

"Want to live in this pussy," Jack said breathlessly, rutting up into me until every last inch of him was in. "You're my perfect, pretty girl."

"Yes," I gasped, bending forward to kiss him, not taking anything for granted as we moved together.

"Don't cry, baby," he murmured, and I realized that water was dripping onto his face as I leaned against him...and it wasn't from my wet hair.

"I'm just so happy," I whispered, and one of his hands came up and tangled in my hair, the other one still gripping my hip, guiding me as I moved on top of him.

"Me too, pretty girl. Me too."

A hand slid down my spine, and I arched my back as suddenly a dick was sliding inside my ring of muscles.

I wouldn't have needed to ask who it was, even if Greyson's tattooed hand hadn't slid up my breasts and encircled my neck as he pulled me against his chest—Greyson was the only one who wouldn't check if I was ready before he shoved his enormous dick in my ass.

Good thing I didn't mind.

He must have lubed himself up already because the head of his cock pushed in smoothly.

"I love your fucking ass," he growled as he surged all the way in.

"Do you love my fucking ass, or do you love fucking my ass?" I teased, my voice coming out breathy and embarrassing.

"Fucking hell, Greyson," Jack rasped, his eyes closing. "Those piercings are a lot…"

"Hey, you've never said that about mine," snarked Sebastian, coming up beside the bed and stroking his own pierced cock slowly as he stared at my breasts.

"It's because of that extra half inch," Greyson said seriously, and then his chuckle had his piercings pressing against something in my ass that had me screaming.

"Extra half inch my ass," Sebastian snarled, his dick all of a sudden in my face.

No inches missing there.

Carter appeared on my other side, not looking thrilled that it wasn't his dick currently fucking in and out of me.

"I hate all of you but Kennedy."

Jack laughed, the sound fading into a groan as I clenched around him.

Sebastian brushed his dick against my lips, and I licked at his slit, desperately trying to get every drop of his precum.

"Fuck," he groaned, his hand sliding into my hair, his thumb brushing the edge of my mouth where his dick was beginning to stretch my mouth wide.

"My turn," Carter said, grabbing my chin so that Sebastian's tip popped out of my mouth, and offering me his own dick—that he'd thankfully washed since it had been in my ass a few minutes ago.

I loved having such a good selection.

They both tasted so good, different tastes, but somehow both my favorite.

Oh, but Jack and Greyson's tastes were also my favorite too.

"Open up, sweetheart," Carter purred as he pushed his dick against my lips.

I opened wide, my jaw still feeling like it might pop as he pushed it in.

Greyson abruptly slapped my ass and I jumped, my teeth grazing Carter's skin.

"Greyson, I will kill you," Carter said, wincing as I gazed up at him apologetically, or at least I hoped that's what my eyes were saying since I couldn't talk around his dick.

Greyson liked a little teeth, but that wasn't Carter's favorite thing—which was why Greyson had just spanked me.

"Just making sure you were paying attention to the man fucking your ass," Greyson said innocently.

Carter scoffed, pushing his dick farther into my throat and making my eyes water even more.

"Such a good girl," he said sweetly, before he pulled out of my mouth and let Sebastian have his turn.

Sebastian palmed my cheek as he slipped between my lips.

Jack and Greyson were moving faster, pounding into me in an exquisite rhythm that had me unable to think. All I could do was feel.

Sebastian fucked my mouth, setting his own pace because I was incapable of doing anything else.

"Love you, princess," he whispered, making the moment romantic despite the fact that I was being split apart by four cocks.

Jack's body was trembling under me, his fingers massaging my clit and making me moan around Sebastian's cock as I came.

"Fuck," Sebastian moaned, erupting as he orgasmed, his cum filling my throat, and spilling down my chin.

He slowly slid in and out of my mouth for a few more seconds before he pulled out.

Sebastian used his fingers to push the cum that had dripped down my skin, back onto my tongue.

"Swallow," he said gruffly, and I obeyed. Opening my mouth to show that I'd swallowed every last drop for him.

His lips crashed against mine and our tongues tangled

together. I wondered if it was as hot for him as it was for me thinking of him tasting himself in my mouth.

Sebastian's grin when he moved away from me said it was.

Jack's fingers dug into my hips and he bounced me on top of his dick, his teeth gritted as if he was in agony.

"Come again," he begged, and I cried out as Greyson bent me forward so that both their dicks were hitting a new angle that set off fireworks in my insides.

Jack captured my cry with his lips as his warm cum filled me up.

How many orgasms was that? A million?

I collapsed against Jack's chest as Greyson continued to fuck into me.

The world grew hazy around us as I basked in Jack's warmth and the painful pleasure of Greyson's dick.

Had he turned into some kind of energizer bunny, though? I wasn't sure that my ass could take anymore.

"Please," I gasped, and Greyson chuckled as he continued to move. My insides fluttered around him in a sudden, small orgasm, and his laugh cut off—because he was much closer to the edge than he'd thought apparently—the smug asshole.

"Fuck, baby," he growled as he pushed forward, sandwiching me tightly between his and Jack's bodies.

I soaked in their closeness like I'd never soaked in anything before.

As was their way though, Greyson was suddenly pulled out of me, and I heard the thunk of his body as he fell off the bed. Jack's dick slipped out as well.

A second later Carter was sliding into my tired pussy—the only one of us that hadn't come.

"Sorry, sweetheart. I'm desperate for this perfect pussy," he rasped.

I moaned, still lying on Jack's chest, just letting Carter fuck me against him.

Jack was whispering dirty things in my ear like how he

wanted a chance to fuck my ass next time, playing with my hair sweetly as his dick hardened between us.

"Don't even think about it," I said in a rough voice, my ability to speak hindered by how many times they'd had me screaming tonight.

Jack laughed, and I moaned at the movement and the way it made Carter's dick slide against my sensitive channels. "Sorry, pretty girl. I accepted long ago that I was just going to be hard every time I was around you. But my dick gets superhuman when you make those hot little noises as you climax against me."

"I can't—" I began, but just as I'd been about to tell him that I couldn't possibly have another orgasm, I came all over Carter's cock.

"That's it, sweetheart, choke my dick," he moaned, his palm smoothing down my back.

Carter's movements stuttered and he swore, and a second later Greyson was perched on my other side.

"That was my fucking kidney," Carter growled, his movements picking back up.

Greyson grabbed my chin gently and turned me towards him, his tongue licking into my mouth even though I was still draped over Jack's chest, and Carter was still pushing into me.

"Love you, Kennedy. Can't wait for you to have my baby," he murmured against my lips.

"*Our* baby," Carter offered, wrapping my hair around his fist and pulling gently so that my lips left Greyson's.

He pulled me all the way up, until I was leaning against his chest as he surged up into me, his other hand lightly squeezing my throat. My mouth dropped open at the view in front of me— Sebastian, Jack, and Greyson—all naked, their cocks erect. My pussy almost got new life...*almost* being the operative word.

The beauty in front of me didn't seem real though. All the abs, the dicks, and the perfect, gorgeous faces.

"I love you," I told them, meaning them *all* obviously.

"Love you too," Carter said roughly as he began to come, his erotic moan filling the room. He buried his face in my neck and took a few deep breaths as I savored the feel of him.

I was truly and completely spent after that, and gentle hands moved me off Carter's dick and settled me onto the bed.

I was vaguely aware of a cool washcloth against my aching core, and arms pulling me close.

And as I immediately fell asleep, I felt completely safe and content.

I was also quite sure...my happily ever after had officially begun.

CHAPTER 2

Kennedy

O ne minute, I was half-asleep and cozy between two warm, muscular bodies. The next, I smelled bacon and the sugary scent of pancakes, and I was suddenly ready for the day.

The warmth of the morning sun filtered through the half-raised shades, casting a soft glow over the room.

Greyson's face was nuzzled against the nape of my neck, his muscular arm draped over my waist. Sebastian's jaw was against the top of my head, and my head rested on his powerful shoulder. I was so cozy and comfortable with them that the idea of ever leaving the bed would have seemed absurd…until there were pancakes.

Greyson stirred behind me. He peppered kisses up my shoulder to my neck. I turned to face him, meeting his ice blue eyes which were lit by a mischievous glint. His dark hair was tousled from sleep, giving him an effortlessly seductive look that set my heart racing.

"Morning," he murmured, his voice husky.

"Good morning," I whispered back.

He captured my mouth with his, in a kiss that started tenderly but quickly ignited. Greyson kissed me with the same intensity he approached everything else, demanding and giving all at once.

His fingers traced the curve of my jawline, tilting my head for better access as he deepened the kiss, our tongues tangling. I could feel his desire press against me urgently.

"Mm," I murmured. Sex sounded so good. So did pancakes. I kissed the corner of his mouth, holding his jaw and feeling the roughness of his dark morning beard against my palm. "After breakfast…we could pick this up after breakfast…"

"I haven't been back to my place in days," he said, rubbing my bare shoulder as if he couldn't bear to stop touching me. "I love being here, seeing you wake up in the morning…But I can't spend my whole life in this penthouse. It's their turf…"

"Aren't we past *my turf* and *their turf*?" I asked.

Greyson raised his eyebrows. But before he could answer, Sebastian stirred beneath me.

"Morning," his voice rumbled, muffled by sleep and warmth.

I turned my head towards him, and our eyes met—his dark blue ones held that soft look reserved for moments just like this. A playful smirk danced on his lips before he reached up, his hand cradling the back of my neck, drawing me down into his kiss. The coziness I felt was now laced with an electric charge, each kiss igniting sparks that flickered through my veins.

Sebastian's kiss was different from Greyson's, somehow both commanding and tender, as if he were savoring each sensation. His other arm wrapped around me, pulling me closer still, and I melted into the connection.

"Hey," Greyson complained mildly, but the complaint was a promise, and his hand drifted over the curve of my side before settling possessively on my hip. He pressed another kiss to my bare shoulder.

Breakfast was the most important meal of the day, but suddenly, this seemed even more important.

Then the bedroom door swung open.

"Kennedy, come on!" Carter's voice broke through our little

bubble of lust. "Breakfast is ready, and I swear if I don't get back in there, Jack's going to burn the bacon."

I was torn from the kiss, a soft gasp escaping me as Carter decisively scooped me out of the tangle of limbs and sheets.

"Hey!" Greyson's complaint sounded a lot more genuine now, and Sebastian made a swipe after him.

But Carter evaded them with the same speed and power that he had on the ice, accompanied with a chuckle. He cradled me in his arms as he carried me back toward the kitchen.

A few seconds later, I found myself perched on the cool marble of the kitchen counter as Carter rushed to take over the spatula from Jack. Jack shrugged and gave me a boyish, mischievous grin, and I grinned back, suddenly sure that Jack was taking advantage of Carter's perspective on his culinary competence.

The rich aroma of coffee filled my senses as Jack approached, his blond hair golden in the morning light that streamed through the window. He offered me a steaming mug before leaning in to press a soft kiss on my cheek.

"Good morning, Kennedy," he murmured, his hazel eyes gleaming with a blend of affection…and lust…since I was wearing nothing but a blanket at the moment.

Carter slid a plate in front of me, and the sight of fluffy, golden-brown pancakes drizzled with maple syrup made my mouth water. "Made these just for you."

"And for me," Jack said, mock offended.

I picked up the fork and took my first bite of soft, fluffy, perfect pancake. I hummed in appreciation, casting a glance at Carter, whose green eyes were fixed on me with a look that could only be described as adoration mixed with a dash of desire. "Delicious!"

Carter grinned goofily. He seemed to love to feed me, which worked out well, because I loved to be fed.

His lips found mine in a kiss that started sweetly but quickly deepened, igniting a fire that seemed to spread through my veins. The world narrowed down to the sensation of Carter's mouth moving against mine, his hands roaming with a possessive tenderness that left me breathless and wanting more.

We broke apart breathlessly, our foreheads resting against each other as we shared a smile that carried all the unspoken promises of the moments yet to come.

"Okay, okay, let the girl eat her breakfast," Jack protested, and I looked up to find he was already eating one of my pancakes. He turned that bright grin on me and fed me another forkful.

"We have a surprise for you after breakfast," Jack added.

"What is it?" I demanded.

"A surprise," Carter said firmly, leaning against the counter with his own plate of food. "Now eat!"

Greyson and Sebastian came in then, both of them grumbling, but apparently willing to forgive Carter once they had their own plates. The guys all stood around, though, no one bothered to move to the eat-in table or the dining room, as if they were in a rush.

I savored my pancakes anyway, curious as I was about the surprise.

As soon as I finished, the plate was whisked out of my hands. I was amused how quickly the guys cleared the dishes, practically tripping over each other to get out the door. I got dressed quickly in jeans and a hoodie, and they barely gave me time to brush my hair before they were urging me out to the parking garage.

Greyson took the lead, his broad shoulders cutting a commanding path to the car. The cool leather of the passenger seat welcomed me as I slipped inside, still mystified.

We drove in a comfortable quiet that allowed me to lose myself in thoughts of what lay ahead. We left the gritty city streets and drove into a cute, sunny suburb with lots of green space. We passed a wide bike path where couples were walking with jogging strollers or towing bike trailers with cute little toddlers inside. I grinned out the window, enjoying the sights as we passed a big public playground and then turned into a fancy development, full of sprawling homes on rolling green lawns.

And then, there it was—the mansion that seemed to have leapt straight from my dreams.

The one I'd whimsically picked out on Zillow as my dream house.

My heart stuttered as recognition dawned on me.

"Greyson…" My voice trailed off, incapable of forming the question that burned on my tongue. He merely smiled, that enigmatic curve of his lips that promised answers without saying a word. I added, "Sebastian?"

Now, I realized Sebastian wasn't casually introducing me to a hobby of browsing Zillow. I twisted in my seat, and he offered me an unapologetic grin.

My breath caught as they ushered me out of the car, and instead of bringing me up the stone path from the driveway to the front door, which was edged with pink and white roses, they led me around the house.

"This is…" My voice faded into a whisper of awe as I stared around at the lush garden in the back.

Stone paths led through the garden, dividing the brightly colored flowers that were everywhere. Lilies and violets bordered our way, leading to an open space where a gazebo stood, with ivy twining up its white posts. At the back of the garden was an enormous swing set, and I grinned at the thought of our future children playing there. Another pair of swings hung from the wide branches of a tree. The backyard was so peaceful and birds sang steadily overhead.

"Are you…thinking of buying it?" I ventured, trying to mask the hope threading through my question. But they merely exchanged glances, a silent pact not to reveal too much, not yet.

"Kennedy, I told you the penthouse will always feel like it's their turf." Greyson gestured to Sebastian, Carter, and Jack, who all nodded in agreement.

"We need something that's *ours*," Carter said. "A brand new house for a brand new chapter—for all of us."

"I love it so much," I confessed, although I didn't just love the garden; I loved them and their commitment to building a life that worked for all five of us.

Soon to be six.

"You haven't even seen the inside," Sebastian teased me, holding out his hand. "Come on."

"I know, but the garden is so perfect," I murmured. "I don't even remember it looking like this in the Zillow pics...this garden is exactly what I dreamed of..."

The four of them exchanged a mischievous smile.

I repeated, "Are you thinking of buying this?"

"Actually," Jack smiled, his hazel eyes glinting with happiness, "we already did."

The admission hit me like a gentle wave, soothing yet utterly overwhelming.

Sebastian's hand pressed against the small of my back, guiding me forward. Together, we approached the French doors that led from the garden into the house.

Inside, the scent of fresh paint lingered, blending with the scent of the lilacs from the garden outside. I wandered in a daze through the enormous but cozy kitchen, the living room with the big stone fireplace where I could just imagine curling up with these men.

But it was the library that left me breathless. Shelves upon shelves rose up to meet the high ceiling, carved from dark wood, and there was a pair of cozy white couches facing each other at the center. It was like a dream.

There were some books lining the shelves, and a pile of boxes and smaller parcels that flowed across the floor.

Sebastian gave me a slightly abashed grin. "I heard some jerk ruined your home library."

"I don't know that I would call him a jerk," I disagreed gently, looping my arm around his lean waist.

He dropped a kiss in my hair as we moved together toward the bookshelves. "I've been going through your Goodreads account. Everything you loved...I've been ordering it. I've been trying to get all the cool special editions."

I ran my fingers over the spines, tracing the titles of novels that had once been dear friends, then pulling out one book to look at the gorgeous painted pages.

My heart swelled with a mixture of nostalgia and newfound joy. These were the kinds of books I'd wanted but hadn't been able to afford.

"Thank you." Tears welled up, unbidden, spilling over as I stood rooted to the spot.

"Kennedy?" Sebastian sounded concerned, alarmed even, as he turned me to face him. His fingers gently skimmed my cheek.

"I can't believe you did all this," I managed to say.

Sebastian wrapped me in his arms. "You know I'll do anything for you."

And then there were more arms, Jack's and Carter's and Greyson's, wrapping around us.

And I was home.

EPILOGUE

Kennedy

The atmosphere in the hockey arena was on fire, the air buzzing with the energy of the crowd and the rhythmic slicing of skates across the ice. Greyson stood beside me, his arm wrapped possessively around my waist as we watched the guys warm up before their game.

Our son, nine months and full of curiosity, wiggled on Greyson's hip, his eyes wide with wonder as he took in the sights and sounds of the arena—or at least what he could hear with the giant noise canceling headphones over his ears.

I was the definition of a helicopter mom at this stage...and what I didn't worry about...his dads did.

My smile was wide as I took in the sight of his chubby cheeks, his tiny fingers reaching out to touch the cold surface of the glass.

Greyson let me go and lifted Ryan up, holding him close to the glass as he pointed out the action on the ice. "Look, buddy," he murmured, his voice soft with affection that melted me every time I heard it. "Look how good your daddies are out there."

My kidnapping, pregnancy, and Ryan's birth had been life-changing for the guys' relationship.

I loved it for the most part, except when they were ganging up on me.

Which was quite often now that their bromance was back in full bloom.

Or at least how I imagined it had been back in the day.

I still hadn't recovered all of my memories, and most of my earlier time with the guys was still a blank wall.

But my life in the present was so perfect...it made up for all of it.

I tracked my men as Jack, Carter, and Sebastian glided across the ice, probably breaking a million hearts as they skated by their fans. I'd seen a bunch of cameras recording Sebastian doing his hip stretches earlier—and I didn't blame them—even if I knew they had an important function, I still got turned on when I watched him stretch like that.

I was only human after all.

As if sensing their presence, our son squealed with delight, his giggle floating through my ears and cutting above the noise of the arena. And then one by one, Jack, Carter, and Sebastian skated over to the glass, their faces alight with joy as they caught sight of our son.

They were all the best dads that anyone could hope for, and I fell more in love with them every day.

And hey, having four...baby daddies meant that I had a lot of help. I had maybe changed four diapers since Ryan had been born.

It was glorious.

Jack took off his helmet and pressed his face against the glass, making funny faces and sticking out his tongue playfully. Our son giggled in response, his chubby fists reaching out to touch his reflection.

Carter skated by next, twirling in circles and blowing kisses. Ryan clapped his hands in delight, his eyes sparkling with complete adoration for his cute daddies as he watched them.

And then, it was Sebastian's turn. He pressed his palm

against the glass, his expression serious for a moment before breaking into a wide grin. He mouthed the words "I love you" before skating away, leaving Ryan cooing and gabbing in delight.

Greyson turned towards me, a content grin on his face. "I think he's going to be a hockey player," he announced.

"Oh, you think?"

"Definitely, wife," he murmured, leaning over and kissing me even as Ryan slobbered all over his sleeve.

Wife. I loved the sound of that every time he said that.

Even if that was one of the small things that had created a little snafu in our perfect life.

When Greyson had kidnapped a priest and forced him to marry us when the guys were at practice.

I couldn't blame alcohol for the fact that I said yes, but at least the rest of them couldn't get too mad at me since I was pregnant.

But Greyson had definitely gotten tied up again.

And then they'd all insisted on forcing other priests to marry me, all of the priests clueless that I was also married to other men.

Greyson had ensured that ours was the only marriage that was actually legal.

But you'd never hear me saying that out loud.

They were all my husbands.

Mine, mine, mine.

And I was all theirs.

THE RICH DEMONS OF HOCKEY BONUS SCENE

Want more of Kennedy and the guys? Sign up for our newsletter and get a bonus scene HERE.

SNEAK PREVIEW

Want to read about some other Rich Demons including Cain and Aurora…a serial killer's daughter? Keep reading for the complete, dark, enemies to lovers, college romance, Make Me Lie. Available on Amazon and KU HERE.

MAKE ME LIE

The world knows me as the Demon's Daughter.

He's a famous serial killer. And I may have been his accomplice.

But no one knows for sure except for me.

The dangerous, cruel men of the Sphinx secret society intend to uncover my secrets…and break me.

Stellan, my childhood crush who lost his sister to the Demon.

Cain, the boy with the face of an angel to who manipulation comes as easy as breathing;

Remington, the playboy soccer star full of secrets.

Pax, the dark psycho who hides behind his fists.

I hoped for a second chance at Darkwood University, only to have my dream ripped away the first time I kissed one of the handsome bastards.

They know who I am.

And they're determined to make me pay.

They should have thought twice about who they were playing with.

Because I am the demon's daughter. And just because they have the power, the connections, the faces and bodies of gods… do they really think they'll win?

I wanted a new life, not a war.

But if they insist, we'll see who ends up playing.

PROLOGUE

GABRIELA

~~DELILAH~~

AURORA

The world ended for me, then started again in technicolor, on a
Tuesday afternoon in fourth grade.

I gripped the doorknob of the back door to steady myself as I
unlaced and pulled off my Converse. My adoptive mother hated
when I wore my shoes into the house, but these high tops took
so long to get on and off, and that made it hard when I was so
desperate to get through the house to my room before my
"brother" Lucas caught me.

The door abruptly jerked open, and I tumbled into the
kitchen, landing on the pristine white tile.

Lucas leered down at me. "What are you doing out there? Come inside, Gabriela. We've got our chores to do."

"I'll do them when Mom gets home," I said. It was safer to wait until she was home so I didn't have to be around Lucas, even though sometimes she'd get mad at me for waiting. If I made it to my room and locked the door, I could do my homework and read my books in peace. Even Lucas wasn't going to risk banging up the door to get to me when Mom's house was her most precious thing—more precious than either of us. Definitely more precious than me.

I edged sideways trying to get away from Lucas, but he pinned me to the wall. "Mom is going to be so mad at you. She told us both that if we didn't do our chores, she was gonna be mad, and you know what that means."

My stomach churned. "I'll get them done."

I tried to get away from him, but he grabbed my pony tail and reeled me against his body. Lucas was seventeen, and he stank of body odor as he pulled me close. I tried to wriggle free.

"Mom said I could spank you if you didn't listen to me."

"No, she didn't." I kicked against one of the cabinet doors, trying to get loose.

"She did, and you're gonna get it from her too if you don't listen." He tried to wrench me with him, and I struggled to get free.

The two of us slipped. I kicked out, trying to get away from him. I managed to land on my feet while he landed hard on his knee and let out a grunt of pain. I ran desperately for my room with no plan but to get the hell away from Lucas while he was so furious at me.

The two of us raced through the hall. He was right behind me as I reached my room. I swung the door shut, but he threw his shoulder into it, and it banged open, knocking me back.

I fell back and slammed my head into the drywall so hard that I couldn't breathe for a second. The world spun darkly around me.

"Oh shit," Lucas said, and now even he sounded scared.

I got to my feet and saw the crack running down the drywall. There was no way Mom wouldn't see that.

"You are so screwed," Lucas said, starting to grin. "Do you want me to tell her that it was an accident? That you tripped? Or that you had a temper tantrum and did it on purpose?"

None of those were the truth.

"Lucas," I said, stunned.

He shrugged. "Up to you, Gabriela."

He always said my name like it was a joke, but everything about my existence seemed like a joke to him.

"What do you want?" I asked.

"Nothing. Let's just get our chores done so she's not mad about that too." He slung his arm around my neck and squeezed, the sour odor of his body washing over me. The affection was confusing. "We've got to have each other's backs, little sister."

I hurried to do my chores, putting away the dishes from the dishwasher that had run while we were at school, vacuuming again, making sure the house was spotless. Lucas had less to do since he pretty much took the trash out and did chores around the outside of the house, but he came over and helped me finish cleaning the kitchen which was nice and unexpected.

When we were done, he pulled out a bag of chips and said, "Come on. It'll be worth vacuuming again before Mom gets home."

She hated for us to have snacks outside of meals, but he rustled the bag with my favorite kind of chips, and my mouth watered. "Where did you get those?"

"I picked them up from 7-11 on my way home. Lunch at the high school sucks. I've been starving all day."

"They're not from Mom's secret stash?"

He grinned. "Nope. But she really needs to get over being so weird about *us* having junk food when she's keeping Hostess cupcakes in her underwear drawer. Come on."

It was unusually nice of Lucas. The two of us ended up

sitting on the couch, watching a television show and sharing chips from the bag. When the bag was empty, I ran and buried it under some trash in the kitchen to make sure Mom wouldn't find it. I sat back down to watch the rest of the show.

Lucas rested his arm around my shoulders, and I leaned into him. It felt awkward but even though he smelled bad, it was kind of nice to be close to someone, even if it was Lucas. Maybe things would be different from now on. Sometimes it seemed like he'd hated me since I moved in four years ago, when I'd been taken away from my first mom. Back then I'd cried all the time, but I'd grown up since.

Then Lucas slid his other hand down my leg. It felt like he was just petting me absently, but I froze, pretending not to notice. It wasn't absent at all. His attention was just as razor-focused on me, on waiting for my reaction.

"Lucas..." I tried to squirm away, and he grabbed my thigh, his fingers sinking painfully into my skin.

"Come on, Gabriela. Remember what I said about how we've got to watch each other's backs?"

"Lucas, please..." I didn't even know what I was begging for, but something about the way he was touching me felt so wrong.

I didn't want him to tell Mom that I'd had a temper tantrum and broken the wall. I didn't know how to fix the wall or hide it from her, even though I'd been racking my brain trying to find a way out ever since it happened. I was going to be in so much trouble, and my stomach ached every time I thought about it. Maybe if she believed it really was an accident though, she wouldn't be mad. Sometimes she could be really nice... just like Lucas.

He pushed up the bottom of my t-shirt and slid his hand into my leggings. Just rested it there, against my bare skin just under the waistband of my panties. I closed my eyes because hot tears were building, threatening to spill over. I'd been lying to myself when I thought I was grown up and didn't cry anymore. I felt small and helpless.

"Shh, Gabriela, it's all right," Lucas said, but I knew it wasn't all right. It wasn't going to be all right. He was just touching me lightly for now, but somehow, I knew it was just going to keep getting worse and worse.

There was the rumble of the garage door, and the two of us jumped apart. I pulled the hem of my t-shirt down, pulling it taut against my body. Lucas knelt next to the couch, trying to sweep up crumbs from the chips that I hadn't noticed when I got up before; they must have been hidden under his leg.

"Shit," he grumbled. "You better hope she doesn't notice any more crumbs."

I turned and ran to my room, afraid of being caught in the living room while he fumbled with the remote.

A few minutes later, as I was turning the pages of my Nancy Drew book and trying to pay attention, I heard a familiar shrill scream. "Gabriela!"

"Coming!" I shouted back, throwing my book down without even remembering to put a bookmark in. I raced down the hall to the kitchen, where my mom was livid with rage, holding the empty chip bag.

"Did you try to hide this from me?" Her voice was the kind of white-hot that meant I was in deathly trouble.

"It's Lucas's," I whispered.

"Right, because they are *his* favorite chips that he always gets for his birthday," she said, tossing them into the trash again. "Where'd you get the money? Or did you steal them?"

"I didn't," I said. "I came right home after school."

"I told her she shouldn't have them," Lucas said from the doorway, and Mom's irritated gaze snapped to him. Before she could bite his head off, he added, "And you should see what she did to her room when I tried to take them from her."

"No, no, no," I begged as Mom towed me by the arm down the hall to my room. Her face went white with rage when she saw the crack in the wall.

She slapped me across the face so hard my vision went red.

"Really, Gabriela, is there *anything* you didn't do today? Lying, stealing, destroying our house?"

"I didn't," I whimpered, but I knew she wasn't going to stop as she dragged me across the carpet to my closet door.

She rummaged through the closet, knocking one of my dresses to the ground as she pulled out a wire hanger.

I caught a glimpse of Lucas in the door, grinning, before I couldn't pay attention to anything but the pain.

That night, I lay in bed, trying to sleep despite the terrible pain. My Nancy Drew book was still lying with its spine open on the floor where it had fallen, and its pages were probably getting creased. I finally managed to get out of bed and pick it up, trying to read by the street light that came in through the window because I didn't dare get caught with my light on. Every once in a while, a car would come down the street and my page would get brighter for a moment with their headlights; I'd read frantically, skimming the page as fast as I could. I put the book under the pillow next to me, raising it just enough to hold the page up so I could drop it and hide the book at a moment's notice.

It was only because I was still awake that I heard the door creak open. I went still, letting the pillow fall, pretending to be asleep.

Lucas came to the side of my bed. He peeled back the blanket and the sheets, and I froze, pretending I was still asleep.

How many times had he come into my room like this?

He didn't touch me again, just touched the front of his pants, then pulled his manhood out. I kept my eyes closed, wanting to scream as he jerked his hand up and down along his pale thing.

Then suddenly, he made a short, desperate sound.

I opened my eyes to see him frozen, one hand still gripping himself, his eyes and mouth wide with horror.

A bright red smile had been cut across his throat, and the man with the knife was standing right behind him. The man touched the knife to his lips, warning me not to make a sound.

Gently, he eased Lucas's dying body onto the bed beside me.

I scrambled back and off the bed, staring at the stranger.

"It's all right," the man whispered. "I'm sorry it took me so long to find you. But nobody's ever going to get the chance to hurt you again."

He reached out his hand to me. I wasn't sure what to do, but his eyes were kind.

"Who are you?" I whispered.

"They call me The Demon," he whispered back. "But you can call me Dad, if you want."

"Where are we going?"

A grin spread across his face. "That's my girl. Wherever you want, darling, that's where we're going. But first, we have to make one more stop..."

I took his hand. He frowned at the sight of the bruises on my body and said, "Why don't you pack a bag while I go have a talk with that woman who pretended to be your mom?"

"Okay," I answered in a trembling, but hope filled voice.

I was putting my books into my suitcase when I heard the faintest start of a scream, so quiet that I didn't think it reached outside the house. I froze for a second, then went on, getting my favorite t-shirts.

He came back in for me, and took my suitcase out to the car while I got dressed in real clothes instead of my pajamas. Then he picked me up, as if I were a little doll, and carried me out into the hallway.

"Don't look," he whispered to me. "Close your eyes."

But I didn't want to keep my eyes closed anymore, and I shook my head, wondering if he would hurt me like everyone else had if I didn't obey him.

But he just smiled.

He carried me into the hallway, where my mother lay half-in and half-out of her bedroom, the carpet stained dark with blood in the dim light.

"You were always only pretending to be sweet and helpless, Gabriela," he whispered in my ear.

"I was?"

"You forgot who you really were, sweet child, because you had to forget. That was the only way for us to keep you safe. But you've always been something more than anyone could realize. You've always been fierce."

I tried to understand what he was saying. Had I always known deep down that I was his daughter, that someday he would come back and claim me? That I was never really helpless, no matter how I felt?

I could leave behind Gabriela, the scared little girl who was locked in closets and beaten with anything handy. She was nothing but a ghost in the house that I was leaving behind, along with the bodies. She wasn't ever real.

The real me could never be hurt, broken...destroyed.

Especially not when I was with my daddy, and my daddy was the devil himself. I smiled up at him, and a slow smile spread across his face, as if he understood what I was thinking. He looked so handsome and strong when he smiled. He pressed a kiss to my forehead.

"My darling, precious, blade of a daughter," he murmured. "The only way anyone will ever see you as a victim again is if you want them to. And at any time, you can pull the blindfold from their eyes and show them you're always the one with the knife."

CHAPTER 1
AURORA

I rehearsed my cover story as I drove to college.

I'd had a cover story all my life, ever since The Demon rescued me. But this time was different. My heart sped as I turned the corner and the stone buildings and green hills of Darkwood College rose in front of me.

I had to come to a stop as I joined a long line of cars waiting to turn into the campus circle in front of the dorms. As I waited, I pulled my sunglasses off and checked my face in the rearview mirror.

I'd been getting worried the swelling and bruising from surgery wouldn't go down in time. But it finally had; there was just the faintest puffiness that I couldn't quite cover with makeup. I mentally amended my cover story: I'd been partying hard the night before, enjoying one last night with my dear friends.

I'd spun my cover story out of a fantasy I'd had when I was a kid, imagining I had half-a-dozen close-as-hell girlfriends who were my absolute ride-or-die besties. Now I was bringing my imaginary friends back, pretending that I'd left them in my hometown, where we'd played lacrosse together. I even had photos starring me and a couple of deep fakes, sitting on the front porch of a house I'd never been to, or standing pink-cheeked with our arms around each other's shoulders and red Solo cups in hand.

The face staring back at me in the mirror was pretty: high cheekbones, delicate nose, large, hooded eyes that were a startling shade of violet. I'd picked my new face out carefully. But I couldn't quite bring myself to put contact lenses over my irises, even though I knew I really should. They were the one connection I had with my birth mother, and I owed her some kind of debt.

It wasn't like me to be so emotional. "You're going to get yourself hurt being stupid," I mouthed at myself, watching my bright pink lips move, before I slipped my sunglasses back on to hide the swelling.

I didn't know then how right I was.

Half an hour later, the line of cars had finally crept forward until I was parked in front of the dorm. I checked in, then popped the trunk of my car and slung my duffel bag over my shoulder. I didn't own much, but I'd definitely have to make more trips.

The sun was shining and the campus was beautiful. The students streaming around me while unpacking their cars with their parents all seemed so happy. It made me feel like an outsider, because I was alone. I wouldn't have wanted to bring my father. Just imagining him in this scene was like imagining the beautiful setting slowly being infested by a dark poisonous blot.

"Let me help you." The voice was deep and sexy, and I spun to find myself facing a tall, good-looking guy with broad shoulders and a powerful body.

He flashed me a boyish smile. "It's a service our frat offers everyone. Whether or not they're a pretty girl."

He'd towed over a bright yellow rolling caddy. Behind him,

another guy was pushing a caddy into the dorm while a girl and her parents walked behind him.

"I might not be a pretty girl, but I'll take the help," I said.

He grinned at me like he knew I knew better, then began to unload the boxes in the trunk into the cart. I stood back and watched him. There was no reason he'd open the tire well and see the weapons hidden inside, but I couldn't help feeling wary.

"What's your room number?" he asked.

I normally wouldn't volunteer any additional information about myself to strangers. In my experience, being casual with your personal information was a great way to end up locked in a wooden box.

Be normal, Delilah…Aurora. Shit.

"Four-twelve," I said, giving him a smile.

When we reached my new room, it already seemed full. A girl with long blonde hair, her parents, and a surprising number of small children seemed to fill the room.

"Oh! Get out of the way, Patrick," the blonde girl said, tugging one of the people out of the way of the frat boy and his caddy. She smiled at me, her eyes crinkling at the corners. "You must be Aurora!"

"You must be Jenna!"

"It's so nice to meet you!" She hugged me.

I'd exchanged a few emails with my new roommate. We weren't really on hugging terms but I was good at adapting to what other people wanted from me. So I hugged her back and smiled. She seemed genuinely warm and sweet just within a few seconds of meeting her, although that could always be an act.

She quickly introduced me to her parents, and to her three younger siblings who had all come along to help her settle into her new dorm.

"Let me get the circus out of here while you unpack," she said, trying to shoo her family out. "Do you have family?"

Here. She meant here.

But I would've said no anyway. I shook my head.

"Okay! Then once I get them to give me some space, we'll go to dinner tonight. Six?" She called over her shoulder as she gently shoved her father out the door.

"Six is good," I answered.

The room felt quiet after they left. I sat down on the mattress, feeling exhausted after only a few moments of being Aurora. My whole life had been a cover story; why was this so tiring now?

Maybe I just wanted to be myself.

Then I thought about what kind of results would come up if I googled *Delilah Kane*, and I knew, no, that wasn't what I wanted.

I just wished I could genuinely *be* someone else.

———

By six o'clock, I'd unpacked my belongings into my room. I was glad that Jenna wasn't here to see me pull the tags from some of my clothing and hastily discard them, covering them up with crumpled paper at the bottom of the trash bin. I'd had to buy everything new, enough to make it look like I had a real past. I'd scuffed up my shoes in a hotel room, washed some of my new clothes and run them through several dryer cycles on hot, but I hadn't had the chance to do that to all of them.

By six fifteen, I thought Jenna wasn't coming back after all, and I was relieved. This would be so much easier if my roommate wasn't nice.

Then the door swung open and she rushed in. "Oh good, you're still here! I'm sorry I'm late!"

"No problem," I said, feeling a sudden sense of dread about heading down to the dining room. "I knew you wouldn't abandon me."

She laughed. "No, freshmen have to stick together. Especially around here!"

I wanted to know why, but she was already kicking the

rubber wedge that held the door open, holding it for me to go with her.

As we headed down to the dining hall, she prattled on, "I wouldn't miss dinner tonight anyway. The frat that helped our dorm move in will be eating with us tonight, and I want eye candy as much as I want some chicken tendies."

I had to smile. "How do you know everything that's going on around here? I'm pretty sure that *eye candy* wasn't in the schedule *I* got from the school."

"Oh, I'm a legacy," she said lightly. "My parents met here and fell in love here! My mom didn't just get her Mrs. degree though, she also did pre-med here."

"She's a doctor?"

She nodded. "And my dad's a mechanical engineer. Don't even get him started talking about gardening—he's engineered all these automatic watering systems and grow lights. If you walk past our basement windows in the spring and see the glow, you'd think he was growing something besides tomato plants."

"What are you going to major in?"

"Pre-med. Not because of my mom," she added quickly. "I want to be a completely different kind of doctor. She's a dermatologist. I am not devoting my life to other people's acne!"

Jenna was easy to talk to, especially since she did most of the talking anyway. The two of us separated in the busy, noisy cafeteria, and by the time I'd begun to load up my tray, I felt a little lost and alone.

But then Jenna waved at me manically from across the cafeteria. She clearly didn't care if anyone side-eyed her nonstop enthusiasm. It was refreshing.

And dangerous.

No, just refreshing, I reminded myself. Just because I knew how dark the world could be, I couldn't stop trying to believe in the happier, brighter version that co-existed right alongside it.

I walked over to Jenna and let her chatter wash over me as I took in the students around us. People were already forming into groups…or trying to. We were such pack animals.

There was a change in the air, a sudden tension, a bit of a hush. I looked up, curious about what had driven the change.

Four of the most good-looking guys I'd ever seen had just walked into the room. But what was fascinating to me wasn't the perfectly styled hair above handsome faces or the broad shoulders and athletic bodies.

It was the way they commanded a room, the way everyone had stopped for a second when they saw them. My heart suddenly beat a warning. They seemed to be in a good mood, getting food, making small talk.

But they bled a sense of power and certainty that I knew. These guys were predators.

"See what I mean about eye candy?" Jenna said, because that girl was oblivious to danger.

"Who are they?" I asked.

"Cain, Remington, Pax, and Stellan." She pointed at each of them in turn, and I sighed under my breath. She was going to draw their attention to us. "Four stars of the school."

"Really? We're not in high school anymore."

"Cain is an amazing quarterback," she gushed.

Maybe we were still in high school. Maybe high school never really ends.

What a depressing thought.

"Pax and Remington kill it on the soccer field together," she said. "And Stellan is the captain of the hockey team."

"Jocks," I said. "Oh, fantastic. I love jocks."

I glanced over my shoulder at them again. They were surrounded by girls.

"Everyone loves them," Jenna added.

"Probably not as much as they love themselves."

Jenna laughed, but I meant it.

I couldn't help keeping a wary eye on them as I continued to get my food.

I hadn't met many men like them in my life, but all the ones I had known?

They were trouble.

Read the rest of the book here.

The Pucking Wrong Number by C. R. Jane

Copyright © 2023 by C. R. Jane

All rights reserved.

Cover Design: Cassie Chapman / Opulent Designs

Photographer: Cadwallader Photography

Editing: Jasmine J.

PROLOGUE
MONROE

"Monroe. My pretty little girl," Mama slurs from the couch. She's staring up at the ceiling, and even though she's saying my name, I know she's not talking to me. Or at least the me that's standing right here, scrubbing at the vomit stain she left on the floor. She's talking to the me from the past, or wherever it is her brain takes her when she's high as a kite.

There's a knock on the door, and I glance at it fearfully, dread churning through my insides. Because I know who it is. One of her "customers" as Mama calls them.

The door opens without either of us saying anything. I'm not sure Mama even heard the knock. In steps a sweaty, pale-faced man that I've seen once or twice before. He has rosy cheeks and a belly that protrudes over his jeans. Like a perverse Santa Claus. Not that I believe in that guy anymore. He's certainly never come to our place on Christmas Eve.

The man's eyes gleam as he stares at me, but then Mama groans in a weird way, and his attention goes to her.

"Roxanne," he says in a sing-song voice as he makes his way over there.

I want to say something. Anything. Tell him that Mama's in no shape for company, but I know it's no use. Besides, Mama would be furious with me later on if she missed out on the money she needs to get her fix.

I leave the room and lock myself in the one bedroom we have in this place. Mama and I share the room, but more often than not, she can't make it any further than the couch.

The disgusting noises I've learned to hate start, so I turn on the radio, trying to drown them out. I fall into a fitful sleep, and my dreams are haunted by the image of a healthy mother that cares more about me than she does about supplying the life she created.

I wake with a start, panic blurring the edges of the room until I can convince my brain that everything's fine.

Except everything doesn't feel fine. It's so quiet. Way too quiet.

I creep towards the door, pressing my ear against it to see if I can hear anything.

But there's nothing.

I slowly open the door and peek out into the room. There's no sign of the man, or my mother. Thinking the coast is clear, I make my way out of my room, only to come to a screeching halt when I see my mother on the ground by the front door, a pile of green liquid by her face.

I sigh, thinking of the clean-up ahead. Again. I hate these men. Every time they come here, they take a piece of her, while leaving her with nothing. It's always like this after they're done with her.

When I walk over with a rag and bucket, I see Mama is shaking, tears streaming down her face. She's a scary gray color I don't think I've ever seen before.

"Mama," I whisper, reaching down to touch her face, only to flinch at how icy cold her skin is. Her eyes suddenly shoot open, causing me to jump. They're even more bloodshot than normal. Her bony hand claws at my shirt, and she frantically pulls me closer to her. Her lip is bruised and bloody. The bastard must've gotten rough.

"Don't let 'em taze your heart," she slurs, incomprehensibly.

"Mama?" I ask, worry thick in my voice.

"Don't…let a man…take your heart," she spits out. "Don't let him…" Her words fade away and her chest rises with one big inhale…before she goes perfectly still.

"Mama!" I whimper, shaking her over and over again.

But she never says another word. She's just gone, like a flame extinguished in a dark room.

And I'm all alone, with her last words forever ringing in my ears.

CHAPTER 1

MONROE

I sat on the edge of my bed, staring out the window into the dark, seemingly starless sky. Freedom was so close I could taste it.

18.

It felt like I'd been waiting my whole life for this moment. For this specific birthday. The thought of finally being able to leave this place, to start my life, on my own terms…it helped get me through each day.

I knew it would be difficult when I left. I only had my scrimpy savings from my after school job at the grocery store to start my life. But I'd do whatever it took to make something of myself.

Something more than the empty shell my mother had left me that day.

I'd been in the foster system since I was ten years old, the day after that fateful night where I'd lost her. Everyone wanted to adopt a baby, and a baby I had not been. I'd gone through what seemed like a hundred different homes at this point, but my current home was where I'd managed to stay the longest.

Unfortunately.

My foster parents, Mr. and Mrs. Detweiler, and their son

Ripley, seemed like nice people at first, but over time, things had changed. They were different now.

Mrs. Detweiler, Marie, had come to think of me as her live-in maid. I was all for helping out around the house, but when they got up as a collective group after every meal and left everything to me to clean up–as well as every other chore around the house–it was too much.

Someday, hopefully in the near future, I would never clean someone else's toilet again.

While I could deal with manual labor for another month, it was Mr. Detweiler, Todd, who had become a major problem. His actions had grown increasingly creepy, his longing stares and lingering glances making me sick. Everything he said to me had an underlying meaning…was an innuendo. He'd started talking about my birthday more, like he wanted to remind me of it for reasons far different than the promise of freedom it represented to me. I'm not sure it had even occurred to any of them yet that I was actually allowed to leave after that day. Both my birthday and high school graduation were the same week. Perfect timing. I just hoped he could control himself and keep his hands off me long enough to get to that point. Some people might not think a high school graduation was anything special, but to me, it represented *everything*.

Ripley was fine, I guess. He was more like a potato than a person, which was better than other things he could be. His eyes skipped over me when we were in the same room, like I didn't actually exist. And maybe I didn't exist to him. As long as his bed was made every day, and he had food on the table, and toilet paper stocked to wipe his ass, he could care less. He was much too involved in his video games to care about the world around him.

I glanced at the clock. It was 4:55pm, time to get dinner started before Mr. Detweiler got home from work. Sighing, I absentmindedly smoothed my faded quilt that Mrs. Detweiler had brought home from who knows where, and headed out to the hallway and down to the kitchen. The house was a three bedroom rambler in an okay part of town. It was nicer than other places I'd stayed, but I'd found that didn't matter all that much. The hearts beating inside the home held a much greater significance than how nice, or not nice, the house actually was.

I'm sure I could have been perfectly happy in the hovel I'd started life in with my mother...if only she'd been different.

I came to a screeching halt, and panic laced my insides, when I walked into the kitchen and saw Mr. Detweiler leaning against the laminate counter. How had I missed him coming into the house? I couldn't recall hearing the garage door opening.

He was nursing his favorite bottle of beer, which was actually the fanciest thing in the kitchen, costing far more than any of the other food they bought. Todd Detweiler was still dressed in the baggy suit he wore to the accounting office he worked at. He had a receding hairline that rivaled any I'd seen, so he brushed all the hair forward, carefully styling it to a point on his forehead right above his watery blue eyes.

He raised an eyebrow at the fact I was still frozen in place. But he usually didn't get home until 6:30, long enough for me to get dinner on the table and hide away until they were done.

"Well, hello there, Monroe," he drawled, my name sounding dirty coming from his lips.

I schooled my face and steeled my insides, taking methodical steps towards the fridge like his presence hadn't disarmed me.

"Hello," I answered pleasantly, hating the way I could feel his gaze stroking across my skin. Like I was an object to be coveted rather than a person.

I knew I was pretty. The spitting image of my mother when she was young. But just like with her, my looks had only been a curse, forever designed to attract assholes whose only goal was to use and abuse me.

I reached into the fridge to grab the bowl of chicken I'd put in there earlier to defrost...when suddenly he was behind me. Close enough that if I moved, he'd be pressed against me.

"Is there something you need?" I asked, trying to keep the edge of hysteria out of my voice. His hand settled on my hip and I squeezed my eyes shut, cursing the universe.

He leaned close, his breath a whisper against my skin. "You've been thinking about it, haven't you?" Todd's breath stunk of beer, a smell that would prevent me from ever trying it, no matter how expensive and nice it was supposed to be.

"I—I'm not sure what you're talking about, sir." I grabbed the chicken and tried to stand , hoping he would back away. But the only thing he did was straighten up, so our bodies were against each other. I tried to move away, but his hand squeezed against my hip. Hard.

"I need to get this chicken on the stove," I said pleasantly, like I wasn't dying inside at the feel of his touch.

"Such a tease," he murmured with a small chuckle. "I love how you like to play games. Just going to make it so much better when we stop." There was a bulge growing harder against my lower back, and I bit down on my lip hard enough that the salty tang of blood flooded my taste buds.

My hands were shaking, the water sloshing around in the bowl. An idiot could figure out what he was talking about.

"Have you noticed how much I love to collect things?" he asked randomly, finally releasing my hip and stepping back.

I moved quickly towards the sink, setting the bowl inside and going to grab the breadcrumbs I needed to coat the chicken breasts with for dinner.

"I have noticed that," I finally responded, after he'd taken a step towards me when I didn't answer fast enough.

How could anyone miss it? Todd collected...beer bottles. Both walls of the garage had various cans and bottles lined up neatly on shelves. There were so many of them that you could barely see the wall—not sure how social services never seemed concerned he might have a drinking problem with that amount of empties. But Todd was never worried about that. He added at least five to the wall every day.

"Virgins happen to be my favorite thing to collect."

I'd been holding a carton of eggs, and I dropped them, shocked that he'd outright said that, shells and yolk ricocheting everywhere.

Just then, Mrs. Detweiler ambled in, her gaze flicking between her husband and me suspiciously. "What's going on in here?" she asked, her eyes stopping on the ruined eggs all over the floor.

Marie had once been a pretty woman, but like her husband, her attempt to hold onto youth was a miserable failure. Right now, she was wearing a too tight flowered dress that resembled a couch from the eighties. It accented every roll, and there was a fine sheen of sweat across her heavily made up face, probably from the effort she'd had to make to get out of her armchair and storm in here. Her hair was a harsh, bottle-black color, and though she attempted to curl and keep it nice, it was thin and limp and I'm sure disappointing for her.

I usually didn't pay attention to looks; I knew better than most they could be deceiving, but Todd and Marie Detweiler's appearances were too in your face to ignore.

"Just an accident, honey," he drawled, walking towards her and pulling her into a soul sickening kiss that made me want to puke considering Marie most likely had no idea where else that mouth had been.

They walked out of the kitchen without a backward glance, leaving me a shaking, miserable mess as I cleaned up the eggs and tried to make dinner.

If that interaction hadn't sealed the deal that waiting for my birthday to leave wasn't an option…the next night would.

I was in bed, tossing and turning as I did every night. When your mind was as haunted as mine was, sleep was elusive, a fervent goal I would never successfully master. I'd never had a night where I could relax, where the memories of the past didn't creep in and plague my thoughts.

It was 3 am, and I was on the verge of giving up if I couldn't fall back asleep soon.

Light footsteps sounded down the hallway by my door. I frowned, as everyone had gone to bed long ago. I knew their habits like they were my own at this point.

Was someone in the house? Someone who didn't belong?

The footsteps stopped outside my door, and shivers crept up my spine.

"Hello?" I whisper squeaked, feeling like a fool for speaking at all when the doorknob tried to turn, getting caught on the lock I was lucky enough to have.

I felt like the would-be victim in a horror movie as I slid out of bed and yanked my lamp from the nightstand, prepared to use it as a weapon if need be.

The person outside fiddled with the lock and it clicked, signaling it had been disengaged.

There was a long pause as I stared breathlessly at the door, waiting for the inevitable.

The door creaked open and a hairy hand—that I recognized—appeared.

It was Mr. Detweiler's.

I didn't think, I just started screaming, knowing I had one chance to get him away from my room.

I needed to wake up his wife. With their bedroom right down the hall, I just needed to be loud enough.

Sure enough, a second after I started screaming, the door banged shut, and footsteps dashed away. A moment later, I heard the Detweilers' bedroom door fly open, and then a moment after that, my door cracked against the wall and Marie's harried form was there. Her chest was heaving, pushing against the two sizes too small negligee she was wearing–that made me want to burn my eyes–and her gaze was crazed as they dashed around the room, finally falling to me standing there in the middle of it, a lamp clutched to my chest.

A red mottled rash spread across her chest and up to her cheeks as anger flooded her features.

"What the fuck is wrong with you?"

"Someone was trying to get into my room. Someone unlocked the door."

I didn't say it was her husband, because that would give me even more problems.

A moment later, Todd was there, faking a yawn with a glass of water in his hand. "What's going on?" he asked casually. Our eyes locked, and in that moment, he knew I knew it was him. His features were taunting, daring me to say something, like his wife would ever believe anything that came out of my mouth when it came to him.

"The girl's saying someone was breaking into her room," Marie scoffed before pausing for a second and examining her husband. "Why were you up?"

The way her lips were pursed, the way her flush deepened— it told me a lot. Apparently, Marie wasn't so unaware of her husband's true nature after all.

Not that she would ever do anything about it.

"I was getting some water when I heard Monroe scream. But I didn't hear anyone else in the house." His gaze feigned concern. "Are you sure you didn't just have a nightmare?"

I stared at him for a long, tense moment before I took a breath. "Maybe that's all it was," I finally whispered, eliciting a loud huff from Marie.

"Get yourself under control, you brat. The rest of us need our sleep!" she snapped, whirling away and leaving, curses streaming from her mouth as she walked back to her room.

Todd lingered, a smug grin curling across his pathetic lips. "Sleep well, Monroe," he purred, a firm promise in his eyes that he would be back.

And that he would finish what he started.

I fell to my knees as soon as the door closed, sobs wracking through my body.

I'd never felt so alone.

He had ruined everything. A month away from a high school diploma, and he'd just torn it from my grasp.

If Todd got his hands on me, he would break me. And I wasn't talking about my body–I was talking about my soul.

The image of my mother's desolate, destroyed features flashed through my mind.

That couldn't be my story. It couldn't.

I had to leave. Tomorrow. I had no other option

———

The Detweilers lived in a small town right outside Houston. I decided Dallas would be my destination, about four hours away. I'd never been there before, but the ticket price wasn't too bad, and it was big. Just what I needed to hopefully disappear. Surely the Detweilers wouldn't try and go that far, not with only a month left of state support on the line. I bet they wouldn't even tell anyone I was gone. They'd want that last check.

I didn't let myself think about what my virginity would be worth to Todd. Hopefully, "easy" was one of his requisites, and he would forget me as soon as I disappeared.

I went to school, my heart hurting the whole day. I'd never been one to make close friends—when you never knew when you'd be moving on, it was best not to make any close connections—but I found myself wishing I had longer with the acquaintances I did have. I walked the familiar hallways, wondering if it would have been hard to say goodbye at graduation, or if I was simply feeling the loss of my dream.

Mama had never graduated from high school. In her lucid moments, though, even when I was little, she would sometimes talk about her dreams for me. Dreams of walking across that stage.

I'd just have to walk across a college stage, I told myself firmly, promising myself I'd get a GED and make that possible.

After school, I went to the H.E.B. grocery store where I worked, putting even more hustle in than usual since I'd be a disappearing act after this shift. The timing worked out, because it was payday, and I was able to get one more check to take with me. Every penny would count.

After my shift, I bought a prepaid phone since I didn't want to take my Detweiler phone with me. Knowing them, they'd probably try and get the police to bring me back by saying I'd stolen their property. A part of me was a little afraid they could track me with it too. I knew I wasn't living in a spy thriller…but still, better to be safe than sorry.

Once I got home, I packed a small bag with some clothes, my new phone, and the cash I'd saved up. And then I sat on my bed, hands squeezing together with anxiety.

I didn't have a good plan. For as much as I'd been dreaming of getting away, my plans were more fluid than concrete. And all of them had depended on me having a high school diploma so I could get a better job, as well as not having to look over my shoulder every second for fear the Detweilers were after me. The state also had a support system for kids coming out of foster care, and I'd been hopeful I'd have that to lean on.

But I could do this.

I cleaned up after dinner. Marie had ordered pizza, so it didn't take as much effort as usual. And then I sat in the corner of the living room, biding my time until I could say goodnight. It was a tricky thing. I had to escape tonight–late enough that they'd gone to bed, but not so late that Todd decided to give me another late night visit.

My departure was the definition of anticlimactic. My mind had conjured this image of the Detweilers running after me as I escaped with my bag out the window, the sound of a siren haunting the air as I ducked in and out of the bushes, trying to avoid the police.

But what really happened was that I slipped out the window, and everyone stayed asleep. I walked for an hour until I got to the Greyhound station, and no one came after me. The exhausted-looking attendant didn't even blink when I bought a ticket to Dallas.

It was nice for something to go my way every once in a blue moon.

The bus ride took twice as long as a car would have. And although I tried to catch a few hours of rest, I kept worrying I'd somehow miss my stop, so I never could slip into a deep sleep. My mind also couldn't help but race with thoughts of what my future held. Would I be able to make it on my own?

Despite my worries, a sense of relief flickered in my chest as the distance between Todd and me grew with each mile that passed.

At least I could cross keeping my virginity safe off my list of to-do's.

When we finally arrived in Dallas, the morning sun was just peeking over the horizon. Even with the dilapidated buildings that surrounded the Greyhound station, I couldn't help but feel excitement. I was here. I'd made it. I may have never been to Dallas before, and I may not have known a single soul here, but I was determined to make a new life for myself.

This was my new beginning.

———

It took about twelve hours for the afterglow of my arrival to fade and for me to find myself on a park bench, debating whether I could actually fall asleep if I were to try. Or if it was even safe to attempt such a thing.

I'd gotten off the bus and was in the process of calling for a cab to take me to the teen shelter I'd found online. And then I'd been fucking pick pocketed while I looked the address up. They'd taken all the cash in my pocket that I'd pulled out for the cab, and swiped my phone right out of my hand.

You can bet I ran after them like a madwoman. But with a

backpack containing all my earthly possessions weighing me down, the group of boys easily outran me.

I hadn't dared to spend any of the rest of the cash I had left, except to get a bag of chips from a gas station that had seen better days.

I'd walked all over for the rest of the day, trying to find the shelter, scared to ask for directions in case anyone got suspicious and reported to the authorities that I looked like a runaway teen.

Obviously, I never found the place, because there I was, on the park bench. Cold, hungry, and pissed off.

And exhausted.

Apparently, when you hadn't slept for close to forty-eight hours, you could fall asleep anywhere, because eventually... that's exactly what I did.

———

I woke with a start, the feeling of someone watching me thick in my throat. Night had fallen, and a deep blue hue had settled over the park. The trees and bushes were indistinct shadows against the darkened sky. The street lamps had flickered to life, casting a warm glow on the path and the nearby benches. The light danced and swayed with the gentle breeze, casting long shadows on the ground. You could hear the rustling of leaves and the chirping of crickets.

I yelped when I saw a grizzled old man sitting next to me on the bench, a wildness in his gaze that matched the tattered clothing on his body. There was the scent of dirt and body odor wafting off him, and when he smiled at me, it was only with a few teeth.

"Oy. I've been a watchin'. Making sure you could sleep, my lady," he said in what was clearly an affected British accent.

I flinched at his words, even though they were perfectly friendly and kind, and scooted away from him.

"Oh, don't be afraid of Ole Bill. I'll watch out for ye."

I moved to jump off the bench and run away…but I also had a moment of hesitation. There was something so…wholesome about him. Once you got past his looks and his smell, obviously.

"This park's mine, but I can share. You go back to sleep, and I'll keep watch. Make sure the ruffians stay away," he continued. Even though I had yet to say anything to him.

I opened my mouth to reject his offer, but then he pulled a clean, brand new blanket with tags out of his grocery sack. When he offered it to me…instead of talking…I found myself crying.

I sobbed and sobbed while he watched me frantically, throwing the blanket at me like it had the power to quell hysterical women's tears. When I still didn't stop crying, overwhelmed by the events of the past few days…and his kindness, he finally started to sing what I think was the worst rendition of "Eleanor Rigby" that I'd ever heard. Actually, it was the worst rendition of *any* song I'd ever heard.

But it worked, and I stopped crying.

"There, there, little duck. Go to sleep. Ole Bill will watch out for ya," he said soothingly after he'd finished the song—the last few lyrics definitely made up.

I was a smarter girl than that, I really was. But I was so freaking tired. And everything inside of me really wanted to trust him. After all, he had called me "little duck." Serial killers didn't have cute pet names for their victims, right?

"Just a couple of minutes," I murmured, and he nodded, smiling softly again with his crooked grin that I was quite fond of at that moment.

I drifted off into a fitful sleep, shivering from stress and exhaustion, and dreaming of better days.

When I woke up, it was far later than ten minutes. It was the rest of the night, actually.

Bill was still there, watching over me, and whistling softly to himself, like he hadn't just stayed up all night. My backpack was still under my head, the cash still in it, and at least I didn't *feel* like anyone had touched me.

Fuck, I'd gotten desperate, hadn't I?

"Do you have a place to stay, lassie?" he asked softly. I shook my head, biting down on my lip as I thought about spending another night on this bench.

"Ole Bill will take you to a good place. It's not as nice as my castle, but it will do," he said, gesturing to the park proudly as if it was in fact an English castle complete with a moat, and he was its ruler.

Despite the fact that he'd at least proven trustworthy enough not to do anything to me after a few hours, it was still pure desperation that had me following him to what I was hoping wasn't a trafficking ring, or something else equally heinous.

I relaxed a little as he took me to a slightly better part of town than where I'd been walking the day before. He chattered my ear off, all in that fake British accent, regaling me with stories about places I was sure he'd never visited.

Before I knew it, we were standing in front of the entrance to what appeared to be a fairly new shelter. The sign read that it was a women's shelter, and the sight made me want to cry once again.

"When you get in there, tell 'em Ole Bill sent you...they'll give you the royal treatment," he chortled, and tears filled my eyes for what seemed like the hundredth time—causing him to take a step away–probably fearing I would burst into hysterics again.

I hesitated for another moment before I finally ascended the steps that led to the shelter doors. Stopping halfway, I glanced back at Bill, who gave me another charmingly snaggletoothed grin. "I see great things for you, little duck," he called after me when I continued to walk.

I knew I'd never forget him. He may have been homeless and slightly crazy, but he was also one of the kindest people I had ever met. He'd watched over me, a stranger, and helped me when I needed it the most.

As I walked inside, exhaustion still stretched across my

shoulders, I strangely felt at peace right then that everything was going to work out.

"Welcome to Haven," a kind woman murmured as I approached the front desk.

Haven indeed.

I could only hope.

Keep reading The Pucking Wrong Number here

ACKNOWLEDGMENTS

And so we've reached the end...Kennedy and her men were some of the most fun we've had writing in a long time. The Rich Demons world, with its red flag men, and courageous heroines, just does it for us...and we hope it does it for you too.

A few thank you's...

To our beta readers, Crystal and Blair. Thank you guys for always stepping in and helping make our words shine. Lucky to have you in our lives!

To Stephanie, our editor, thank you for your hard work in making our baby beautiful. This manuscript is what it is because of you!

To Caitlin, thanks for supporting us every day.

And to you, the readers who make all our dreams come true. Thanks for embracing our crazy book boyfriends and allowing us to have fun for a living.

ABOUT C.R. JANE

A Texas girl living in Utah now, I'm a wife, mother, lawyer, and now author. My stories have been floating around in my head for years, and it has been a relief to finally get them down on paper. I'm a huge Dallas Cowboys fan and I primarily listen to Taylor Swift and hip hop…don't lie and say you don't too.

My love of reading started probably when I was three and it only made sense that I would start to create my own worlds since I was always getting lost in others'.

I like heroines who have to grow in order to become badasses, happy endings, and swoon-worthy, devoted, (and hot) male characters. If this sounds like you, I'm pretty sure we'll be friends.

I'm so glad to have you here…check out the links below for ways to hang out with me and more of my books you can read!

Visit my **Facebook** page to get updates.

Visit my Website.

Sign up for my newsletter to stay updated on new releases, find out random facts about me, and get access to different points of view from my characters.

BOOKS BY C.R. JANE

www.crjanebooks.com

The Pucking Wrong Series (Hockey Romance Standalones)

The Pucking Wrong Number

The Pucking Wrong Guy

A Pucking Wrong Christmas (a novella)

The Pucking Wrong Date

The Pucking Wrong Man

The Sounds of Us Contemporary Series (complete series)

Remember Us This Way

Remember You This Way

Remember Me This Way

Broken Hearts Academy Series: A Bully Romance (complete duet)

Heartbreak Prince

Heartbreak Lover

Ruining Dahlia (Contemporary Mafia Standalone)

Ruining Dahlia

The Fated Wings Series (Paranormal series)

First Impressions

Forgotten Specters

The Fallen One (a Fated Wings Novella)

Forbidden Queens

Frightful Beginnings (a Fated Wings Short Story)

Faded Realms

Faithless Dreams

Fabled Kingdoms

Forever Hearts

The Darkest Curse Series

Forget Me

Lost Passions

Hades Redemption Series

The Darkest Lover

The Darkest Kingdom

Monster & Me Duet Co-write with Mila Young

Monster's Temptation

Monster's Obsession

The Rich Demons of Hockey Duet Cowrite with May Dawson

No Pucking Way

Our Pucking Way

Academy of Souls Co-write with Mila Young (complete series)

School of Broken Souls

School of Broken Hearts

School of Broken Dreams

School of Broken Wings

Fallen World Series Co-write with Mila Young (complete series)

Bound

Broken

Betrayed

Belong

Thief of Hearts Co-write with Mila Young (complete series)

Darkest Destiny

Stolen Destiny

Broken Destiny

Sweet Destiny

Kingdom of Wolves Co-write with Mila Young

Wild Moon

Wild Heart

Wild Girl

Wild Love

Wild Soul

Wild Kiss

Stupid Boys Series Co-write with Rebecca Royce

Stupid Boys

Dumb Girl

Crazy Love

Breathe Me Duet Co-write with Ivy Fox (complete)

Breathe Me

Breathe You

Breathe Me Duet

Love & Hate Co-write with Ivy Fox (complete)

The Boy I Once Hated

The Girl I Once Loved

Rich Demons of Darkwood Series Co-write with May Dawson (complete series)

Make Me Lie

Make Me Beg

Make Me Wild

Make Me Burn

Make Me Queen

BOOKS BY MAY DAWSON

May Dawson's Website

The Lost Fae Series

Wandering Queen

Fallen Queen

Rebel Queen

Lost Queen

Their Shifter Princess Series

Their Shifter Princess

Their Shifter Princess 2: Pack War

Their Shifter Princess 3: Coven's Revenge

Their Shifter Academy Series

A Prequel Novella

Unwanted

Unclaimed

Undone

Unforgivable

Unstoppable

The Wild Angels & Hunters Series:

Wild Angels

Fierce Angels

Dirty Angels

Chosen Angels

Academy of the Supernatural

Her Kind of Magic

His Dangerous Ways

Their Dark Imaginings

Ashley Landon, Bad Medium

Dead Girls Club

The True and the Crown Series

One Kind of Wicked

Two Kinds of Damned

Three Kinds of Lost

Four Kinds of Cursed

Five Kinds of Love

Rich Demons of Darkwood Series Co-write with C.R. Jane

Make Me Lie

Make Me Beg

Subscribe to May Dawson's Newsletter to receive exclusive content, latest updates, and giveaways.

Join Here

ABOUT MAY DAWSON

May Dawson lives in Virginia with her husband and two red-headed wild babies. Before her second career as an author, she spent eight years in the Marine Corps and visited forty-two countries and all seven continents (including a research station in the Antarctic). You can always find her on Facebook in <u>May Dawson's Wild Angels</u> or on the internet at MayDawson.com

Made in United States
Troutdale, OR
04/05/2024

18982483R00209